Tally-Ho, Cornelius!

Tally-Ho, Cornelius!

Carter Kaplan

MUSTARD LID PRESS
Hyde Park, New York

Published by The Mustard Lid Press: Hyde Park, New York.

ISBN: 978-0-615-24220-0

Library of Congress Control Number: 2008907474

Cover illustration by Kai Robb

Climb into your time suits, temperature jockeys! This month's installment from the Second Ether Library will leave you shivering for some time to come. How's that for a *warm* up? Ha, ha, ha! Now comes the part you've been waiting for (drum roll, please). Ahem! Proudly offered for your consideration, we bring you the super team-up of Jerry Cornelius and the Corsairs of the Second Ether, presented together for the first time in any magazine—and exclusively for the readers of *New Worlds Global*. The critics just might find something to chatter about, too!

Excelsior!

Warwick Colvin, Jr.

Warwick Colvin, Jr.'s

Corsairs of the Second Ether

Chapter 47,455: "When the Stars Threw Down their Spears"

The story thus far: After rescuing Professor Pop from the Boomwap, Cappy Cahtah Kohenum orders his team of maverick chaos engineers to effect the transversal mass maneuver that slings his mighty clipper *Bifurcating Monofilament* across the Second Ether to within an instant of the End of Time, exceeding by millions of exponents the designated fractal level imposed upon him by the grand order of the Cosmic Balance. In this way confounding Old Reg the Original Insect, Cappy's hubris has succeeded in adding yet another stratagem to the Playbook of the Just—the Just who stand always with Spammer Gain herself, and who will sacrifice all to win the Game of Time!

But Cappy's actions don't pass unnoticed by the Cosmic Balance. And old Reg, too, his angry antennae whipping back and forth across the eons, is not content to allow his own pride to be eclipsed by the arrogance of the legendary Daredevil Corsair. In an unprecedented maneuver, the Original Insect and the Balance form an alliance that combines their powers together—powers such as the multiverse has never seen! As lovely Spammer and her fishlings beat a quick retreat into the seas of the late-Cretaceous, Cappy finds himself the target of a very diabolical compound eye slung from the pans of a very cross Balance. Although defiant and resolute in their gladness that their sacrifice has made Spammer's escape possible, Cappy and the crew of the *Bifurcating Monofilament* are suddenly dazzled by the explosion of the allied cosmic wrath. They find themselves exiled from the multiverse itself, and possibly forever!

Now read on!

From atop the elliptical control podium came a ding and a dong, then: "Jeepers! What, what, what was that?"

Engineering Department Supervisor Little Billy Blake strained his head back to glimpse the figure of his glorious commander, Cappy Cahtah Kohenum glaring down from the command dais on high. Already the situation had grown too real. "It's the engines, Captain Kohenum. The Pegasus drive is throwing its shoes!"

And to be sure, the rest of the crew—some just then emerging full-grown from the azure brow of the Daredevil Corsair to whom they all owed blood allegiance—were not a little moved by the new crisis facing the *Bifurcating Monofilament*. Her sub-woofers were pounding against the flow of the great black—what was it, *singularity*?—that had so suddenly engulfed them.

"Brave new conjuncture!" The splendid commander of the Lost Corsairs called down from his high pedestal, "Who and whence are we?"

Professor Pop woke from a momentary daydream of books, books, and more books: "Hallo, Cappy! But did you call for a conjecture?"

Lt. Baudrillard nervously ran his pincers along the frame of the tri-color synoptic sequence viewer. What was this? Sparkles? "Captain!" he cried. "I see the appearance of sparkles!"

"Sparkles!" in unison cried Adam and Vadim, the Simulacrum twins, and after being admonished by the booming voice sounding from the dais on high, they acknowledged their new orders before bolting from the control room to see if they could draw up some impressively astute plan to reinforce the constant reconstruction of the new moment.

"And have a look round for those shoes while you're down there!" cried Cappy. Then he frowned when Billy affirmed the shoes were indeed flying overboard, and in a manner and with a force not unlike that which had just moments before propelled the *Bifurcating Monofiliment*—

"—out of the multiverse!" Cappy couldn't help finishing Billy Blake's sentence. "Then where are we?"

Billy looked up from the glaring throat of his furnace. The orange light wavered against his strained titanium skin. Billy glanced over at Lt. Baudrillard, who hesitated a few moments before nodding his agreement.

"Well?" cried Cappy.

Billy Blake shrugged. "It's the universe a'right! U.N.I."

"Uni!" cried Cappy. Immediately the control room began contracting.

Even the ever-phlegmatic Professor Pop swallowed. He stroked his grey beard anxiously as he over and over repeated, "Uni, uni, uni, uni, uni..."

"But the *universe*?" demanded Cappy. "I always thought such a thing was purely McTheoretical?"

Professor Pop ceased his senseless repetitions. "Ah, did somebody say McTheory? Have we spotted the arches?"

Cappy nodded. "Ahoy, Lookout! Hast thou seen the gilded arches?"

Lt. Baudrillard depressed the Hijab pedals with both his feet as he squinted into the reticule. He swallowed and then reported. "The moonbeams are gone! All iconography has completely exceeded the old calibrations. No fractal dust, no self-similar patterns, no scaling stations—" Baudrillard was by now anxiously pumping the Hijab pedals "—indeed, the multiverse is gone!"

Billy Blake stood, outraged and indignant. "Impossible!"

"See for yourself!" returned Lt. Baudrillard.

"Belay that!" cried Cappy. The command dais settled down into its recess in the floor and the Captain of the Lost Corsairs, spurs jingling, damp boots squishing, marched over to view the screen. He tapped his holstered attenuator with irritation. It was true. The Mandelbrots were gone. Not a trace of fractal dust. Nothing but— "What are those things?" asked Cappy, and he rippled his aura at the screen.

Professor Pop nodded with an air of loss and tragedy. "Stars. Shining stars against a field of sable. I almost wish I was back in the Boomwap."

"My goodness!" Cappy angled back and stared with fascination as his tentacles assumed the shape of human arms and human hands. "And what are these?"

Professor Pop looked at Cappy's hands and shook his head. "Apparently you are assuming a *universal* form.

Lt. Baudrillard nodded after examining his own hands. "We are assuming *His* image?"

"Allah?" said Cappy, evidently astounded. "Then Allah be praised!"

Professor Pop was more philosophical about the transformation. "But if we are now in Allah's image—" he looked at Billy "—then Allah must be a tad ugly."

Cappy agreed, "And clueless as well."

Lt. Baudrillard couldn't take it anymore. "Help! Help! Help!"

"Steady, man!" Cappy moved to give Lt. Baudrillard a sharp slap across the chops. He was certainly within his rights to do so. But he thought better of it and instead rubbed the lookout between the shoulders and told him to cheer up, which produced the desired effect.

Meanwhile, Billy Blake was kneeling with his head inside the forge. As he pulled it out orange drops of flame splashed against the hydrostatic deck membrane. For a moment the nanobots danced on the surface of his shinning face but then gave up the struggle against the engineer's new form and retreated. "There went the last one, Captain! We'll have to re-shoe the soft drive of the Pegasus engine if we ever hope to see the multiverse again!"

Professor Pop tilted his head. He was remembering something. "Impossible!" he pronounced. "Worlds, time, old friends, parents, habits, love—yes. But corsairs themselves are never lost!"

Cappy knelt by the forge and stuck his head into the flames. The drive was broken down, alright. He pulled his head out and shook the flames from his eyes. "What a mess!"

Billy agreed. "It will take some time to repair. And we'll have to run the Cornelius Loop to get everything on-line again. But even assuming the drive does get fixed—" Billy shook his head.

"Out with it, man!" Cappy steeled himself for the worst.

Blake spanked his leather apron. "The navigation problem is irresolvable! How are we going to find our way back to the multiverse?"

Cappy shrugged. "The Cornelius Loop can solve any navigation problem."

"Aye." Billy nodded. "An impressive bit of code, to be sure. But as to solving *any* navigation problem—that's only a myth."

"Myth?" Cappy laughed defiantly. "Ha! I'm counting it!"

Suddenly the *Bifurcating Monofilament* struck something soft.

"Nebula?" demanded Cappy.

"No, sir," replied Lt. Baudrillard. He twisted back the zoom. "Tar pit! And if I'm not mistaken we've got company."

Cappy pushed his cap back and scratched under his command leotard. What was growing all over his body? Hair? But what was more, smiledons had surrounded the ship. "Oy!" cried Cappy. "What's that smell?"

Professor Pop was looking at his hands. He sniffed them.

The roaring of the smiledons was shaking the ship as they opened their dripping maws and turned their saber-teeth to glisten in the starlight. The situation really did appear hopeless.

Cappy smiled at the old scholar and chuckled to break the stress. "Ha! You know, this is just *my* kind of challenge, old son!"

Buoyed by his commander's courageous enthusiasm, some of the old trademark twinkle returned to the Professor's eyes. He shook his head. "Ah, me. All bets are off this time, Cappy. *Challenge*, you say? I wish it were so simple; but in the meantime, we need to run that loop!"

"Right!" cried Cappy, and he drew down the Omniphone. "Now hear this! Turn back the clocks—" The ruggedly handsome commander of the

Bifurcating Monofilament looked for confirmation in Pop's face. The old scholar heaved a big sigh and nodded at Cappy, who took a deep breath before cheering on his crew: "All the way to zero!"

To be continued....

Chapter One

Contes Deux Fois Racontées

"Come," said I to my friend, startling from a deep reverie, "Let us hasten hence or I shall be tempted to make a theory, after which there is little hope of any man."

—Nathaniel Hawthorne, *The Hall of Fantasy*

Sitting in the window facing the Hudson River—it was Apartment "C," twelfth floor, 104 Riverside Drive, Morningside Heights, Upper West Side, New York City—The Reverend Dr. Jeremiah Cornelius selected "shut down," waited a few moments for the machine to line up its ducks, then reached for the power strip and depressed the rectangular button that arrested the flow of electricity to the ensemble. He was having another good day. It was another good day again! So good he didn't feel like working! As a younger man he had been always desperate to put down the words, absolutely grim in his discipline and puritanical work habits. At the age of 45 he had under his belt ten books (three titles in religion, two in physics, and five in something falling in-between), and as well four degrees (BA in mathematics, MA in theology, MA in physics, PhD in physics)—and no children. He had a wife, however. Catherine. And she was as beautiful as she was—

Barren.

The Reverend Dr. Cornelius sighed as he pressed his hands together and placed them before his face so they divided the steam flowing against the cold window.

The Hudson River was broad and cold and it looked beautiful out there and he didn't care how much work he missed or how cold it was. He was going out. It was all out there and he didn't want to miss it. He gazed across the river at the panorama of the grey sky cut horizontally by the dark rectangles of apartment buildings standing along the steep bank on the New Jersey side, then lowered his eyes across the water (the Hudson was rather fresh that December morning) and like a hawk he looked down through the twigs and bare branches of the patient trees that stood above the park where a man walked a dog, and the man fumbled as he guided the dog using both the lead and the plastic stick with the bag at the end. The awkward dog walker amused the Reverend Dr. Cornelius. He had to get out there into that cold world. That's where the life was. But not yet. He could feel it. Not yet, but he was going out.

Catherine had left at 7:30 that morning to help with the preschool group at the Cathedral—that would be the Episcopal Cathedral of St. John the Divine, boasting the longest nave in the world (a tenth of a mile long), six blocks away; a cathedral, in fact, to which the Reverend Dr. Cornelius was loosely "attached" as he finished his current book project and prepared for, as a few voices were promising, his own cathedral—that would be Christopher Wren's masterpiece cathedral, St. Paul's of London.

New York or London?

London? He could hardly picture the place. It made him feel a bit tense. But why not? No bother. He was in New York, and he easily pictured New York just then like a branching tree. Lower Manhattan—especially Wall Street—was the base of that tree, the roots coming from deep in the ground. From here Manhattan reached up like the columns facing the Stock Exchange, or the columns of the Federal Building—oh, that amusing statue of George Washington standing before it in the same place he stood over two centuries ago. Rather bold of those bankers to break away from Blighty the way they had. But for now the Reverend Dr. Cornelius passed over Blighty. Back to New York. Back to Wall Street—those absurd and somewhat horrid looking policemen with their camouflage fatigues, flack jackets, helmets, boots and automatic rifles. But all very necessary with the war on. Then on up the street a bit, the trunk rises—and here at the top of Wall Street, right here on Broadway stands Trinity Episcopal Church— Anglican, of course, ahem—a respectable pile of gothic building in ruddy stone with a proper church yard, tall handsome steeple, and thank the Lord for something old in this New World—here the trunk really reaches up, up Broadway mostly, and past St. Paul's Chapel—Anglican again, and why not? St. Paul's was indeed quaint, colonial, old—thank the Lord again—and it stands right at Ground Zero, actually. Never mind, thought the Reverend Dr. Cornelius, he had talked about that enough anyway, he had made the case for scepter and country, fair enough. Enough. And then here, again, again, the Reverend Dr. Cornelius saw the tree thrusting upward, further up, further into Manhattan, past Canal Street and through Chinatown and right beyond the trendy streets of Soho until it penetrated Houston Street, where there was a wonderful change, a steep shift in the sense of the place, where the numbered streets began—First, Second, Third, and so on—where the first branches, yes, spread out—to the west and the quaint gay swirl of Greenwich Village, where the successful queens with bags of money went to age, and then to the east and the somewhat sprawling tenement utopia of the East Village, once a "low-zombie/high-zombie" paradise from Tompkins Square through Alphabet City, land of needles, mapped with tracks, but now blighted with the not altogether unwelcome worm of gentrification, boasting a mixture of Puerto Ricans (on their way out) and artsy-enough-looking "types" (on their way in) swaddled in black cotton and leather and pulling in at least 150,000 a year to afford those flats, while the devilish ghosts of the "high zombies" who were hip and the best and the beat, the fallen star intellectuals, the freaks, the fags, the feeling, the failing—together with those broken bits of cosmic debris orbiting round them like asteroids, a sort of shadow tribe of painted-up kids from the waste lands of suburban New Jersey, and it might as well have been all the suburbias beyond the Hudson, beyond New Jersey, beyond Pennsylvania, and on and on to whatever suburbs might exist out there in the midst of that cemetery of factories, corn fields, island cities and deserts; the Reverend Dr. Cornelius did not care—all the zombies were fading along with whatever youth culture had existed before the country got old, or had invented more efficient ways to push out the young, the not-so-young, consume the youth, reject the weird, and eject the poor. Strange thoughts for a twenty-first century theologian, a barnstorming vicar, a postmodern divine, but that's why he loved New York. The Reverend Dr. Jeremiah Cornelius could think anything here. New York could take it. But he wasn't thinking about London. He did not have to and so he did not. Between the villages and in the middle of downtown was NYU—where he had introduced himself to a brilliant physicist, a boring philosopher, and an amiable historian, with mixed results—and here, too, was Astor Place and the neighborhood was absolutely bursting with bookstores. Further up—and the Reverend Dr. Cornelius had walked all this course in fits and starts, in bits and pieces, blocks and sections, in sun and rain, in snow and in the wind many times so that he had patched this map, this route, this tree neatly together—further up, further into Manhattan, past the bustle of 14th Street and the swelling puissance of the 20s and 30s until the Empire State Building announced the advent of midtown—"you better prepare, just a few more blocks, where 42nd shall rise before you"—and here the branches spread out towards train terminals and squares and libraries, where the tourists marched up Broadway and Fifth, while between them the great glass boxes marched up Sixth—the Avenue of the Americas—where the corporate powers vied to pronounce a more impressive statement of uniformity, but only to be overshadowed by the grandeur of Rockefeller Center, like a messenger from some alternative capitalist dimension proclaiming "my way is better" and indeed the facade and the sculpture might prove the claim. Times Square is somewhere buried into the fabric of this place, opening herself, those exploding lights, those heights, those crowing animated adverts—when viewed from the avenues—so that from blocks away—but best from the blocks above, right down the line of some avenue—it was like staring into a circus of giants lit by floodlights from the moon, while when you approached it from the streets—pow! Times Square pounced and instantly you were one of those illuminated giants looking at other giants, and look at that Chinese man, and look at that Russian, and look at that cop, look at that Lebanese by his Gyro cart, look at that Jew—his beard, curious dark coat and odd dark hat, what kind of uniform is this?—look at that young brown girl with the long black hair, those impossible shoes and her possible glance, and look at that sailor, and look at that tourist, and that tourist, and that tourist. And further on the Reverend Dr. Jeremiah Cornelius marched until at last Central Park stood in the way and the city forked. The city grid was parted by the most energetic green space in the world, where the city dwellers became some tribe of healthy, athletic forest people with nothing to do but play in the meadows and woods and promenade the puzzle of those winding pathways that brought them round and round a sort of festival of serenity and adventure, or round and round nothing at all, if you prefer.

The Reverend Dr. Cornelius clapped his hands softly before his face. He had fogged the window. As he drew his handkerchief and rolled away the dew he recalled his theory that the best way to explore New York was to simply pop on the train and then wait for the angel of expedition to come and pop you off—"Here's your station, off you go, enjoy yourself, that's what this place is for." He could hear that angel calling him to put on his scarf and coat. He was ready, but not just yet.

To the west of the park the walker's best bet was the march up Central Park West along the pavement on the park-side to view the long wall of apartment buildings, among them the Dakota, which stood out from the rest (the San Remo, the Beresford, the El Dorado not among the rest, albeit said) its singularity as much to do with John Lennon as it has to do with the sort of hyper Tudor features that garland the dark and beautiful building. Then further up the Society of Ethical Culture and then the Unitarians have their little shows going, as does the New York Historical Society, but then—and this was after all the postmodern divine's greatest discovery in New York—

the entire city fell away before the most splendid place in the world—the American Museum of Natural History. The Reverend Dr. Cornelius wasn't impressed either way with President Theodore Roosevelt, but he always entered the museum through the Roosevelt Rotunda. And more of that museum anon. Here the walker would be advised to walk one street over to Columbus Avenue and continue to press deeper into the folds of the Upper West Side, glancing down the streets at the brownstones in the 80s between Columbus and Central Park West, which—the Reverend Dr. Cornelius had an odd feeling—just might be the best place to live in the entire world. And so on and along this way you would end up in his neighborhood, Morningside Heights, the environs of Columbia University—where he had met nobody interesting, not even some agreeable exile from England—and here was the Cathedral of St. John the Divine, his home away from home. Riverside Church was up here too, and inside that tall mausoleum he had once given a sermon that was politely received as it fell into the sea of dark faces. But, anyway, back again to Central Park South and that great fork in the trunk. We've been up the West side, now to the East. According to the Reverend Dr. Cornelius, the best way to proceed up the east side was in fact to cut through the east side of the park, past the skating rink, between the statues of those two Scottish poets, up the mall, turn at the drum circle, cross the road, run the gauntlet of the model boat pond, Hans Christian Anderson and the bronze Alice, and so on; but one could—and he had done so on several occasions—choose instead to cross the park's southern boundary and then head up Fifth Avenue, strolling along with the apartments of the super rich on one's right hand—this time walking not beneath the trees hanging over the pavement, but along the other pavement before the buildings. While they possessed more treasure, certainly, than their artistic and bookish counterparts to the west, the east side dwellers lived in palaces that suggested some futuristic Italian Renaissance bourgeoisie, as if the Medici had popped into a time machine that had crashed them into the 20th century, whereupon they darted a glance up Fifth Avenue and called, "We shall build our palaces here!" The home of J. P. Morgan might fit this description—sort of a squared-off fortress for bachelor sensibility is Morgan's mountain of stone. But one should not dismiss the tastes of the crass American robber barons too soon. A little further up and the peripatetic epicure must confront the former home of Robert Frick. Did someone say the American *nouveau riche* have no taste? Go inside this home and witness the folly of such slander. As far as the Reverend Dr. Cornelius was concerned, Frick's home was it. Exquisite. Regardless of how

16

Frick made his fortune, Frick's taste was well nigh perfect. The closest thing in concept London had—the Russell—was rather dry in comparison. But enough on that. Further up the buildings became statelier and more Roman in grandness, fitting counterweights to the museum on the west side of the avenue, the Metropolitan Museum of Art, which was a wonderful recourse for the spirit indeed. The energy of this compartment of civilization was unaccountable. The Reverend Dr. Cornelius had never met with such a good feeling. Even if he wasn't in the mood for art and exhibitions, he would return here again and again with a book to seek out a snug gallery or a buzzing hall where he might be alone in a crowd and fall like an angel into the curling flames of a good read. Further up Fifth was the Guggenheim, whose spiraling gallery was worth a visit no matter what the exhibits might be. Further up still was the Jewish Museum, then across the avenue again were the Conservatory Gardens which the Reverend Dr. and Catherine once visited in the summer and promised to come back to, but one thing led to another. And so on up until Fifth Avenue was topped off (along with the park) by Harlem, which was an alien though surprisingly respectable looking place. To the east the city declined, eventually becoming altogether barbaric across the river in the South Bronx. Above Harlem and the environs of Columbia, northern Manhattan branched away in every direction completely, blowing outward into a million vague impressions but with one sort of nest—or tree house—perched in the uppermost of Manhattan's waving branches: Fort Tryon Park and the Cloisters Museum. Higher and higher still upon a hill atop Manhattan, this beige compound of transplanted Medieval art and architecture, cloistered walks and orchard trees crowns the spirit—or rather spirits—of Manhattan, as if in climbing up through the great tree of the greatest city of the Earth—the planet's very capital—the metronaut can peek through the topmost branches and spy afar off the empyrean heavens—or, better still, look across the Hudson River and here, far above the George Washington Bridge, gaze with a mixture of humility and pride at the broad waters of one of the world's great "young" rivers, and, above them, the tall and majestic Palisade Cliffs that guard northern New Jersey from nothing clearly seen.

What time was it? The Reverend Dr. Cornelius saw that it was almost noon. He thought to hurry off before Catherine came home for lunch, but instead decided to arm the kettle and wait for her.

And in a little time she showed up, bringing with her a parcel containing rolls and cheese, a tomato, and two lovely grapefruits.

17

"You-hoo!" said the Reverend Dr. Cornelius as Catherine's key scratched the lock.

"You-hoo!" she replied. She entered. At the age of forty-one she was beautiful, the ribbons of grey rather enhancing her black hair like lightning bolts through a black night. She was a little too "practical" to bear the thought of hair dye. Besides, she was reasonably confident in her pretty round face and slim figure, and the grey only made her appear more striking. For his part the good reverend quietly and conscientiously patched up the silver threads in his own dark hair, being in the public eye and wanting to represent the Church as best he could.

The postmodern divine took the shopping from her. "Well done. What have you brought us then?"

"Something good, I think. The most gorgeous stilton, Jeremiah."

"Your stilton's not the only one." And the Reverend kissed his wife with a kind of mechanical condescension.

She kissed him back innocently. "Jeremiah, we have found us with a new boy today and he is soooo adorable. Everyone's fallen in love with him. He's an orphan from Brazil, but he speaks English like he's been to university. Some of us were a little spooked, actually."

"Hmm. A verbal little nipper, eh? How old is he?" The Reverend Dr. Cornelius snapped on the kettle.

"Well, it's very sad. He doesn't know. He's very short, but sometimes we think he might be as old as twelve, he speaks so well. But I'm afraid he is also very immature. Early on he had a fit when he was told to do something, and generally he is very forceful. Oona has dubbed him 'Little Commander.' It was decided to put him in with the preschool group for the time being. Actually, he's not naughty—at heart, anyway. And he helps with the little ones. They love him, too, even as he orders them about. He lines them up and makes little speeches on how to behave!"

The Reverend Dr. Cornelius paused with the tray. "It sounds very odd mixing him in. Some sort of American education thing? 'Mainstreaming,' I think they call it?"

Catherine shook her head and said, "No. Don't be silly." But then the kettle went off and she moved to pour the hot water into its pot. "He's an orphan. He's had a rough go of it, that's all. Poor thing. He's such a sweetie. At night he stays in the cathedral's family shelter."

"Sounds like a monster. Twelve years old, and in with the preschoolers by day? A package of proper difficulty's what you got there."

"I rather think he's an angel."

18

"Here's to your angel then." With a pleasant smile the Reverend Dr. Cornelius bunged the last of the lunch things to table. "Be sure to remember him as you say grace, please."

As they ate the subject changed to the postmodern divine's current project.

"Actually," he said. "I've done nothing all morning. I have been planning a walk. I shall thank you for the butter, please."

Catherine shoved it over to him and said, "Good! Once more New York saves the day! What a lucky man you are, Dr. Cornelius, to be sent on your mission to the tribe of the Manhattans."

"Providential, to be sure." With his knife he slapped the butter back and forth across the face of his roll.

"You have worked too hard for too many years. You owe it to yourself—us—to let up from your prolific—" she lost the momentum.

"'Evidentiary record of meritorious contribution'?" He laughed.

"Precisely what I was about to say, word for word!" She laughed. "I shouldn't mind if you set aside your meritoriousness forever, and then see you happy resting on your laurels, Jeremiah."

"Mmm. All morning I've been thinking I should like to go out, but I can't make up my mind where to go."

Catherine was having difficulty making the crumbly cheese sit on the roll. She popped a piece of tomato on top and that seemed to do the trick. "Just march over to the tube and make that important decision once you're on the train."

"That had crossed my mind." He paused a moment to work a piece of stubborn cheese from between his teeth. "Darling, I have been thinking. I am really very happy in New York."

"So am I. We should think about staying. Something could be worked out at the Cathedral, I'm sure. It's a big place, a growing place, all sorts of programs, full of youth and life. They could make room for us, I think. Besides, they absolutely adore us."

"Mmm. Of course they do." The Reverend Dr. Cornelius sighed. "There is, however, that slight matter of St. Paul's Cathedral. The position of Dean is coming open and we've been told—"

"Yes, yes, Jeremiah. But would we really be happy in London, especially after New York? I don't know, Love. You have been so awfully happy here. And after all that traveling we've done."

It was true. There wasn't a continent, save Antarctica, where they hadn't caught fever, matched wits with bandits and mafia, suffered broken bones, had become lost, were bullied by petty bureaucrats, threatened by local police, and on and on over the course of following his career round the world. "It would be rather amusing if we ended up in America, of all places!"

Catherine smiled guiltily. "Remember the shameful laughs we had before we came? Gosh! Horrid, the things we said!"

"Mmm! My Love, we were diabolical." The Reverend Dr. Jeremiah Cornelius sniffed and nodded purposefully. "Right! Let's not burn any bridges, but at the same time keep your ear to the ground. Who knows what might turn up? Something good, maybe?"

"I shall be like a Red Indian with my ear to the ground!" Catherine held up her hand and said "How!"

"Red Indian!" My dear girl, watch the way you speak. Someone from Columbia University might overhear you and they'll send in the Lobby of Rectitude to check up on the political onus of your grammatical impropriety." With his knife he pushed the butter back and forth across the face of a second roll.

Catherine nodded. "Remember when you said 'colored' when you were referring to that black man?"

The Reverend Dr. Cornelius shuddered. "Nearly beheaded for that one! Ah, well. I had what the American's glibly call, ahem, 'a learning experience.' Dreadfully ironic, too, considering all I've done to promote multiculturalism in the Church."

They finished and began clearing things away. At length Catherine asked, "Jeremiah, what are you going to do this afternoon? Go back to work then?"

"Dunno. I still have ambitions to go off somewhere. I suppose I'm waiting for that light bulb to appear above my head."

"Good."

"How's that?"

"Well—" Catherine wiped her hands from cleaning the dishes. "Oona has been after me for days to read her poetry. If you went out I could ring her up and she could come over."

"An afternoon of American female poetry?" he said gravely. "I should say I've discovered my inspiration!"

"I'm afraid it's been forced upon you." She looked very pretty as she smiled and tilted her forehead.

He reached for his coat and scarf, gave Catherine a kiss, and then sprang heroically through the door.

Warwick Colvin, Jr.'s

Corsairs of the Second Ether

Chapter 47,456: "The Antinomian Gambit"

The story thus far: Upon crashing against the slowly swelling surface of the miasmic super-carbon tar pit at the center of the strange, laws-of-physics-defying universe, Cappy Cahtah Kohenum of the *Bifurcating Monofilament* orders the immediate re-shoeing of the Pegasus engine, necessitating the throw-back of all ship's thermochronometers to absolute zero, and so simultaneously (and paradoxically) initiating *and* terminating the dialogic flow within the core of the Pegasus engine itself, bringing not a few chaos engineers to doubt if the re-shoeing will be completed in time to run the Cornelius Loop. Meanwhile, as the temperature converges upon the beginning of time, the super-carbon tar thickens, and holds fast the paws of the advancing smiledons.

Now read on!

Cappy Cahtah Kohenum nodded with satisfaction at the tri-color synoptic sequence viewer. "That will hold those kitties for a while. Right! How much time until re-shoeing is complete?"

Little Billy Blake, ship's blacksmith, was unsure. "It's the forge, Cappy! What hand dare seize the fire?"

"Belay that, Billy. The New Jerusalem wasn't built in a day. Believe in yourself. One foot in front of the other, lad, like the Little Choo Choo Who Could: 'I think I can... I think I can... I think I can...'"

Professor Pop had seen Cappy drive the men too hard before. "Cappy, Billy is doing the best he can. The duration of the current synopsis is approaching absolute zero—"

"—there will be time enough withal, to be a rock and not to roll!" Cappy couldn't help completing Pop's sentence.

Winking at the greybeard, Cappy turned to his other responsibilities. Once more Lt. Baudrillard doubted the authenticity of the images coming through the tri-color synoptic sequence viewer. Baudrillard chose his next words carefully: "As we approach absolute zero, modernity keeps slipping,

slipping, slipping, into the future. Therefore, all that is about to happen is an imitation of what we anticipate. Under such circumstances, how long do you think we can maintain the illusion of signification? Our expectations were all fulfilled long ago. We've consumed it all before, you know?"

Cappy momentarily lost his patience—but in the nick of time (not a commodity they had a lot of, incidentally) he realized he was *reacting* when he should have been *responding*. Maybe Pop was right? And for a few moments he thought to do a mitzvah... but he just couldn't bring himself to go through with it. Mitzvah-schmitzvah, he thought, he'd hoist Baudrillard with his own petard! "Do you want to discuss postmodernism, *again*? We've already consumed that discussion before." Cappy shook his head. Why he of all the skippers of the Chaos Brotherhood should be stuck with such screwballs...

Ah, what the heck, they were lovable screwballs!

Professor Pop puffed his pipe with a piquant sparkle in his eyes. He knew the skipper well, so well that he could read his thoughts. If time wasn't converging upon absolute zero, he could have precisely anticipated Cappy's next move.

Cappy stood shaking his head as he anticipated Pop's next speculation; but, after all, he hadn't the time to bother with academic inanities. He had a ship to run. "Billy!" he ordered, "Grab your chain and anvil. It's cool enough by now. I'm going out to get the brains of one of those tigers!"

The tension deflated for a few moments. Baudrillard looked back and forth between the image of Cappy in the tri-color synoptic sequence viewer and the "real" Cappy in the compartment beside him and decided that he was having trouble drawing a distinction. The metal digits in the thermoclock turned over more slowly. Clank... clank... clank... clank... Cappy was climbing into his insulated silver time suit. From the throat of the forge the fire roared.

Professor Pop crammed his thumb into the bowl of his pipe and extinguished the smoldering white sage that had done so much to purify the transforming atmosphere—smudging the good ship and her crew each time he drew a puff. But by now their life support had taken on a definite *universal* tang. He wondered for a few moments how their bodies might react to the rarefied expanse of this new space. He decided they better not take any chances. "Cappy, you don't intend to go out like *that*, do you?"

"What do you mean?" asked the determined leader of the Lost Corsairs.

Pop shook his head. "You look a might fey, golden boy. Don't you think you ought to dye your hair?"

Cappy could only laugh. "Blonds have more fun. Besides, my aura is combed. I'll represent the *Bifurcating Monofilament* with honor, dear fellow!"

Billy Blake looked up from his forge and snapped his iron pincers. "Begging your pardon, Cappy, but you wouldn't be going out like that if we were back in the multiverse!"

Cappy narrowed his eyes at Billy Blake—and then blinked at the pincers. "That's 'Captain Kohenum' to you, dude!"

"Well, quite actually," said Professor Pop, "your mother was a gentile, and according to the rules you're no more kosher than that aura you've been bragging about!"

Cappy wasn't about to split hairs with the good professor—besides, he had left his Talmud in his other time suit. "If I've told you once, Professor, I've told you before," and Cappy recited a tit-bit of ancient advice he once received from his sage father: "'The Rabbis don't make up the rules, *we* do!'"

Pop shook his head. "What? Are you an antinomian Cohanim, Kohenum? One of those Paul-reading Jews for Jesus?"

"No, Pop, I'm with that other outfit—Jesus for Jews!" And jabbing his index finger upward at Allah for emphasis, Cappy entered the airlock, which slammed behind him with a deep shuddering clang and defiant hiss, as if the entire structure of the *Bifurcating Monofilament*, roots and branches, was resonating in agreement with the iron resolution of the mixed-blood antinomian peregrine of time.

But once he was outside alone standing on the frozen tar, Cappy wondered if perhaps he should have dyed his hair. Those smiledons weren't frozen after all. They were moving!

"Dog-gone-it!" exclaimed Cappy, "I don't care if I have to tear it out through one of their blasted mouths. I'm not going back inside without a brain!"

To be continued....

Chapter Two

La Nature de Mes Occupations

The impious presumption of legislators and rulers, civil as well as ecclesiastical, who being themselves but fallible and uninspired men, have assumed dominion over the faith of others, setting up their own opinions and modes of thinking as the only true and infallible, and as such endeavouring to impose them on others, hath established and maintained false religions over the greatest part of the world, and through all time.

—Thomas Jefferson, *The Virginia Act of Religious Freedom*

Early Saturday morning following his exploration of Manhattan (continued) and her celebration of unremarkable and ugly poetry (passive civility in the clutches of provincial maneuver), the Reverend Dr. and Mrs. Cornelius were awakened by the blare of their American telephone.

The hand of the postmodern divine reached out from beneath the duvet to pluck up the receiver. He answered, "Hello, Dr. Cornelius."

Catherine Cornelius opened her eyes to measure the light level in the room, then closed them again as she listened to her husband:

"Hello... Oh?... Yes, a bit surprised... Really?... Really? My goodness... Yes, I am very impressed... Yes... Yes... Well, good!... good... good... good... good... Oh, I see. He's with you... Good then... eight days? You should stay with us... I see... Still, you will be here early. Can you have tea with us?... Good... I have a service tomorrow in Lower Manhattan ... Really, it's no bother... Good... See you then... I shall send her your love... Yes, Francis, goodbye." And the Reverend Dr. Jeremiah Cornelius replaced the receiver and said, "Mmm."

Catherine's eyes were now wide open. "That was Francis? Is he coming?"

"Yes, said the postmodern divine. "Bishop Francis Cornelius is indeed coming. And he's got an African Bishop in tow; no less than Bishop Achebe—"

"Jeremiah," hissed Catherine. "You don't mean an African bishop will be *here* tonight for tea? How could you?"

"Oh, no. Just Francis. He's flying in on a Gulfstream business jet. Imagine! What posh creatures these bishops be. Both will stay at the Rectory at St. John's, but Francis says he'll be able to have tea with us. Their big dinner is Tuesday night, and we're invited."

"Sounds like a long day tomorrow."

Jeremiah nodded. "I shall finish that sermon straight away."

Catherine got up to help her husband get the day going. As she dressed she noticed he was staring at her. "What are you looking at?"

"My attractive wife."

"Stop it. You make me feel like an object."

The postmodern divine pursed his lips at this, but let it go. He averted his eyes. "It must be the New England thing."

"What?"

"The African bishop, Bishop Achebe. He's been a keen opponent of the homo bishop from New England."

"*Gay*, you mean. Don't forget we're in America, darling."

"Of course. *Gay* bishop." The Reverend Dr. Cornelius got out of bed and reached for his bathrobe. "What a politician, that Francis, flying African bishops round the world. I shouldn't be surprised if he's arranged a meeting between Achebe and the bishop from New England. That's what this is all about. He couldn't say so because the bishop was with him on the aeroplane."

Catherine went in the bathroom. "Well, good for Francis. What time will he be here? I have to do shopping."

He gave the knot on his bathrobe a reassuring tug and called after her. "Four or five. He shall call if his plans change. His aeroplane gets in at eleven. They are off to lunch together with people from St. John's."

"Well, I didn't have any plans anyway. Still, your brother can be imposing, can't he? Popping in out of the blue?"

"I suppose he's used to it."

Catherine came out of the bathroom. "Well, it's not a terrible bother. He works very hard."

The Reverend Dr. Cornelius leaned forward to kiss her, but she dodged under him and went to the other room. He listened as she drew her coat from the cupboard, jingled her keys, and went out the door.

"Well," he said philosophically. "I suppose I have time for a quick shower. Better make it a cold one, Cornelius."

The sermon and the shopping were finished by noon, lunch was mechanically consumed, and the Cornelius family, fondly waiting for the advent of their third member, busied themselves with minor occupations. Catherine chatted over the telephone with Oona, their chief subject was the new Brazilian boy and his charming capers. Then Catherine pushed her husband off the Internet—he popped out to buy a newspaper—and she found a real estate site and gazed at pictures of apartments in Morningside Heights. When he returned she took the bait, and he once more got on-line.

The Reverend Dr. Cornelius was a purposeful person on the Web, which for him represented not a library or a source of superficial entertainment, but rather a grand tool whose first purpose was to bring the world's people together as one worshipful congregation of humankind. And if he had anything to do about it, that congregation would be shepherded behind the crook of his organization. An idiosyncratic but nonetheless visionary physicist, he knew full well—and better than most other people—the real significance of the Internet. While he was content to leave the Earth's population to the superficial symbols of their local religions, belief systems and customs, he was committed to the idea that only one church should superintend the spiritual purpose to which the Internet was invariably heading. And that church was going to be—had to be—the world-wide Anglican Communion.

At half-four Francis rang to say he was on his way. Lunch and the meetings had gone as expected, and he would tell them all about it when he joined them. Catherine and Jeremiah filled the ice bucket, poured a bag of crisps into a bowl, and swung wide the doors to the liquor cupboard.

Twenty minutes later Francis was on the intercom and Catherine "buzzed him up."

The Reverend Dr. Cornelius opened the front door so that Francis might walk straight in after he stepped off the lift—which was soon easing up its shaft to the twelfth floor. The doors slid open, and they could hear Francis out in the hallway. He evidently spied their open door straightaway—

"You-hoo!"

Catherine called back, "Hoo-hoo!" And as Francis walked in muttering something about rocket boosters, acceleration, space satellites in orbit and fast American lifts, the Reverend Dr. Cornelius stood up and said, "Well done. Well done. What have you there, anyway? Something wet, I think."

"Oh, what a lovely bow. Francis!" Catherine embraced the bishop and took the bottle from him in one remarkably deft maneuver. "Jeremiah, look what Francis has brought. Isn't it a lovely bow? Thank you so very much, Francis!"

"Absolutely breath-taking!" The Reverend Dr. Cornelius advanced and shook his brother's offered hand. "Not gin?"

Francis shrugged. "A single-malt, by way of variety. Something for after dinner, I think."

"I'll put him with the others," said Catherine, and she walked the bottle over to the liquor cupboard, all the way petting the bow with her fingertips as if it was a lovely thing indeed. She came back and embraced Francis again and he gave her a warm hug and a cold kiss even as he very nearly shoved her off him. The bishop was a big man, a bit taller than his younger, slender brother, who was himself quite tall. But while Jeremiah was rather boyish and thoughtful-looking—in a Hollywood matinee idol sort of way, a sort of aged James Dean with thick black hair—Francis presented the picture of an ancient force of nature. He was very strongly built, and his face was rugged and handsome. In fact, he looked very like John Wayne had at the same age. John Wayne in the *Green Berets*, that was Francis to a "T."

"Right. What's everyone drinking?" cried Catherine.

"Oh, Earl Grey for me, thank you very much," said Francis. "I had four glasses of sherry this afternoon and I'd like to sit a while and leave the wind to dry me off."

"Tea for me, too, please," said the Reverend Dr. Cornelius. He stared at Francis's clerical collar. "Good heavens, you must want to take that thing off."

Francis reached up and felt his collar. "It's grown into my neck! I've had this on since five this morning—London time." And Francis removed it and handed to Catherine, who knew just where to put it. As she started the kettle the two brothers walked together into the sitting room talking about aeroplanes.

"Did you say 'Gulfstream' this morning?" asked the Reverend Dr. Cornelius, and he indicated any seat his brother might desire.

"Ah, Gulfstream *Five*, you mean." Francis looked round. The flat was sensibly decorated. Catherine had done very well with the plants, as usual. Most of them had been placed under the windows, which commanded a respectable view of the Hudson and, beyond that great flood, the hills of New Jersey. The bookshelves were ample—they were veritably "stuffed" with books—and covered the entire far wall, save an opening to the hallway leading down to the bathroom and the bedroom. There were a few Russian icons on the wall, a copy of a rather neatly done 15th century Dutch painting of the Annunciation, one of those very American sketches of the savior praying, and, over the sofa, a framed poster from a Jackson Pollock exhibition that had been at MOMA in the 90s. Francis stared a moment at Pollock's madness, and then sat beneath it on the sofa. The Reverend Dr. Cornelius alighted upon the little divan before the wall of books.

"Gulfsteam Five? Isn't that a big one?"

Francis smiled dismissively. "Well, it was hauling two bishops."

"*Hauling?*" The Reverend Dr. Jeremiah Cornelius was amused. "C'mon. Just how big is a Gulfstream Five, then? And, more to the point, sir, just what has the Church of England to do with posh executive jets?"

Francis explained that the Gulfstream Five (or "G-V" as he preferred to call it) was a very-long-range business jet that could carry up to nineteen people. This one had a very nice flight crew—two very military-looking pilots—and a resourceful cabin attendant from Jamaica, whose name Francis couldn't remember just then. "Goodness, my mind is slipping."

"Well, what do you think of the flat?" Catherine was suddenly standing in the entryway.

"Comfortable," said Francis. "Does it belong to the Cathedral?"

Catherine nodded. "They wanted to put us in a flat on the fourth floor of the Rectory, but Jeremiah bluffed our way out of it."

"Thank goodness," added her husband. "Can you imagine all the extra work they would have dreamed up for us if we were living next to the Cathedral?"

Francis nodded. "They would have had you, all right. By your vestments."

The kettle suddenly howled. Catherine shot away to snap it off, and even from the sitting room they could hear the water lapping into the teapot.

Francis returned to the subject of aviation. "As for owning this posh jet, no. It's on loan from the Beesley-Flyinghorse Foundation. The same folk who give you grants to write your books."

The Reverend Dr. Cornelius nodded. Beesley-Flyinghorse was a joint Anglo-Arabian group formed by a very quiet (but huge) British insurance company, and a Saudi-Arabian philanthropic organization. Indeed, the insurance side of the foundation was the British government's underwriter against terrorist attack. "But what need has the Church of England for a business jet—and a big one, too, by the sound of it?"

The bishop blinked his eyes slowly to communicate that he very much enjoyed his brother's curiosity. "I was just getting to that. Beesley-Flyinghorse has provided the use of this G-V jet—and three more, incidentally—to support our efforts bringing people together to heal the world. That's the mission. To this end, one of the most visible roles for our jets is to conduct what are called 'angel flights'—an American phrase, actually. These angel flights are little errands of mercy; usually carrying sick children round to hospitals for special treatments, and so on. Absolutely wonderful from a public relations standpoint."

The Reverend Dr. Cornelius nodded. "I should say so. Ah, here's Cath."

Catherine came in with the tea tray and placed it on the coffee table. They gathered round and as they passed the milk and teapot Catherine asked about the economics of corporate aviation. "It is very expensive then?" She sat on the sofa beside her brother-in-law.

"Very," he said. "An enormous write-off for Beesley-Flyinghorse, to be sure. Of course, our Arab friends have no shortage of resources, and this is such a good thing to do to create trust amongst people, particularly with this horrid war going on. Everyone is very happy the way the Church is reaching out."

The Reverend Dr. Cornelius nodded and took a chocolate biscuit. "Well, good then. What a very good thing."

"Isn't it amazing," agreed Catherine.

Francis nodded. "And we owe not a little of this good fortune to the work Jeremiah's been doing. Things have been moving back in jolly old England."

"Really?" asked the Reverend Dr. Cornelius, and he elevated his right eyebrow.

"That last book of yours has set things in motion, my dear. The voices of reason are being heard in the General Synod, and the prevailing feeling is that the necessary legislation—both by Canon *and* by Measure—will in fact be passed. Preliminary negotiations with publishers have already taken place."

The Reverend Dr. Cornelius was looking like the cat who ate the canary, though he was feeling very satisfied about it—as so too did that cat. "Gosh, imagine the committees that will have to hammer it all out."

Francis nodded. "They have not been formed yet, but the willing people have been identified. And it could mean a lot of work for you."

Catherine looked at her husband, who stared ahead blankly. His poker face was nothing short of masterful. At length he shook his head and sighed. "Mmm. Well, it looks like I have established my legacy then."

"Legacy?" said Francis. "You haven't even started, my boy."

"Ohhh—" slowly began the Reverend Dr. Cornelius. "—I rather think I have, Francis. I have done quite a lot for the church, and heading up a project like this—sitting on committees—gosh, gosh. I am an idea man, Francis, a physicist, not an organization person."

"But as Dean of St. Paul's—there, I said it—you would be in a wonderful position to lead the effort. You would be everyman's Dean, everyman's church reformer, working right there in the capital, showing up where people should see you every Sunday morning marching in the procession, and people would whisper—'there's the person who's doing so much to make the church reach out'—not to mention the perks, Jeremiah. Lots of time to work on your projects, travel, meeting the rich and the curious."

"We very much like New York," said Catherine.

Francis looked at her and said nothing, then turned to his brother. "Not to mention the gratitude of generations to come. After all, there is a war on, and history might show that what we are now doing is the one decisive thing that prevented the war from becoming a world war—a fourth world war."

"Francis, this is getting a bit much, don't you think?" The Reverend Dr. Cornelius shook his head. "Heading off World War IV does not ride on *my* shoulders. Indeed, if the situation is that serious then I am the last person you're looking for. I am not one to sit on committees smiling round at everyone. I am an idea person, a dreamer, as I've said. My interests are physics and computer modeling."

"Really, Francis," added Catherine, "Don't you see Jeremiah is better suited to other things. At the same time, though, we have discussed St. Paul's. We have dreamed about that. Oh—" she shook her head. "It's all happening so fast."

"My academic jobs in Alexandria and Prague were interesting—at first." And the Reverend Dr. Cornelius went on to explain that while he enjoyed preparing his lectures, after actually lecturing once or twice the novelty had worn off and he found himself very bored with it. "And then on top of it were those absurd meetings." He shook his head.

Francis nodded. He realized that he mustn't appear to be pushing things. Instead he needed to maneuver his brother into the position of wanting the job for his own self. And, the bishop thought to himself, his brother probably wanted it anyway. That was it. The dormant desire wanted to be nurtured—and flattered.

"Your books?" asked Francis. He stood and moved his large frame to the bookshelves. "My goodness, all the physics and computer books? Where's the theology?"

"'T' for theology," said the Reverend Dr. Cornelius. "They are arranged alphabetically by subject."

Francis's large figure leaned forward at the shelves as if he meant to intimidate them. "I see. But where do you fit your own books, falling under multiple categories as they do?"

Catherine laughed. "Ah, I put them dead in the middle—hovering at the epicenter of the vortex of knowledge. They are arranged left to right in order of publication."

"I see." Francis adjusted his mass forward to read the titles on the spines, beginning with the earliest book first:

The Solace of Physics and the Physics of Solace

Order Out of Chaos: How We Shall Learn to Live Together, Or Else

Chaos and the New World Order: Good News for Working People

The First Trumpet Blast of the Global Redemption Download: Computer Modeling the Revelation of St. John, and Other Fun Things to Come

Armageddon 2.1: A Cheaters Guide Including the Latest Codes and Passwords

The New and Improved Second Coming: Good Clean Fun with Those Loveable Nanobots

Roadtrip with Jesus Down the Information Superhighway: Easy Steps for Creating a Winning On-line Worship Strategy

A Brand New Broom: Do the Thirty-nine Articles have any Future in the Church of England?

A Survey of Emerging Global Comfort Industries and the Role of the New Church: An Investors Guide with Charts

Good Neighbors Say "Allah": How Inclusive Multiculturalism Will Promote the C.O.E. Amongst Our Special Friends

"The last book is laminated," said Catherine. "The vomit wipes right off."

Francis nodded as he turned away from the shelves to face her. "How very clever. What will they think of next?"

The Reverend Dr. Cornelius smiled at Catherine proudly and turned to his brother. "Really, Francis, I think I've done my part, don't you?"

The bishop had to agree. "But still, think of what you have left to achieve. Nothing has done as much as your books, Jeremiah, to keep the church alive in the new millennium. If not for the well-being of others, think of your own self and how helping others helps you."

Catherine raised an objection. "You mean a posh sinecure at St. Paul's?"

"Nonsense," said Francis. "I meant what it does for Jeremiah's sense of fulfillment. Virtue is its own reward, what? Even if St. Paul's wasn't at issue, Jeremiah has done tremendous *good* in this world, and that is more than most of us can say. More than you or I can say, and I do say so humbly. Our Jeremiah is a giant. Goodness! He is one of the contemporary world's leading theologians. That must count. It simply must. Draw a line right under that. Moreover, being Dean of St. Paul's is certainly not a sinecure. If Jeremiah goes there—as I hope he should—then it shall be because he can do *more* good from being there."

The bishop sat down with them and lifted his cup to his lips. "Mmm. Can someone warm this, please?"

"Of course." The Reverend Dr. Cornelius glanced at Catherine equivocally as he poured tea for Francis. "Oh, bother—cold. I'll make some new."

"I'll do it," said Catherine, and she got up to fill the kettle.

"Better still," said Francis and he carefully mispronounced his words: "'ow about some ginz insteadz?"

The Reverend Dr. Cornelius peered out the window at the setting sun, "What, is it past noon already?"

Francis looked at his brother and his eyes fairly twinkled. "I think we're safe."

"Well, if *you* say so, Bishop."

"Oh, you boys!" said Catherine, and she changed course for the cupboard where the liquor lived.

"We've become very happy here," said the Reverend Dr. Cornelius.

"The Cathedral of St. John the Divine?"

"Manhattan." And the postmodern divine went on to describe his walking expeditions and the haunts he liked best: bookstores, museums, parks, riverside pathways, and the unique churches and synagogues—many quite old in fact—that contributed to the city's endless array of diversions.

Tea was rather casual—they sat in the same chairs they'd been at all evening—and the conversation was without incident. Old friends were discussed. Francis reported the inevitable list of people who had passed on. An architectural discovery or two was mentioned. The war wasn't spoken of, and the church was avoided, until after dessert, when as they sipped more tea Francis finally opened up about his meetings that afternoon, the purpose of his visit, and his struggle with the African bishop, Bishop Achebe, whom Francis characterized as rigid, inflexible, bull-headed, and thoughtlessly conservative. "His opposition to changing the liturgy is like a concrete wall."

"Hang on," said the Reverend Dr. Cornelius. "I thought his big crusade was against the gay bishop from New England—Bishop Marvel?"

"Well, indeed it is," explained Francis. "Ironically, Bishop Marvel is also against the revised liturgy. Bringing them together, you see, just might cancel out their opposition, if you see what I mean?"

Catherine was narrowing her eyes at this.

The Reverend Dr. Cornelius was nodding. "I see. Francis, you're a genius."

"I don't understand?" said Catherine.

"First," explained her husband, "when the two are brought together then the African bishop will see that he has an ally in the gay bishop, and then perhaps he might no longer be such a rigid old monster on the gay issue."

Francis nodded. "Second, if the African bishop decides he still doesn't like the gay bishop—if the anti-homo issue carries his conscience—then he just might come over to our side on the issue of the liturgy. Finally, the third possibility: if the African bishop remains both opposed to the gay bishop and to the liturgy, well then that's good, too. It will stopper him up, because, after all, he and the gay bishop agree on the biggest question facing the church, and why call attention to this, as it will embarrass his 'standing firmly together' with the gay bishop in their opposition? He doesn't want to be seen on the same side of anything with his foe."

"What I call a win-win-win situation," said the Reverend Dr. Cornelius.

"I rather call it cynical," said Catherine.

The two brothers shrugged.

"These are matters of principle, after all," insisted Catherine. "And, anyway, how do you *really* feel about the gay issue? I want to know."

"Me?" asked Francis.

"Yes."

"It doesn't matter what I feel. Don't be ridiculous."

Catherine knitted her brow at this. "What do you mean, 'doesn't matter'?"

Francis shrugged. "I mean it is a political issue. I am on the side of consensus. I have to be. I'm the bishop."

"Francis!" Catherine insisted.

"Look here," he said. "Europe is changing. The church either changes along with it, or it shall be left behind. Now do you understand?"

Catherine nodded and then shook her head. "Gay people should be embraced. Surely, the Lord loves them as much as He loves any of us."

"I don't disagree with that."

"But you don't come right out and agree either." She looked at her husband. "And how do you feel about the rights of gay people? How do you *really* feel, Jeremiah?"

The Reverend Dr. Cornelius looked alarmed. "Catherine, my last book and my current project, too, are all about inclusion!"

Catherine nodded skeptically. "Yes, yes. And it's what's best for the Church."

"Now look here, Catherine." Francis looked fairly cross by now. "I don't know what kind of soppy American emotionalism has got into you, but I am your brother and I have had a very long day, and these are very difficult problems. And I am old, too. Please."

Catherine sighed. There was quiet for a few moments.

The Reverend Dr. Cornelius looked round the situation with the precision of a stopwatch. At just the right instant he said, "Tea?"

Both his brother and his wife said "yes" and further tragedy—or was it farce?—was averted.

"Anyway," said the Reverend Dr. Cornelius, again at the best possible moment. "We are in for an interesting week together."

Francis confessed that he had no better friends to see him through than his brother and sister. They all agreed to that, and love was restored.

Francis explained that at dinner Tuesday evening the African bishop would be seated at the big table together with the bishop from New England, but they wouldn't be placed close enough where contact might be necessary. That should come later, in the study afterwards where everybody would be drinking. "I'll push them together with me own bare hands," laughed Francis, and Catherine and the Reverend Dr. Cornelius couldn't help but have a scream at Francis moving his large arms round like a bear.

"I wonder," asked the Reverend Dr. Cornelius as his laughter died down. "With the C.O.E. coming aboard, just how opposed can the African bishop be to the new liturgy?"

"Well," chuckled Francis, Bishop Achebe hasn't gone so far as to suggest the Church of England should be thrown out of the Anglican Communion!"

As the laughter again subsided the bishop thought to check his watch. "Ah, eight o'clock—Eastern, what? And our long week begins tomorrow. Very early."

The Reverend Dr. Cornelius agreed. "I must be up at half-five for that service I have at Trinity. I have a forty-minute tube journey just to get down there."

Francis added, "I have a walk-on part tomorrow at the Cathedral. I shall be carrying a borrowed crook in the procession."

"Did you not bring yours with you on that big aeroplane?" quipped the Reverend Dr. Cornelius.

"No. I am to choose one from some enormous crook-cupboard at the Cathedral."

"I'll ring you a taxi, Francis." Catherine stood to find the telephone.

"How far is the cathedral?" asked Francis.

"Six blocks," said the Reverend Dr. Cornelius.

"I'd rather walk," said Francis. "Bother the taxi, Catherine. I've been sitting all day and I need to stretch me legs."

The Reverend Dr. Cornelius offered to walk his brother over.

"Thought you'd never ask."

As they stepped out the Reverend Dr. Cornelius was saying, "Actually, Francis, I'd like to return to the work I was doing in my middle period... that's where the future really lies—"

Catherine had the phone in her hand. Why not? She rang Oona to tell her about the day.

Warwick Colvin, Jr.'s

Corsairs of the Second Ether

Chapter 47,457: "The Appearance of Enlarged Perceptions"

The story thus far: Against the backdrop of the infinite void of the strange, laws-of-physics-defying universe (which even now was crystallizing to within mere nanoseconds of absolute zero) Cappy Cahtah Kohenum of the *Bifurcating Monofilament* has made the command decision to venture forth alone upon the surface of the super-carbon tar pit with just one object in mind—the retrieval of a smiledon brain to be used in re-shoeing the Pegasus drive. Having exhausted all other options, the heavy hopes of all the Lost Corsairs rest squarely upon Cappy's shoulders in this, their last-chance play. Indeed, their desperate ambition amounts to nothing less than to run the fabled Cornelius Loop, that wondrous program of infinite regressions, which, with a little luck, could restore them to their abode amongst the branching moonbeam buttresses of their beloved eternally self-similar multiverse.

Now read on!

Cappy Cahtah Kohenum of the *Bifurcating Monofiliment* raised his attenuator at the sluggish smiledons dragging their great paws through the congealing tar. The beginning of time was proving not so difficult to negotiate after all. His own feet, wrapped in the glossy silver fabric of his impervious time suit, moved deftly across the tar, which hardened beneath his super-cooled adamantine boot soles as his clever tactics brought him in an arc around the growling prehistoric tigers, their mighty fanged maws opening, closing, and shaking back and forth in a display of boiling anger that seemed directed as much against the universe as it was against Cappy.

"Take it easy, kitty," he said, and he slowly holstered his attenuator as the last of the big, saber-toothed tigers came to a stop and stuck fast in the tar.

"Well, bless this creation!" exclaimed Cappy, and he looked across the tar pit from horizon to horizon, and then gazed upwards to behold the stars as they gravitated towards the coalescing quasars which appeared as irregular blobs against the black firmament, increasingly crisscrossed with streaks of lavender and mauve as the stars fell into them.

Cappy knew the temperature was close to zero by now. He called to the *Bifurcating Monofilament,* which was half-sunk in the frozen surface, her massive tentacles ensnared in the tar, her antenna towers and sensory dishes clustered with glittering ice and moonwebs. Something of the multiverse was pulled through after all. Cappy certainly was very encouraged.

"Cappy to *Monofilament,*" said the mighty explorer as he toggled the transmit lever at his collar. He stomped his feet once or twice against the frozen tar. "Cappy to *Monofilament.*"

"*Monofilament* to Cappy. Go ahead, please."

Cappy smiled behind the dome of his time helmet. "You-hoo! Hello, *Monofilament!*"

"You-hoo. This is *Monofiliment.* Hello, Cappy. How are you, please?"

"Fine, thank you very much!" said Cappy playfully, and he added another "You-hoo!"

"You-hoo," again replied the *Monofilament,* and the exchange would have gone on in this jolly way for some time, but suddenly Cappy felt a little warm.

"Hello, Cappy? Are you still there, please?"

Cappy was busy identifying the source of that warmth. He cocked his eyebrows and looked this way and that inside his time helmet. It was coming from the chakra in his chest. He called the ship. "Hello, *Monofilament.* I am standing on the most remarkable frozen tar pit you could imagine. But—"

"You-hoo," said a new voice from the *Monofilament.* It was Professor Pop. "Hello, my boy. What do you see? Over."

Over! Cappy smiled at the professor's old-fashioned transmission manners. "You-hoo. Hello, Professor Pop? Is that you, please?"

"Yes, why I think it is? I mean, I should think I am! How are you, dear? Over."

Cappy was feeling very warm. "Problem—something—hang on—"

There was a pause at the other end. "Problem? Come again, my boy? Over."

Cappy was now feeling very very warm indeed. In fact, he was lifting his feet up and down they were so hot. He was saying, "Something in my—" when flames suddenly enveloped his suit.

Cappy's aura had caught fire!

"My goodness!" cried Cappy, and as the flames ate through it Cappy began brushing away pieces of his time suit! But then he came to a sudden realization. If only he wasn't too late! He reached up to toggle his transmitter and cried, "Everyone out of the ship! And hurry! Don't bother putting on your time suits! Abandon ship! Abandon ship!"

"Say again, please?" said Professor Pop. Evidently there was an emergency of some kind. Pop then realized he should hand the transmitter over to one of the young people. He thrust it at Lt. Baudrillard.

"Lt. Baudrillard, sir. Come again, sir? Did not copy that?"

Cappy was feeling very frustrated. His suit had nearly completely burned away. "Abandon—" he cried, but that was all. His flaming aura quickly consumed the rest of the suit and his equipment: his boots, gloves, helmet, his attenuator, and the transmitter too. He couldn't tell what the crew had understood of his transmission.

He stood on the surface of the frozen tar with his aura flaming. The smiledons were roaring again. Stuck in their tar as they were, their roaring was baleful and gloomy. Before him was the ship. It was suddenly glowing. "Dog-gone-it—"

And then the ship burst into flames. The combined heat of all the crews' auras igniting in unison set the *Bifurcating Monofilament* alight, explosively. In seconds it was a blazing inferno. The skin burned off first, followed by the antenna and sensor towers, which, with remarkable haste, crackled apart and fell away. Then the glowing orange support structure, a sort of branching broccoli of irregular form, began falling inward as the ship was consumed, while all about the flaming wreck the naked figures of the crew—each enveloped in spinning fire, and each glowing after the color of their personal self-concept—ran helter-skelter until safely away from the ship, when at last they turned and, safely enveloped in their burning auras, they watched the *Bifurcating Monofilament* cave in under its own weight and fall into a heap of fire and broken ruin.

When it was done they gathered together to organize a salvage party, which went into the smoldering wreck to recover whatever equipment had survived. Billy Blake's forge, the reticule from the tri-color synoptic sequence viewer, and the core of the Pegasus drive were all that remained.

"At least we managed to salvage the drive," said Billy thankfully.

Pop agreed that it was an important piece of equipment, but otherwise he was feeling much shaken and very old.

If there is any doubt, rest assured that Cappy more than rose to meet the occasion. His first task was to mend the morale of his crew, and he did so admirably with assurances that their auras would keep them going so long as they kept them lit. All the crew had fortunately survived. Indeed, the fire had exposed crew members who hadn't been seen in years. There was Professor Pop, of course, and familiar favorites like Little Billy Blake, Lt. Baudrillard, and Adam and Vadim Simulacrum; but also there were relatively mysterious corsairs like Sylvia the Plathological Anorexic, Pope Nobody the Twenty-third, Johnny Tesco, Pedantic Joe Philistine, Vicenté the Presidenté, Laughing Jack Calvin, Mary Make-Believe, Trailer Park Shane the Bling-Baring Gangsta Wanna-Be, and Sid the Freak.

Cappy looked deeply into the auras of the Lost Corsairs and decided he just might be able to pull it off. He wasn't about to let the situation slip out of control, despite how ridiculous it all looked. Anyway, the inevitable was the least of Cappy's concerns. Plainly and simply, he had to take inventory of what there was to work with and then make a plan. His identity had never remained so consistent for any similar period in all his life, and moreover being just one person was yet very strange to him, appearances notwithstanding. And this was a thing not going unnoticed by Lt. Baudrillard, who, nodding in Cappy's direction, muttered to Billy, "Strike that man where you will and he rings true."

To be continued....

Chapter Three

De sa Condition Présente et de sa Destinée

Remon. No one Clergie in the whole Christian world yields so many eminent scholars, learned preachers, grave, holy, and accomplish'd Divines as this Church of *England* doth at this day.

Answ. Ha, ha, ha.

—John Milton, *Animadversions upon the Remonstrants Defense against Smectymnuus*

One theory that does much to explain the efficacy of the Reverend Dr. Cornelius's trademark preaching style, in particular the unique experience of his sermons, proposes that a shepherd and his flock—the person in the pulpit delivering the sermon and the worshippers patiently attentive in the pews who listen to it—form a temporary though unique interpretive community—mediated by the institutions of the church and promoted by the especial architectural vernacular of its buildings—and bound together in worship by the participants' shared assumptions about what constitutes a truly inspired sermon. Thus in accordance with institution, tradition and shared interpretive conventions, the community of devotion is joined together by an internalized theological competence that allows them to respond appropriately to their scripture lessons, and indeed to any worshipful concept they encounter. By this formulation, any sermon (so long as it satisfies the congregation's internalized conventions) is empowered to advance the most outlandish claims even as the preacher operates the most peculiar stage effects, so that even in challenging the rules—so long as the architecture is right—bizarre representations, even awkward manners, satisfy the congregants' expectations and sets them free to emotionally celebrate the priest's simply being there and saying what amounts to *nothing*. Such a church virtually rattles with released tension as all just authority and reasonable truths are dismissed, as if thrust up and out the metaphoric "spout" of the church steeple, so that hallucinatory identifications with the poor, the suffering, the displaced, and the marginalized create within the sanctuary a temporary political alliance that can be as swiftly concluded as it was convened—through the simple expedient of banging an iron bell.

But this is by no means to be construed as yet another echo of the claims of certain critical churchmen, that the Reverend Dr. Cornelius haphazardly performed his services without a set of consistent assumptions or techniques. Dismiss such criticisms immediately. For the record, the Reverend Dr. Cornelius was in possession of a sophistication that transcended the pedestrian sensibilities of his obtuse (and jealous, ahem) detractors. The Reverend Dr. Cornelius was indeed most consistent in the practice of his oratory, and moreover, considering his formidable genius, it should come as no surprise that his practices were in keeping with the actual intellectual material of his sermons. Thus not only did the sermons of the Reverend Dr. Cornelius return again and again to his central thesis—that near-chaotic complexity triggers self organization—but the structure of the sermons themselves, and their delivery, were also configured according to the cosmic explanation implicit in the meaning of his thesis. Not only were his sermons significant grammatically, but they resonated performatively as well; that is to say, whilst he stood in the pulpit (or before the congregation in the aisle, his preferred stage—or *orchestra*) he was a man who actually practiced what he preached. In the execution of his sermons the Reverend Dr. Cornelius employed a series of recurring devices that he triggered at strategic moments both in the text of his discourse and in his delivery. These devices included:

First, *the construction of complexity and organizational depth*: he would use obscurity, vagueness, overlaying concepts and actions—all contributing to a general cluttering of his ideas and his presentation.

Second, *multivalent signifiers*: he would tell cryptic parables featuring characters, themes and plots that stood for a multiplicity of concepts, all of which were intermittently transforming and intermittently reflexive.

Third, *feedback technique*: he would select figures and themes that served as metaphors for the process of divine revelation, inspired speaking, and the exalted interpretation of heavenly signs.

Fourth, *catastrophe, folding, landslides, and phase transitions*: he would introduce sudden and disruptive changes in image, concept or scene.

Fifth, *scaling*: here he would employ parallel images, personalities and themes, altering their contours but evoking their self-similar connectivity through citing—indeed projecting upon a silver screen above the high alter—the mathematical proofs of Mandelbrot's famous equations and the dazzling graphic dramaturgy of fractal geometry.

Something more must be said of his demonstrations. The Reverend Dr. Cornelius was famous in the church for his integration of scientific exposition and audio-visual technology with the liturgy. Indeed, astounding revelations of physics aside, his signal "autograph" was the use of visual aids as he worked the pulpit, the altar, or (again, his preferred platform) the front of the aisle before the congregation. It is not difficult to picture the Reverend Dr. Cornelius at the outset of his career as a preacher, like a young Christopher Lee—tall, stern, determined, the consummate man of skill—surrounded by bubbling flasks and steaming beakers, pendulums, inclined planes upon which rolled shining steel balls, van der Graff generators, parallel wires that supported a constant series of snapping blue sparks that climbed between them—meanwhile the man himself cutting a heroic figure with a pair of goggles protecting his eyes and a lab coat over his cassock as he lit a Bunsen burner on the high altar to heat the Eucharist wine and produce a miraculous steam so that he might simultaneously celebrate the miracle of transubstantiation whilst chanting an explanation of the process of evaporation, and all the while not firmly establishing but rather slyly implying, and rather mystically, some analogical connection between the two processes. One of his techniques was to employ a sort of secondary altar, or sub-table, which he placed centrally in the midst of the congregation. Here he would employ a child volunteer from amongst the flock, and whom, with an expression of pastoral delight, he would introduce to the assembled worshippers together with a little of his own chat with the child, which was designed to make the child look foolish to the degree and for the effect that even the most stupid blockhead sitting in the pews could feel that there was at least one person (albeit a child) in the sanctuary whose ignorance exceeded his own.

Handing the child a toy beach pail and shovel, the Reverend Dr. Cornelius would proceed to pour sand from his own pail, which he replenished from a wheel barrow that another assistant, usually the prettiest girl in the choir, had moments before pushed up from the back of the church (nearly tipping the barrow several times and producing further amusement amongst the congregants, as well as prompting a discreet cackle from some large woman in an ostentatious hat, or a cough from an old toper who was minding his watch in anticipation of that highball he'd be enjoying with Sunday brunch). The Reverend Dr. Cornelius would pour the sand upon the table and proclaim "Ah ha!" as it began forming a mound. As more sand was added and the mound increased in size, slides and avalanches occurred along the mound's sides. As the Reverend Dr. Cornelius explained, the sides of the mound were "at the edge of chaos" so that only a few grains of sand added to the top could create massive disturbances—avalanches—lower along the sides of the pile. The Reverend Dr. Cornelius would demonstrate the process, again looking like a commanding and intense Christopher Lee as he towered over the mound, the pretty girl, and the child, who might have wandered off by now (more cackling); meanwhile with his fingers slowly dropping pinches of sand on the mound, the postmodern divine would suddenly alter his tone and his persona—if addressing a middle class congregation, he would speak as a mild mannered university lecturer, or, if his congregation was of the laboring classes, he would speak in the shrill tones of a low church enthusiastic beholding the marvel of God's handiwork; and so addressing the faithful in his tone-of-the-moment, he would observe: "As a management model our growing mound evokes images of elite actors exercising control over a broad domain of holdings through the careful tweaking of variables at the top of the mound, much as our intrepid financial leaders are hard at work balancing the global economy." This was of particular interest if there had been a recent factory closing, or if the town's biggest employer had recently "outsourced" one of its departments—Accounting, for example—to an outside provider; and the demonstration would especially capture the attention amongst such worshippers—mothers, fathers, the supporters of households—as were wondering where the next pay check was coming from. The Reverend Dr. Cornelius would drop more sand on the pile, produce further avalanches, and continue: "Catastrophic disturbances occur along the sides of the pile until self organization—a sort of 'order for free'—asserts itself, and the pile grows *larger*, all the while retaining its shape." The postmodern divine would then seek at this point to reassure the doubtful, again asserting that the growing mound and the avalanches were proofs of a cosmic balance, that the Lord had created a "multiverse" of possibilities in which anything could happen; but, indeed, wherever and whatever may befall, His underlying balance was at the end of the day *the* underlying order and *the* physics of all things—from chaos must emerge new order and stability, and all should thus be well and fit to the divine purpose of the Lord. And after pausing dramatically, the Reverend Dr. Cornelius would pronounce a most posh and breathless "Amen!"

His "Mound of Sand" sermon—entitled "Order Out of Chaos"—in fact became the basis of his ground-breaking (and highly technical) second book, which subsequently spawned a tremendously popular sequel.

Laboratory coats, safety goggles, electric sparks and stained test tubes were one thing, but where the Reverend Dr. Cornelius really excelled was in his use of sound equipment and light projectors. His taste in background music was impeccable—and this was the celebrated opinion of the director of the Academy of St. Martin-in-the-Fields, an organization, it must be pointed out, that knows a thing or two about music, and absolutely *everything* about excellence. Also remarkable was his use of illuminated images, graphs and moving designs. His PowerPoint presentations could evoke tears from even the Coroner of the City of New York! But where the Reverend Dr. Cornelius really wowed them was in his use of an orchestrated amalgamation of sound, projected images and human theatre. The number of services in which he staged multi-media events are too numerous to record here, but special mention must be made of the celebrated "Passion of Physical Reality" service he staged in the Millennium Dome, and which was attended by the late Queen Mum, Allah rest her soul, who, although she didn't express much interest in meeting the postmodern divine, did yet acknowledge, "This Reverend Cornucopia has the most amazing wardrobe. I must recommend his seamstress to the Archbishop. That multi-colored cassock bearing those delightful fractal designs is such good fun!"

Her oldest grandson was also present. He nodded absently as he was distracted just then by the Brazilian dancers running about in the fetching brevities of their bikinis with those abbreviated "strings" between the dancers' gluteus maximoids. He simply nodded nervously and mumbled "good heavens," and then thinking he had heard something *else,* he looked at his grandmother with a shocked expression and said, "What! The Archbishop in a bikini?"

But such spectacles actually belong to the Reverend Dr. Cornelius's early career as an architect of the new worship, and the service he directed on the Sunday morning that concerns this tale was fully disabused of projected images, sound effects, scientific apparatuses, laboratory coats, safety goggles, and so on. Indeed, the Reverend Dr. Cornelius compressed all his talents for innovation into the sermon itself, which was titled, "What Need of Understanding when Through God All is Explained?"

The thesis of his sermon was straightforward and memorable—memorable to an appropriate degree. As was usual for the Reverend Dr. Cornelius, his sermon that morning at Trinity Episcopal Church was ingeniously yet sensibly connected to that morning's scripture readings. A rather awkwardly dressed (over-sized, boxy, square-cut American suit—besides it was tan, in December!—and it was wrinkled!) elderly African-

American gentleman read the selection from the Old Testament. It was Genesis 3.1-7, which tells of the serpent and the temptation in the garden. The reader garbled the cadence of one or two lines but was otherwise fine—"at least it sounds natural" was the best the Reverend Dr. Cornelius could say to himself as he followed along. But then as the reader described our first parents experiencing the opening of their eyes and the reader stumbled upon the word "naked"—which he pronounced "neck-ked"— the Reverend Dr. Cornelius groaned so audibly that the reader's wife, who was sitting in the front pew, poor thing, felt her fuse ignite, so that later that afternoon she admonished her husband for being a complete embarrassment in front of the congregation, though not so awful, she admitted, as "that snob preacher from England," whom she alternatively called "Sir Sniff-A-Lot" and "Dr. Frightenstein."

The reader of the New Testament selection was rather more fluent. Not a member of Trinity, she was a regular attendee of St. John's and had come all the way from the Upper West Side to hear the Reverend Dr. Cornelius. Indeed, the Reverend had a small following at the Cathedral and several of them, along with the reader, had made the trip down that morning to hear their "fair dominé" as they called him (completely to his bewilderment); though, to do them justice, they also called him their "irrepressible English genius" (which he modestly accepted: "Well, dear ladies, if you insist, but don't tell my wife you call me that or she will withhold my supper until such time as I write another *ten* books! Ha, ha, ha, ha, ha, ha…"). She was very much a creature of St. John's in her lace-up boots, black mid-length skirt, and flowing, colorful Macintosh rose pattern scarf, which she made a big show of throwing over her shoulder as she stepped up to the stand supporting the oversize scriptures. As she read from II Timothy 3.1-7 her voice was rehearsed and elegant, though from the perspective of the Reverend Dr. Cornelius it was typical of those infantile American personas barking out vain, puffed-up and sanctimonious ninety-second "essays" as heard every evening from Washington DC on National Public Radio's parade of twee nobodies. Normally she was a person who would choke on something as sexist as that morning's New Testament reading, but it was a favor for the Reverend Dr. Cornelius, after all, and there was always a method to his madness, and so she was fully enthused with drama and in complete, driving sympathy with Paul in his second letter to Timothy as she read of those misleading charlatans who "make their way into households and captivate silly women, overwhelmed by their sins and swayed by all kinds of desires, who are always being instructed and can never arrive at knowledge of the truth."

The Reverend Dr. Cornelius's thesis, as alluded to earlier, was direct and sensible to all who would listen. His purpose, as always, was to bring faith to the hearts of the congregation, and thus to illustrate the goal in mind his central strategy was to draw a distinction between those who possess faith, and those who do not. Faithful people were those who embraced the Lord as the *explanation* for all things; whilst people lacking in faith were seeking some kind of vague *understanding*—of what they did not know, nor did they know it when they found it. The quest for an explanation was a quest for the truth, which must always be the Lord, and it was selfless. "Like a cup empty of itself, the Lord only can fill it truly," was the trope he used to sway the believers into the spirit of the thing, that is faith, which as he explained was the terminus of trouble and an end to all suffering. On the other hand, however, was the quest for *understanding*, which was a self-centered and self-involved chasing of ghosts and illusion. "For," as he said, "understanding can go only so far as catching a shadow glimpse, here or there, of where one stands in relation to the thing he or she contemplates. Understanding can go no further than to understand where one is situated in relation to the thing one contemplates. Understanding is thus rooted in the self: understanding does not acknowledge the Lord as the explanation of all things, and it is vain."

Key to the postmodern church doctor's distinction was what he called "why people" and "how people".

"Why people," patiently intoned the Reverend Dr. Cornelius, "want to know why something happens. Free from the diversions of speculative moonshine, they want to know why something happens so they can address the root cause of things. 'Why people' are the bold solvers of problems. For example, a physician does not seek to *understand* a disease, but rather seeks an empirical *explanation*; for it is through arriving at this explanation that a proper treatment can be prescribed. Thus 'why people' are pious and obedient. They are wise to acknowledge that there are things on this earth and in this *multiverse*," as he phrased it, "that are beyond human ken, and that all human knowledge is so vast that our one slim hope is to look to divide up the great multiverse into departments of explanation, and place the search for explanation into the hands of specialists, of scientists, of pious leaders in government and business, our generals and warriors, and into the hands of the bold speculators who have embarked with the human race into the great self-regulating marketplace of information. We are beholden to the intrepid leaders in all the scientific fields and the arts who are laboring to uncover the explanations to all the varieties of experience, and who are thus bridging the gap between our ignorance and the one true explanation that is the Lord."

The Reverend Dr. Cornelius looked sternly round to affirm the congregation was paying close attention.

"How people—" and here the Reverend Dr. Cornelius sniffed and exhaled with measured but patient disapproval "—how people, on the other hand, are like Eve and Adam in our reading this morning from the first of the old books of Moses. The Paradise they lived in, I should have you to understand, was actually a Paradise of *explanation*. Just as Adam named the animals—their names coming trippingly and automatically over his tongue—so too were all things known to Adam and his helpmeet Eve. Our first parents required no understanding of the Paradise around them, for their state was one of grace with the explanation that the Lord was the explanation to all things. When Satan tempted our first mother, as it is written in the Holy Scriptures, he tempts her with two deadly tools, like the two prongs of his forked tongue: a lie and an illusion. He lies thus to Eve: that if she consumes the deadly fruit, 'You will not die.'" And here the Reverend Dr. Cornelius nearly gasped. "In truth, Adam and Eve lived, as scripture reports, long lives, but they did alas in the end *die* for their sins. Next, Satan says, 'your eyes will be opened, and you will be like Gods, knowing good and evil.' And this is the second prong of Satan's forked tongue, the prong of illusion. For what knowledge is this of which Satan speaks—a *knowledge* of good and evil?" And at this point the Reverend Dr. Cornelius held his hand aloft and paused to build effect, then brought his hand down to brush smoothly forward over his sermon and then out in the direction of the congregants, in some subtle but unmistakable indication of matters important and issues grave. "When Satan promises knowledge he actually delivers nothing but that obscure, self-centered, revolving, circular quest for understanding. Let me say this again. The Lord has provided for all the needs of Adam and Eve, including an explanation, *the explanation* of all that Adam and Eve need to know; indeed, the explanation for all there is to know. All questions have been answered. So what can Satan's promise of knowledge be but a one-way trip round the self-centered and godless quest for understanding? And so, too, again as Paul warns Timothy in our reading from the New Testament: we must beware of that charlatan who steals into our house and instructs us as to that thing called *understanding*, which ever leads us round and round everywhere but can never ever, as the inspired apostle writes, 'arrive at a knowledge of the truth.' Thus we have our choices before us, dear people: a pitiful and mortal *understanding* that can only understand where itself stands in relation to other things, moreover with the Lord withal. Or, indeed, the *explanation* that is the Lord withal, the Lord withal—" and here the Reverend Dr. Cornelius elevated his gaze and the pitch of his voice in homiletic gusto "—and we can accept the Lord and embrace his explanation, his love, and a life beside His Son everlasting. Amen."

And here the postmodern church doctor lowered his head.

The rest of the service came off a snap. The Reverend Dr. Cornelius was a bit irritated, however, by his assistant who presided over the Eucharist, as after Holy Communion he revealed himself to be one of those persons whose sense of church ritual and priestly procedure bordered on superstition. He insisted upon cleaning off the chalice thoroughly and completely—rather like a good butler to a good home polishing the good silver. He licked the chalice and gave it the eyeball—began to lick again but checked himself to eyeball it once more, then, satisfied, ran out his tongue again and licked the chalice over and over with grand determination; his tongue pressing in and out and round and over, then drawing back into the priest's mouth to orbit a few turns against the pickets of his teeth, when it was ejaculated again into the cup, again to go round and round until it was withdrawn again into the priest's mouth where it again preformed its service—as a shocked Reverend Dr. Cornelius could tell from the odd motions of his fellow churchman's lips and cheeks—before once again the man spit his tongue out in a spasm of movement and whitened saliva into the ceremonial chalice against the odd chance that there might yet remain one more precious and holy drop of Eucharist wine, the Savior's blood, or one more microscopic particle of the Christ's body that had somehow been missed the last time his grotty old tongue had swabbed the filthy silver cup. Countless times the priest stuck his tongue into the thing and sloshed it about and round and then the tongue was withdraw inside his mouth once more, out, in, out, in, out, in, out, in… The Reverend Dr. Cornelius, fully alarmed and petrified by the maniacal ravenousness of his fellow churchman's acrobatic tongue, quite expected that at any moment the tongue might snake forth from one of the man's nostrils, pour down into the cup, flip out across the alter, drop to the floor, race down the aisle, dash the front doors aside, hesitate left and right before Broadway, and then plunge down Wall Street before its elasticity had been truly exhausted, whereupon with a snap it would explosively withdraw again up Wall Street, cross

Broadway, shoot back betwixt the un-hinged doors, zip up the aisle and slurp inside the priest's nostril and down into the steaming sewer of his mouth before once more flooding out again into the holy chalice to begin the process afresh.

After worship had concluded there was a delightful coffee and tea service in the common room inside the quaint white building that stood between the church and the rectory. The Reverend Dr. Cornelius appeared at the front door with his cassock draped over his arm. A deacon took it from him to hang up, and not a few heads turned to watch the statuesque churchman pour a cup of tea and select from the array of Pepperidge Farm biscuits that had been carefully arranged on the tray. No doubt many of those turned heads were wondering who would have the favor of sitting with him and enjoying his conversation. He turned with his tea and biscuits in either hand and gazed quickly across the room pretending not to notice the smiling faces of his admirers, and absolutely not acknowledging those persons who were moving their mouths in a pantomime of, "Oh, here he is!" or, what was truly pathetic, "Come sit with me."

Not content to be arrested in their pursuit of his attention, the ladies who had come down from St. John's called out as he rolled past them, and fairly drowned him with appreciation and proprietary allusions to his brilliance. The ladies insisted on making a big show of letting everyone sitting in the common room know they were down from the Cathedral of St. John the Divine exclusively to hear their resident English genius, and moreover they mixed in with their clucking and gossip certain phrases like "well done" and "good show" and "cracking good sermon" so that in order to avoid further embarrassment the Reverend Dr. Cornelius took the offensive and singled out for special praise the woman who had earlier read from the New Testament.

"Oh, did you really like the way I read this morning, Doctor?"

"Magic. Simply marvelous." And the Reverend Dr. Cornelius slipped beyond the table as the women trained venomous smiles upon she who had been thus anointed by the churchman's pleasant attention.

Under his breath he congratulated himself for so suavely deflecting their boring chatter: "Well done, Cornelius!"

But then whom did the Reverend Dr. Cornelius sit with? He avoided the other churchmen, and the little African-American man whose wife was looking up at the postmodern divine with the hapless expression of a person watching a bird fly into a window. He also avoided the widow with the inviting gaze, who was no doubt inspired by something she had read in I

49

Timothy—which she had paged through and read during the sermon—a book which has a lot to say about the urgings and fit usages of widows, and which no doubt played a role that morning in awakening this particular widow to the possibilities.

Who the Reverend Dr. Cornelius actually chose to sit with was the architect, Lovechild, who was something of a celebrity in his own right. This Lovechild was the person who had submitted the winning design for the reconstruction of Ground Zero, and who had met twice before with the Reverend Dr. Cornelius: their first meeting was at a conference in Scotland in the early-nineties where complexity theory and computer modeling were the subjects of an exuberant (and elegant) series of meetings that addressed the frontiers in architecture attending the advent of computer modeling, chiefly sophisticated drafting programs like AutoCad. The seminar went beyond the instrumentation and focused specifically on new possibilities for representation and subject matter, and at that time it was thought that rather than the flattened architectural vernaculars that had done so much to make the buildings of the eighties appear cheap and kitsch, the seminar promoted the idea of drawing upon science and mathematics for the patterns that were to be celebrated in the architecture of the new millennium. Many of the world's leading architects had attended, as had the Reverend Dr. Cornelius, who had read a paper on complex equations and modeling various Cabalistic codes. The seminar was rightly regarded as the signal event in shaping the architecture of the new century. Indeed, both Lovechild's winning design for Ground Zero, as well as the new subway transportation center designed by Calatrava, with its great reptilian spines and articulated, motor-driven, fin-shaped roof, were roundly influenced by the subject of the seminar, which was fondly remembered by the attendees to the degree that participation made one a member of a sort of special society, so that even many years later the people who had been there, upon even the odd chance meeting, always felt drawn to one another to talk intimately with a mixture of the easiness of old friends and the pride of belonging to an exclusive club—an international society of geniuses!

The Reverend Dr. Cornelius had also come across Lovechild on Rector Street earlier that autumn—it was October, actually—and the two men— one a dashing European smiling broadly with teeth flashing beneath his trademark Armani eyeglasses; the other a tall, erect Englishman in alligator boots with a seventy dollar hair-do, shoe-horned into a tight, double-breasted suit coat and wearing about his long aristocratic neck a silk kerchief that flew occasionally in the autumn wind as round them the financial capital of the world thrust its teaming buildings up, up, up into the cloudless shimmering sky. The two had almost walked past each other, and then stopped, did a double-take—the architect pointed, the priest shrugged and nodded— "Yes, alas, it is us!"—and then the two extended their hands, and bowing to one another briefly, ejaculated the seminar's name and then agreed that they had to go off together and have a talk straightaway; but, unfortunately, the architect had a meeting with the Ground Zero Development Corporation that afternoon, and much as he would like to cancel it—and they both nodded and smiled wisely at the double-entendre—the architect said that he was sorry but he could not just then pop off for a chat. The Reverend Dr. Cornelius invited the architect to drop by Trinity that Sunday, as he was filling in and doing a sermon, after which they might talk over coffee; and the architect agreed that he would try to make it. But that had been several months ago, and now as they sat together Lovechild explained that he had been called away on that particular Sunday back in October, and he had felt so bad about it that he had been literally checking the sign on the church *daily* (the architect's office was actually just down Rector Street) hoping to see the announcement of a return engagement. During their chance meeting in October, the Reverend Dr. Cornelius had neglected to tell the architect that he was attached to St. John's; and, had the architect known, he would have taken the subway up and met with his friend there. For his part, the Reverend Dr. Cornelius was, thanks to the newspapers, very aware of the bumpy ride the politicians, the Ground Zero Development Corporation, the "landlord," and the victims' families groups had been giving Lovechild; otherwise, he would have aggressively acted upon their chance meeting, and would have persisted in making an appointment for luncheon. Meanwhile, the Reverend Dr. Cornelius was grateful for the architect's thoughtfulness in checking the sign regularly, and was moreover doubly thankful the architect had stopped by on this particular Sunday, and thanked him, too, for the opportunity to join with him for a refreshment just as they—with a sniff of amusement after sorting all this out—had agreed to in October. In response, the architect mentioned that from his office window he could see the steeple of Trinity Church, and whenever he saw it he thought of the chance run-in he had had with the Reverend Dr. Cornelius, and how extraordinary that had been, as he rarely ran into people anymore who had been up to that important seminar in Scotland. On his side, the Reverend Dr. Cornelius confessed that when he read the newspaper articles about Lovechild's fortunes, he sometimes grew a little cross over the way that he, Lovechild, was being treated. After

51

reading one such article, indeed, the Reverend Dr. Cornelius almost sent a supportive e-mail to the architect, but at the time concluded such an action would have been too forward; furthermore, in the wake of their chance meeting on Rector Street, it might have looked even peculiar. The architect said, "Nonsense!" and invited the Reverend Dr. Cornelius to e-mail him anytime. Now the Reverend Dr. Cornelius alluded once more to the awkwardness he felt that previous time he was about to e-mail the architect, and then quipped that in the wake of this particular conversation they were enjoying just then, might not e-mailing him now, also, and in the same way, seem likewise a little peculiar?

They both laughed out loud.

Such was the substance of their talk, which was one of the more civilized conversations the Reverend Dr. Cornelius had been part of in America, where, it seemed, everyone was busy shouting some bit of information *at* one another, and where people really didn't have the time or the inclination to relax and enjoy the art of conversation. Lovechild—who, as mentioned before, was from Europe, and who in fact was looking forward to returning to work there after his relationship with the politicians, the Ground Zero Development Corporation, the "landlord," and the victims' families groups had dissolved—agreed that he would probably treasure this conversation with the Reverend Dr. Cornelius as one of the few happy memories he would take away with him when he departed for Europe—a confession for which the Reverend Dr. Cornelius expressed the profoundest sympathy, before himself confessing that the life of a genius was a life lived alone, a life spent apart, and rare indeed were civilized conversations, or civilized people, to be found.

Thus the Reverend Dr. Cornelius was feeling a little melancholy as he rode the Number Two express subway to Morningside Heights. The wind seemed particularly verbal as if chatting on and on about nothing whatsoever as he charged up 103rd Street to his apartment building on Riverside Drive.

Once inside his apartment he was greeted by Catherine and her friend Oona, who had brought along—gosh!—her horrid Rottweiler, which was called, strangely enough, "Lampoon." How a woman could live alone in an apartment with a monster like Lampoon was something the Reverend Dr. Cornelius couldn't understand, much less approve. As usual, Oona was a bit lofty with the Reverend Dr. Cornelius. She sat there with her long fringes or "bangs" (in front) and closely razored nape (behind) wearing her blue jeans, ivory wool jumper, and scarf—another of those scarf outfits; uniforms, he thought. She called him "ma'lord" and "guv'na" and always deferred to him in a condescending fashion, as if in asking for his consensus or his opinion she really meant his consensus or his opinion was immaterial. When they had first met she had been a bit timid, but as she discovered his mild nature she found she couldn't help pressing things more and more; and try as she might she couldn't tell if he was simply a pushover, or if instead he had a very long fuse. She could hardly expect him of actually being ahead of her game. Way ahead.

When he entered the flat she began mocking him immediately: "Good afta'noon, guv'na"—and it took intervention from Catherine to rein her in, but then of course only for the time being.

The conversation, such as it was, hardly bears recording. It was all an even thing, an indifferent matter. The dog's comments—at one point he yawned—were as interesting as anything the humans had to say.

Catherine, however, asked the Reverend Dr. Cornelius to join her, Oona, and the children from the preschool group that Tuesday morning for an outing. The Reverend Dr. Cornelius was uninterested. Moreover, Tuesday evening was the dinner up at the Cathedral with all the struggling bishops. But when Catherine explained that the outing was to the American Museum of Natural History, the Reverend Dr. Cornelius found the corners of his mouth elevating slightly—tugging, as it were, at the better side of his imagination.

"The American Museum of Natural History, did you say?"

"Right-O, your Lawdship," said Oona, and not without something that might be construed as friendliness. "We could use your help with the kiddies. You game?"

The Reverend Dr. Cornelius preformed a quick time-benefit analysis. If he remained at home Tuesday he could work on his book, but that would mean hours spent staring out the window at the tops of bare trees, at the Hudson, at New Jersey, and all the while waiting for that dinner at the Rectory which would loom over the afternoon like a black cloud ready to fall down on him. On the other hand, he could go to the Museum and muck about with the children, which activity would satisfy his appetites for both science and confusion; and it would be a good place to be—far away from the Cathedral and that inevitable dinner.

"Right! Its sounds a good thing. I will go, Catherine."

Catherine said, "Good. I am so glad you will be coming. And it will give you a chance to meet Capricorn."

"Well, good then," said the Reverend Dr. Cornelius, not knowing what she was talking about.

Oona pressed her lips together. "You people sure do say 'good' a lot."

The Reverend Dr. Cornelius raised his eyebrows at this. "Of course we people do, Oona. It's the Lord, you know. We are blessed in our good lives, what? And we should all think to remind ourselves."

And she had no answer to that.

Warwick Colvin, Jr.'s

Corsairs of the Second Ether

Chapter 47,458: "The Genealogy of Civilizations"

The story thus far: Surrounded by the burned wreckage of the *Bifurcating Monofilament*, the Lost Corsairs are exposed to whatever terrors the laws-of-physics-defying universe can throw at them. After the mighty conflagration that almost instantly consumed their ship, only three key tools remain: the smoldering forge of Little Billy Blake, the reticule of their once far-seeing tri-color synoptic sequence viewer, and the core of the Pegasus engine itself. The core is useless, however, unless it can be re-shoed and made to run the fabled Cornelius Loop program, which can, or so it is believed, solve any problem of inter-transitory navigation. Some of the corsairs doubt any possibility for salvation, but fortunately they have a man among them who does not doubt. He is their commander, Cappy Cahtah Kohenum, scourge of all that is superstitious or born from thoughtless custom, and thus one who is rightly known across all the myriad scales of the Second Ether as the Daredevil Corsair.

Now read on!

The scene had been set. The Lost Corsairs stood at attention, shifting their feet occasionally as their burning auras melted the tar beneath them. They looked at each other as their commander encouraged them with his counsel. For the time being the smiledons had grown quiescent. It might be said that the big saber-tooth cats were as attentive to Cappy's words as the corsairs. Above, ominous, glorious, and moving with unspeakable purpose, the last of the stars were joining with the great wobbling, blob-like quasars that shimmered brightly as the temperature of the universe inched yet closer to the beginning of time.

There was one Corsair, however, who insisted upon interrupting Cappy's speech—an incident hardly worth noting except for the significance it lends to events related later in the story.

"Supwiddat?"

It was Trailer Park Shane, the Bling-Baring Gangsta Wanna-Be.

Cappy glanced momentarily in the direction of Trailer Park Shane, but otherwise ignored him and continued his speech.

"Yo! Cappy getting iz mack on real strong and people actually start to believe it, but it's all a front!"

Cappy had reached the end of the ranks and now he turned slowly around to look at Shane, who stood at the other end of the line. Shane swung his hands up in an exaggerated motion as if to embrace the air, and shrugged his shoulders. "Supwidat?"

Cappy squinted his eyes and leaned forward. "What's up with what?"

"Yo!" said Shane. "None of uz iz pimpnotized by your stale rap."

Cappy began scratching his head. "You talking to me?"

"Yo!" Shane turned up his index fingers before his face. He felt rather naked without his blings (which along with his grills and 300 dolla bathin apes had burned away in the conflagration) but he was nonetheless bold in his manner. "Yo! I'm tahkin to you, ya little wanksta."

Cappy stopped scratching his head and became very stern. "Who you calling 'little wanksta'?"

"I be calling you 'little wanksta,' little wanksta." said Shane, and then he folded his arms and struck an arrogant pose with his legs splayed out dramatically.

Cappy controlled his anger. It could be that Trailer Park Shane wasn't really trying to dis him, but instead was only seeking to get some attention from the other corsairs, who in the past had never really paid much attention to Shane, or his blings for that matter.

Lt. Baudrillard glanced significantly at Billy. The other corsairs remained facing forward at attention.

"Now look here, Shane." Cappy spoke firmly but diplomatically. "We all have to pull together here. We are only as strong as the weakest link in the chain."

Professor Pop thought this was a very reasonable thing to say, and he was greatly at odds to understand Trailer Park Shane's unpleasant behavior.

And it was unpleasant. Shane wrinkled his lips in a royal pout, and then he raised his middle finger in Cappy's direction. "Wha'd'ya tink about dat, Cappy-wappy!"

Cappy swallowed—he gulped! But he wasn't going to react to this. He studied the situation for a few moments as he formulated his response. He wasn't insensitive to the fact that his attenuator had been destroyed in the fire; he would have to improvise if the situation got touchy. As for Trailer Park Shane's behavior, it just didn't make sense.

Suddenly Cappy's eyes dilated. He couldn't believe the conclusion that had just popped into his brain, but there it was: Trailer Park Shane the Bling-Baring Gangsta Wanna-Be was actually Old Reg the Original Insect in disguise! For an instant—but only an instant—Cappy was terrified at the implications. But then reason prevailed and actually the phenomenon of the Original Insect manifest in the persona of the absurd corsair before him was a stroke of good luck.

Cappy sprang over to a nearby smiledon, snapped off its saber-tooth, and then raced back to face Shane. "Thought I wouldn't see through your little masquerade, eh?" and Cappy laughed.

"No fair!" cried Shane. "Help eberybody! Help eberybody! Dat nut gotz a big toof!"

Little Billy Blake was little, but he was bold after all. "Cappy, what are you doing! That tooth isn't fair!" Lt. Baudrillard pulled Billy back and cupped his hand over the engineer's mouth. When corsairs were about to scrap it was NOT a good thing to get involved, and especially if one of the combatants was the captain!

Cappy heard Billy and spoke to him while keeping his watchful eyes on Trailer Park Shane. "Steady, Billy! This is no ordinary Lost Corsair. Observe closely: See his eyes? We all have human pupils, but Shanes eyes are—"

"Compound!" Billy blurted out the word as Lt. Baudrillard eased his grip.

"Exactly!" cried Cappy. It's old Reg the Original Insect, all packed up into human form and painted up with a fake aura for a decoy!"

"Help! Help!" cried the naked trailer park devil. "Cappy tryna go crazy and gettin' hyped up!"

Now smiling—but it was a grim, desperate smile to be sure—Cappy lunged forward with the saber tooth and beheaded Old Reg on the spot!

Cappy was old school in action. Old Reg was cleanly decapitated like it was business as usual. His body fell and flopped about like a fish, while his head—crying "Supwidat! Supwidat!"—went rolling across the tar pit. Then both pieces of the diabolical imposter were still, the flaming aura round them dying to an unpleasant green glow. From across the tar pit the head began calling once more, "Supwidat! Supwidat!"

In the ensuing moments Cappy took a metal shaft from the burnt debris of the *Bifurcating Monofilament* and marched off across the tar pit. He collected Old Reg's head along the way and a hundred yards from the corsairs he stuck the shaft in the tar and impaled Reg's head upon it.

"There now," said Cappy. "Here you'll serve as a reminder."

"You trippn'!" cried the head as Cappy turned it away from the direction of the Lost Corsairs, off to face the darkness. The head glowed an ugly green and sent aloft a dim flame that snaked to and fro as it drifted away through the night.

"In the multiverse you are real enough," said Cappy. "But here in the universe you are no more than myth." Cappy nodded forthrightly at a job well done.

"Supwidat! Supwidat!" said Old Reg, but Cappy turned his back on the abomination and returned across the tar pit to join his compatriots.

Corsairs are an emotional lot, and the crew sent up a great cheer when Cappy returned. They had a long, caper-filled dance to celebrate. As they hopped up and down the tooth was passed around and everyone had a go pretending to be Cappy beheading Trailer Park Shane.

Afterwards a smiledon was sacrificed and there was a great feast of cat meat, which cooked up nicely in the flames of their burning auras.

After the celebration more tigers were slaughtered and their bones and skins were transformed by the crews' clever hands into all sorts of ingenious tools and implements that would prove wonderfully useful, both for repairing the Pegasus drive and for providing the corsairs with various comforts and luxuries to improve their condition in the universe—luxuries, alas, that made their universal condition comfortable indeed!

At one point Cappy observed Lt. Baudrillard amusing himself with, of all things, a toy puppet he had made. The puppet was in the image of the great Spammer Gain herself, and Baudrillard delighted at being able to hold her form up to his chest. He clutched the little doll with harmless affection, and with not a little amusement, too, at his own sentimentalism, which was certainly movingly evoked by the small doll that resembled a particularly cute cuttlefish, "Ah!" said Cappy, smiling to see Baudrillard occupied in this happy way. "It appears modernism has its rewards after all, eh, Lieutenant?"

It has been said that nobody rises to the occasion like corsairs under fire, but strangely enough (though understandably, if you think about it) there is really very little acknowledgement of just how stellar corsairs can be when they muck in and get things accomplished together when the situation is going well and there is plenty of simple, honest work to be done. Ah, those noble corsairs, what an industrious folk they are!

But perhaps "industrious" is an understatement, for, working harmoniously as they did, the corsairs soon had Blake's forge roaring; then, with plenty of tiger bones and tendons providing the raw materials, the Pegasus engine was rebuilt and ready to run the Cornelius Loop!

"But how do we do that?" Billy flipped his tiger bone hammer at the tar. "All the manuals have been lost, destroyed in the fire."

"But will it work?" asked Cappy.

Little Billy nodded. "Aye. The Pegasus drive will work, Captain, t'be sure! But how are we to run a program we do not possess? I, for one, don't know a single line of that code. And neither does anybody else."

Cappy considered this. "Are you sure? Have you asked everyone?"

Billy nodded again with much frustration. "I've asked everyone."

Cappy glanced at Professor Pop, who shook his head in confirmation.

"Hmm." Cappy stepped back from the Pegasus engine and eyed it up and down. His aura, usually golden—even as it had been while he fought with Old Reg—seemed to loose a bit of its luster. Indeed, for a few moments it looked almost a dark orange, and then became a rather gloomy reddish-brown. Cappy was sounding the deep recesses of his worst doubts. But then his left eyebrow arched significantly. His aura blossomed once more into glorious gold.

"Correct me if I am wrong, shipmates, but is it not true that the Cornelius Loop was written by a human?"

Lt. Baudrillard was scratching his head. Billy was kneeling, tapping the head of his tiger bone hammer with his palm. By his expression you could tell he thought this path of inquiry useless.

"I believe that to be true." It was Sylvia the Plathological Anorexic.

Cappy smiled archly "And?"

Professor Pop snapped his fingers. "Of course! Cornelius, the original author of the Loop which bears his name—this is only myth, mind you—dwelled for some time in a realm known as 'Ko-O-Ko.' Now, 'Ko-O-Ko' is a word derived from an old Martian dialect—a very difficult dialect, I can assure you. Ha, ha, ha. Ahem. Anyway, 'Ko-O-Ko' means—"

Cappy smiled. "—universe?"

Pop shook his head as he marveled at the sureness of Cappy's intuition. "Well done, my boy. Well done!"

Cappy stepped closer to his friends. "That's just where we are!"

59

Lt. Baudrillard raised his Spammer doll and gave it a kiss. "*Zoot alors!* What a stroke of luck!"

"Remarkable," was all Pop could say.

Cappy shook hands with several of the appreciative corsairs. Working together as they had since the beheading of Old Reg, many of the signs of rank and the formalities of discipline had been all but forgotten.

"I guess it's up to me," said Cappy. He stared up at the black dome of the sky and regarded the quasars, which even now seemed to be moving towards each other, though their motion was too slow to be detected with the unaided eye. A glance through the reticule, however, confirmed the universe was indeed contracting. "We don't have much time."

Of course nobody wanted Cappy to leave.

"At the very least," insisted Pope Nobody the Twenty-third, "We should all go together."

"No," said Cappy, and he explained that he didn't want the others to venture with him beyond the tar pit and risk losing somebody out in the universe. "Then nobody would be able to go home. I, for one, could never bring myself to leave anybody behind. And I don't want to spend eternity looking for one of you oddballs should you become misplaced out here in the universe."

"But you can't leave us alone, Cappy!" Little Billy Blake threw down his hammer and stood. Not a few voices joined in to agree.

Cappy was not unmoved, but he was also resolved.

"Ohh! Pleeeeease!" said the Lost Corsairs in unison.

"No!" said Cappy and it was final. The command persona had returned. For the last time Cappy told them he was going out to seek out Cornelius— alone.

"Gosh, anyway," complained Adam Simulacrum, sniffling.

Professor Pop was nodding sadly.

"Well, gosh, Cappy!" cried Vadim Simulacrum. "Can't you at least sing us a song before you go? Can't you at least sing us a song!"

"Yeah!" said Adam. "Cappy, please sing us a song!" A chorus of voices joined in begging for a song.

How could he refuse them? "Alright, but just one, and then I have to go."

There was no unanimous "Hurrah!"—which, quite frankly, Cappy would have enjoyed—but the Lost Corsairs had at last settled down. A few of them dried their damp eyes and wiped their noses as together they sat in a half circle around their beloved commander. A few put their arms over each other's shoulders or joined hands, but before he sang them their song he gave them instructions on what was to be done while he was gone. He advised them to exercise a prudent stewardship of the smiledons and not deplete their population. Also, he placed Billy in charge until he should return, and he ordered them to assist the engineer with the Pegasus engine, which, as their only means of escape, was to be their top priority. "Finally," he said. "No past-life regression until I return."

He made them all promise to follow his instructions, and then he sang:

> The tar pit is ancient
> The universe is born
> The tigers are tasty
> So don't look forlorn!
>
> The quasars are congealing
> We don't have much time
> So my message to all:
> Behold the cosmic design!
>
> Between this moment and the next
> I shall return, it is true
> As Barbara Cartland has written:
> I swear by my life, I love you!

All those dried eyes and noses were again wet. Cappy turned away and marched straight off across the tar pit, right past the impaled green head of Old Reg—who was still blabbering, "Supwidat! Supwidat!—and then a mile or so further on, as far as the corsairs could see, he was swallowed up by the darkness.

As he strode along, his aura a golden beacon that lit his path through the universe, Cappy couldn't help but snicker at their gullibility.

To be continued....

Chapter Four

Un Petit Peu Dérangé

One day at about three in the afternoon he had a vision. He distinctly saw an angel of God, who came to him and said, "Cornelius!"

—Acts 10:3

As he sauntered down the slope of 103rd Street the Reverend Dr. Jeremiah Cornelius cut a striking figure in his brushed suede safari coat, tan bush trousers and rugged kangaroo-skin riding boots. Upon his head he wore a sage oilskin cowboy hat with the left side of the brim bent up and snapped against the side of the crown in the manner of an Australian "digger" hat. The kerchief he wore that morning sported a leopard print, so that as he emerged from the shadows of the street and burst suddenly into the sunshine beating down on Broadway his giant form might strike the innocent passerby as a big game hunter who had misplaced his rifle, or (and more probably) an exuberant Broadway choreographer who had misplaced his inspiration.

The children were gathered together at the preschool, which was down amongst the corridors, classrooms, dining rooms, common rooms, meeting centers, administrative offices, libraries, and storage cupboards that fitted together in a jigsaw maze beneath the Cathedral. There was even a kitchen and a neglected darkroom, which, in the advent of the digital age, was somebody's projected computer graphics and video editing studio. The Reverend Dr. Cornelius had been asked to look in on progress when he first came to St. John's—he poked his head into the "studio," was shocked by the disarray, and excused himself to the smiling American hobbyist, claiming "I was looking for the library and I think I've lost my way."

As the Reverend Dr. Cornelius entered the classroom Catherine and her three colleagues were reviewing plans for transporting the nine children to the museum. The One-Nine Local stop at 110th and Broadway was just two blocks from St. John's, but the 86th St. stop, the stop on the One-Nine closest to the museum was eight blocks away from their destination, and three of those blocks were those very long walks between Broadway,

Amsterdam, Columbus and Central Park West. It would be an impossible hike for the little ones. On the other hand, the C and D stopped right at the museum, and also there was an entrance to the museum actually inside the 81st St. subway station. What this meant was they would walk the children to 110th and ride the One-Nine down to 59th St-Columbus Circle, where they would transfer to the C or D local, which they would ride back up to 81st and the museum.

The women hardly saw the Reverend Dr. Cornelius enter the room—except for Oona, who spotted him immediately and bit her lip to keep from laughing as she nudged Catherine with her elbow. Catherine looked up; she might as well have looked *through* her husband; but anyway they were ready.

The Reverend Dr. Cornelius remained aloof, nodding quietly but firmly as he was instructed to follow behind to mind the stragglers, and thus he waited as the group of Lilliputians was herded out into the corridor. Once out, he shut down the lights and closed the door.

They soon found their way up the steps, and crossed the narthex beneath the brilliant round stained glass window that hovered some five stories above them in the giant cathedral.

As the hydra of children and adults pushed through the swinging glass doors the Reverend Dr. Cornelius watched Oona produce a length of knotted washing line. As he went outside he discovered this was intended for four of the very smallest children, who the Reverend Dr. Cornelius now observed were very young indeed. They were mere toddlers, scarcely two or three years old. He thought it odd that such young children should be taken to the museum. These very small children were told to grasp the cord and walk in single file, connected together like mountaineers or—as the Reverend Dr. Cornelius thought—prisoners on a chain gang. Then as they began walking slowly together with the cord in their tiny hands, barely understanding where they were in the world and mindlessly obeying their minders, the Reverend Dr. Cornelius winced to behold something that he compared in his imagination to a scene out of Dante. He thought to say something to Catherine about it, but like the rest of the adults and the older children she took it all in stride, and thus he stood silently in horror as he wondered where could be the parents of these lost souls?

Just then the Reverend Dr. Cornelius felt something grasp his fingers. He snatched his hand away and looked down.

Staring up at him with a somewhat tense expression was a little boy cradling his hand next to his chest. That hand, the Reverend Dr. Cornelius realized, had been the thing that had just touched his own—and he had snatched himself away from the dear little boy who had obviously, in the most innocent of childish gestures, sought to grasp his fatherly hand! The Reverend Dr. Cornelius stared awkwardly, but only for a moment or two. The boy was very short, with black shoulder-length hair, a dark tan face, very large brown eyes, and he was in possession of very fine features. He wore denim trousers and a russet wool coat that was over large, and his hand, still clutched next to his chest, was nearly lost in the folds of that coat, which, as the postmodern divine observed, had not been properly fastened— but rather than fasten it, his first thought was to make amends:

"Why, hello! I'm sorry. Was that you who just now touched my hand?"

The little boy nodded. His mouth was horizontal and fixed. He didn't appear frightened of the tall churchman, but just the same he appeared somewhat guarded. "Padré, don't you want to hold my hand?"

"Why, of course I do! Allow me to introduce myself: I am Catherine's husband, Dr. Cornelius."

"I see," said the little boy. And he tentatively moved as if to offer his hand, but then drew it back.

The Reverend Dr. Cornelius assumed an expression so wonderfully civilized as to be charming. "It is my very good pleasure to meet you. What is your name, my friend?"

The little boy blinked his eyes slowly at the giant's hand as it reached down towards him. He looked at the hand carefully and then smiled and grasped it. "My name is Capricorn."

"Really. That's a very impressive sounding name. I have heard good tales of you."

"You have?" Cappy stood there with his chest out as he shook the enormous hand. His voice was flat and business-like. As Catherine had promised, Capricorn sounded very much older than he looked. It was uncanny. "And what good tales have you heard?"

The Reverend Dr. Cornelius was impressed. "Well, I have heard that you are a very very clever little boy."

Cappy released the giant's hand. "Yes, but I am not a boy. I am really an angel."

"Is that not an unsuitable thing to tell an Anglican priest?"

"In one way, perhaps."

"And how's that?"

"Well, if you were a Catholic nun, you might actually believe me. Do you think nuns are more perceptive than Anglican priests?"

The Reverend Dr. Cornelius couldn't help chuckling, nor was he slow in confiding in his new little friend. "Well, I should hope so. Truth be told, Anglican priests are very silly people."

Cappy motioned with his index finger. "You know, Padré, that's just what I was going to say."

Catherine was calling from ahead: "Come on, slow coach! Jiffy it up!"

The postmodern divine took Capricorn's hand and they hurried along to join the others. They made good progress down the Cathedral steps, across the street and most of the way down 112th, but as they walked along the Reverend Dr. Cornelius found that he had to step very carefully round the boy, who for some reason—to taunt him?—kept walking in front of his legs. He could see that they should make another arrangement, and soon.

The impressions of the postmodern divine were not without foundation; just to see what might happen, Cappy suddenly stepped right into the giant's legs. "Ouch! Don't step on me, Padré!"

"Walking under my feet isn't doing either of us any good!"

"Will you carry me?"

The Reverend Dr. Cornelius leaned forward slightly to see if the boy's shoes were clean, nodded with satisfaction, smiled at the boy, and then with his two enormous hands lifted the boy up to the sky.

Then there was a bit of a struggle. As the postmodern divine sought to shift the boy over to his side and sit him upon his right arm, the boy wiggled his body and thrust his knees in whatever direction the giant was seeking to move him. Any possible progress was in this way obstructed. The boy looked up into the postmodern divine's face and smiled at the effects while at the same time ignoring Catherine, who was again calling for them to pick up their pace. Picture the postmodern divine with the small boy in his arms shifting against all reason, gouging his knees into the churchman's chest, and all while the postmodern divine seeks to acknowledge in a cultivated English accent the criticisms of his impatient wife—and moreover this great towering theologian dressed as a big game hunter gently seizing his hands round the struggling boy while their combined mass blocks the door to the Labyrinth Bookstore, whose patrons are checked as they seek to move out the glass doorway—two of them growing especially annoyed: the first being a pimply-faced female gender-studies student with a pronounced forehead enhanced by her hair drawn tightly back in a pony tail so that her horn-rimmed glasses project a mile in front of her face, along with a rather dilapidated cultural theorist with an "international" reputation—both standing impatiently inside and unable to push open the glass door because of the gargantuan obstruction on the pavement outside that is rocking back and forth and calling in a desperate pitch, "Help, Catherine! Help! I'm doing the best I can! It's like wrestling a rabid orangutan!"

Catherine ran up and pulled Capricorn off her husband and placed the kicking boy on the pavement, whereupon Capricorn cooed as if making some new discovery, shot over to the door of the Labyrinth Bookstore, looked in at the gender-studies student and the dilapidated cultural theorist and began slowly blinking his eyes up and down as if he was staring at two curious marine specimens inside a big aquarium.

Flustered as he was, the Reverend Dr. Cornelius was impressed by the boy's sudden fixation, so that he too pressed up against the glass door and glared curiously inside, so that the gender-studies student and the cultural theorist rocked back with fright and toppled over an African-American woman with a parcel under her arm who had all this time been standing on tip-toes to see what was going on outside. The Reverend Dr. Cornelius saw by the commotion inside that someone had fallen, and vaguely fearing further delays, or perhaps even a lawsuit, he grasped Capricorn firmly round the waist and shot off down the pavement to the corner, bolted across Broadway, absolutely streaked along the great street (a wonder chips of pavement weren't struck off by his heels), flew down the steps, and waited for his wife and the rest of the group inside the 110th St. subway station.

When Catherine and the others joined them she was somewhat exasperated. "Honestly, Jeremiah; you can be so awkward!"

"Well, I suppose you won't be calling me 'slow coach' for some time," was his hushed answer, and he took off his hat, smoothed back his hair, and replaced it feeling very fit and ready.

The silver train was soon roaring into the station. Adults and children joined hands—the four toddlers, indistinctly aware of their responsibility, tightly clutched their rope—and the Reverend Dr. Cornelius and little Capricorn eyed each other with the same superior expression on their faces, and each feeling that he (and he) had showed the other a thing or two. Heeding Oona's admonishment, they joined hands and an instant later simultaneously squeezed each other's fingers in mutual affection.

The train squealed to a stop, compressed air hissed through an assortment of hoses and the doors sprung open. The group boarded without incident and they cooperated smartly as they took their various places inside the nearly empty car. The minders helped the toddlers up to the seats while the other children quietly heeded Oona's instructions and sat together in the seats opposite. Once the children had located themselves, the other minders,

Debbie and Trinique, sat down. Catherine and Oona stood in front of the toddlers. The Reverend Dr. Cornelius remained standing along with his new friend, who was bobbing his head up and down to imaginary music.

"And why do you not have prams for the little ones?" asked the Reverend Dr. Cornelius, and he added, "Please stop that enthusiastic dancing, Capricorn, it is disrupting my conversation. Thank you very much."

"Oh, I am very sorry," said Cappy, and he waited for the postmodern divine to smile down at him, whereupon he resorted to bobbing his head once more.

The brakes released and the standing passengers picked their feet up and down and leaned forward into the direction of travel as the train accelerated. Soon the posts supporting the station ceiling were flickering by and just as quickly the lights of the station dropped behind as the train fell into the tunnel.

Oona conferred momentarily with Catherine, who was standing with her back turned toward her husband. Apparently this was the first time Oona had heard the word "pram" which is the British word for what Americans call a "stroller." She looked at Catherine's husband and said, "Do you want to push them around all day? We've done this before and it's easier this way." She adjusted her rucksack and looked out the window as the train flew into the light of the 96th St. station. The voice of the conductor scratched over the speaker to announce the downtown One-Nine would not stop at 59th due to construction. The conductor instructed the riders to switch to the express and take it to 42nd, where the uptown local One-Nine was running. Meanwhile, the blurred silver of the express Number Three was waiting across the platform. The minders eyes darted back and forth to find the number, spotted it, then called to each other. "There's the Number Three!"

"Should we? Should we?"

"We should!" decided Oona.

"All right, children," called the minders together. "Everybody stand up, please. We are going to change trains. Come now! Get up! Get up!"

The children were up instantly and the toddlers were automatically crawling off their seats and clutching each other and Catherine and Oona as the train began braking and their momentum caused everybody to rock back and forth. The other two minders, Debbie and Trinique, told everyone to get ready to step off.

The train finally stopped and in the midst of the adults' admonishments to hurry the children matched out the door. Oona and Catherine each held two of the toddlers under their arms and they laughed as they warned the children to "be careful" and "hold hands" as they hurried across the platform to the express train.

"Drama!" laughed Catherine as she hurried across the platform with the two little ones dangling under her arms.

"Drama! Drama!" laughed Oona, for a moment speaking with long vowels—not the first time the Reverend Dr. Cornelius had heard her imitate a British accent in that horrid American way. But notwithstanding his irritation at her pathetic phonetic bounding, he felt left out of this little fun, and as they stepped inside the train he was sufficiently enough caught up in the spirit of the adventure to awkwardly say "Drama," but only to cause Catherine to wrinkle her nose at him. She turned to smile at Oona, as, along with Debbie and Trinique, they directed the children to sort themselves.

The express train was also relatively empty and together the group repeated their seating drill. It was very impressive how well the children cooperated, and the behavior of the little toddlers was nothing short of miraculous.

The doors slid shut and over the speaker the conductor announced their next stop, 72nd St. Capricorn, who once more stood hand in hand with the postmodern divine, had ceased his irritating head bouncing. As the train sped up once more he stood very still and looked back and forth between Catherine and Oona, all the while slowly blinking his eyes—first at Catherine and then at Oona—and he repeated this several times. Then he looked up at the giant holding his hand and smiled. "Will you take me around at the museum? We could leave the others and do what I want?"

The Reverend Dr. Cornelius agreed. "Looks like things are going in that direction. However, we will do what *we* want. There are things I should like to see too, little Capricorn."

"Ah, Padré! Don't get too generous."

"Generous? Are you attempting to *amuse* me?"

"Don't be ridiculous." Capricorn tugged sharply on the postmodern divine's hand, as if he was re-setting a mechanism. "Seriously, Padré, are you going to buy me a toy?"

"That's a rather forward request, don't you think?"

"Do you have a little boy at home you buy toys for?"

"For crying out loud, guv'nah!" It was Oona. "Tell Capricorn you'll buy him a toy!"

The Reverend Dr. Cornelius drew a splendid bead on her and tilted his head disapprovingly, and then he looked down at Capricorn smiling. "My dear little chap, as a matter of fact I do not have a little boy at home. But I wish I did—" here he glared victoriously at Oona, and then smiled mildly once more upon Capricorn "—because I should very much like to buy a toy for that special lad who shared my life. And in such a spirit I promise to buy a toy for you—"

"Yay!" interrupted Capricorn.

The Reverend Dr. Cornelius held his mouth open patiently during this interruption and then as Capricorn subsided said, "—if you are good."

The train shot into the 72nd St. station where it braked so sharply people were variously stomping suddenly backwards or leaning steeply forward in the direction from whence the train had come. As the train stopped and the doors flew open a great number of people boarded. Although it was after the morning rush hour it was a weekday and the express Number Three was approaching the outer periphery of midtown.

Cappy looked up at the faces as they crowded in above him. With an effort he tugged his hand away from the postmodern divine and then squeezed himself in amongst the toddlers, who automatically shifted to let the boy sit with them. He closed his eyes tightly, only occasionally opening them to quickly peer at the people, who he didn't view so much with distaste as he did with frustration, as if looking at them all together was proving too much for him to grasp at one time. When he finally seemed to be accustomed to the compressed collection of beings he was very slow in his movements as he stared at each individual facial feature, each expression of character, each posture and each gesture with an intense fascination, as if in face, feature and figure there were a myriad of subtle signs that required careful examination and analysis. Again he employed that peculiar eye blinking of his. It appeared almost mechanical and was accompanied by all manner of odd facial ticks, sudden half-smiles, and near-grimaces. The Reverend Dr. Cornelius was himself fascinated by it, until he realized that rather than some exotic phenomenon, Capricorn's odd mugging was actually evidence of deeply-placed psychological problems that were unquestionably the consequences of neglect, loneliness and abuse.

At 42nd St-Times Square the group disembarked, walked up the steps and crossed to the uptown platform. Once more Catherine and Oona held a toddler under each arm. The group moved rapidly and in good order. Although relegated to the rear echelon, Capricorn and the postmodern divine were especially gratified to see reflected in each other something of their mutual sensitivity to good form and the importance of a strident carriage and bearing. They all but marched though the station, and almost simultaneously they thought to enhance the crashing of their footsteps by stomping. Catherine, who was evidently used to this, glanced back to upbraid them: "No clomping please. The concrete is fragile."

Oona warbled once more in her *faux* English accent. "Oh, no! We've got *two* of them!"

The group descended the stairs and gathered together to wait for the uptown One-Nine. Nearby was a conga player whose tapping drew odd expressions from Capricorn, who at last turned to his giant friend and said, "Why isn't anybody dancing?"

The postmodern divine looked very arch. "If you've noticed, they aren't singing either?"

The boy nodded. "Maybe they don't know the words?"

Catherine repeated this to Oona, who began cackling.

Then the uptown One-Nine flashed into the station. Its brakes squealed volubly and the postmodern divine found himself drawing the boy close to his legs. It occurred to him that his nearly unconscious desire to be protective felt wonderful.

They boarded the train and in moments it was accelerating forward. Once more the standing riders were picking their feet up and down and leaning into the direction of acceleration. The posts supporting the station were flashing by and then suddenly the silver train was sucked into the darkness of the tunnel.

At one point the lights inside the train went out and Capricorn called to reassure the group: "Steady on, my friends! Steady on, brave hearts!" He spoke clearly and he spoke well. Although they didn't think much of it— and it did sound a little silly after all—everyone was made to feel very good by the ring of absolute confidence in the boy's voice.

Once more they found themselves pulling into the 59th St. station, this time of course from the other direction. The doors slid open, the group disembarked in good order, and like experts they moved efficiently though the station to the platform for the C and D uptown local trains. Once more the care of the toddlers fell upon Catherine and Oona, who marched cheerfully along with a child under each arm. Debbie and Trinique took charge of the four older children, who walked along to either side holding their minders' hands, while the Reverend Dr. Cornelius and his little friend brought up the rear of the party, also hand-in-hand and enjoying the impression of being the overseers.

"Yo-ho!" cried Cappy suddenly and in response the other children cried "Yo-ho!" Catherine and her colleagues exchanged amused glances as they hurried along; and so they made their happy way to the platform for the C and D.

The train—a large "C" inside a blue circle glowing on the face of the first car—was soon rumbling rather slowly up the tracks. The breaks squealed softly, the wheels made a muffled grinding sound as their steel pressed down against the steel rails; then the train gently halted and the doors slid open. The group filed inside the crowded car where they found they had to stand. Then it was off, prompting them to lean this way and that as they clutched each other—the train accelerated and was soon shifting and bouncing under their feet. On this leg of the journey, Capricorn appeared comfortable with the crowd of passengers. He seemed for the time being occupied with shoes and feet, for he looked all round the bouncing floor. From the perspective of the postmodern divine, whose cowboy hat with the folded left brim nearly grazed the ceiling, the boy was comparing his own feet and legs to those of the passengers who stood round him. Then Capricorn ducked for a moment to take in the kangaroo-skin boots, and then he looked up at the giant and laughed, "Ha!"

The train rifled into the 72nd St. station and Oona announced the next stop was the museum. A number of people stepped off and though there was more room in the car the preschool group and their minders remained standing. The Reverend Dr. Cornelius felt his little friend tug upon his hand.

"Next stop, Padré!"

"Yes, it is."

"How long did it take us?"

The Reverend Dr. Cornelius checked his watch. "Thirty-two minutes."

"Not bad."

"Not at all."

"Are we going off together at the museum?"

"I'll ask Catherine once we're inside."

But Cappy wasn't content to wait. "Catherine!" he announced. The doors shut and she acknowledged him as the train began its career forward.

"Can the Padré and I go off together at the museum?"

"Yes," she said. "But you two boys wait until everyone is inside and we make our plans, please."

It was the first time that day Capricorn and the postmodern divine had been referred to as "boys" and the sound of it fell indifferently upon Cappy's ears, but the name stuck and as the day unfolded it developed into to something of an irritation to the bigger of the two boys.

71

The "C" uptown local shot into the 81st-American Museum of Natural History station. Back at 59th the women had thought to lead the group to the end of the platform where they could board the last car, so that as the train shuddered to a stop they found themselves directly opposite the stainless steel turnstiles that stood before the museum entrance. Children and minders filed out excitedly and hurried to the turnstile, with Oona turning as they did so and calling, "Let's wait for the boys! Hurry up, boys!"

Cappy was rather gleeful as he stepped off the train and discovered the colorful mosaic images of living things that were set amongst the shining white tiles of the station walls—even life-size bronze casts of dinosaur bones as they might appear protruding from the living rock of the Urals, or from the grassy sands of the high plains and badlands of Montana. Half acknowledging the minders who were waiting on "the boys", the postmodern divine and his little friend slowed their advance across the platform to give the colorful mosaics and model specimens a proprietary (however brief) inspection.

"Boys!" implored Catherine, now standing with the others on the opposite side of the turnstiles. The postmodern divine and his little friend picked up their advance and tumbled through the turnstile. The group moved through the heavy brass doors and filed down the short stairway to the ticket desk. Oona produced the appropriate documents, and everybody was waved forward through another set of doors where they found themselves in a large foyer with a low ceiling. There were restrooms to the right, an ice cream parlor to the left, and, thirty yards ahead, the "Dinoteria" lunchroom.

"I have to go wee wee," announced Capricorn, and several of the children agreed that they had to go too. Cathrine, Oona, Debbie and Trinique took the girls and the very little ones into the women's room. It was up to the Reverend Dr. Cornelius to escort the three older boys, including Capricorn, to the men's room, and not surprisingly the postmodern divine made an expert show of it, even when Capricorn asked for help pulling up his trousers—but then only to turn away from the giant's hands and shuffle off with his trousers and his y-fronts down about his feet as he laughed: "Runaway boy! Runaway boy!"

"Honestly, Capricorn! Cease this horseplay or I shall turn you over to Oona for the rest of the day."

The little chap stopped and turned. Appearing sufficiently abashed, he waddled up and obediently allowed the postmodern divine to pull up and fasten his trousers. The two other boys looked on blankly. They had learned to be patient with Capricorn's little pranks, and, as they were also used to his verbal and physical superiority, they saw this as simply more proof that it was Capricorn and not the adults who was really in charge of affairs.

After this bit of fun they were once more standing outside waiting for the others. When his wife and the children came outside, plans were hastily agreed upon. Debbie and Trinique would take the toddlers to the museum's day care center. Catherine and Oona would take charge of the four older children and tour round the museum, while Capricorn and the Reverend Dr. Cornelius would be set loose to go off on their own. At noon everyone would meet back at the Dinoteria for lunch, and at that time plans for the afternoon would be made.

"But we can stay no later than two, as we have a dinner to go to tonight," said Catherine.

The Reverend Dr. Cornelius was then surprised to learn that Oona would be there, too.

"We shall talk about that later, Jeremiah."

The postmodern divine leaned forward to give his wife a kiss, but she dodged round him and, along with Oona, took charge of the older children and they went off.

"Be good, boys!" admonished Oona, and she and Catherine and their charges disappeared round the corner on their way to the lifts. Debbie and Trinique might have taken notice of Catherine and Oona's apparent disregard for the postmodern divine, but if so it was secondary to their fussing over the toddlers, who were again clutching that horrid rope. The Reverend Dr. Cornelius was used to leading the way. Now he experienced a vague sensation of being left behind, so he took his little friend by the hand and struck off for the stairway as if he was in charge of everything, which, he reasoned, he probably was.

The stairway was tall and it was quite a climb for little Capricorn, but he pressed on happily. About halfway up he shook his hand free of the giant, picked up his pace smartly and leaned purposefully forward and assumed, in miniature, all the spirit of adventure and British capability that was expressed in the stature, bearing and garb of the Reverend Dr. Cornelius, who produced no few stares amongst the startled museum patrons as his prevailing legs thrust up his tall figure two steps at a time, his leopard print kerchief pulled spectacularly to one side of his collar, his hat behind his back dangling from its lanyard, his coat open and sailing in the breeze created by his movement, and his kangaroo-skin riding boots reporting jubilantly against the white granite stairs.

They went up one flight and found themselves on the first floor. To their right was the entrance to the museum store and Capricorn smiled and picked up on his toes in his excitement to see though the entranceway.

"Capricorn! Come along, thank you very much."

"Padré, you said you were going to buy me a toy?"

"When we are ready to depart the museum, I shall buy you your toy. In the meantime, be good."

Capricorn grunted and took exaggerated steps toward the giant, who shook his head disapprovingly at his little friend's little display. Once more in formation, they moved down the corridor. They looked to their left at the entranceway to the Hall of North American Mammals, but instead of entering they turned right, again toward the front of the building, and stepped into the Theodore Roosevelt Memorial Hall. In the center of the hall was a membership and information desk. Along the walls were displays celebrating the life of Teddy Roosevelt, the great visionary patron of American conservation, a man whose love for the outdoors and whose respect for the richness and the grandeur of the natural order was the guiding genius of the museum. At each of the walls along the longer measurement of the hall were four great dioramas, each sixteen feet wide by a dozen tall. The postmodern divine and his little friend moved to their right and the first exhibit they came to was a perspective of Roosevelt's Elkhorn Ranch in the western badlands of North Dakota. The two friends stared up from the sand and scrub immediately behind the glass, while the splashes of paint against the back wall representing the distant hills and ranch buildings made them feel they were staring out from the edge of a steep incline. The uncanny impression of austere remoteness and rough living was evoked to good effect. The Reverend Dr. Cornelius hummed in approving recognition of the feeling, while his little friend stood transfixed, as if he was suddenly experiencing himself actually standing out alone atop the dry, windswept elevation.

They went round the far wall where there were free standing cases containing memorabilia from Roosevelt's political career, primarily his work as the Police Commissioner of New York City, where he was as vigilant against the corruption inherent to the city's system of political patronage as he was against the wrongs of the underworld, which at that time were two fangs in the same wolf. But there were also artifacts from his tenure in the highest office in the land. Capricorn drew the postmodern divine's attention to a curious placard beneath one of Roosevelt's hats—the thing was barely visible from above. The postmodern divine stooped down to read. It was a passage taken from the journal of the President's son, Quentin Roosevelt, and it read:

Father says that scrap of paper [Cromwell's autograph] is the most valuable thing in the White House except mother.

The Reverend Dr. Cornelius could only imagine why Capricorn had drawn his attention—amongst all these items—to this little inscription, which actually had no relation at all to anything else in the case. What must Capricorn be wondering about? The persona of the boy who had been the son of the American president? Had the word "mother" attracted his attention? Did he wonder what the purpose of the inscription might be, placed as it had been inside the case with no relative significance to the other articles there? With such questions passing through his mind, the postmodern divine was fully unprepared for what Capricorn's question turned out to be: the postmodern divine's opinion of Oliver Cromwell.

"Oliver Cromwell!" he said with a start. "I really have no opinion whatsoever. He was a very strong man, to be sure. Today we should call him a dictator, I suppose."

Cappy raised his finger. "I see. Did he do anything bad?

"Well, he chopped off the head of the justly anointed English King."

"Was that not a good thing to do? Kings are bad, aren't they?"

The Reverend Dr. Cornelius shook his head. "Oh, no. A king is a very good thing, Capricorn. They give people someone to love. Since a king symbolizes a subject people's country, a king focuses a subject people's love upon something that is warm and human, and thus the subjects' love for their country becomes warm and human, too."

"But America does not have a king?"

There was something uncanny about the smile Capricorn wore on his face. The Reverend Dr. Cornelius had up to this point accepted that Capricorn was unusually verbal, and that he was singularly mischievous, but all that had been rationalized into his picture of the little boy as a little boy, however unusual. But this line of questioning together with his saturnine expression was altogether suspicious. The postmodern divine thought perhaps to confront his little friend directly, but upon turning the matter over he instead decided it would be better to question his little charge in a roundabout fashion. He asked Capricorn about his own mother. For his part, the little fellow remained nonplussed. He blinked his eyes once, twice, and continued:

"For Mr. Roosevelt to say that Oliver Cromwell's autograph was nearly the most valuable thing in the White House means that Oliver Cromwell was an important person, don't you think?"

"Well, maybe Roosevelt liked history? I can't imagine why people would keep such things in the White House. Anyhow, I did not go to an American school, so I don't know."

"Do you think someone who went to an American school would know?"

The Reverend Dr. Cornelius felt various ideas sound through his head. He stood, bored with Capricorn's questions. "These days, I should doubt that anybody going to an American school knows much of anything, least of all anything about an unpleasant, seventeenth-century politician whose autograph, a century ago anyway, was kept on file in the White House."

Another placard inside the case listed some of Roosevelt's administrative achievements. Cappy read them aloud: "Pure food and drug laws, meat inspection act, child labor laws, railroad rate regulations, the regulation of the trusts."

The postmodern divine appeared momentarily pained. "Such enthusiastic rulings speak volumes about a lack of confidence in society's just leadership; moreover, a meddlesome impedance to our faith in He who watches over all. I cannot approve." Done with the subject, the giant walked to the next display.

It was another broad diorama set into the wall. It showed Manhattan Island as it might have appeared in the days of Dutch settlement, when the city—if it could be called a city—was known as New Amsterdam. The display portrayed Broadway at its south-most terminus in lower Manhattan: it was a dirt road running from the grass-surrounded walls of the Dutch fort on the left, then crossing the center of the diorama where the action transformed from a painted background to a three-dimensional scene, and then on up to the right and to the north, where once more the scene was rendered with paint on a flat surface. On the opposite side of the road and painted on the back wall were a series of quaint houses, and, beyond them, the Hudson River and the green hills of what today is called Jersey City. A trio of tawny Indians with great triangular noses were approaching from the bank of the Hudson—one of these was painted upon the back wall, while two were life-size manikins, naked but for loin cloths, and sporting fanning Mohawk hair-cuts and stoic (though altogether amiable) expressions. The first member of this party stood with his arm extended to offer long cuts of tobacco leaf draped over the palm of his hand. On the left, the European they greeted, himself a large-nosed manikin, peg-legged and supporting himself with a crutch, and characteristically garbed in the fashionable but practical dress of the new mercantile middle classes, was none other than Peter Stuyvesant, the last Dutch Governor of New Amsterdam (and who should not be confused with the first governor, Peter Minuet, who is the chap celebrated in history for purchasing Manhattan Island from the natives for twenty-four dollars in trinkets). The execution of the display was particularly effective, and as the giant read the explanatory placard his little companion walked all the way to the left of the glass so that he might have a better perspective of the view up Broadway.

Continuing along, they found themselves near the entrance, and the natural light coming through the windows in the doors worked for some reason upon the duo like a repulsive magnetic force. They turned at right angles and walked across the floor of the memorial until finding themselves once more in the corridor. Immediately before them again was the entrance to the Hall of North American Mammals. They both hesitated, not just then knowing their minds. On the wall opposite was the museum floor plan, and they gravitated toward this to decide where next to go.

"Well, what's your pleasure, Capricorn?" The postmodern divine adjusted his leopard print bandana and, finding it suddenly uncomfortable, decided to remove it.

"Can we check our coats, please, Padré? I feel a little warm."

It was agreed. The nearest coat check was up on the next floor in the Theodore Roosevelt Rotunda. They retraced their steps several feet and mounted the stairs. Once more little Capricorn leaned purposefully forward and assumed in miniature all the spirit of adventure and British capability that was expressed in the stature, bearing and garb of the Reverend Dr. Cornelius, who again produced odd stares amongst the startled museum patrons as his prevailing legs thrust his tall figure up two steps at a time, his leopard print kerchief trailing from his hand, his hat behind his back bouncing on its lanyard, his coat open and sailing in the breeze created by his movement, and his kangaroo-skin riding boots reporting jubilantly against the white granite stairs.

They went up one flight and moved round to their right. Once more Cappy slowed and lifted up on his toes as they passed the museum store, but this time he said nothing and, correctly reading the situation, slid his feet forward rapidly and was once more walking in formation with the giant. They made their way down the corridor, glanced together to their left at the entrance to the Hall of African Animals, but instead of entering they turned right, again toward the front of the building, and stepped into the Theodore Roosevelt Rotunda.

Capricorn felt vaguely impressed by the great space while the postmodern divine accepted it as granted that such a grand hall should serve as a backdrop, such as it was, to the movements of his towering figure. Dominating the center of the room were the fossil skeletons of several dinosaurs—the largest of which was a brontosaur of some kind—these days they were calling it "Barosaurus"—posed so that it was rearing on its hind legs. It was a most unlikely pose indeed; and, for that matter, when the exhibit was opened there was much controversy over the curators' decision to fix the specimen in this dramatic stance. At her feet—for surely she was a "mother"—was her young brontosaur offspring huddled behind her hind legs, while forward and just beneath her upraised forelegs was a large Allosaurus posed in full canter as it attempted to circumvent the rearing mother and attack the youngster. While the effect of the mother's head extending on its long curving neck to a height several stories above the floor was breathtaking—especially the contrast of the stilted pattern of vertebrae against the consistent geometric lattice in the curved ceiling—the lack of any grounding in scientific fact was nothing less that an affront to the sensibilities of the Reverend Dr. Cornelius and his youthful charge. No, Barosaurus did not rear up on her hind legs. No, Allosaurus did not attack brontosaurs that were over ten times his size. The scenario was as ridiculous as a three-hundred pound crocodile attacking a three-thousand pound African elephant.

"I once read," said the Reverend Dr. Cornelius, "that the exhibit was supposed to affirm the ideal of mothers protecting their young; rather a political statement somehow ironic in the city of fatherless households."

"If a culture has to create absurd totems like this to celebrate the maintype of maternal protection," pronounced Capricorn at length, and thrusting his finger upward to evoke the authority of Allah, "then that society in fact has completely failed at preserving it. This exhibition is a vain and conceited expression of wishful thinking: as purposeless, as tragic and as pathetic as the Ghost Dance ritual of the Native Americans five generations ago."

They checked their coats and took a brief tour of the Rotunda. On the east and west walls chiseled into the rectangular mason stones were aphoristic statements of TR's personal philosophy. The subjects included Youth, Manhood, Nature and the State. If they could be condensed into one or two lines, they should seem to echo the sentiments of Pericles in his funeral oration, but more so; improving on even Thucydides best language in this regard, TR conveys something of a greater democratic sentiment, a greater spiritual profundity, for his notion of the "good life" was of a kind elevated from worldly to cosmic principles—and in this way corresponding also to Jefferson's revision of Locke, where Mankind's inalienable duty to preserve the Rights of Life, Liberty and the Pursuit of Property were revolutionized as a defense of Life, Liberty, and the pursuit of *Happiness*. Evidently TR thought happiness was to lead a life very much the way he led his own— active, robust, fecund, a wrestling match with nature, a game of reaching almost quixotically for some ineffable and shifting "truth" of existence. From the perspective of the 21st century and the masters of creation who dwell safely within its simulations, it seems a furious and dramatic quest, but in Roosevelt's own time—eschewing the mythology of rearing fossil skeletons—the nation seemed to agree.

On the north and south walls were colorful murals celebrating the proud lineage, the ideas, and the legacy of Theodore Roosevelt. Surrounded by two-dimensional festoons of geometric patterns, patriotic bunting and botanical garlands, there were images of reformation and progress: power lines, steam shovels, tropical canals, Rough Riders, agriculturalists, ancient Dutch patriarchs in puritanical costume, coats of arms, diplomatic accomplishments, and magnificence on the battlefield and on the high seas. One image was particularly attractive to Capricorn and he led the postmodern divine to examine it closely. It showed a scene from the peace negotiation that concluded the Russo-Japanese war. The iconography portrayed a pair of Japanese diplomats conferring with a triumvirate of Russian diplomats. Labels written in Japanese and Russian characters identified the diplomats by name. Standing before them—the letters "TR" indicating his identity—the great man himself was proffering the olive branch; and, to be sure, the mural wonderfully conveyed the important role his delegation played in bringing the Russians and the Japanese to conclude their peace. Capricorn indicated the figure of one of the Russian diplomats, and as the Reverend Dr. Cornelius read the Cyrillic letters a look of wonderment appeared upon his face. "Nabokov?"

Capricorn nodded proudly. "The novelist's uncle, actually."

The postmodern divine blinked several times as he thought about this. "Well then, we are keeping good company today. Small world, what?"

Capricorn pointed down at their feet. "We are standing just above the case containing Quentin Roosevelt's allusion to Cromwell. I should like to believe the *feng shui* is very good on this spot. Very good indeed."

The time had come once again to make a decision about where to go. They went round the corner to consult the directory. Along the way they once more passed the Museum Shop, prompting Capricorn to observe that he was being "a very good boy."

"Yes and no, Capricorn. I think you are being less than honest with me about your background." This prompted the little boy to point out that, on his side, he wasn't about to make forward inquires as to the Reverend Dr. Cornelius's antecedents, and thus at the very least he should expect the same courtesy extended in his own direction; which prompted the postmodern divine to stare at the little chap who had said this so earnestly and in every way conveying the most gentlemanly assumptions about good manners, so that the postmodern divine could do nothing but respect his friend's wishes. Yes, the Reverend Dr. Cornelius might have been an absurd buffoon, a manipulative schemer, an opportunistic, self-promoting, amoral and ruthless hypocrite—but he was firstly and above all else an Englishman.

Thank goodness.

As they stood before the directory on the wall they exchanged much fluent debate over which hall to visit. The Reverend Dr. Cornelius was rather in a mood for safari that morning. He favored visiting the dioramas portraying the mammalian specimens in their natural habitats. He wanted to visit the Hall of African Mammals. On his side, Cappy was in a mood for anthropology and pre-industrial cultures. He wanted to visit the Halls of Asian and Pacific Peoples. Then in the ensuing debate both friends expressed the same courteous desire to see to it that all of their interests were satisfied. "Indeed," pronounced Capricorn, "I'd like to go through the entire museum at once."

"If it were only possible."

They decided to flip a coin. It came up heads—the Reverend Dr. Cornelius won the toss. They passed through the entrance just behind them and entered the lower floor of the Akelley Hall of African Mammals. They strolled along without remark. Each display—be it cheetahs stalking through tall grass, giraffes sharing a water hole with baboons, mountain gorillas beating their chests, chimpanzees hiding in dark forests, rhinoceroses wallowing in mud holes, wild dogs prowling across a lurid twilight landscape and catching the scent (and possibly the sight) of a straggling zebra in the distance—each diorama was provided at either side with descriptive signs: one describing the natural history of the displayed animals and the drama of the scene; the second advancing a description of the "group environment"—the geographic backdrop against which the scene was played. The Reverend Dr. Cornelius was particularly interested in these "group environment" descriptions, and he spent very little time actually examining the dioramas. For his part, little Capricorn was transfixed by the displays. Each time he stared into them he was instantly transported half way round the world as his imagination was stimulated by the sight of the posed creatures, the expertly preserved and arranged foliage, and the vividly painted backgrounds. After a few moments he could actually feel the wind, the heat. He could hear birds and insects, the rustle of branches and footfalls. He could even plunge himself into the breasts of the preserved animals and experience their lives, their emotions, their sense of movement and vitality, and their appetites.

After looping completely round the gallery one and a half times they moved through the entryway at the far end. Immediately before them on the wall was a large map of Africa showing geographic regions, elevations, climates and rivers. The Reverend Dr. Cornelius was not insensitive to the fact that the map, as wonderful as it was, yet nonetheless was forty or fifty years old. It displayed no political divisions, it is true, but the Africa the mapmakers had pictured in their mind was not the Africa of the 21st century. It was an uncomfortable observation. He found himself feeling nostalgic for the 20th century, which despite its wars was something to be yearned for ecologically. How might a contemporary map of Africa presenting population, deforestation, migration, warfare and genocide change the experience of walking through this passage? He turned back to face the Hall of African Mammals.

"Yes, Padré, that Africa in there is dying."

The Reverend Dr. Cornelius offered his palm to the child. "Then we must tread softly as we pass."

They went down the corridor. On the wall was a temporary display of digitally enhanced photographs prognosticating the effects of rising ocean levels upon coral atolls in the Pacific. In some cases the ocean waters had completely swallowed the atolls, which existed as dark circles and sickle-shaped shadows beneath the waves. The skies were breathtaking scenes from a South Seas romance, but along with the waters they seemed to be swallowing the world, drowning the universe in flaring blue light, brilliant clouds, miles of trackless and meaningless space.

At the end of this section of corridor there was a back entrance to the Museum Shop. Again Capricorn went up on his toes to see more of what waited inside. They turned to the right and stepped lightly through a narrow corridor with a small blue-lit dome in the ceiling. The confined space was hushed in comparison to the halls and corridors they had been passing through, and Capricorn made soft sounds reflecting his impressions of compression and expansion, like he was a quivering atmospheric instrument, a living barometer of architectural spaces. They turned to the left again and found themselves in the Hall of African peoples. Immediately ahead was a diorama portraying tall Africans slaughtering a small cow. From where he stood it was possible for Capricorn to see the manikins' long, uncircumcised penises, and he stared at them in a very scientific way, completely indifferent to the embarrassed shock or hushed guffaws that such long uncircumcised penises would normally produce in a young boy, particularly a boy who came from a constellation where circumcision was such an important part of the plan.

Just around the corner was another diorama. Portrayed inside was a troop of pigmies in their rainforest. Garbed in loincloths and brightly decorated, they were at work gathering food, examining the rainforest around them, making their living after their own fashion. Capricorn felt somewhat nostalgic for the figures. With a sort of odd miniature manly assurance he pronounced, "Looks like a good crew!"

"Crew?"

"Aye," Cappy said wistfully. "A right good crew of corsairs." Cappy nodded at the manikin pigmies. "I could lead these people places, I could."

The Reverend Dr. Cornelius thought this was a ridiculous thing to say, but there was something just then in Capricorn's bearing that he noted down for further consideration.

They moved more deeply into the hall. In the center was a little cul-de-sac formed by glass cases containing relics of the sub-Saharan spirit world. The soft music just then coming over the speakers was a mournful chanting accompanied by the tapping of some sort of ringing wooden blocks. The angry masks in the cases, the little fetish carvings, the mad little arrangements of feathers and sticks used for various shamanistic practices riveted Capricorn's attention. He stood peering into the Second Ether in a new way, and he regarded the articles, too, the way he would any piece of sophisticated technology. That they really "worked" or not was immaterial to him, the thing that captured his imagination was his understanding that people behaved as if they worked. That was the key point. His meditations along these lines were rewarded then as they stepped past the cases and in the large displays against the wall beheld a collection of dancing costumes used by the Yoruba peoples in their ceremonies. One was an elaborate costume made of dry brown grass, completely covering the manikin who wore it, and making the manikin appear like a kind of two-legged thatched cottage. Another costume was made entirely of red snail shells. And so on— bark, animal skins, bits of cloth, feathers, sticks, leaves, bones, beads—the costumes were unique expressions of Yoruba mythology. To the eyes of an outsider, or to the eyes of a religionist whose jealous God has vanquished (or through his Son, called Reason, has tamed) the infinite pantheon of the human mind, the costumes were childish and incredible; to Capricorn, however, the demons living inside the dancing costumes were real, possessing their own wills, and standing ready to advance out of time, out of space, out of the Second Ether—and once more hold sway over the dreaming mind of Man.

They walked around the corner and found the antithesis to the sensibility and the industrial level represented by the dancing costumes. Here were small dioramas—or rather models—of six-inch-tall Africans minding various basic irrigation systems: ditches, water wheels, Archimedean screws—technologies that the farming Africans had been using in their agriculture for thousands of years. There was a simple symmetry to it, a sensible balance of human ingenuity and the land. The little scaled-down models of African agriculture gave every impression of good sense, a space in which to live, and simple but ample wealth—a far cry from the Africa of the 21st century, which is rather an argument for the principles of Malthus, or the systems of the anti-Christ.

Around the corner they found a diorama portraying Bedouins dwelling in the High Atlas. It is early dawn—the sun has not yet risen but the sky is glowing blue-grey and in it many stars are still shining. The landscape is desolate rocky desert. In the background are a mountain ridge and an ancient fortification as dry and as hard looking as the rock-strewn basin composing the scene. In the foreground is a Bedouin in traditional dress as he might appear in the 19th or early 20th centuries, and sitting with a long barrel musket in his lap as he regards the sky. Just behind him a veiled woman is preparing coffee on the fire. That is all. The image is beautiful. The beauty is stark. The climate after all is extremely hostile. This glimpse of life before the emergence of the furnace of the sun shows a world as it would best suit a visitor from more temperate latitudes. But when the sun rises the brutal and repressive heat will blast away the twilight ecstasy, and the scene will once more become the thirsty, hard-scrabble landscape that has over centuries hardened Bedouin sensibility to a fever of suspicion and duplicity that, to a shattered mind, would rival the most accomplished

European politician, lawyer, or even bishop of the Church—and whether that model bishop be Anglican or Roman is an indifferent matter.

The outer entrance to the hall was just behind them and they moved through it and passed rapidly by the Birds of the World.

They boldly climbed the stairs to the next floor and found themselves surrounded by primates of every variety. At one time this glass-walled cavern of apes would have been considered a straightforward collection—a menagerie of stuffed specimens carefully grouped according to the character of their relations, but as the Reverend Dr. Cornelius began to lecture his little friend on the action of complexity and the interplay of chaos and order upon the ontogeny of species, the collection of apes rather looked more and more like a shed of discarded prototypes—possible vessels to carry the intelligence and guile that would finally emerge in Humankind, and propel that species, Homo sapiens, to conquer and vanquish all competing life forms on earth, and moreover transform those that remained into instruments and tools of further conquest, whereby intelligence and information were joined into a complex interplay of interactions in which intelligence itself was exalted into a kind of dialogue of survival—the persistent and meaningless perpetuation of nothing but itself.

Capricorn led his giant friend to a case where, at the bottom, the skeletons of a human child and a young ape stood side-by-side. Capricorn slowly blinked his eyes as he regarded the two skeletons and noted carefully the relative size of their arms, and compared this to the relative measurement of their skulls.

"The ape child is certainly more robust than the human child," remarked the postmodern divine, "but upon the survival landscape where these two once met, the larger cranium of the human child was the decisive instrument of survival. But what happens inside that cranium? What characteristics does it possess? I believe it is sophistication; in the terms of information science, that sophistication is what we call 'Complexity.'" And here the postmodern divine advanced his thesis that near-chaotic complexity triggers phase transitions, self-organization, and advancement to higher and more complex order. He explained that this self-ordering process is seen again and again: in complex self-organizing molecular systems, organisms, economic systems, technological systems, and cultural systems. It was this same penchant for self-organization in the drying, molecule-rich puddles of primordial earth that ignited the flame of life. "Life was no accident," he asserted. "We were expected. Think of it, little Capricorn; where is this complexity leading? Could it be that the emergence and the evolution of intelligence within the multiverse is part of a larger process whereby the multiverse itself is becoming an intelligent thing? *The* intelligent thing?"

Capricorn looked up at the giant. And then of a sudden enthused, Capricorn raised his finger toward the ceiling and shook it with a vengeance. "The praise you speak is for Allah!"

The Reverend Dr. Cornelius had been smiling during his little dissertation, but now Capricorn's expostulation caused him to knit his brow, twist his lips back and forth, and otherwise look rather disconcerted as different ideas raced though his sophisticated mind.

Capricorn once more had to use the restroom. There was one just to their left. This time he didn't require assistance fastening his trousers. If he was guilty of any peccadilloes in this instance then it would have be his playing with the sensor switch that activated the faucet, which he delighted in repeatedly tripping with his waving hand. But, to be fair, he was due this little occupation whilst he waited for the Reverend Dr. Cornelius to finish smoothing a little lock of hair that had somehow boldly curled up from the side of his head. It took a little water and some persuading, but soon the postmodern divine was once more in control of his hair-do, and then they walked out the door.

The stairway was just around the corner. On the wall was a directory and they paused before it to choose their next destination. "I defer to your preference," announced Capricorn, and the postmodern divine patted him on the head.

They went up one more floor to see the dinosaurs. Immediately in front of them as they breached the top of the stairs was the Café on Four. It took just a suggestion on Capricorn's part to coax the postmodern divine to buy him a bottle of water and a brownie, which he ate with exaggerated relish, as if he enjoyed puffing out his cheeks and moving his jaw up and down as much as he enjoyed the chocolate treat itself. The Reverend Dr. Cornelius drank a cup of tea, and as he sat at the tall table with his little friend he thought once more to make inquiries as to Capricorn's origins.

"Well, alright, Padré. But you go first."

As if to provide an example, the Reverend Dr. Cornelius grinned toothsomely and appeared perfectly happy to share something of his background. He introduced his parents though brief references to their occupations and publications—his father had been a National Health Service oral surgeon, his mummy had been a translator of German instruction manuals for high-fidelity stereo equipment, which, he added, their house had been packed with when he was a little boy. He then presented himself as a consecutive issue, emphasizing a series of letters and dates somehow corresponding with the character and the time frame of his accomplishments at university, and in rattling off these codes he spoke rather more fondly—or so it seemed to Capricorn—than he had when he spoke of his own parents. As he began describing his brother the little chap interrupted him.

"Ah, you mean the bishop who visited the preschool yesterday, Padré. He came with another bishop." Capricorn explained that one of the bishops had been introduced as 'Cornelius' but since his back was turned at the time— Capricorn claimed to have been immersed in Saul Bellow's novel *Ravelstein* during the introduction of the bishops—he was unaware of which of the two bishops was the Reverend Dr. Cornelius's brother. "Padré, is your brother the black bishop or the white bishop?"

The Reverend Dr. Cornelius coughed on his tea. "Really, Capricorn, don't be ridiculous."

"Well?"

"I refuse to answer on the grounds that you are not being honest with me."

"Very well. Quite frankly, I couldn't be bothered to know which of the two bishops your brother was." Capricorn returned to eating his brownie, this time pursing his lips, puffing his cheeks, and moving his jaw up and down all the more.

The Reverend Dr. Cornelius asked Capricorn to take his turn and describe his family. Capricorn checked himself as he raised the last bite to his lips and insisted "black or white?" and then he crammed the rest of the brownie into his mouth, puffed up his cheeks, pursed his lips, and began slowly chewing up and down.

The Reverend Dr. Cornelius was fully aware that Capricorn was playing the fool, but rather than become irritated he thought to turn the table. "Why . . . the black one."

"I thought as much."

"Now see here!"

"Capricorn swallowed his brownie and then caught the attention of an African-American woman sitting nearby at one of the lower tables. Her baby was sleeping quietly in her pram while the mother ate a yogurt. "Madam." Cappy hooked his thumb at the postmodern divine. "This guy just told me his brother was black."

The woman took it all in stride—she viewed Cappy's statement as nothing but childish nonsense and she smiled with her eyes and continued consuming her yogurt. The Reverend Dr. Cornelius sat back and viewed Capricorn like a safecracker who had been confronted with next year's impenetrable model. He gave it up, but not before suggesting that Capricorn had smeared chocolate all over his face, and that he was just then looking rather black himself.

Capricorn chuckled triumphantly. "Ha! Ha! I got you!"

Such exchanges characterized much of the "to and fro" between the postmodern divine and the little boy during their expedition round the fourth floor, which was conducted counter-clockwise, or backwards through time. They began with the Milestein Hall of Advanced Mammals, then entered the Hall of Primitive Mammals, where Capricorn was rather more interested in the Astor turret, through the windows of which they could take in the prospect of Central Park, the tall apartments and Midtown buildings standing along the park's southern border, and then, in the distance, the taller east side structures like the Citicorp Building, Trump Tower, the Trump Palace, and—further up along the park and standing almost alone above the bare trees—the Carlisle Hotel.

Next they went into the hall of Ornithischian (bird hip) Dinosaurs. The animated triceratops head presented a momentary diversion, but both the postmodern divine and his little companion where so deeply occupied flinging impractical words at one another that the fossil treasures passed their notice without producing reflection or commentary. At the end of the Hall of Ornithischian Dinosaurs, however, Capricorn suffered a setback. Here, just beyond the entrance, they found themselves facing the Dinostore. Capricorn was suddenly checked in mid-sentence, and as the lad confronted the error of his ways the postmodern divine chuckled and shook his head saying, "Tsk, tsk, tsk. Toys are for good little boys, Capricorn, or wasn't that our agreement?"

"Oh Padré." said Capricorn, trying to affect indifference. "I'll be good, but you sure make it hard for me the way you come off being so clever *all* the time."

They were marching together down the corridor to the next hall. The long legs of the Reverend Dr. Cornelius were nearly springing out of his kangaroo-skin boots. "Oh, you're forgiven my friend! I promise, today a toy shall be yours. Um, so tell me—rather fancy a plastic ball?"

"Touché, Padré. Touché!"

They burst upon the Hall of Saurischian (lizard hip) Dinosaurs. The Reverend Dr. Cornelius felt in full possession of his little party and he marched along expressing confidence and command. In many ways the two were of the same mind. The postmodern divine felt he was fully in control of Capricorn, while on his side Cappy felt he was in control of himself, too. But this hypothesis ruptured when Catherine and Oona came at them from the opposite direction with their four children in tow. This little group presented a striking contrast to the team of Cornelius and Capricorn. The children escorted by the two women were walking slowly along admiring the exhibits. They stuck close to the women, and deferred to them as they pointed out salient features of the fossil skeletons. The children would often pause to ask questions and share ideas—pausing earnestly as a dedicated community group to fully appreciate together some new discovery one of them had made.

In striking contrast, the Reverend Dr. Cornelius and young Capricorn trotted round with their heads turning everyway, as if they were competing with each other to view and to *compute* as much of the fossil record as possible. Rather than sharing ideas, they kept their thoughts to themselves and only exchanged their "findings" when one of them had come across something he believed the other had overlooked. Their project was a sort of hasty inspection. They were interested not so much in visible facts nor the opinions of the paleontologists; they were rather looking for clues to the solution of some cosmic mystery, and in respect to what they sought they would have done as well to look into a bowl of porridge as to study the fossilized skeletons that stood round them, and so far as Cornelius and Capricorn were concerned the dinosaurs' naked bones had been picked clean by other minds and thus could be of little value to such original geniuses as are interested only in their own discoveries. They had made it quite half way through the dinosaur halls, and the Reverend Dr. Cornelius was already impatient to visit the dioramas and read more about the geographic vagaries of his "group environments," while Capricorn, too, shared something of this desire, as he wanted to look once more into the dioramas and enjoy the experience of actually feeling himself transported into the illusionary imagery of those representational spaces. Now with Catherine and Oona approaching, the postmodern divine felt himself even more distant from the thing he sought to know. For a moment he thought to hide behind the skull of Tyrannosaurus Rex, but seeing that he had been spotted he suffered himself to say "hello" to his wife and her friend.

Oona had been the first to spot the party. "Well, hello boys!"

The Reverend Dr. Cornelius ignored her and greeted his wife. Hello, my love."

"Jeremiah, have you two been good?"

"Well, I should think so."

"All right then, but remember: we are to meet at noon downstairs in the Dinoteria Café." Catherine brushed her long hair aside as she checked the position of the child whose hand she held. She knew her husband wanted to be off on his own in the museum, but she was also sensitive to the fact that he would like her to ask him and Capricorn to join them. She was in no mood, however, to flatter his conflicting desires. "Aren't you going in the wrong direction?"

"Ah," said her husband, "Would you like us to join you?"

"No, Jeremiah. I was just wondering if you might gain more from the experience if you were to take Capricorn properly though the exhibits, as Oona and I are doing with *our* children."

The Reverend Dr. Cornelius smiled pleasantly—until Oona barked out in her coarse American laugh, "Haugh! Haugh! Haugh! Haugh!"

"No thanks, just the same. Capricorn and I were just now headed for the early vertebrates. We are hot on the trail of a new discovery." He leaned forward to give Catherine a peck, but she held him back with her hand. "Not in those boots, Jeremiah. It might upset the development of the children's eye-hand coordination. They are very impressionable at their age."

Oona croaked again, "Haugh! Haugh! Haugh! Bye, guv'na!"

Either side of the postmodern divine's mouth drooped down and he narrowed his eyes with a kind of indignation that was at bottom meaningless. "Right, see you soon then."

Capricorn watched all this transpire with pursed lips. He exhaled "phaw" after the other group had begun moving slowly on. Oona thought to turn once more and wave. "Bye, boys!"

"That woman—" said the postmodern divine.

"Yes?" said Cappy.

"Silly American," was all the Reverend Dr. Cornelius could say, and he moved along with his follower backwards through biological time.

The Hall of Vertebrate Origins was a little more suitable to the needs of the two explorers. The exhibits they found particularly stimulating were the flying reptiles, a painting of Tylosaurus—half crocodile, half porpoise— engaging a giant sea turtle for lunch, and finally the first of the really big vertebrates: hanging from the ceiling at the far end of the hall was Dunkleosteus, a placoderm sixteen feet long, a large primitive fish with big angry teeth and a helmet for a head. In a case nearby were fossil specimens of even older early vertebrate fishes. Cappy viewed the large, bony, tadpole-like forms and the transport he experienced wasn't so much forced by the speculations of his imagination as by the re-kindling of old memories.

"The Cambrian Explosion, 550 million years ago—a vast sudden increase in speciation and the emergence of new life forms." The Reverend Dr. Cornelius used his arms to describe in the air a sort of imaginary box—to Cappy it had no relation whatsoever to anything at all. Indeed, it was as odd as if they were standing out on the street and an escaped lunatic suddenly walked up, held his arms forward to describe the shape of an invisible box, and then out of the blue pronounced: "The Cambrian Explosion, 550 million years ago—a vast sudden increase in speciation and the emergence of new life forms." Nor did it make things any clearer when the lunatic—that is the Reverend Dr. Cornelius—continued his inspired monologue: "At this unique time, organisms burst into the biosphere in a variety of forms. Speciation is diverse and mutations are radical and dramatic as life forms take great leaps in design in order to explore new ways to maximize their chances for survival. As fitness increases, life settles upon the forms of simple variants that continue to seek refinement in more subtle ways. It's kind of like a factory improving its products over time—like cars becoming better and better with each successive model year." And in a scene that suggests a Chinese socialist realism propaganda poster portraying Chairman Mao kneeling beside laughing, pig-tailed youngsters, the postmodern divine kneeled beside his little friend and gently placed his hand behind his little back, and together in a kind of reverie they looked up at the big fish with the helmeted head.

"Now there is something I simply must show you...." said the Reverend Dr. Cornelius, and he led his little follower from floor to floor, from exhibit to exhibit as together they chased their ineffable theme.

It began, naturally enough, after coming fully round once more to the Café on Four. They took the same staircase that led down to the primates, but this time descended past the third floor and returned once more to the second—they now found themselves looking again at dioramas, this time showcasing a host of birds in their natural environments. They selected their dioramas in a kind of haphazard lottery. The first scene they came upon offered an enormous Peruvian Condor flying high over the Andes with its vast wings spread out across the upper half of the display. Its companion stood with wings folded, skulking on the bare rock with its naked head bent crookedly like some kind of bald Prussian Junker. With a monocle shoved into one of its eyes the association would have been complete.

The Reverend Dr. Cornelius cupped his hand and in a gesture suggesting an intimacy with all things gentle and true, indicated the great expanse of the condor's floating wings. "Does," he asked earnestly, "does the emergence of intelligence—of the new cosmic intelligence that now waits at our shores—does it transcend even the evolution of beings that can fly?"

His little companion responded with the fingers of either hand pressing softly beneath either side of his chin. "Eureka, Padré. Show me more."

They stepped excitedly across to the other side of the hall. The diorama they came to presented a scene from the Alps at 7000 feet. Here the environment was a high alpine meadow dotted with delicate summer flowers. In and amongst the bulbs and fans of purple, white, crimson and violet were birds more accustomed to the Arctic, birds such as the rock Ptarmigan and Common Redpoll that had been there since the ice age had withdrawn their habitat to the far north, stranding their ancestors here upon this ice age island in the sky. The green mountain meadows opened out to the valleys below. Just above, the rock burst through the mossy tundra, where snow and glaciers framed the tops of the ridges that were broken by the taller alpine peaks, and among them was the Matterhorn thrusting its mighty column of rock to the roof of the sky.

"Did you know, Little Capricorn, that atop that tall and precipitous tower there exists rock formed in such a jagged manner as to resemble a miniature replica of the entire range of the Alps? I have seen it! Rocks resemble mountains, mountains resemble mountain ranges. Go to the rocky coast of any landform, and you will see the same thing along the shoreline."

"Can we tie it all together?" asked his little friend. He looked at the diorama and the painted mountain and dreamed of the miniature replica at the top and he knew the toy was within his grasp.

"I think I can. I think I can," said the giant, and he led his little friend to the next diorama.

It was a wooded park scene—from good old England! It was the New Forest in late spring and what a lovely day it was. The companions grew very quiet as they beheld a beautiful English day calling forward in every way to the coming summer, a whiff of vapor in the air, gorgeous clouds, gorse bursting with yellow blooms, enormous three-hundred-year-old beech trees stretching their winding branches lazily through the moist and pleasant air, whilst below in the shade of their rich green leaves a narrow ruddy stream slowly obeyed a curving path, and all about the grass were bluebells springing madly like memories, and the stillness was as palatable as the sounds of the voices and footfalls echoing in the museum corridors and the postmodern divine sighed and Cappy was traveling through time and what were those voices saying and where were those footfalls and both of them were out of their heads!

"Bluebells!" cried the Reverend Dr. Cornelius, gently remembering and doting like a blind man enthused with a dead nostalgia. Cappy looked up to see the giant standing with his hands clasped as he twisted his waist to the side and turned his leg this way and that upon the toe of his kangaroo skin boot like a schoolgirl fawning over a boy who had never existed.

"This way, Padré, and before it's too late!"

They stepped over to the next diorama and the noble volcanic cone of Mt. Fuji swept up majestically to remind them of the need for balance and decorum. The Reverend Dr. Cornelius unclasped his hands and bowed slightly, while Cappy approvingly said "hmm" deep inside his throat, and as the Zen influences seeped into their bones they regained their composure just in time to escape the scrutiny of the tourists and the museum guard who, not a moment before, had half-consciously sensed something like a silent earth tremor and had turned in unison toward the Reverend Dr. Cornelius and his little companion, but to behold nothing at all but two nondescript tourists, one tall and somewhat awkwardly dressed, the other a long-haired man in miniature, an orphan boy-of-color, a little brown elf from a mystery world they couldn't even begin to comprehend.

"England?" said the postmodern divine with a dire melancholy.

"It is gone."

"How?" The giant looked up toward the ceiling of the corridor. "How shall I remember her?"

"Now that you should know better than me."

The Reverend Dr. Cornelius thought a moment and, at last resolved, placed his fist softly but firmly into his palm—ah, but gentle as the gesture was it was nonetheless as robust and obdurate as true English resolution.

"Yes?" urged Capricorn.

The postmodern divine nodded. "Constable. Definitely Constable."

"Where?"

"Gosh, the Metropolitan Museum of Art. Across the park."

"Do we dare?"

The postmodern divine checked his watch. "Drat! We have only an half an hour before we're due to meet Catherine. Perhaps after lunch?"

"I will be ready."

"Steady then. So shall I." He repeated himself for emphasis. "And so shall I!"

What to do with their half an hour? Capricorn expressed his desire to visit the Margaret Mead Hall of Pacific Peoples, which they would meet if they just followed the corridor to the next stairway, went up one floor, and then carried on in the same direction through the Halls of the Eastern Woodlands and Plains Indians. The Reverend Dr. Cornelius expressed his desire to move down rather than up. On his side, Capricorn argued that the photograph on the directory corresponding to the Hall of Pacific Peoples showed a large Easter Island head, and that head was something his ambition had been set upon ever since the first time they had deliberated over the directory. He was very quiet and in earnest as he pleaded his heart's desire, and when the postmodern divine again vetoed the Pacific Peoples, the little fellow cheerfully conceded. His gracious acquiescence impressed the giant, who had been on guard for a debate on the issue. Had Capricorn at last distinguished the light of adult authority? As they struck off together toward the stairs he was quite pleased, as was his little friend who was contemplating the acquisition of a toy.

And so when they met the stairway it was down rather than up. The Reverend Dr. Cornelius lifted his hands at his sides and cut the outline of a flying spirit as he sailed down the stairs darting his eyes this way and that with proprietary satisfaction and humming softly to himself. His friend was a shadow in miniature as he too moved his hands lightly at his sides, skipped once or twice as he descended the stairs, and hummed the "pom pom pom" of a brass band burping merry melodies over a village green.

At the landing between the floors they paused to view Knight's painting of "Cro-Magnon Artists of Southern France," who were appropriately hirsute and uncombed as they labored industriously inside a limestone cave. They were putting the finishing touches on a mammoth they had applied to the wall. The chap standing before the painting held aloft a burning brand as his counterpart used a small swab to add pigment to the figure. It was an innocuous painting—both the mammoth on the cave wall and the circumscribing cave scene hanging on the wall in the stairway of the museum. Both were unevenly executed, though it could be said of the former image—the mammoth, which, incidentally, should have been a bison—that it represented something entirely different to the caveman than what the painting itself represented to the postmodern divine and his youthful charge, who registered it superficially and without comment, until Capricorn softly quipped, "And thus the Second Ether was born."

"What? 'Second' what? What was that you just said, my boy?"

"The realm of maintype images and abstract transformations."

93

The Reverend Dr. Cornelius cocked his head to the side. He was lost a moment and then thought of Plato's notion of ideal forms. "Is that what these fellows are up to?" He waved his inquiring hand at the painting.

"What they are doing we can never know truly. Perhaps they are planning a hunt, or maybe they are lost in some symbolic ritual praising the animals their economy rests upon. What's remarkable is they are entering the Second Ether."

"I see. And these fellows are inventing your Second Ether, are they?"

"Not inventing. And I can't say for sure if these people at this stage have even discovered it in what they are doing. It's the capacity of true intelligence to experience an existence that does not exist. It is a blessing and it is a curse."

"Can something that does not exist be experienced?"

"If survival depends on it? I should say, 'yes.'"

The Reverend Dr. Cornelius nodded his head knowingly. "Your abstract realm, shall we say, is nothing short of the evolution of consciousness from the infinite complexity of all existence. As this complexity approaches chaos a phase transition occurs and a new higher order of being is the result."

The little boy shook his head. "But why should complexity on its own be so important? Consciousness is an essential expression of the mingling property of matter. Complexity is a component of this property, but it is not the thing itself that brings about the emergence of consciousness, or the ability to willingly enter the Second Ether."

They eyed each other carefully and continued down the stairs.

As they stepped down to the first floor they found their passage was blocked by scaffolding that painters had erected in the arched opening to the foyer at the 77th St. entrance. To find their way round to the hall the postmodern divine had set as their destination, they turned round at the base of the stairs and walked through a narrow corridor that was lined at either side with case upon case of seashells. The brilliant little jewels—for that's how they appeared, and more, to Cappy—were arranged behind the glass according to their taxonomic families; the method of taxonomy was based upon their shapes, so that each shell was placed close to its formal relatives, and in turn these families of formal relatives were arranged beside their closest clans, and so on; taken together the collective sweep of the corridor was a true spectrum of form.

The postmodern divine again took up their argument. "Form seeks consciousness and consciousness seeks form. Plainly, at this level you can

94

see how form is seeking to find its way into consciousness, like an actor behind a curtain trying to force his way through to the stage. In these species, however, form itself is too strong a counterbalance to consciousness, and so consciousness will never be attained. These forms aren't quite right. Consciousness will have to emerge elsewhere, upon a stage of greater complexity and higher form."

As he walked along Capricorn was bent over slightly with his hands joined behind his back. In the exhibited shells he was seeing other matters, and he found the giant's observations intrusive, if not downright tasteless, but he let it go.

Further down the corridor they found the entrance to the Dana Education Wing. To their right was a small passage that had been made into a little memorial to the naturalist John Burroughs. They passed though without regarding the photographs or the artifacts and swung aside the door that admitted them to the Hall of Northwest Coast Indians. This is the museum's oldest hall and it presents the artifacts recovered by the museum's first major field expedition conducted in 1897 to 1902 by the Museum president Morris K. Jessup, and Franz Boas—the latter widely acknowledged as the "father of American anthropology." The expedition had been organized to investigate the cultural and environmental connections amongst the people living in an area stretching from modern day Washington to the Gulf of Alaska, the aim being to determine if Asians had been the original inhabitants of the Americas. Dominating the exhibits representing the main tribes of the Pacific Northwest were sections of enormous totem poles cut down to a height of twenty feet to fit beneath the ceiling. The totems stood at the dividing walls separating the various tribes whose customs and artistry were preserved in such articles as clothing, tools, ceremonial devices, household utensils, even tall wooden racks on which simulated pink fillets of salmon were set to dry.

Above the doorway they had passed through was a great winged carving, a grimacing face twelve feet across that represented some ocean spirit which figured significantly in one of the tribe's colorful pantheons. It was difficult not to stop and stare, and indeed the progress of the postmodern divine and his little friend was checked as they felt themselves magnetically drawn to the charismatic carvings that called out to them from inside the many glass cases that ran along the walls of the dark and spacious gallery. In the section devoted to the Kwakiutl people they found a special rug decorated with magical emblems and used as an appliance to ward off the bad effects of household demons, particularly in those circumstances where a father was possessed by a malignant spirit that led him to beat his children. The rug was an implement used commonly to check this spirit, and it was employed in an expedient and sensible manner: when the spirit invaded the household and possessed the father, the mother rolled up her little ones snugly in the thick rug, and thus the demon was prevented from striking them.

They walked round to the next section and found themselves facing a case containing a host of masks belonging to the Bella Coola people. Dancers wore these masks during the Bella Coola winter ceremonies that lasted for many nights and consisted of a mixture of mythological dramas expressed in song and elaborate choreography. The movements of the dancers were thought by the Bella Coola to imitate the movements of supernatural beings in the world above. The wild and colorful masks suggested many mythological ideas, from simple nature spirits to more sophisticated deities that represented the process of myth making itself. The Reverend Dr. Cornelius spoke with great care and used his posh voice to wonderful effect as he articulated the names of the masks:

"The singer of the house of myths; the originator of Bella Coola arts and crafts; a powerful ocean spirit; the sun; an echo mask with five mouths; owl; thunderbird; killer whale; eagle; moon and sun; wolf mask; hermaphrodite; the fusion of an eagle and a chief's son; a mythical sea monster; a white goose."

Cappy found the giant's voice especially pleasing as its precision and resonance smoothly liberated the possibilities contained in the brief identifications. They stepped back together and nodded. Stopping here had been worth it.

They turned now and walked down the hall, pausing only twice; the first time to examine a model of a fishing trap the Haida people had used to catch the running salmon—an ingenious affair woven together like a giant basket and thrown across a swiftly rushing stream: on the downstream side the trap had a series of round chutes channeling the fish to the interior, where, unable to make any further progress and lacking the wherewithal (and the intelligence) to find the openings at the ends of the chutes, the fish were trapped, and speared easily by the fishermen through openings in the top of the device.

They stopped also before the Kwakiutl village model. It was built entirely of wood and clearly demonstrated how the people possessed a technical and material mastery over their world that had made life very comfortable. The Reverend Dr. Cornelius and his little friend thought the same thing. Looking at those vast shed-like homes, tastefully decorated with striking carvings, a stately totem pole before the foremost building, and all built upon a handsome steep bank that stood right over the water, it was easy to imagine lives that had been naturally vigorous but also blessed with richness and plenty.

They marched through the gallery and out the double doors to find themselves in the foyer of the 77th St. entrance. Before them was a seagoing Haida canoe, sixty-three feet long and crewed by a dozen manikins garbed in clothing befitting their respective social stations. They were variously handling paddles, the tiller, or exerting a commanding presence—as was the situation of the richly garbed fellow surveying their progress from the back of the open vessel. Perhaps they were off to a potlatch, as the bundled goods that filled the canoe might serve to show. There was nothing war-like about the boat, which fact struck the postmodern divine and the little boy at the same time. They looked at each other and nodded significantly.

They moved along to the left and passed through a small vestibule (running at one side part way under the stairway) devoted to the polar expeditions of the Norwegian explorer Roald Amundsen and his American counterpart Lincoln Elsworth. But following the marching pace set by the man in the kangaroo boots they pushed on without stopping, and thus careered boldly into the Hall of New York State Environment.

"Where are you taking me?" Capricorn was glancing right and left. Around him were all manner of dioramas and displays calling for his attention, and he was delighted to see that above New York City there was an Arcadia truly flowing with milk and honey. Glowing wonderfully, the quaint exhibits celebrated the sensible cultivation methods used to sustain agricultural productivity year after year.

"Forward!" cheered the postmodern divine. "Forward to the North American forests!"

"But I am interested in learning how agriculture has been developed in this area," objected Cappy, and he cast his eyes round at the processes of soil conservation, crop rotation, the use of natural fertilizers in the soil, and the life of the soil itself.

"Bah!" said the postmodern divine. "These exhibits are fifty years old. The agricultural philosophies celebrated here have been overturned by the true science of free markets and the physics of complex economies, which together have integrated the landscape even more efficiently into the global economy. All these so-called 'natural' techniques were little more than sentimental precursors to the truly 'scientific' revolution in agriculture made possible by biotech and the new innovations coming down from the petrochemical industry." The postmodern divine cast his eyes about skeptically. "Agriculture has moved beyond all this nonsense. We have invented a new nature, and it is better."

They moved into the Hall of North American Forests and the postmodern divine turned to the right. A few more feet and they stopped before a diorama showcasing the desert outside Tucson, Arizona. Scarcely taking time to view the diorama, the postmodern divine fixed his eyes upon the sign describing the "group environment." Capricorn stood back from the diorama and rather than appraise the scene he appraised the postmodern divine. To Cappy's left were dioramas depicting Monument National Park and Ship Rock, also in Arizona; and then a diorama portraying Glacier Park in Montana. The postmodern divine read each of the illuminated signs describing the group environments, occasionally mumbling to himself as he debated some matter or another.

"What are you doing?" asked Cappy.

"Ah? Well, you see," began the giant, "I am interested in comparing the key environmental maxima and minima that define a survival landscape. Temperature, solar radiation and moisture are the key values. Any given survival landscape can be defined depending upon how these values are attuned. Elevation and the inclination of the landscape are important variables as well, but in terms of energy and the adjustment of survival coefficients they are of secondary importance."

The giant nodded with tremendous satisfaction, then turned and, calling to Capricorn, struck off once more, this time heading down the corridor that led to the Hall of Biodiversity. Along the way he paused to peek in at the diorama showing a section of soil and loam, over which marched giant creatures—a daddy long legs three feet across, a millipede five feet long, and assorted shoebox-size ants, squash-size grubs, ponderous earthworms, and an army of other creatures scaled up to monstrous proportions—aphids, mites, lice, flies, ticks, fleas, pillbugs, nematodes—all of them creeping, crawling, squeezing, stomping, pushing, slinking, skulking, stalking and milling about, over, though, under and over and over again the rotting leaves, acorns, broken sticks, mosses, fungus, lichens and what-have-you debris of the forest floor.

Immediately upon entering the Hall of Biodiversity, Cappy was struck by the darkness and then by the clutter and noise of the flickering lights of the multi-media displays. It was as if the designers of the hall were interested primarily in exciting the visitors' senses; conveying knowledge and encouraging an understanding of the natural world were secondary concerns. To the right was the flicker and chatter of a film documentary—the volume was much too loud—describing various problems in the Everglades. On this side of the hall a series of computer terminals ran along the far wall, while TV screens and cluttered diagrams and signs on the near wall battered the visitor with data on pollution, population, and climate change.

In the center of the hall was a walk-through tropical rainforest, but rather than providing a clear sense of what the rainforest was like—as many similar rainforests were clearly presented by the dioramas in the museum's older halls—the rainforest here was unnaturally dark, backed not by finely executed painted renderings but rather recorded video projections of plain, distant and indistinct trees, and bordered by glass walls that provided no clear sense of the exhibit's perimeter. Moreover, the few sources of illumination were brilliant spotlights mounted high above, so that it was nearly impossible to look up and view the upper reaches of the simulated rainforest without having one's eyes blinded. There was no glass partition protecting the exhibit from the pathway, so that the inevitable succession of school children, careless patrons and loutish passers-by had littered the dark floor of the rainforest with bits of paper, candy wrappers, and odd particles of rubbish. Cappy entertained a disturbing suspicion that the exhibit designers had intended to create the mess he saw before him for the devilish reason of actually discouraging any serious appreciation for the important subjects the hall was meant to explore, but then he suspended his unpleasant imaginings and decided the sole reason for the disarray was that the designers had simply been motivated by the desire to do something "new." Never mind usefulness or the importance of clearly fulfilling the hall's purpose, the designers were first interested in doing something "flashy" to promote themselves; and the museum directors, pretty much on the same wavelength, had allowed them to go ahead with it. This wasn't natural history. This was science entertainment. The Reverend Dr. Cornelius thought it one of the best exhibits in the museum.

After passing through the pathway leading through the rainforest the pair turned to the left and found themselves facing the "Spectrum of Life" display dominating the wall surrounding the entrance to the Hall of Ocean Life. The Reverend Dr. Cornelius and his young friend stopped to review the main points of the family tree of life—called a "cladogram"—that was cluttered over with many grotesque specimens superimposing more of the confusion that seemed, once again, to be the designers' undergirding aesthetic principle in slapping together this regrettable hall. Not surprising

Cappy one bit, the postmodern divine spoke in glowing terms of the cluttered cladogram as he once more dissertated upon the evolution of life from simple to complex forms—all leading irrevocably to the emergence of dominant biological forms and the spirit of intelligence to which the process of evolution irrevocably leads. Cappy rather compared the cladogram to some sort of production diagram, and complained that it portrayed life as the result of some technological trajectory, as if the process of life was an industrial process culminating in the on-going fabrication of upgraded "products." Missing the critical point entirely, the postmodern divine expressed approval for his little friend's level of comprehension, which he characterized as being "remarkably acute."

"But what of the play of chance?" observed the little fellow. He surveyed the cladogram. "Who is to say that rather than vertebrates instead in-vertebrates might have emerged on earth as the life form that gained intelligence: crustaceans, insects, or mollusks, for example?"

"Mollusks?" laughed the postmodern divine. "Hardly. As we have seen here today, the defining variables are temperature, moisture and solar radiation, and no matter how these variables are adjusted across a wide range of environments, the cladogram shows the forms that emerge and assume the dominant role are determined to do so by their level of com-plexity."

They still had a few moments before lunch, and to reward his little friend for being so cooperative the man in the kangaroo boots agreed they could take a quick peek inside the Hall of Ocean Life.

A life-size blue whale suspended from the ceiling dominated the two-story hall; the fellow's long forehead sloped toward the entrance to greet the visitor with the benign image of a gentle giant from another world, and Cappy immediately felt at home. They advanced to the rail and looked round at the dioramas circling the lower floor. The dioramas on the upper floor were fewer and smaller, while much of the space was given over to various displays dilating on environmental or evolutionary themes, so that the bottom floor with its dioramas invited the visitor to understand, while the top floor advanced something in the order of an explanation, or, as Cappy quipped to himself, the mystical pretense of an explanation.

They went downstairs to take in several of the dioramas. The Reverend Dr. Cornelius remarked that this particular museum kept its halls much darker than its counterpart in South Kensington, and Cappy wondered why it had taken him so long to make this observation. The first diorama they stepped up to presented a polar bear walking across the frigid white plain of the icecap. The rugged icepack stretched off into the horizon, broken only by the abbreviated peaks of ice mounds twelve to twenty feet tall whose tops had been sculpted by the wind into sharp fingers that glowed blue and green against the smoldering sky—such colors and sights as drew the little boy deeply into the dazzling drama of cooling red and burning orange. In the foreground an angry polar bear was about to seize an unfortunate seal that was, alas, just a few feet away from the hole in the ice that could have provided sanctuary in the chilly waters.

"Minus fifty degrees Fahrenheit!" suddenly ejaculated the giant divine. "That's near the bottom of the envelope!"

His little friend felt himself pulled back from the blazing Arctic skies, back like a falling spirit on failing wings, back to stand firmly on the floor of the exhibit hall. He looked up at the giant. "There are more things that make up a landscape, Padré, than are dreamt of in your philosophy."

"Yes, and I have heard that before."

The postmodern divine was still in the mood to accommodate his young friend's capriciousness, and they walked across the floor diagonally and somewhat aimlessly, pausing to look up at the whale from beneath its belly—then the little boy saw something he thought he recognized. It was in the corner opposite the polar bear, and as he picked up his pace he saw more of the form that revealed itself to be a giant squid hovering in the dark ocean abyss.

"Oh, my!" He stopped not ten feet from the diorama and then sped rapidly forward to view it closely, and not without a measure of upset. What he saw inside that had so startled him was a thing sharing the diorama with the giant squid—the great squid was not alone. Indeed, in the darkness of the abyssal depths the squid had company and, as Cappy could see, it was the great block-shaped head of a sperm whale that had closed its formidable jaw against the poor squid's tentacles, which were wrapped round the whale's head in a fierce struggle with the dark form that sought to make of it an evening meal.

"Quite a battle," remarked the postmodern divine, who was not so obtuse to fail to notice the emotional effect the deep-water theater had upon his young friend, who presently looked up at the giant and as quickly regained his composure: "It is almost lunch time."

The postmodern divine nodded at the diorama. "Apparently so!"

There was a stairway immediately to their right and they went up it. At the top of the steps they found themselves opposite and across from the main entrance, which they now moved toward. Before they took their first turn, however, they came upon a small display—a diorama six feet wide by four high—portraying a sea floor of the late Cretaceous sea populated by a variety of prehistoric mollusks. Dwelling together in the primordial scene were a variety of curious bivalves and snail-like gastropods crawling about on the sandy, pebble-strewn floor. Surrounded by slender strands of seaweed with tiny leaves winding round like jewels of yellow and purple-red were all manner of exotic tentacled creatures from the shelled family of squid-like nautiloids and cephalopods: long and thin Baculites clutching the sand with their tentacles, their long tapering spindle-shaped shells angled aloft in the clear water; a solitary Helioceras with its tentacles resting on the pebbles like the thick whiskers of some undersea bearded wise man, meanwhile its dark plum shell with its lovely lilac fringe spiraling above with a most pleasing and aesthetic twirl, as if growing that beautiful shell was sufficient reason for this wisest of all creatures to exist, a living apostrophe calling to his friends, "A shell of beauty is a shell forever!" which was itself a sufficient point of departure for understanding much much more; and, at last, governing the scene with her all-forgiving acceptance, a beautiful great Ammonite—like a spiral nautilus of modern times but much larger—viewing the life of the ancient waters through her patient and loving eyes.

The little boy said nothing to his giant friend. He simply turned to face him and smiled archly; and then checking his watch the postmodern divine announced they had better beat a quick retreat to the Dinoteria or his wife might be of a mind to chop off his head.

They marched round the Hall of Ocean Life, passed though the entrance, and once more found themselves in the cluttered Hall of Biodiversity. As they passed though the portal Cappy looked up to behold the rippling form of a life-sized squid suspended beneath the ceiling. He "hmmd" quietly in a sort of resolved affirmation. Then they stood once more in a vaguely familiar space. It was a corridor. To their left and about forty feet away was one of the entrances to the Museum Shop. Just ahead was the entrance to the Theodore Roosevelt Memorial Hall, and just around the corner, as Cappy took delight in reminding his friend, was that cryptic line about Cromwell taken from Quentin Roosevelt's journal. The postmodern divine was so concerned about the time he barely heard his little friend. He stretched his neck this way and that, and quickly decided to press on to the left and down the corridor until they found the opening to the stairway that led down to the Lower Level and the entrance to the Dinoteria.

They held hands briefly at the top of the stairs and then let go each other and descended rapidly like a pair of sure-footed mountaineers who had conquered some impossible peak and, possessed by some new and joyful energy, were sliding down the scree in a state of exuberant and humble delight.

They met the others in good time inside the Dinoteria. All the children wanted pizza, except Cappy, who expressed his desire for "a big mess of cat meat." While the other children laughed and the adults cautioned him not to be silly, Capricorn said that in lieu of cat meat he might settle for "a big mess of salmon."

"How big, Capricorn?" asked Oona, evidently used to this little routine, and the little boy said, "Big to the point of excess, Oona!" and all the adults laughed, including Catherine, who just then appeared very young and very pretty to her husband, who suddenly thought to say, "I should like a large salmon as well!"

Nobody laughed but Oona, who rather laughed *at* him. "Sorry boys, there's no salmon here. You have to have pizza, too."

Vaguely sensing a number of opportunities, Capricorn reached up to clasp the postmodern divine's dangling hand. "Padré and I had a wonderful time. And I was a very good boy!"

"Were you?" chirped Catherine. "Then I should think you two will be going up to the shop after lunch; but you two boys will have to hurry because we are going back to the Cathedral soon after lunch. The little ones didn't take a nap this morning and you know what that means."

The postmodern divine related the plan he had made with Capricorn to nip across the park and visit the collection of Constables at the Met. "If you can manage this lot, we'll make our way back to the Cathedral an hour or so behind you."

Catherine verified this with Capricorn and after conferring with Oona the request was granted.

"But before we leave we have to stop at the shop," said Capricorn, childishly mindful of his toy.

The Reverend Dr. Cornelius reached down and patted his little lad several times on the head.

The two friends joined Catherine in the pizza line, while Oona collected small cartons of milk together on a tray. It fell upon Debbie and Trinique to sit with the children, who they placed round one of the long and attractive crescent-shaped tables near the entrance. The table was low and provided easy access for the children.

Oona was the first to join them with her tray, and then Catherine and her husband were advancing with the pizza. The table was awhirl with chatter and calling children, incongruous noises and occasional shrieks. Capricorn was on his very best behavior and his example set the pattern for the others. The adults were happily aware of his leadership, while Catherine and her husband couldn't help remarking to each other that children as strong and as secure in themselves as Capricorn, in their experience, were only the sort that came from very very wealthy families. The Reverend Dr. Cornelius shared his favorable impression of his verbal ability, and then added further inquires into his background should be made. Meanwhile, he would like to take Capricorn off for an afternoon sometime soon.

"Oh, I should like that very much!" cheered Capricorn.

Oona shook her head. "Now look what you've done, guv'nah. He's speaking the King's English."

The Reverend Dr. Cornelius rarely "took shots" at people, but he couldn't resist on this occasion. "Why, yes, Oona. He takes it up quite readily. Now if only we could get the rest of your country up on the step; though, to be honest, I think we are too late, so instead you'll have to settle for on-going colonial status."

These were trifling and meaningless words, but as Catherine looked back and forth between her husband and her best friend it seemed to Cappy that Catherine looked very much like the monkey in the middle.

"Make sure you get something nice," said Oona, and she tossed a challenging glance toward the postmodern divine. "And don't you boys be stingy. You only go around once."

The Reverend Dr. Cornelius turned and, not knowing what to say, said it in an ambivalent tone: "I am looking forward to seeing you tonight, too, Oona."

Oona smiled unpleasantly and then looked at Catherine, whom she would take it out on later.

The postmodern divine and his youthful charge once more mounted the stairs and flew up to the first floor. At last Capricorn had made it to the doors of the Museum Shop!

The Museum Shop climbs three floors through the center of the museum. The first floor is taken up by the children's section, the second floor is for books and recordings, and the third floor is given over to souvenir items from around the world—crafts, clothing, jewelry, musical instruments, cards and posters. The Reverend Dr. Cornelius was discouraged to think his young charge might want to examine every article in the place, but then he was suddenly relieved to see Capricorn immediately identify his "toy" and moreover express absolutely zero desire to spend another moment in the shop. So what did he select? Near the first floor entrance there was set, upon a sort of island, a display of hard plastic animals. One side of the display was devoted to living animals that dwell upon dry land—lions, tigers, eagles and so on. The second side was devoted to prehistoric animals—so popular with the children—dinosaurs and so on. The third section held animals of the sea—whales, fishes, sharks, jellyfish, lobsters, octopuses, eels, and—

"A squid?" The Reverend Dr. Cornelius took the red plastic model and turned it over several times. The body was about seven inches long, the eight flexible arms were each about six inches, while the twin bendable tentacles with wires inside to assist in posing them were nearly a foot long, so altogether the little model, which was hefty and evidently well-made, was over twenty inches long. The Reverend Dr. Cornelius looked at the price. It was modest after all! "What a very good toy you have selected, Capricorn."

"Thank you, Padré. I love her."

"And how do you know it is a she?" asked the postmodern divine. Capricorn wrinkled his lips as if the giant had said something that was not only foolish, but also embarrassing. Capricorn stood there blushing. "I think we just better buy it and go, Padré, before somebody sees us and wonders what we're up to."

So with a somewhat mystified expression on his face the postmodern divine purchased what many people, could they have looked into Capricorn's mind, would have understood to be a kind of Kewpie doll!

The postmodern divine and his youthful charge exploded from the shop, assaulted the stairs and flew up one more floor to the Roosevelt Rotunda where they collected their coats and bundled up—the Reverend Dr. Cornelius took great pleasure in gently helping his little friend into his coat, which he then carefully fastened as he smiled quietly and warmly—and then they burst though the heavy brass doors to find themselves standing atop the steps and looking down upon the light afternoon traffic on Central Park West running left and right just beyond the burly statue of Theodore Roosevelt on horseback.

They marched down the stairs, saw the light was with them, crossed the road and then turned to follow the pavement up to 81st St. where they found the opening in the wall to their right and swung into Central Park and walked briskly and manfully for the Upper East Side.

They said little as they went along, once or twice acknowledging the landmarks as they passed them. Capricorn picked his ears up in the midst of the postmodern divine's acknowledgement of Delacorte Theatre, especially as in glowing terms he described the "Shakespeare in the Park" program offered in the summer. Then amusing the giant with his confidence, Capricorn related that he hadn't read any Shakespeare but would directly catch up on The Bard so they might discuss his plays next time they got together. As they cleared the theatre they could view Belvedere Castle standing high above the turtle pond on its black cliff. To their left the baseball diamonds of the Great Lawn were empty. The duo marched steadily on, coursing deliberately like a pair of his majesty's battleships stalking some German commerce raider, resolved to enjoy each other's company in radio silence until they came round the curve when the postmodern divine extended his palm to their right and in kind and solicitous tones suggested, "This way, please."

They followed the pavement down a shallow incline that brought them under a lovely arched bridge that served neatly for a little gateway to the environs of the Metropolitan Museum of Art—which now stood before them like a grey citadel of good promise. In a few more moments they came round the building and gained the pavement along Fifth Ave. They turned left and continued their hike admiring the luxurious dwellings that stood on the opposite side of the avenue.

"I very much love to come here and read," observed the Reverend Dr. Cornelius as they mounted the steps and paced up them with a most confident and attractive alacrity, like a pair of world class Olympians who by chance that afternoon were seen by the public taking their exercise together, and whose movements exhibited such grace and command as should evoke much sparkling approbation from their admirers.

Once inside they had to pass before the tables where the guards were checking peoples' bags and rucksacks. The Reverend Dr. Cornelius and his young charge had nothing but their coats, but nevertheless the guards thought it necessary to draw the plastic squid from Capricorn's coat and turn it over several times as they sought—obviously—not so much to check it for security reasons but because they wanted to play with it.

After passing through the gauntlet of this embarrassment, Capricorn observed that the guards were duffers, and that his little squid could have been filled with enough plastic explosive to take out any gallery in the museum, and all the people in it. Moreover, any bulky winter coat could be lined with enough explosive to take out any three such galleries.

The Reverend Dr. Cornelius was plausibly shocked to hear his little friend talk so. "Really, Capricorn, the security people are professionals; they know what they are about."

Now that he had won his toy, Cappy was emboldened to confute the giant. "Nonsense. This city is wide open. With ten men even I, a little boy, could bring this metropolis to its knees. And the implications of this fact are obvious. There are no terrorists coming, and if there were, those idiots aren't worth a toot," nodding back at the guards at the tables.

"Ha, ha, ha! How you talk, my young friend!" But noticing his little companion was in earnest he addressed the boy's bitter criticisms. "Ah, of course I doubt you are wrong; but with the war on the security people help everyone to feel safe, and they help to bring the community together to focus on the war effort. People need to be reminded that these are dangerous times."

Capricorn thought it might be prudent to pick up this disagreement another day. There was only one thing he liked more than a quarrel, and that was choosing when and where that quarrel took place. The giant's time would come. He looked up and nodded. "If you say so, Padré."

The postmodern divine presented his credentials at the membership desk; they fastened their little lavender buttons to their coats and then moved on to the great central staircase that ramped grandly up to the second floor and the entrance to the European Galleries. Suffice it to say the companions made a memorable impression as they moved steadily upwards with an almost predatory deliberation. The postmodern divine threw his hat back to bounce on its lanyard against his shoulders, vividly loosened the leopard spot kerchief encompassing his neck, and then swung his arms regally as he looked up forebodingly toward the second floor as if he intended not only to conquer the top of the stairway but maybe also tear it out of his way if it dared to budge even an inch beneath the resonant crashing of his kangaroo skin boots. His little companion stomped his feet several times but it was a tall stairway and a long climb, so he produced his squid, pointed its tail in the direction of travel, pursed his lips and went "Woosh! Woosh! Woosh!"

Once at the top of the stairs they marched rapidly through the galleries and at last entered Gallery 15, the English paintings. The gallery held rather pedestrian examples of Constable and Reynolds. Capricorn could barely stay focused as the giant dilated upon Constable's 1826 painting of Bishop John Fisbury with his saucy-looking young wife posing for their portrait on the green behind Salisbury Cathedral, one of many landscapes Constable made featuring the cathedral's straight and splendid spire.

The giant leaned his long body forward to consider the figure of the bishop's wife. "She must have been beautiful."

Cappy was faintly cutting. "The force that through the green fuse drives the flower, to be sure."

"Exactly what I was going to say about the spire," agreed the postmodern divine, also somewhat cutting. He broke away to view the other paintings.

Cappy fully yawned when the giant nodded towards Reynolds's work, and they exchanged a few unforgettable words about the pasty manikins that populated these canvases, the only life in them being the mortal arrogance they soporifically expressed—but then the two friends suddenly expressed strong interest in the works of Gainsborough, generally considered the lesser master of the three. To the acute sensitivities of the Reverend Dr. Cornelius and his young companion, Gainsborough emerged as the painter who best merited their extraordinary powers of polite and attentive inquiry. Never mind his affinities with Goya, his lack of sophisticated intellectuality, his rococo tendencies, or his obvious debt to Dutch landscape. In the first consideration Gainsborough was an inventor, a true original, and Capricorn and his giant friend were delighted to celebrate their insightful observation that Gainsborough fully anticipated (and surpassed, ahem) the greatest inventions of Turner, and indeed what was more, they affirmed that the poetry of Gainsborough's compositions not only preceded but also *fully surpassed* Wordsworth's comparatively chilly efforts at evoking the stark beauty and pathos of rustic life.

Before them was Gainsborugh's sentimental masterpiece "The Wood Gatherers." The composition was simple yet delicate, portraying a trio of young children, the third not much more than a baby. Evidently they were abandoned in the world, young orphans scuffing together a living by collecting small sticks and branches for some villager's hearth—or is it for their own fire that they shall soon need to warm themselves? Their faces appear angelic, patient, and if not hopeful they are at the very least faithful. Is there something wistful, too, in those hollow-eyed expressions? Could it be there is fright in their hearts, prompted by the same autumn wind that tugs upon the ragged tree branches reaching toward them from the darkling sky? Their poverty, their meaningless labor, and their dire situation contrast ignobly with their innocence, and like Adam unjustly thrown out of paradise they might rightfully protest even to Allah, petition for redress, and go so far as to indignantly reproach the creator of all things for so coldly elevating them to misery.

Capricorn heaved a sigh and quoted Milton: "Did I request thee, Maker, from my clay to mold me Man, did I solicit thee from darkness to promote me?"

The Reverend Dr. Cornelius was not unfamiliar with the line. He looked down at his little friend. "Come come, Capricorn. What a dark thing you suggest. I think you debase this simple and lovely painting, which expresses nothing more than a quaint sentiment, and that is all."

Capricorn swept his squid through the air. "The melancholy situation of these children is not presented here for our pleasure, Padré. A thousand injustices hemorrhage through these pigments. These young people are castaways in a wilderness of hurt. Their quaint innocence to me is salt in the wounds."

The Reverend Dr. Cornelius thought that if his little friend liked to speak in adult tones, then it might be appropriate to reply with adult wisdom. "I beg your pardon, Capricorn, but these little orphans, as you style them, taken collectively and advanced into the real world in such political movements as you would assume for them should actually amount to a wave of marauding destruction. You have heard of the French Revolution, have you not? The devastation, the murder, the terror—all perpetrated by hordes of your little wood gatherers grown up and turned loose. Nay, my little friend. Take your heart off your sleeve and check your enthusiasms, honorable as their source may be." Wearing an expression of dark and manly perspicacity, the postmodern divine nodded up at the three children in the autumn painting. "Your little wood gatherers are nothing short of Frankenstein's monster in triplicate; moreover worse, in that the monster, lacking a mate, was impotent, while these urchins are able to reproduce themselves exponentially, and abruptly drown entire civilizations in a flood of prodigious numbers."

Cappy stood silently staring at the painting; then he sighed heavily. "Well, as for what you say, I prefer to elevate my gaze at least to the horizon." And that was that.

If on other occasions the appearance of our two figures coming down great stairways has evoked images of explorers banging down the gangways of sailing ships just returned from the Pacific Ocean, or treasure-laden Englishmen sliding down towering beanstalks, or mountain climbers descending from the roof of the world, the Reverend Dr. Cornelius and his young friend this time tumbling down the splendid grand stairway of the Metropolitan Museum of Art now exceeded themselves, for they evoked to the fullest extent possible such *gravitas* (and *vanitas*) as should reasonably follow what had been their grand tour through natural history and philosophical investigation. Leaning this way and that dramatically, thrusting their legs in sidelong exaggerated sweeps, galumphing along while giving free reign to every emotional twitch their heightened sense of purpose and dignity could excite—the two companions reproduced with their movements the incongruous strut Lionel Jeffries affected in his role as "Grandpa Potts" in the film *Chitty Chitty Bang Bang*. And like their model they carried themselves with all the satisfaction fully owning to those retired soldiers what had so bravely upheld the curling flag of Victoria's good empire, and who rightfully swaggered before kings and councilors to collect their honors, and, again harkening to Lionel Jeffries' Grandpa Potts—just, dignified and resolute exponent of the British everyman—they could unflinchingly sit down to tea even with the Maharajah!

Once separated from each other, however, "tea with the Maharajah" meant different things.

To Capricorn, tea with the Maharajah included enjoying his own isolated company beneath the long nave of the Cathedral as he sat and stroked his plastic squid, moving occasionally to another and then another of the hundreds of empty wooden chairs that on Sunday would be full of worshippers. Then around five in the afternoon, as per usual, he made his way to the family shelter two blocks away, where he had dinner before repairing to his room—a snug little den where he lay down to read in the lower bunk beneath a succession of hapless refugees who intruded sometimes in the smallest hours of the morning. And (not occasionally but usually) tea with the Maharajah meant rolling out of bed in the wee hours when, after confirming that staff had gone to bed, he would sneak out to explore the city on his own—or to surreptitiously peek in upon any odd meeting or dinner party that might be held in the nearby rectory.

To the Reverend Dr. Cornelius, tea with the Maharajah included sitting alone in his apartment waiting for his wife, who called round half-four to say she was over at Oona's and would proceed directly from there to the dinner at the rectory, and, finally, that dinner—but rather than an opulent Eastern potentate surrounded by viziers, tea was shared that evening with a collection of artful bishops, crack theologians and able churchmen.

There was light talk in a small common room as the diners arrived. The talk was pleasant and meaningless, with Bishop Cornelius naturally dominating the scene and assuming the role of host. The dinner, after all, was his baby. Much to the delight of those who were concerned, the gay bishop from New England (Bishop Marvel) and the homophobic bishop from Africa (Bishop Achebe) greeted each other amiably and exchanged a few words touching on the afternoon meeting at Fordham University, and then compared their views on several fine points that really had to be raised in the response they were composing to the Pope's latest encyclical. No detail escaped the sharp eyes of Bishop Cornelius, who was gauging just how far he might push things forward that evening, and so far things were looking very good for a hard push. At one point he went up to Oona and Catherine and asked them to each grab one of the bishops and persuade them to sit opposite the women, and thus next to each other, at table. The women readily agreed, and the Reverend Dr. Cornelius, who was standing with them when his brother made this request, trained his attention upon the mystery as to why the director of the daycare center had been invited to the dinner. As he watched his wife and her friend descend upon the hapless bishops he sought to question his brother, but just then Francis had stepped out to the loo.

The other diners were the Reverend Dr. John Hamilton, Dean of the Cathedral, who for some reason would lapse into some kind of southern American usage and call the Reverend Dr. Cornelius, of all things, "Dr. Jeremiah," or, what was really odious, "Doc;" then there was Hamilton's boisterous wife Margaret, who like any other female creature of St. John's (saving perhaps Oona) worshipped the ground Dr. Cornelius walked upon, and which might explain the funny names her husband had invented for him. Also present was the Reverend Dr. John Temple, the prolific theologian from Princeton's Religious Studies Department, who was uniformly respected throughout all controversies *du jour* by both liberals and conservatives, but whose books were completely lost upon (if not indeed fully loathed by) the Reverend Dr. Cornelius, now meeting Temple for the first time, and who was also discovering a similar dislike for his haircut. Then there was Brother Michael Sylvester, the winsome, savvy, almost "street-wise" Jesuit. In the estimation of the Reverend Dr. Cornelius, Brother Michael might have been only a "fairly competent" historian of the early church in Africa, but nonetheless the postmodern divine would admit to Brother Michael being a gifted linguist. During the last several days the Jesuit had struck up a friendship with Bishop Cornelius, who had invited him to tag along to the dinner from the meetings at Fordham. Then there was Dr. Tom Abernathy, who was a physician and a leading contributor to the Cathedral, and his wife, Mary, who had finally converted from the Roman Church to her husband's Episcopalian Church several years earlier when the child abuse scandal was exposed. For many years she had maintained a thriving psychiatric practice in Manhattan, and had only recently retired to devote herself to Cathedral fundraising and her orchids. Finally, there was the Reverend Dr. Cornelius and his wife, and Oona, who was that evening on good terms with the postmodern divine, going so far at one point as to smile at him like a "buddy" and affirm that she thought the party was "fun."

"I am having so much fun. Hey, that bishop from Africa has a degree in primary education."

The ears of the Reverend Dr. Cornelius picked up at this and he smiled at his buddy, then glanced across the room, found his brother speaking with Brother Michael, caught his eye, and nodded. The meaning of the eye contact was lost for a moment on Francis, but when he spotted Oona talking to the postmodern divine he nodded almost imperceptibly and without interrupting his own conversation.

The seating went smoothly. Catherine was having trouble with her gay bishop from New England, but Francis came to the rescue and took him by the arm and fairly forced him to sit opposite her. Oona managed her African bishop very easily, and he was so gleeful in talking to the young woman with the short and attractive hair-do, that as he sat alongside Bishop Marvel his smile did much to soften the social space between them, and if any small flame of personal animosity yet existed between the two because of their theological differences, it was fully extinguished by that wonderful smile. Oona celebrated the good influences of her comportment by turning to Catherine and saying, "I am really having fun!"

The wait staff provided by the caterers was Peruvian this time, and they did a lovely job hurrying things in and out of the dining room. The crab appetizer elicited few comments, but the leek soup nearly won an ovation, as did the Waldorf salad, which caused Oona to shake her fork in the air and cry, "Mmm. I love it!" Whereupon Bishop Marvel was delighted with her exuberance and, caught up in the excitement, drew up several inches in his chair, batted his eyes up and down, and flatly stated, "I think this is wonderfully remarkable." Bishop Achebe went even further: "Africa needs many things, and this Waldorf salad is one of them!"

Sitting to Catherine's right, the Reverend Dr. Cornelius studied this closely and rather grimly wondered how the lot of them might appear sitting behind the glass of a museum diorama. Sitting beside him, his brother smiled up and down at the diners and—completely oblivious to American table customs—freely and shamelessly expelled the compressed gas that had gathered inside his large intestine. Oona burst out laughing. Her chortles and snorts were so voluble that Bishop Achebe looked round confused, while Bishop Marvel thought to raise his napkin to cover his smiling lips. The postmodern divine turned to his wife and softly growled through the corner of his mouth, "Is that your friend laughing, or did a stuffed hyena follow you home from the museum this afternoon?"

The other diners acknowledged no impropriety and—thank goodness—the wait staff was bringing in the main course, which provided the postmodern divine and his brother the postmodern bishop with an opportunity to distract everyone's attention with small talk over the cabbage.

"I should like to know," pronounced Francis, "can a boy descended (in part) from Alsatians resist the lure of *choucroute* and *bière*?"

The postmodern divine shook his head. "I can not. I even go to such extremes as brewing the *choucroute* myself."

"Do you use any additives whilst boiling and bubbling the *choucroute* in your alembics?"

"To be sure, Francis. I like to add a bit of Armagnac. The joys of applied chemistry!"

And then dashing behind a veil of charming laughter the Cornelius brothers averted further disaster.

Knowing Oona and Bishop Achebe shared a background in early childhood education, Catherine thought to raise the subject. She also hastened to add—clever girl—that her husband had just that afternoon joined the little ones on a "field trip" to the American Museum of Natural History.

"Took the whole day off for the adventure," boasted the Reverend Dr. Cornelius. "The children were delightful."

Bishop Achebe agreed this was very good and without hesitation observed: "Anything that might take the Reverend Dr. Cornelius away from his particular task is a good thing." And he let the postmodern divine dangle and squirm from his hook before charitably adding: "I trust you will return to your important work tomorrow refreshed by your recess with the youngsters."

The Reverend Dr. Cornelius grinned broadly. "Why, thank you, Bishop. I certainly intend to."

"Jeremiah was simply wonderful today," said Catherine. She turned to her friend. "Wasn't he, Oona? We have a very special little boy who just loves Jeremiah."

The two bishops ceased poking their plates and trained their benevolent eyes upon Oona.

"Oh, that would be Capricorn, our little orphan boy from Brazil. Poor thing. He is a very bright little boy but his behavior can be horrible. He's so strong minded."

Mary Abernathy asked if a psychiatrist had looked at the boy.

Oona didn't consider this an intrusion upon her turf, but her antennae were quivering nonetheless. "Why, no, Dr. Abernathy. He isn't exhibiting any serious symptoms. Actually, he was so good today that Dr. Cornelius rewarded him with a toy."

The postmodern divine wanted to avoid all talk with Dr. Abernathy whatsoever. He deflected her with a positive report. "Actually, his behavior today was lovely. Quite frankly, I should be proud if my own little boy— should the Lord bless me with one—behaved so well."

"Are we talking about the little boy from the family shelter who sometimes sits alone in the Cathedral?" asked Reverend Dr. Hamilton, the Dean.

"Yes," said Oona, and the postmodern divine watched to see how she would wiggle out of this one. "Isn't he a little star?"

"Well, said the Dean. "I suppose he is, but I was just discussing him with the director of the family center this morning and they still haven't learned anything about his background."

"I should like to visit the little fellow," offered Bishop Achebe.

"Actually," said the Reverend Dr. Cornelius sensing some vague opportunity, "I have arranged to take little Capricorn on an outing Thursday. I'll press my inquiries from that end. I am making great strides toward winning his trust."

"Still," offered the Bishop. "I would very much like to meet with this boy, too. For that matter, my visit with the pre-school yesterday morning was so enjoyable that I should like to spend more time with your group, if that would be alright, Oona?"

"That would be great!"

Catherine smiled as she worked her knife and fork. "That is so very kind of you, Bishop. Thank you very much indeed."

Since he was sitting right there, Bishop Marvel thought it only fitting to contribute his own energies; he reached out for a prop—and Dr. Abernathy looked like just the thing. "You know, my background is also in psychology. Perhaps you would agree to visit the boy with me, Mary?"

Bishop Achebe raised his hands. "We can all go together?"

114

"Oh," said Oona. "But you will still visit us at the pre-school, won't you Bishop?"

Bishop Achebe smiled mildly. "Of course, my dear. Perhaps I can take the little fellow for a walk; and, as Dr. Cornelius has done, I might also make a constructive breakthrough?"

The postmodern divine smiled. "Oh, as I found out today, he will do anything for a toy, Bishop."

"What toy did you buy him, Dr. Cornelius?"

"Why, it was a plastic squid!" And the whole table laughed.

The Reverend Dr. Cornelius happened to turn just then to find his brother beaming.

And well he should. Earlier that afternoon Francis had been bombarded with some rather unpleasant phrases like "racist hegemony from the north" and "bloody sharia law" and "won't stop until they make dimini's of us all" and "rape" and, what had been truly unpleasant for Bishop Cornelius, Bishop Achebe had raised the specter of "genocide."

"Twenty-five-thousand Christians were crucified last year just to the north of my country's borders. This year, seventeen-thousand were murdered."

Francis had his face controls set somewhere between "grin" and "grimace" as he digested Achebe's insinuations. "Well," he said at last. "I think we need to consider these figures carefully, Bishop, and look to the positive side of things. In the wake of twenty-five thousand, seventeen-thousand is a remarkable improvement, don't you think?"

But that was all behind them now. Sitting there in the midst of the sociable dinner, surrounded by friends making new friends—friends making plans to get together with each other, plans to work together to help the children—it was all coming up roses. And this is what the postmodern divine found—or rather what he *chose* to find—when he turned and saw his brother beaming at all the friendly chat.

So much for tea with the Maharajah.

Warwick Colvin, Jr.'s

Corsairs of the Second Ether

Chapter 47,459: "Between this Moment and the Next"

The story thus far: Now with Cappy away on his quest for the author of the famed Cornelius Loop, the Lost Corsairs must alone face the challenge of surviving in the hostile, laws-of-physics defying universe. Although Cappy's parting orders were plain, Professor Pop is concerned that his shipmates could yet fail to sustain their little oasis of civilization, and he knows the struggle inside them is going to be as fully challenging as their struggle against time, against temperature, and against the inescapable advent of Absolute Zero!

Now Read On!

"I say!" called Professor Pop. "I say, Mary! Fancy a walk round the tar pit, my dear?"

"No thank you." Mary Make-Believe was pushing her head down into the tar to soften it beneath her hot aura. The tar began bubbling as she finally succeeded in pushing her head in past her chin.

To pass the time (what little there was!) the Lost Corsairs were busying themselves with various projects, discussions, and amusements. They had their responsibilities to the community, and Cappy's parting instructions had to be followed, but in all other ways they were free to follow where their interests led. One of the difficulties they encountered was adapting their Second Ether sensibilities to the linear, sequential flow of existence within the strange, laws-of-physics-defying universe, and hence Mary Make-Believe's current experiment. As things went, her curiosity was typical of what drove the others in their occupations.

Sid the Freak was probably the most dynamic in his pursuit of amusement, finally deciding he was most satisfied studying the quasars, which he imagined to be moving together faster than they really were, whereupon he pumped up into a panic over the thought of the advent of absolute zero, which, as he reminded everyone who would listen, could occur at any second.

"At this rate? A second could take a million years!" Lt. Baudrillard gestured dismissively and kept walking.

Sid the Freak found in this all the more reason to panic. "True! True! And just what are we going to do with ourselves for a million years, eh?"

Vicenté the Presidenté, Laughing Jack Calvin, and Pope Nobody the Twenty-third formed a little debating society, and they took turns arguing from a variety of perspectives a wide array of insignificant matters touching upon the meaning of existence, their lack of complete and total knowledge, and the real motives behind their desire to debate such issues—and that is assuming there were any motives.

When it came to choreographing these amusements, perhaps the most ambitious of the Lost Corsairs was Sylvia the Plathological Anorexic, who for a while succeeded in corralling Pedantic Joe Philistine and Johnny Tesco into her little gourmand club. She was *maitre d'*, chef and serving person rolled up into one, and she took great pleasure in proposing menus, preparing smiledon meat, propping it up decoratively, and serving it to the two corsairs. They hesitated until she joined them, but she was not satisfied until they accepted her refusal—"Oh, I don't have to eat"—and so they weakly started without her.

She stared at them as they ate, her shoulders and chest heaving up and down in a kind of rapture; she was almost gloating. They took a few mouthfuls and chewed slowly as they looked at each other dumbly wondering why she wasn't eating with them.

Johnny Tesco was the first to break the silence. "Sylvia, this is really weird. Why aren't you eating?"

"Is it good?"

"Well, yes. Of course it is," answered Pedantic Joe Philistine; and, as if he was a bit insecure over whether it really was good, he looked across to Johnny Tesco for confirmation.

Johnny Tesco had a funny feeling about Sylvia. He put the food down. "Nah. I don't wanna' eat right now."

Sylvia turned her back on them.

Johnny Tesco knew something weird was going on and he spit out whatever remained in his mouth.

"Sylvia, it's good. It's good," pleaded Pedantic Joe. Her response was to move several steps away, where she then stood in place, her back to the two men.

"Sylvia?" Pedantic Joe set down his smiledon surprise and stepped up to her. She turned away from him and he sought to get in front of her. She turned once more and took several steps away and stopped. Poor Joe. He thought he had done something wrong. Once more he sought to move near her. She had the end of a lock of hair pinched between her fingers, and she peeked around her arm watching his progress. It was impossible to tell if she was looking because she was frightened or because she was checking to confirm he was following. He stepped up beside her.

"Help! Help! Pedantic Joe Philistine is chasing me!" cried Sylvia as she once more began walking away, moving her feet rapidly but taking very very short steps so that she all but waddled.

None of the other corsairs responded. Some looked in their direction but most remained indifferent and concentrated on their own projects in the tar pit.

"Sylvia?" Pedantic Joe was thoroughly confused.

She had stopped once again, and now she turned to see if he was following. Again she peered around her arm as she twisted a lock of hair in her fingertips. "Aren't you going to finish the lunch I made you?"

Pedantic Joe Philistine was in a quandary. He looked back and forth between Sylvia and the smiledon meat he left on the floor of the tar pit. Johnny Tesco was standing and slowly shaking his head. Pedantic Joe hesitated, and then he began to walk away. Sylvia looked back and with an absurd cry she threw up her arms theatrically and fell to the ground. This alarmed Pedantic Joe and he ran up to her.

"Sylvia! Are you all right?!"

Her response was to roll her head away from him and curl up in a fetal position.

"Sylvia? Sylvia!" Pedantic Joe Philistine ran around to look at her face, but she only tightened up more closely, all the while shifting so her hair fell and covered her face.

"Help!" cried Joe. "Something's wrong with Sylvia!"

By now all the corsairs had stopped what they were doing to watch the show. As Joe cried out they all laughed. Joe looked back and forth between Sylvia and the corsairs.

"You got that right, Joe. Something is wrong with Sylvia!" cried Lt. Baudrillard, and the corsairs laughed again before suddenly tiring of the caper.

Pedantic Joe looked down at the curled up woman, finally figured out she had a screw loose, and then walked away with his aura blushing his embarrassment.

Soon realizing there was nothing more to be gained, Sylvia the Palthological Anorexic stood up and sought something else to do.

The Simulacrum twins, Adam and Vadim invented for themselves a sporting amusement. Seeing Mary's success melting the tar with her flaming aura, they turned their own flames upon the tar to soften it and make balls—tar balls—which they let cool and harden, and then as rapidly as possible (lest their flaming auras melt the tar again) they snatched the balls up and threw them with all their might at the green head slowly smoldering in the distance.

Trailer Park Shane—his head impaled on the pole, that is—was facing away from the corsairs and was thus taken by surprise when he heard the impacting sounds behind him and then saw the tar balls rolling across the ground below.

"Suppwidat?" said Shane.

Soon Adam and Vadim got his distance and the tar balls were whizzing over, beneath and to either side of Shane's head, which made him cry out again, "Suppwidat! Suppwidat!"

One of the balls struck the pole and his head rocked back and forth several times until the pole stopped swinging. "Yo! S'up! S'up! Chill! Chill!"

Professor Pop watched this with some concern. "Lads, do you think you should be doing that?" Looking at each other, the Simulacrum twins shrugged and laughed and continued throwing. Since Billy Blake was in charge, Professor Pop turned to him and asked him to stop Adam and Vadim. "I don't think this mischief is very wise," said Pop.

Billy stood up by his forge and watched Adam and Vadim hurl the balls, which flew magnificently from their strong arms and sailed across the stars before coming down once more to impact near the green head, whose calls were just barely perceptible and tinny-sounding in the air that had nearly reached absolute zero. Cappy had laid down no rules against this kind of sport and it had nothing to do with the Pegasus drive, so Billy shrugged his shoulders and resumed his work. Pop thought next to appeal to Lt.

Baudrillard, but when Baudrillard went over to examine the balls, and then began throwing them too, Pop gave up.

What finally put a stop to the sport was Sylvia the Plathological Anorexic, who had come around from the side and had nearly reached the burning green head before they saw her. Pop finally had enough and demanded they cease, and then, uttering a muffled curse or two, he struck off across the tar pit to bring Sylvia back.

By the time Pop reached her she had struck up a conversation with the green head; as Pop realized this he shook his head knowing no good would come of it. Furthermore, Pop had never crossed Sylvia's path before, so he was a bit apprehensive as to how she might respond to his requests. As it turned out, however, his fatherly persona worked a charm, and after giving Shane a peck goodbye, she took the greybeard's hand and walked back with him demonstrating all the obedience she thought due his fatherly figure. Then she shook free of his hand and ran ahead, running from him in the spirit of the little happy daughter she had never been.

The way they had ignored Pop, the tragic situation of Sylvia the Plathological Anorexic, Cappy's lingering absence, not to mention their lost condition—these things had a devastating effect upon the emotional corsairs, whose rugged wildness was mixed in with a moody sense of indignation and ill will that, according to the nature of most wild people, was ever ready to fire off in any direction, or in all directions at once. They stared at each other sullenly as they were torn between feelings of guilt and shame. The whole situation came falling down on them, and collectively they grew irksome and were soon as annoyed as the smiledons, who with their paws still stuck in the tar again raised their baleful roaring and lingering growls at the quasars, which were swelling still larger as the stars slowly oozed towards them, falling slowly towards absolute zero and the beginning of time.

At last the Lost Corsairs came to understand the only way to get along in the strange, laws-of-physics-defying universe was to be totally disgruntled, irritated, petulant, contemptuous, peevish, impatient, suspicious, scornful, angry, frightened and bored. In short, the only way to carry on was to be completely and totally unhappy. Anything else was intolerable.

To be continued....

Chapter Five

Des Paradis du Feu

I cherish the greatest respect towards everybody's religious obligations, never mind how comical, and could not find it in my heart to undervalue even a congregation of ants worshiping a toad-stool; or those other creatures in certain parts of our earth, who with a degree of footmanism quite unprecedented in other planets, bow down before the torso of a deceased landed proprietor merely on account of the inordinate possessions yet owned and rented in his name.

—Herman Melville, *Moby-Dick*

In order to nurture within the mind of young Capricorn a sense of appropriate respect and appreciation for the roles people must play in the world, the Reverend Dr. Cornelius decided to wear his dark suit with the clerical collar, or "dog collar" as it is sometimes informally called. The Reverend Dr. Cornelius had always felt indifferent to the white band of his office—"rather suggesting," as his brother once quipped, "a halo that slips down round the neck to choke the unsuspecting." Besides, the Reverend Dr. Cornelius rued being mistaken for a priest of Rome, which was an institution that, while sharing many of the outward forms and worshipful ceremonies of his own church, and fully all of the same claims to priestly orders, was nevertheless, in the considered estimation of the Reverend Dr. Cornelius, not only a fully wrong-headed organization in its resistance to human progress, but also a rascally one as well.

St. John's family shelter was located two blocks south of the Cathedral and the staff roundly welcomed the Reverend Dr. Cornelius as he came inside to collect Capricorn. The "dog collar" exerted a formalizing effect upon the psyches of the family shelter people, and instead of the usual (and preferred) "Dr. Cornelius," on this occasion they affectionately called the postmodern churchman "Father Cornelius." His height, his austere and reserved good looks, and his dark suit worked together in a combination that was overpowering. As usual, he found "Father Cornelius" a bit embarrassing and his reaction was a bit cold; but then little Capricorn came tumbling down the stairs with that mischievous smile of his, laughing at literally everything—the walls, the furniture, the steps, the people—his bright eyes blinking, indeed, his eyes suddenly popping open like round parachutes when he saw his favorite churchman—like an unfastening of the boy's soul, especially when he stopped and waved from the landing—"Oh, Padré!"—and then bound down the stairs and ran up to the Reverend Dr. Cornelius's legs to embrace them and then look up innocently with an open-mouthed expression of total trust and love that epitomized the best human beings had to offer one another. Even the staff, accustomed as they were to a steady diet of heart-wrenching family dramas, were nearly overwhelmed by the sight, and afterwards looked upon the Reverend Dr. Cornelius—who like no other person could move difficult little Capricorn, one of their hardest cases, to such a sweet expression of affection—with something not short of complete love themselves. While they sometimes thought little Capricorn was the very devil in his mischievous ways, after this joyful greeting at the stairs they pronounced a perpendicular oath upon the person of the Reverend Dr. Cornelius, who was now to their hearts very much more than the genius from England. Indeed, he was now every inch "The Angel of St. John's Cathedral."

Seeing himself in the public eye, the Reverend Dr. Cornelius went into spectacle mode, and smiling with his eyes at the beaming staff he leaned forward ever so slightly (the staff thought he looked both majestic and noble—"absolutely royal," as one woman described it later) and looked down upon the boy who now rested his little hand upon the knee of the churchman's dark trousers: "Well, my little chappie, where would you like to go today?"

"Let's just jump on the subway, Padré, and we'll cross that bridge when we come to it!"

The Reverend Dr. Cornelius reached down and caught little Capricorn's fearlessly upraised hand, all the while sharing lovely smiles and sparkling eyes with the assembled staff persons, several of whom moments before had entered from other rooms, where, suddenly sensing something, they had abruptly left their respective tasks to see what was happening in the foyer.

As the tall form of the Reverend Dr. Cornelius passed through the front door gently guiding the little boy by the hand, no few of the staff actually curtsied, and not a one of them didn't have a lump in her throat. There were a few absurd smiles, and then someone pronounced: "We should be terrible fools if ever we let Father Cornelius leave the Cathedral and go back to England!" The older woman who would later use the word "royal" in connection with her reflections upon the person of the towering churchman fully sighed, and then, suddenly inspired, thought to cry out what was surely on the minds of all the younger women pressing with her round the empty doorway: "God, what a man!"

Marching proudly together in a sort of mutual admiration society, the duo went to 110th St. where they boarded the local One-Nine; whereupon at Capricorn's instigation they changed at 96th to the express Number Two. The train shook along, and they said little to each other until at 72nd the Reverend Dr. Cornelius posed the practical question: "Well then, where shall we begin our adventure? We are plunging deeper and deeper into Manhattan, little Capricorn."

Cappy was busy assessing the other riders, whom he subjected to a thorough scrutiny marked by his curious, deliberate eye-blinking as he experienced the full range of sensations that were produced as he gazed upon them. Evidently their faces were producing all sorts of internal commotion—Cappy would wrinkle his lips, raise his eyebrows, frown, tilt his head with circumspection, burst out laughing, glare, shake his head with amazement, suddenly pull his head back in shock and purse his lips, squint his eyes with something like angry approbation, stick out his tongue with disgust, moan while smiling wickedly—all of which reactions were apparently produced by little more than the impression of the peoples' physical appearances upon his young mind.

"You know, little Capricorn," advised the Reverend Dr. Cornelius. "It is not polite to stare like that."

"Why's that, Padré?" Cappy took out a piece of gum and began chomping up and down on it volubly.

"Capricorn?" said the Reverend Dr. Cornelius slowly.

"Yes?" Capricorn chomped on the gum and shifted his weight as the subway car lurched and swayed.

"Friends who care are friends who share."

Capricorn gave the postmodern divine a stick of gum, which was taken inside the large hands, carefully unwrapped, and then pushed into the large, smiling mouth. Pleased with Capricorn's generosity of spirit, the Reverend Dr. Cornelius patted the head of the boy, who in an eruption of glee all at once stood on his toes, bunched up his shoulders, squeezed his eyes tightly closed, and grinned with the gum protruding from between his teeth. Then with an unnerving suddenness, one of the eyes dropped open and slowly blinked once, twice, three times at the postmodern doctor of the church.

"Really, Capricorn, you shouldn't look at people that way. It's very naughty of you."

"Oh, I should never wish to be naughty," said the boy.

The Reverend Dr. Cornelius again felt something uncanny about the boy, that same feeling he had at the museum. He was curious about how he might prompt Capricorn to speak with that strange intelligence of his.

"You know, I really enjoyed our good talk the other day at the museum."

Cappy nodded. "Oh, I've had better conversations than that."

The Reverend Dr. Cornelius nodded. "Mmm. And I should like to know with whom?"

Cappy bent his knees deeply as the train began swaying in earnest. It was in fact moving very fast down the tunnel. "Lots of people."

"Yes?"

"Yes."

"Who, for instance?"

"Who, for instance?"

"Are you mocking me?

"What?"

"Are you mocking me?

"What?"

"Are you mocking me?"

"What?"

"Ah! I found you out, cheeky!"

Cappy burst into such charming laughter that the postmodern divine was forced to purse his lips to supervise the rebellious smile that tugged all the way to his ears.

The train slowed as it approached the 42nd St.-Times Square station. When the doors opened the sound of echoing conga drums could be heard. A crowd of people boarded the train and Cappy was forced quite close to the postmodern divine, who was sitting in the seat with his knees framing the boy at either side.

"Are you interested in discussing Shakespeare?" said Cappy.

"Why, yes," he said with big eyes.

"I think Shakespeare stinks."

"Now, why would you say that?"

"It's the same thing over and over again."

Wondering where this could have come from, the Reverend Dr. Cornelius spoke patiently, "Oh, and what would that same thing be?"

"Well, in Shakespeare's universe people are supposed to play their role. And when people don't play their roles the social equilibrium is upset. Then the people who don't play their roles all die—maybe it's a tragedy, but somehow they deserve it—and then the people who sheepishly play their roles take over and the social equilibrium is restored. End of story. Every one of his stupid plays follows the same formula."

"And?"

Cappy eyed the postmodern divine. "Well, don't you think that's a rather stupid way to view life? Anybody who'd preach that message would want things to stay just the way they are. Kind of underhanded, too, isn't it? That's not what life is really like to minds that are free, but Shakespeare wasn't interested in setting minds free. He was rather poet for the brain police—"

"Brain Police!"

"Look at poor Cordelia. She tells her stupid old dad that he's playing the fool—and he is—but in Shakespeare's universe *she* is in the wrong because telling the silly old goat he's a fool means she's gone outside her role as daughter. So, even though she's right, Shakespeare has to kill her off because that's his code. By the middle of *King Lear* they're all acting outside their roles, and the silly Bard of Avon has the temerity to suggest this is a bad thing—all those stupid allusions to witchcraft, old wives tales and madness—then equilibrium is restored and everyone who transcended his or her role has to die—all so Shakespeare can make his point that everybody must conform to the status quo. Same thing with Hamlet. He dies and the person who is willing to play his role takes over; and as in the play *Henry V*, the people who correctly play their roles and who restore the social equilibrium are mass murderers who wear crowns. How's that fit in with your New Testament, Padré?"

"And just where did you learn this, Capricorn?"

Cappy nodded. A map of the New York subway system was behind the postmodern divine, who turned his large body to glimpse it, and then he turned once more to face the boy, who said:

"I've been wandering the moonbeam roads a long time. I know freedom, and I know the ravings of the brain police, Padré."

Just as Cappy said this the silver train flew into the 34th St. station. The doors slid open to admit more passengers. The conductor was barking over the speaker. As the people shuffled in Cappy was pushed right up into the postmodern divine's face. Cappy's eyes were looking right into the eyes of the Reverend Dr. Cornelius. Slowly, very very slowly, Cappy blinked his eyes. Then the train lurched, strained forward and began accelerating rapidly along the tracks. Outside the window, the station slid by faster and faster, its lights winking as the station support columns stuttered by, and then the station lights dropped away as the wall of the tunnel once more ran along just inches from the window, which had become a dark glass where Cappy saw the packed forms of the subway riders huddled together like zombies racing to their respective appointments with the same thing, which was something completely insignificant—but anyway, he thought, who would be so boring as to bother over that?

He trained his eyes once more into the eyes of the postmodern divine and slowly blinked.

"Capricorn." The postmodern divine winced slightly and sat back. "You can be very awkward sometimes—down right intruding. You must learn to respect people's persons."

Cappy ceased his slow blinking. "I've heard of a people person, but people's person? Padré, are you going to get Lacanian on me?

"Lacanian! Now see here, Capricorn. You are an unusual little boy and I want you to tell me where you've learned all these things!"

Once more Cappy nodded at the subway map. "Riding silver moonbeams, as I said. And the way you shamelessly spout off all that Lacanian psychology—and in public, no less—I'd say you've been around the moonbeam block a few times your own self. And, indeed, where else but in a web of moonbeams could you have learned to recognize yourself inside the shell of this absurd illusion I see before me?"

Cappy said this at a very high register—artfully mocking the postmodern church doctor's posh accent.

The train once more shot into the brilliance of a station. It was 34th St. The brakes squealed angrily as everything came to a stop. The doors flew open admitting the roar of the station; across the platform the local One-Nine closed its doors and shuddered forward. Enough passengers got off the express so that Cappy could step back and make room for the postmodern divine's persona.

Then the doors of their own train were sliding shut and the train once more began accelerating along the tracks. Outside the window the station slid by faster and faster, its lights winking as the station support columns stuttered by, and then the station lights dropped away as the wall of the tunnel once more ran along just inches from the window, which had become a dark glass where Cappy saw the forms of the subway riders scattered about like zombies racing to their respective appointments with the same thing, which was something completely indifferent—but anyway, he thought, who would be so boring as to bother over that?

At the 14th St. station some NYU students carrying signs on long sticks boarded the train. Evidently they were going to a protest of some kind. They appeared animated and happy in their winter coats and colorful knit hats. The train started off once more and was soon passing beneath SoHo. It stopped at Canal St. and the Reverend Dr. Cornelius reminded his little friend that soon the train would be heading under the East River and into Brooklyn if they didn't soon make a decision about their destination.

"Let's change to the local," said Cappy, and they—along with the students—stepped off the train at Chambers. They stood on the platform looking down the tracks for the lights of the local, which soon appeared as a glow and then bright blobs of shimmering glare reflected in the white ceramic tiles that covered the station walls, and then the train itself was rumbling up like a shining, mindless monster. The brakes barked sharply, the train stopped and from beneath it a breath of compressed air shot from some unseen source. They stepped on and rode the nearly empty train to South Ferry, where the line meets its terminus.

"Best deal in New York," said Cappy as they emerged from the subway stairs and found themselves on the very wide street that curves round Battery Park and the terminal for the Staten Island Ferry.

"Oh," said the Reverend Dr. Cornelius. "We needn't bother about expense, Capricorn."

"Really?"

"Of course not."

"Will you buy me a toy, Padré?"

"I bought you a squid just the other day. Have you tired of it already?"

Cappy shook his head. "Of course not. I just wanted to know if you would buy me another toy, hypothetically?"

The Reverend Dr. Cornelius eyed Capricorn coolly as he organized his suspicions. He had decided the best way to probe the mystery of Capricorn's precociousness was to give it free reign so that the verbal little boy might show his hand and the explanation should be revealed. "Within reason. But mind you. We're here for exploring Manhattan, not for a shopping expedition."

Cappy agreed. "Well, alright then."

"You were speaking of the best deal in New York. Do you want to go for a ride on the Ferry?"

Cappy hesitated for a moment and then decided he was in the mood for architecture rather than sea adventure. "Not really."

"Good. Nor I."

As they walked into the park Cappy reached up to grasp the offered hand of his tall companion, who had to stoop slightly as they walked. They presented a picture variously touching, comical and bizarre. Cappy's black hair blew around his shoulders but even from a distance his exaggerated little march was unmistakably masculine. It was necessary, however, for the Reverend Dr. Cornelius to take abbreviated steps and his little friend often walked in front of his feet, further complicating the business of negotiating the pavement, so that soon the combination of proceeding with a stoop and making short, uneven steps was tugging on his back.

"Goodness, Capricorn, this isn't going to work." And before Castle Clinton, the ancient battery fort that gives the park its name, they let go of each other's hands.

As the postmodern divine rubbed his back they considered walking over to the American Museum of the Native American, installed temporarily in the old Customs Building where it is administered through the Smithsonian Institution. It was a tempting possibility, but they were resolved their outing should be spent out-of-doors and so instead followed the winding path to the edge of the water where they gazed across New York Harbor. The wind was fresh, the water was active and occasionally the sun heated the grey overcast till it glowed brightly and filled the cold day with a sort of life that etches itself into the minds of time travelers and maniacs alike. Brooklyn sat across the waters, from their perspective falling away until the insular world of Governor's Island steeped into view at the front of the watery stage. Beyond the Coast Guard dormitories and facilities, the far end of the island plunged into the harbor where many miles away the distant heel of Brooklyn came into view before itself plunging beneath the waters of the Verrazano-Narrows, over which the enormous bridge of the same name sweeps suspended from its two towers to connect Long Island to Staten Island, the dark mass of the latter looming obscure in the distance and serving as a backdrop against which the grey and dull red of distant tankers and cargo ships, the white specks of tiny pleasure craft, and the quaint yellow forms of two of Staten Island's ferries could be seen variously at anchor or creeping stubbornly over the skin of the grey harbor like vague forms upon the surface of some impossibly polished and ever-changing plane of steel. Then there was the obscure clutter of New Jersey: the cranes of the far distant Marine Terminal miraculously visible behind the less distant Navy

Terminal, then the obscure outlines of Bayonne which seamlessly flow into the similar but larger outlines of Jersey City to form an uninteresting quasi-industrial-urban backdrop for the green figure of the Statue of Liberty lifting her golden torch with effortless permanence and, a little closer, the Victorian onion domes topping the grand, red brick building on Ellis Island.

The pair traveled right round the tip of Lower Manhattan, their pathway running directly beside the water so their bodies were possessed by the motion and the steady music of the harbor as it slapped up against the concrete wall at their feet, while their eyes moved slowly along or came alive suddenly and fixed together upon some phenomenon with a kind of predatory interest as in chopped sentences they assessed the thing that called to unite their discreet attentions.

They continued along their course, which soon turned them north and brought into their view the Hudson River and the long wall of new buildings that stood along the Jersey City side of the water. Before they could comment on the architecture, however, their attention was drawn to the pyramidal stone building before and to their right—the Holocaust Memorial and Museum. The postmodern divine pointed out the new construction to the right of the pyramid and asked for Capricorn's opinion on the addition. Cappy regarded it carefully and noted that while the work was tasteful the statement made by the pyramid standing alone must have been more forceful than it was now with the blank wall of the addition curving behind and mitigating much of the pyramid's former outline. Then he swelled himself up like a miniature Dr. Johnson and observed that, "While I don't as a general thing approve of memorials, particularly memorials celebrating wars, violence or the cult of martyrdom (or, its diminutive sibling, the cult of victimhood), surely the horrid phenomenon of the Holocaust demands some token of architectural recognition."

"Beyond a memorial, what do you think of a *museum* devoted to such themes?"

Cappy teetered on his heels and nodded to himself. "Tear it down, sir. Tear it down." Then Cappy paused as if he suddenly remembered something. He shook his head. "But I am afraid this particular planet must do with a strong reminder."

The Reverend Dr. Cornelius was not unimpressed. "What do you find most significant about the Holocaust? What to you is most striking?"

"Beyond the terrible suffering of those poor human beings?" Cappy touched his little hand upon his chin. "I believe the most significant thing to be the cold bureaucratic normalcy of the killers' methods. The people who perpetrated those atrocious acts of mass murder were in their way very banal and conventional creatures, and not the monsters depicted in the popular imagination. That to me is most terrifying."

"To what then do you attribute the Holocaust?"

"Conformity, complacency, and self-satisfaction in knowing one's place and playing one's role in it."

"Do you object to playing your self?"

Cappy answered directly: "Not at all, sir. I object only to being satisfied with the role. Finding contentment in one's soul, I should add, is another thing entirely. Moreover, that should be a difficult thing to find locked in the human form—the divine image of Allah, shall we say."

The Reverend Dr. Cornelius started at this. He looked off through the distance to reflect. "Can you suggest another form then?"

Cappy tugged on the trouser leg before him until the giant looked down. "Jesus."

They began strolling again together like cozy old confidents, a pair of peripatetics who had struck off together in Athens 2500 years ago and were still walking today.

The Reverend Dr. Cornelius didn't know what to make of his little prodigy. He was once more tempted to inquire into Capricorn's background but decided he would rather continue the fascinating conversation. "Tell me," he said at length. "Who do you hold accountable for the crucifixion: the Jews or the Romans?"

Cappy smiled slyly. He looked up at his tall friend. "The Jews? Jesus was a Jew!"

"Well—yes. Yes of course, but—"

"Jesus wasn't out to create a new religion. He wanted people to be good Jews. Even people who weren't Jews could be good Jews as far as he was concerned. Good people, that's all."

"Granted. But let me re-phrase my question. Do you think it was the Romans or the Pharisees who are culpable in the death of the Savior?"

Cappy hooked his thumb over his shoulder to indicate the Holocaust memorial behind them. "Neither. It was the human race, Padré. The Homo sapiens did it."

They walked along quietly now and gazed at the large buildings that had gone up along the New Jersey side of the Hudson. The tide was flooding, and as it does at this time of day the river actually appeared to be flowing north. Many of the buildings on the New Jersey side were new, and the building boom that had begun there in the late 1990s had been accelerated by the World Trade Center disaster. The appearance of the area was breathing and alive. The buildings were shining, angular, robust, clad in bright metal and white. The dreadful kitsch architectural fashions of the eighties and early-nineties were scarcely evident, and the impressions produced as the two friends gazed at the new construction were positive and optimistic, even "futuristic" in some very good sense of the word.

The promenade was interrupted now by the large plaza of the World Financial Center. In the middle of the plaza was the World Financial Center Marina. Except for a handful of excursion craft and the small sloops belonging to the New York Sailing Society, the marina was empty, a far cry from other seasons when yachts from round the world tie up to afford their owners and crews a unique berth in Manhattan. Set back and surrounding this artificial lagoon, the tall buildings of the World Financial Center were blighted by just the sort of architecture that was absent across the river. Formerly, the Twin Towers had acted as counterweights, reducing the scale of the World Financial Center with its dreadful eighties vernacular of conformity and that self-consciousness that hides behind the mirror-mask of its own pretension; but even in their absence the Twin Towers arguably balance out these unpleasant elements, as history, too, has a way of placing new values over things. In the wake of the towers' destruction, the architecture of the World Financial Center was made a living thing; it came out from behind its postmodern mask and was thus redeemed through meeting up with its own obsolescence.

There was one feature that transcended the controversial architecture of the unimpressive buildings—the Winter Garden. Situated in the center of the World Financial Center, the Winter Garden was a large framework of curving steel covered in light-catching transparent panels. Before the Twin Towers came down it had been accessible at the far end through an enclosed bridge that spanned the West Side Highway to join the Winter Garden to the base of the World Trade Center, the great plaza there, and the vast below-ground galleria that had been a city beneath the city within the city. But those were times that fell before those times that concern this tale.

Cappy and his tall friend went in the revolving doors and through the little glass-wall vestibule and stepped out beneath the curving transparent roof. Beneath their feet was the Italian marble that had replaced the marble that had been destroyed when the towers came down—these polished slabs were identical in pattern to the marble they had replaced, but not red and cream in color, rather a brown and light beige. To a person who knew the marble floor of former times, the change was suggestive of parallel worlds or parallel dimensions, where the basic outlines of reality are exactly similar in both places, but nonetheless exhibit slight discrepancies in the finer details.

Much of the central floor was given over to an orderly array of green metal benches, from the midst of which ascended the uniform columns of palm trees—trunks of a grayish beige that lifted the bright green fronds forty feet into the air. In tune with the season, amongst and above the fronds hung long lines of bright lights that created an effect like a nebula of stars hanging in the "sky" of the Winter Garden. The lights were bright yellow and so numerous and suspended so deeply that the effect was nothing short of soothing.

To either side where they stood at the front of the Winter Garden were escalators angled up to meet the second floor, which ringed the great structure with a sort of balcony. Between the escalators a stage had been set up and upon the stage was Santa.

"Sit on that fellow's lap? I think not," said Cappy, and the giant's indicating hand was withdrawn.

After surveying the structure at that end, they moved toward the great steps that dominated the other side of the building. Layered in the same Italian marble as the floor, the convex semi-circular layer-cake of steps rose fifteen feet to a circular landing, and then raised once more in a convex amphitheater of steps to the second floor, which was actually the main corridor of the entire center giving access to its many towers. For the nonce they remained on the ground floor and followed the circular corridor beneath the steps where they viewed behind the glass a series of displays given over to describing the history of the World Trade Center, its fall, the architectural competition to which the world's leading architects submitted their designs, the selection process, and, finally, to Cappy, the misguided project for designing the World Trade Center Memorial.

"Instead of a memorial," suggested Cappy, "They should build a jail in which to place the politicians who let this happen."

"Charity, Capricorn."

"Such charity belongs in the solid state of heaven, and not upon the face of this turning earth." Cappy's attention was captured by a video recording of politicians and architects meeting to congratulate one another for the selection of the new design. As the story unfolded Cappy blinked his eyes very slowly, but then suddenly shook his head with disgust at the landlord and the representatives of the victims' families group. "Why they were permitted to participate in the process I shall never know. The landlord's

132

design for the so-called Freedom Tower, tra la, completely spoils the vision of the original architect. And all that space given over to a memorial is maudlin and repulsive. Do you have such a memorial in London devoted to the blitz?"

The Reverend Dr. Cornelius held his head up proudly. "Certainly not. We defied the dastards and got on with our lives."

Cappy nodded. "Exactly. Harrumph. As for this—" and here Cappy moved his little hand in a reluctant circle to indicate the display "—they should have disabused themselves of this nonsense and straightaway got on to rebuilding the Twin Towers, and bigger and better than they were before."

Now the TV screen was showing some kind of celebration of the winning designs. A half dozen dancers representing as many different cultures were performing their various hornpipes—African, Indian, Native American, Eastern European, Latin—even a ballerina in a tu-tu had been imported from some culture sweatshop or another.

Cappy blinked once, twice and then looked up at the giant. "At the very least somebody should be held accountable for this!"

They walked back into the main area of the Winter Garden and went up the steps. About half way up the second section they turned to view the prospect. The gallery of suspended lights was so enticing they sat down for a few moments to dream in the light—until Cappy's tummy sang the song of the hungry little boy. They stood and went the rest of the way up the steps, during their ascent agreeing they should both benefit from lunch.

At the top they were greeted by the tall windows that stand at the street side of the Winter Garden—and they could see, beyond the street, Ground Zero.

They took in the view quietly. The grey "bathtub" that had held the river out of the galleria beneath the Twin Towers was empty and desolate. A large construction ramp angled in from the right. The cornerstone for the "Freedom Tower" had been set, and gravel had been spread over the former footprints of the towers, but otherwise it was a gutted and stark-looking ruin. On the left, glass-clad Number Seven had been rebuilt and was already admitting tenants. Some preliminary work had been done on Calatrava's station, but the rest of the stone-age site was the same blasted mess it had been since the rubble was first cleared away.

"I think I'd put it there," said Cappy pointing vaguely into the bathtub.

"And what's that, Capricorn?" The Reverend Dr. Cornelius grinned at the foolish child.

133

"The jail for the politicians."

They walked off and had lunch in one of the many feeding nooks housed in the labyrinthine structure. The Reverend Dr. Cornelius asked the waiter for a bowl of minestrone and a small salad. When Cappy was asked he patted his belly and said, "A big mess of cat meat."

"The boy will have your grilled salmon," said the Reverend Dr. Cornelius, and scarcely hiding his amusement he shook his head at his facetious little friend.

As they ate the conversation was of the sort one should expect between a small boy and a world-class theologian. They discussed Cappy's life at the family shelter, his interests—chiefly his toy squid and sitting alone in the Cathedral—and his resistance to going to a school with the "big boys." No matter which clever strategy he employed, the postmodern divine could not persuade his little friend to discuss the idea. When he tried to bring up Capricorn's origins—Brazil? Family? Parents? Any brothers and sisters?—Capricorn turned his nose up, tapped his fork against his teeth, and made more of his tired efforts at eating his fish.

When Capricorn announced that he was done the Reverend Dr. Cornelius observed that he had barely touched his fish.

"It didn't meow when I cut into it."

The postmodern church doctor paid for lunch with his charge card.

They dodged out a side door and were somewhat startled by their submersion into the cold—but just as suddenly relieved to be once more out-of-doors. They found and climbed the steps leading to the covered pedestrian bridge, and walked though the bridge along the northern boundary of the World Trade Center site. Then they climbed down the steps to the pavement and walked over to check on the commotion before the PATH station. It was a protest. The Reverend Dr. Cornelius thought they were all rather silly people, but nonetheless admired their expressed desire for peace. But then he became irritated by their angry suspicions and the absurd accusations they hurled at the administration, and he just couldn't bring himself to understand their lack of common sense.

"They are rather naive, aren't they?" said Cappy. "I shouldn't pay much attention to them."

The Reverend Dr. Cornelius was pleased to hear some good sense coming from the small boy, but when Capricorn then asserted that the real culprit was an international "cabal" hostile even amongst its own membership and consisting of Arabs, Persians, Pakistanis, Israelis, British financiers,

American spies, oil companies, big banks, corporate socialists and a new avant-garde imperial system, the postmodern divine could only balk.

Cappy jabbed his finger upward to evoke the authority of Allah. "They all have a seat at the board of directors, where they glare at each other waiting for someone to blink. The only thing they agree upon is that the world should be run with intimidation and fear. Is that preferable to the alternative? To peace? Maybe it is? For the only sure way to achieve peace would be for the Europeans and the Americans to throw their politicians in jail and then invade South Central Asia with a vengeance, put the kings and the mullahs to the sword, burn down all the mosques, indifferently murder two-hundred million people, and then when its all over seize who's ever still standing—or crawling—and teach them to read the New Testament and play baseball. Until that happens, you are going to have this." And Cappy indicated the empty pit before them.

The Reverend Dr. Cornelius would have been alarmed if the words hadn't come from a small boy. "I should remind you, little Capricorn, that there is a coalition that has invaded Iraq and Afghanistan, and their plan is achieving the desired results, and without the horrors you would bring down upon all those poor people." Citing elections in Afghanistan and Iraq, the good reverend added the plan had already made impressive strides toward restoring security throughout the world.

"Afghanistan invaded? To what end? Has the poppy crop been destroyed? Do women still walk around wrapped like mummies?" Cappy shook his head. "Until such time as ALL kings, mullahs, warlords and poppy farmers have their intestines cut from their stomachs and thrown into their children's faces, there is going to be war and hatred enough on this planet to last a hundred—no—a thousand years. Meanwhile, as your politicians adhere to their illusion of a "War Against Terror" the cabal of Arabs, banks and oil companies will bleed your civilization until it finally collapses into the cesspool of its own stupidity. Your vain Homo sapiens complacency forbids you from seeing over the horizon." And with that Cappy turned his back upon the horrified postmodern divine and resumed his study of the buildings.

One of the protest organizers was chanting through an electronic megaphone: "No war for oil! No war for oil!" and the people in the crowd were responding unevenly. Cappy remained indifferent to the process—he was keenly occupied with the architecture. But when he actually turned and glimpsed the protestor with the megaphone he halted and pointed with something approaching an ecstatic fit:

"The Grand Wazoo!" he cried. "The Grand Wazoo!"

The Reverend Dr Cornelius followed Cappy's pointing hand. "What? Do you mean the megaphone?"

Cappy was hopping up and down, "An exact replica of the Grand Wazoo—scaled down by a factor of hundreds—no—thousands! And here it is in the universe! I can scarcely believe all of it could fit into one tiny place, let alone be light enough for a frail human being to lift it so easily."

"Don't be silly. It's only a megaphone."

"Let us think of a way to take it away from that person. The Grand Wazoo is not to be trifled with."

Again the Reverend Dr. Cornelius explained the common nature of the device, pointing out that megaphones were available throughout the city.

"Are they?" asked Cappy. "Where!"

The Reverend Dr. Cornelius pointed up Fulton Street. "There is a Radio Shack just a few blocks that way."

That strange (and now familiar) curiosity seized the Reverend Dr. Cornelius yet again, and he obliged Cappy's demand to visit the Radio Shack.

"You'll buy me one?" asked Cappy.

"Hang on. They can cost well over a hundred dollars."

Cappy waved his hand dismissively. "C'mon, you promised you were going to buy me a toy. Besides, you have always wanted a son to spoil. You said so yourself."

They crossed Broadway. As they passed the Fulton St. Subway station—a gaping cave mouth choked with commuting protestors, the cluttered tables of African vendors, shuffling tourists, busy shoppers and nimble office workers—Cappy commented on the congestion and the thoughtlessness of the city planners for not better organizing the space. "Chaos," he said. And he glared significantly at the Reverend Dr. Cornelius. "So where's the phase transition? Where's the leap to a higher level of order?"

"This, young Capricorn, is an epicenter of specified activity, a vortex of ad hoc co-creation existing inside a larger complex system that in fact exhibits the very emergent order you seek."

Cappy was just then bounced aside by a charging woman in a light blue business suit and white tennis shoes. "If you're speaking in terms of geological time, then perhaps I agree with you. Otherwise—take me to the Wazoo!"

The Radio Shack was just ahead. Cappy stopped and nodded for the Reverend Dr. Cornelius to open the door for him, and they entered.

136

The good churchman advanced to the counter and began to make inquires as to electronic megaphones. Meanwhile, Cappy went round taking things from shelves and off the wall. Rather than replacing them where they belonged, he simply pushed the articles into whatever crack or crevice was most handy, and in his path the shelves were left a clutter of displaced merchandise.

"Hey, kid! Wa'da'ya think you're doing?" One of the salespeople swung out from behind the glass counter and marched over to straighten the shelves that Cappy had disturbed. Cappy stopped his inspection and slowly blinked his eyes as he calculated how far he might push the human.

"I'm looking for the Grand Wazoo, mister."

"Grand Wazoo? What are you talking about?"

Cappy concluded his study of the salesman's character, then resumed his inspection of the merchandise, replacing the articles as haphazardly as before.

The Reverend Dr. Cornelius had made some progress with his salesperson, and he was lifting a megaphone into the air to show his little companion. "Capricorn, is this the Wazoo you are looking for?"

Cappy turned to see what the Reverend Dr. Cornelius had found, but then he spied something on the clearance table that more closely matched his specifications.

The Reverend Dr. Cornelius and the two salesmen stared as Cappy swaggered over to the sales clearance table and fumbled with a cardboard box. It contained a cheap plastic microphone—over-sized and obviously designed for a child. The barrel was yellow and the round business end was a bright pinkish-red. It was equipped with a spring that created a mechanical reverberation when the user sang—or shouted—into the mouthpiece. Cappy turned it over and over with an expression of glee beaming from his tan face. He hummed into it a few times, licked the red plastic, and then cried into it: "Abandon ship! Zero! Zero! Zero! This is Zero the Hero! Watsupwidat! Watsupwidat!"

The Reverend Dr. Cornelius waved the electric megaphone. "Capricorn! I've got your megaphone here. Hello!"

The salespersons thought these proceedings a bit odd, but it was New York after all and they were easy.

Cappy called into the plastic microphone: "This is the Captain speaking!"

The Reverend Dr. Cornelius advanced with the megaphone. Some of his little friend's spontaneity had rubbed off on him, and he bothered to switch on the megaphone and say, "Hello! Look, I have the Grand Wazoo!"

"No you don't!" Cappy said into his plastic spring-activated reverb microphone. Besides being somewhat distorted, his voice was tinged with a stern command presence. "My Grand Wazoo is more to scale than yours."

"But my Grand Wazoo is louder," said the Reverend Dr. Cornelius.

"Volume is unimportant," said Cappy. What matters is how many scales you can reach at any one time. Besides, mine is a lot better looking than yours."

"But my Grand Wazoo is far more expensive than yours. And I've got a horn." The Reverend Dr. Cornelius lowered his megaphone and hit the horn button. BLAW! BLAW! BLAWWWWW!

Still holding the plastic microphone to his mouth, Cappy yelled, "BLAW! BLAW! BLAWW! WAUGHHHHH! WAUGH! WAUGH! EVE! LYN! WAUGH!" Cappy lowered his microphone and said, "See. It doesn't matter how loud you are, it's the meaning that counts."

"'Blaw! Blaw! Blaw! Evelyn Waugh!' is meaningless," retorted the amplified voice of the Reverend Dr. Cornelius, once more in megaphone mode.

Cappy was unimpressed. "Don't be silly, you get extra points for nonsense, for what can indeed be more significant than nonsense?" And then he tossed the plastic microphone to the salesperson. "We'll take it. Gift wrapped, please. Pay the man, Padré!"

The Reverend Dr. Cornelius purchased both the plastic toy voice-altering microphone and the expensive electronic megaphone—which the two salespersons carefully re-packed in plastic, re-inserted into boxes, gift-wrapped, and placed in plastic shopping bags—and then Cappy and the postmodern divine went out the door with their devices thus neatly packaged, gift-wrapped, and bagged. Once back on the street they went down to the first rubbish bin they saw (just down the street at the southeast corner of the empty building that had been home to the Strand Bookstore annex) and pulled their purchases from the bags, tore away the innocuous holiday wrapping paper, drew the wazoos from their boxes, and then rolled everything together—the boxes, the innocuous holiday wrapping paper, the protective transparent plastic bags, the red and white plastic Radio Shack shopping bags, the little packet of moisture absorbing poison that kept everything dry, the Styrofoam inserts, the instructions, the warranty, the registration card, the discount coupon, the Radio Shack two-page megaphone catalog, the bright orange identity theft warning flyer, the bright yellow State of New York Statement of Consumer Rights, the Spanish instructions, the Spanish warranty, the Spanish registration card, the Spanish discount coupon, the Spanish Radio Shack two-page megaphone catalog, the bright orange Spanish identity theft warning flyer, the bright yellow Spanish State of New York Statement of Consumer Rights, and the receipt—all rolled up madly together with the boxes and the plastic bags and the wrapping paper and the documentation—all slapped quickly and mechanically into a large ball, which they thrust unceremoniously into the bin.

"Attention, New York! Attention, New York!" Cappy cried into the Grand Wazoo in a sort of anxious monotone. "Abandon city. This is no drill. Abandon city. I repeat: this is no drill. I am a ventriloquist dummy made up to look like a human boy. I am made out of plastic explosives and I am set to detonate upon receiving a short burst of radio waves broadcast from the Department of Homeland Security at such time as the President's popularity rating falls below the committee's recommendation!" Cappy lowered the Grand Wazoo from his lips and said, "Right, let's go back up to the protest!"

The Reverend Dr. Cornelius laughed and said, "I think we can give the people a better message than that, don't you?" and the churchman raised the megaphone to his lips and said, "Keep the faith! Stay the course! Be at ease! We have nothing to fear but terror itself!"

Cappy didn't know whether to be irritated at the giant for the complacency of his message, or to admire him for making what was, after all—from the giant's perspective anyway—no little disturbance in the public street.

"Well, what do you think?" And the Reverend Dr. Cornelius clicked off his wazoo.

Cappy shrugged. "Well, as I said, never underestimate the significance of nonsense."

They turned and walked back up the pavement to the Fulton St. Station. They avoided the big cave mouth entrance and went down the less frequented and narrow stairway across the street from the Radio Shack. Once down in the station they resorted once more to their Wazoos and made absurd noises as they walked along the tunnel and through the turnstile and at last lingered awhile on the platform and waited for the uptown express. The station was filled with protestors, a few European tourists, and working people. There were few young people. A sociologist interested in demography might note that most of the people were black, that most of the "white" people were Hispanic or students, and that most of the unhappy people were probably Russians, but even as tired as some of the Russians

139

appeared it was hard for Cappy and the good reverend to really feel that anybody in the great city had to work very hard, and if they did work hard, or, worse, if they were *worked* too hard, then it was their own fault because the big job—really, the only job—to being in New York was simply being—being in New York, being dressed warmly enough, being in good spirits, being happy in the station amongst all the people who were just going where they were going like anybody else—just being, just being there, just being period—BEING—and that's all there was to it. If anybody got uptight they had brought it upon themselves, or, even worse, if anybody rushed or worked too hard, or let anybody bring them down, that was too bad, because here in the Greatest City on Earth time was made for the people, and a civilized person should know to do anything he or she wants, and if anybody got in your face it was their problem and—

"Watsupwidat! Watsupwidat!" cried Cappy into the Grand Wazoo and the Reverend Dr. Cornelius slowly spoke into his Grand Wazoo in the most posh, slow, disinterested, amused, winsome, high-altar tone imaginable, "What is up with that, ahem." And then he bounced his eyebrows up and down at his little friend and posed the musical question: "Why kaaaant the English luuuun to speak?"

Cappy cried into the Grand Wazoo: "Squeek! Squeek! Squeek!" and then he cried out shrilly: "Eeeeeeeeeeeeeeeeeeeeeeeeek!"

And except for one or two quick glances directed at something vaguely incongruous about the sight of the Reverend Dr. Cornelius's clerical collar, nobody paid much attention.

Cappy wasn't satisfied with that.

His opportunity to push the envelope emerged at the next stop—City Hall/Brooklyn Bridge, where everyone was asked to be patient because of a "police problem" in one of the cars at the front of the train. But the true nature of the situation was really anybody's guess because after being stalled there a few moments the conductor cracked in over *his* wazoo to announce the train was out of service and everyone had to get off.

"I knew we should have taken the Two-Three," said the Reverend Dr. Cornelius.

"Ahhhh," said Cappy through the reverberating wazoo, "But this way we can stop at Grand Central and go down stairs and look at the big station for the Number Seven to Flushing. Then we can take the shuttle to Times Sq. and catch the A there. I love riding the shuttle.

The Reverend Dr. Cornelius depressed his horn button. WAUGH! WAUGH! WAUGH!

A pair of sheepish policemen momentarily looked at the postmodern divine, spotted the dog collar, concluded he was a Catholic priest, and therefore whatever he was doing—even depressing the horn button and blasting the Grand Wazoo inside a crowded, echoing subway station—was somehow copasetic.

Cappy raised the plastic microphone to his mouth and was about to shriek—but the train started off with a wizzz wizzz wizzz wizzz wizzzzzzerrrrrrrrrummmmmmmmmpppppooooo and a woo woo wooz wooz wooz wooooosssssssssssssh! and a grumblerumble-brumbble-dumble-um-um-um-ack-ack-ack! and was soon roaring and clanging and squeaking like some metal-clad incarnation of Electrosquirm the Mile-long Dys-systematic Centripetal Centipede—so Cappy waited a few moments for the competition to drain out of the station pulling its kabooty antennae and wriggling legs behind it, and then he began imitating the train's squeaks and shudders through the Grand Wazoo.

The Reverend Dr. Jeremiah Cornelius held his wazoo against his chest admiring little Capricorn and pretending—why not, it was New York?—that the little tan fellow was his own son and bosom buddy and father's wee chappie and dad's earnest lad—

—until Cappy's opportunity to push the envelope emerged.

Cappy slowly lowered the Grand Wazoo from his lips and stood with his mouth open. His eyes blinked slowly up and down as he gazed upon a group of men garbed in long black coats, black suits, black hats with pronounced brims, and sporting also long black beards, black shoes—everything was black but their pale faces and hands, their un-tucked shirts, and the dangling white threads of the knotted tzeh-tzeh that emerged from beneath their shirt tails.

"Look at them," cried Cappy at length.

"The Hasidim, you mean?" asked the Reverend Dr. Jeremiah Cornelius.

Cappy shook his head. "Oh, strictly speaking they are not the Hasidim. They are very Orthodox, yes, but they are not the Hasidim." Cappy looked up at the postmodern divine. "My father very much disapproves of their insularity, but is otherwise a commanding presence in their midst. Give me that!"

Before the postmodern divine knew what was happening, Cappy snatched the electronic megaphone and advanced several steps closer to the bearded gentleman, who were now only fifteen feet off. Cappy raised his plastic microphone up to the mouthpiece of the megaphone and so augmented the mechanical reverb with the power of electronic amplification—a bigger, more competent Grand Wazoo if there ever was one—and depressed the trigger:

"Clansmen! Avast, ye blasted swabs! I am Captain Cahtah Kohenum, son of Rabbi Dada Kohenum, who was high-priest to all the Pleiades. By my father's direct command—and transgressing the law requiring a Jewish mother, indeed, setting a new precedent under the direct auspices of Allah's revealed plan for planet Earth—I, Captain Cahtah Kohenum of the clipper *Bifurcating Monofilament*—I say, I am my father's successor and direct messenger. As such, I charge you to hear my words! I have read the reverberating writings of certain apostate intellectuals who stride like superheroes before the Gentiles. Indeed, I see in their words a thinly-veiled xenophobic attack upon the Protestant homunculus of western civilization, which, I say, Allah willing, is the true New Jerusalem! These intellectuals have besmirched the wise and love-borne legacy of Arminius and Socinus, Milton and Locke, Mayhew and Jefferson. For this vandalism shall we be held accountable? And thus my admonishment contains a forewarning. Hear me. My words are of your eternal salvation. I have read your Theodor Adorno, your Max Horkheimer, your Leo Strauss, your Stanley Fish, and your Allen Ginsberg! And what a lot of *mamzeyrim* they are—soaring acrobatically skyward in their gaudy tights and flapping capes, the rivals of Allah's joy and the foot-to-ground Reason of His only Son! Amen! Amen! And I warn you the attempts of these grove jesters to glibly subvert the holy wisdom of John Milton, The Declaration of Independence and the U.S. Constitution shall be revealed to the nation of E Pluribus Unum, and it will be an embarrassment to all our people. Shame! Shame! These university intellectuals—many who had themselves fled the persecution of the *übermenschen*, but then only to turn round and bite the back of the nation that had given them sanctuary—I say, thinking of their vulgar appeals to the legalistic illusions of metaphysics and 'scientific' authority—I can say only this, and heed my words: You can take the Jewish intellectual out of Germany, but can you take Germany out of the Jewish intellectual?" Cappy paused a moment for emphasis. "Now just think about that as the next train pulls up, and thank Jesus that train is taking you for a jolly round the Big Apple rather than back in time to an *übermenschen* detention camp. Behold the sword comes out of my mouth. And change those awkward black clothes, and—"

The postmodern divine snatched the electronic megaphone away from Cappy. He has been so amazed at Cappy's outburst that he had hesitated,

142

but when he realized the full portent of the little orphan's oratory he thought it prudent to intervene.

"Why did you do that?" Cappy was speaking into his plastic wazoo. "I was just warming up."

"Surely, when you brought the detention camps into it you had fully peaked, I should say."

The two policemen were back and the Reverend Dr. Cornelius cleared his throat and stood upright as they approached.

"Is something the matter, Father? That kid was saying some pretty crazy things. Do you think you ought'a let him play wi'dat thing?"

The Reverend Dr. Cornelius patted his megaphone by way of indication. "Oh, he snatched it away from me. I shall keep a tight grip on it henceforth, I assure you. Like a vise, officer. Like a vise."

The two policemen were stuck as they computed the posh English accent. "Well, a'right, father, but this is a public place, remember. We all gotta get along here. Jeesh." They walked off in front of the group of Jewish gentlemen, who had by now established the connection between Cappy and the postmodern divine, and who were also training some rather resentful eyeballs upon the megaphone, and—much to the postmodern divine's chagrin—training some rather resentful looks indeed upon the clerical collar he wore about his neck. He decided they should leave the station, and as they went up the stairs he grinned to think the Orthodox gentleman, like the police, might have mistaken him for a representative of the Roman Church.

Outside they found themselves at the east side of a thin wedge of city park that was bordered on the west by Broadway and then, thrusting its green roof up so that it floated above them like a folly in the sky, the Woolworth building. In the other direction the street led up to the gothic arches and steel webs of the Brooklyn Bridge. The pair crossed the street and marched along the pavement that led to the pedestrian causeway that followed over the arched roadway. As they ascended from Manhattan they were exhilarated by the cold wind. At the peak of the arch they stopped to turn round and take in the prospect of Manhattan, the East River, Brooklyn, Manhattan again, and the tall ships, not several hundred yards off, that were on permanent exhibit at the South Street Seaport Museum.

Cappy began: "All I ask is a tall ship—"

"—and a star to steer her by," concluded the Reverend Dr. Cornelius. The moment was unique—and conducive to a rather candid discussion about some very personal matters. At length the Reverend Dr. Cornelius confessed that while the view was very striking, it was also very cold in the wind.

They returned to Manhattan and took a taxi all the way back to the Upper West Side. The postmodern divine had spent nearly two hundred dollars that day—quite one-hundred pounds. It made up, he thought, for some of his life-long parsimoniousness.

"I wish I had had a son," he said softy after leaving little Capricorn with his minders at the Cathedral family shelter. "I should spend all my money on him, and I should wish to burn for eternity in the bad place if I left this world without spending every last penny I had upon him."

The Reverend Dr. Cornelius thought to use his keys and make a detour through the Cathedral. He entered through the eastern middle doors by the crossing. He went inside and stood beneath the great dome and looked up at the sanctuary till his eyes settled upon the high altar. BLAW! BLAW! BLAW! went the Grand Wazoo as three times the postmodern divine depressed the horn button, and then shouted "Evelyn Waugh!" so the sound echoed round the dark empty blimp hanger, up and down the nave from the narthex to the Chapels of the Seven Tongues.

Then he went home to his wife.

Warwick Colvin, Jr.'s

Corsairs of the Second Ether

Chapter 47,460: "The Saga of Zero the Hero"

The story thus far: The struggle to survive on the tar pit beneath the coalescing quasars has been difficult, but the Lost Corsairs have so far prevailed. Through careful husbandry of the smiledons, the grim company has managed to preserve civilization. Indeed, not only the basic elements of survival, but the essence of their culture has been nurtured too, and with no small thanks to Professor Pop who has been tireless in satisfying their appetites for mental occupation. But how long will it be before Cappy returns? And without their beloved commander, how long shall last their desire to go on? Such essential questions mark the contours of their very existence.

Now read on!

Professor Pop found the corsairs assembled together on the tar pit looking rather listless. "I know," he announced. "I miss Cappy too."

Pop's observation was met with many sighs—even groans—of agreement. Little Billy Blake was sitting on his anvil beside the Pegasus drive. Lt. Baudrillard stood near him, leaning against the forge. The rest were sitting huddled together with legs crossed, hunched over somewhat, and looking—according to their unique dispositions—variously bored, irritated, forlorn, cross, stupefied, anxious, hopeless, agitated, simmering, depressed, or, in the case of Mary Make-Believe, apparently withdrawn into a state of complete catatonic disaffection.

Pope Nobody the Twenty-third was particularly contemptuous of their situation. "I don't think Cappy will ever return."

Lt. Baudrillard picked up at this. "Avast, shipmate. Belay such talk. Cappy would never leave us."

Pope Nobody the Twenty-third dismissed Baudrillard with a grunt.

Billy and Professor Pop exchanged glances with each other, and the Simulacrum twins, Adam and Vadim found the eyes of the engineer and the old greybeard and let them know that they too, no matter how miserable they felt, were sticking through to the very end.

Vicenté the Presidenté looked up and caught his shipmates glancing at each other and he gave them his nod as well. He was in for sticking it out, no matter what. "Señors and Señoritas," he said. "I, Vicenté the Presidenté, the greatest public speaker in all of the multiverse, I for one am ready, Allah willing, to see this through."

Laughing Jack Calvin laughed.

"Why you laugh?" asked Vicenté the Presidenté.

Laughing Jack Calvin shrugged. "Because I'm Laughing Jack—"

"—laughing's what I do," said Lt. Baudrillard, completing Laughing Jack Calvin's sentence. And then he groaned from boredom.

It was at this point that Pedantic Joe Philistine said, "It would be a lot easier to deal with our predicament if we had some kind of explanation of what's really happening. Surely our situation has been studied before? Harrumph! If only I had access to some refereed journals, like the collection we once had aboard the good old *Monofilament*." He cast a mournful glance in the direction of the burned out wreckage.

Little Billy Blake had just about enough of this bellyaching. He exchanged a significant nod with Pop, who stood up and said:

"Come to think of it," clearing his throat, "our situation does have some interesting parallels with certain episodes from the Saga of Zero the Hero."

Everyone lifted their faces towards Pop. Even Mary Make-Believe, who had appeared most withdrawn, was suddenly very alert. She sat there with blinking eyes as the rest of the crew demanded to hear the story once again.

"Zero the Hero," and Pop chuckled ironically for effect. "There's a story you don't often hear these days. "Mind you, though, at one time the story had quite a following across hundreds if not thousands of scales." Pop took a deep breath. "It all began long ago in the earliest days of time travel when even the Pegasus drive was yet to be invented. Why, in those days people traveled through the Mutliverse encased in slabs of solid super-carbonite. It could take weeks to pass through even a handful of scales. Into such a primitive state Zero was born. His origins are obscure and the scholarship is full of contradictions, but according to one source that many commentators suspect to be reliable, he was the son of a minister who kept a small church out in the frozen moors of Northumbria, and Zero's mother in fact was a witch."

The corsairs looked at each other with wide eyes and wiggled their backs and shoulders excitedly.

"What source do you refer to?" interrupted Pedantic Joe Philistine; but Johnny Tesco, who was sitting next to him, punched him in the shoulder.

"Avast! Shut thy belching biscuit hole, shippy! Pop's just getting to the good part."

"Indeed," said Pop. "Zero's origins may be obscure, but his status has been well established, and there is a uniform and unanimous consensus amongst the scholarship that he was Old School."

The corsairs "oooo'd" because "Old School" meant that Zero had to have been among the first time travelers to wander across the moonbeam roads, and, moreover, one of the few immortals whose parents had passed on before the discovery of eternal life. People whose parents were immortal were of course referred to as "New School," while people who had no parents at all and who had been created through one generative process or another were affectionately called "fishlings" or "Spammer's Kids" and were loved all the more.

"As a matter of fact," said Professor Pop. "Cappy himself is Old School. As you know, there aren't many of those folk around."

The corsairs "oooo'd" again.

"Gosh," said Sid the Freak. "Who would have guessed?"

"Poor Cappy," sniffed Mary Make-Believe. "I feel so sorry for him. His parents are all gone."

Professor Pop smiled at Mary, his eyes twinkling. "Oh, you find other people to love." And the corsairs realized that Pop was Old School too, and they decided to stop being so soppy and let the venerable greybeard get on with his story.

"Zero," said Pop, "was a quiet enough chap, earnest, thrifty, hard-working, kind-hearted, and capable as the next man of making mistakes. What set him apart, though, were two qualities: perception and courage. He saw things for what they were, and he wasn't afraid, as the old saying goes, 'to speak the truth to the face of falsehood.' Now as he grew into a young man these qualities lead Zero into all sorts of trouble. While he enjoyed some notoriety amongst the other schoolboys he ran and played with in and about the rolling fells of Northumbria, when Zero came of age and mixed in with the wiser world of commerce and trade, his honesty was viewed as a kind of insipid egoism, and Zero found that even the schoolboys who once followed him were no longer about. His early years were very lonely, which was moreover very painful to Zero because he was very much an earthy man and he needed a kind woman with whom he could share his love. But who would have him? What woman could love a man who was perceptive about the ways of things, and moreover who shot off his mouth about it?"

"Oh, I should love him! I should love him with all my heart!" cried Mary Make-Believe, and the others shushed her.

"Oh, it is a very long saga, and the episodes are endless." Pop shook his head, as if in his mind he was turning over a wistful thought or two. "And the episodes are told differently at different scales...." Pop continued to drift off.

"Is that it?" demanded Lt. Baudrillard.

The Lost Corsairs wanted Pop to tell the rest of the story.

"Let me see if I can capture the gist of it." And Pop rubbed his hands together. Suddenly he arched both eyebrows and said: "Long ago—this all took place long ago, as I said—travel across the scales was very new, and there were certain long-time occupants of the multiverse who cast suspicious eyes upon the young races of beings who were discovering time travel and the technologies that allowed them to traverse the silver roads. Old Reg, Manley Mark Male, Fearless Frank Force—even the Balance— were suspicious of the new creatures that were scaling up across the fields of time. However, if there was one champion of the fledgling time travelers, it was Spammer Gain, who at all scales is the true friend of all living things, and whatever their origins."

Lt. Baudillard clutched his little Spammer puppet as Pop continued:

"Led by Old Reg and the Balance, the Machinoix—who, as you know, have in the past been known to throw an iron bar or two across Cappy's rails—were enlisted in a plan to create a political reaction amongst the new races of time travelers so as to prevent them from traveling the moonbeam roads by extinguishing in their hearts their desire to do so. Oh! Old Reg— and the Balance too—were clever in pursuing their nefarious objective. And the Machinoix were nothing sort of ingenious in the expedient they hit upon to implement the diabolical plan."

"Ah!" ejaculated Baudrillard who was completely caught up in the story. "The irrationalization of the Nazareth formula!"

"Shhh!' hissed Little Billy Blake. "I like the way Pop tells it."

"Mmm," Pop nodded knowingly. "So you've heard it before?"

"Just go on. Go on," said Lt. Baudrillard, and he anxiously squeezed his Spammer doll to his chest.

"Oh, it was a diabolical plan," said Pop shaking his head. "As you know, before a species of intelligent life can make that evolutionary leap into the Second Ether, that species must embrace Reason as both the guiding spirit and the underlying instrumentality of its culture. Indeed, the structure of the Second Ether itself was originally constructed to be impregnable—or so it was thought—to the invasion of any irrational species. And this was the very reason Old Reg invented the Singularity Program—or, as it is also known in its camouflage form: the Dialectic of Reactionary Closure."

A hush fell over the corsairs. This was getting serious. Pop saw that he had their complete attention and continued:

"The Dialectic of Reactionary Closure was designed to penetrate and subvert the very same reason that would allow species to evolve into forms which could enter the Second Ether. It varies from system to system, but the contours of the Dialectic and the way it takes hold of a species are the same. First, a tragic historic event is seized upon, and in describing the causes of that event the Dialectic of Reactionary Closure places blame squarely at the feet of Reason and freedom. Reason and freedom are made into a straw man, a villain. Reason is portrayed as instrumental and technocratic, as an overarching philosophy of history based on the notion of the domination of nature, and it argues that any civilization, impelled by the instinct of self-preservation, will destroy itself and the world though the technology that Reason allows beings to create. Although Reason overcomes the terrors of nature, the illusions of magic, and the deceptions of myth, the Dialectic of Reactionary Closure attributes to this same spirit of Reason a sort of technological barbarism that frightens entire civilizations and deceives them into rejecting the spirit of Reason *in toto*.

Lt. Baudrillard shook his head emphatically. "And they don't call Old Reg the Anti-Christ for nuthin'!"

Professor Pop nodded politely at the interruption. "Why, that is very true, my young friend. How very clever of you to make the connection."

"But what about Zero the Hero?" asked Little Billy Blake. "How does he fit in with all this?"

"Ah," said Professor Pop. "I am glad you asked that. And allow me to respond by asking you a question. Do you know how the Omniphone came to be invented?"

Little Billy Blake sat on his anvil scratching his head. "I should. But, confound it. No. I don't know that story."

Lt. Baudrillard shook his head and admitted, with some embarrassment, that he didn't know the story either. In fact, none of the Lost Corsairs knew it.

Professor Pop put his hands behind his back and contemplated things from within his flaming aura. "Well," he began at length. "The Omniphone had a predecessor. It was called the Grand Wazoo. Oh, it was a tremendous device, hundreds of miles long, and capable of existing at many hundreds of scale levels at once, and moreover capable of broadcasting to scales numbering into the thousands! A far cry from our Omniphone, which as you know can broadcast to ALL the scales of the multiverse simultaneously. But, nonetheless, for its time the Grand Wazoo was a formidable tool for those who possessed the knowledge—but more importantly the courage—to use it."

"I bet I know somebody who had the courage to use it!" cried Sid the Freak.

"Who?" said Pedantic Joe Philistine anxiously. "Who!"

"Who?" began Professor Pop, somewhat incredulous at the question. "Who but Zero the Hero himself!"

"I knew it!" Sid the Freak clapped his hands. "I guessed it before anybody here!"

"Ah! Sí! As the greatest orator in all the multiverse, I should have known theese!" Vicenté the Presidenté nodded as he held out his hands and shrugged.

"Well," said Lt. Baudrillard. "What happened?"

Professor Pop tilted his head. "Well, Zero found out about the plot to promulgate the Dialectic of Reactionary Closure across the multiverse and corrupt the young races who were about to embrace Reason and migrate into the Second Ether."

"And? And?" cried a chorus of voices.

"Zero was determined to warn the young races about the Dialectic of Reactionary Closure. He raised his lips to the Grand Wazoo—"

"Yes? Yes? Eh, eh?"

"And he cried!"

To be continued....

Chapter Six

Une Splendeur Triste

> I shoved the whole thing out of my head; and said I would take up
> wickedness again, which is in my line, being brung up to it, and
> the other warn't. And for a starter, I would go to work on stealing
> Jim out of slavery again; and if I could think up anything worse, I
> would do that, too; because as long as I was in, and in for good, I
> might as well go the whole hog.

> —Mark Twain, *The Adventures of Huckleberry Finn*

Here now is an occasion for great moralists to ponder and debate. How did the Reverend Dr. Jeremiah Cornelius separate from his beautiful wife Catherine?

It is tempting to find fault and place blame, but who can say with any exactness what actually passes between a husband and wife in those times that gather them alone and place them apart from the rest of the world? Take, for example, a boisterous couple. In public we see them argue often, keenly and with apparent derision, yet when closed up together they in consort fuse like a pair of angels winging aloft through endless skies singing harmonious praise to the font of all light. Surely their public would be amazed to see that Allah, the blessed, the merciful, is a loving presence with them! Then there is the other couple, the *happy team* who in the civic eye always presents evidence of matrimony's true joy: they fawn and dote on one another, touch, laugh together, perform as a pair of oxen in the blissful yoke of marriage, yet when absent from the crowd and removed alone to the milieu of their true matrimonial state, they become like scorpions and snakes, sting each other in the eyes, drive fangs into each other's hearts, and fill the minds of one another with such venom that their spirits wither into bare wisps that fly out of their bodies, forever powerless to return.

And then there is the third kind of couple consisting of mixed-up people, like most of us children of time, who combine inside themselves both modes, sometimes friends, sometimes rivals, now troubled, once more making their peace, then doubting, often confused, but always ready to forgive again. The postmodern divine and his beautiful wife could easily appear to be of this party, in which case their separation should have to be attributed not to fault—which is a dubious enough proposition when considering men and women to begin with—and instead attributed to the class of things called "problems." And as the tale has shown, the list of problems might be readily drawn.

The physicians first diagnosed Catherine's barren womb when the pair were still in their twenties, married quite two years and still so full of youth that the reality of the situation failed to seem true. There had been vague talk of eventual adoptions, defiant promises to "keep trying anyway" and desperate weekend visits to family and friends who were then having children—all of which became embarrassing as they passed into their thirties, and reason for the spouses on the outside of these relationships to complain about the odd Cornelius couple—"your soppy friends from university who want to visit as if we are still chummy postgrads." Then they were following the postmodern divine's career, and in one far flung corner of the earth or another there were children of some kind to build relationships with, relationships that always ended unhappily as the Corneliuses—Catherine looking off into space, her husband clenching his teeth—boarded a taxi, a train, the bus for the airport, never to return again. During the experience of publishing his first book—a sloppy re-write of his PhD thesis—the Reverend Dr. Cornelius was delighted to discover that making a book and then having it published were actually easy things to make happen. It was a game of form and structure and all you needed was enough time to come up with *something*. If you played the game correctly there was no end to the rubbish publishers were willing to print, and it came as sort of a joke to the postmodern divine and his wife that publishers were in fact desperate to make books—the perception (rather than the fact) that a book was good was all that was necessary for the publishers to sit up obediently with their paws outstretched. And so the books came rolling out, all ten of them, and as they did so the far flung corners of the world became more agreeable. Whatever modest burden of church work there was became less and less demanding. The improving prospects became conducive to greater ambitions. Anything seemed possible, and after just one more book, one more relocation, one more year, and then they should adopt that child.

Nothing came of it. Their career had prevented them from growing up. Moreover, the Reverend Dr. Cornelius was an egoist of the first magnitude. He could never love a child that didn't reflect his especial mystique. Indeed, the fact that he married a tall, slim, fair, dark-haired woman who might well have been mistaken for his sister (and it happened no few times) does much to indicate that in domestic matters the postmodern divine combined both tribal and mythological tendencies. In his heart he dreamed of a family that reflected his image; his daughters and sons should represent a different aspect of his genius—scientist, theologian, exhibitionist—altogether raised under a thatched-roof temple that was staffed not by children but by miniature priests who in drawing down the gods represented youthful reflections of his own image, with the household cries of their upbringing a sort of brassy trumpet music within the pantheon of his vanity. Catherine, and actually he noted this early on, would be incapable of providing him with the beings he needed to staff this temple.

In the meantime she was an agreeable enough helpmeet. Her beauty is already well established, but she also provided other "practical" services to the postmodern divine. She was an agreeable conversationalist, possessing excellent rhetorical skills that were comfortably inferior to his own. She could cook and clean rapidly, was tidy, and she didn't mind doing more than her share of shopping or laundry. She would leave him alone when he was writing, and before he switched exclusively to the internet for his sources she was an able and efficient research assistant, being able to nip up to the nearest library, or, in more remote corners of the earth, ever willing to hop on a bicycle and pedal across ten miles of rice paddies—or round ten miles of terraced mountainsides—and find a train station post office to pick up some book he had ordered through the third-world mails. Wherever they had lived she had proven an able politician and partner. She played the preacher's wife well, never alienating even a donkey. Her pale skin and colorful cheeks, bright round eyes, red lips, dark eyelashes and lofty brow altogether with her health and youthfulness rendered make-up unnecessary so that she was perpetually presentable, which was a wonderful benefit. With the time they shaved off waiting upon her toilet they could entertain twice as many people as any other couple, who could never be as ready to entertain as the Corneliuses, a couple who were perpetually ready to amuse company with their brilliant conversation. They were the eternal postgrads. Their home—their presence anywhere—was an on-going hippie party where visitors could come for an easy dose of youth, religion, science, and spontaneous laughs; and it was a "reality" (if it could be called that) which was devoid, too, of the reality of children. No less than their guests and acquaintances, the Reverend Dr. Cornelius and his wife had enjoyed that party too. Meanwhile, at more private altitudes, marriage had provided the postmodern divine with plenty of opportunities to accustom himself to the habits of connubial exploration, and within a year or two he had become familiarized, as do most husbands, to the mysteries of the female outline, and so he could hardly blame Catherine for *that* lost sense of adventure, but he wondered, too, again as most husbands do, if perhaps in regard to attractiveness his wife was after all not so wonderful as he had thought before they married? After all, provided as he was with the ample attentions of many admiring women, as well as the expressed envy of many male friends, the postmodern divine had many reasons to believe that it wasn't entirely outside the realm of possibility—in terms of animal magnetism and earthly appeal—that in Catherine the Reverend Dr. Cornelius had an inferior match.

These might be foundations for many problems, but problems without troubles are not problems at all. And, what was a confounded thing, perhaps, was the Corneliuses had no troubles. Certainly the Reverend Dr. Cornelius was not the sort of person who invented troubles. Rather, he was the sort who would prefer to invite troubles from the outside, and then cultivate them. Thus, in keeping with the postmodern patterns of his thought and the postmodern practices of his friends in the world of commerce, he decided to outsource the manufacture of his troubles. Nor, in keeping with a principle of thrift and economy, would he countenance the use of hirelings to bring in these troubles. There was something in that sort of intention that struck him as vulgar. If he was going to employ a troublemaker it would have to be the genuine article, a committed home-wrecker, a reputable practitioner of the art of marriagecide—that is if all this is to be believed.

It is an easy thing to slander a great man; even easier to slander a great man of the public. That the Reverend Dr. Cornelius was a man other men envied is self-evident. A world traveler, author, public speaker, preacher, theologian, the husband of a beautiful woman, a genius—any of these qualities alone are sufficient reason to make for the postmodern divine more enemies than a dog has fleas. Moreover, taken in aggregate these qualities are sufficient to stuff even a saint into the blackest of sepulchers, over which the covetous stone cutter might contemptuously mock the voice of the ghost inside, and chisel the ironic line: "Look on my list of publications, ye mighty, and despair!" To what point does this lead? It can be only this. Any person who would cast doubt upon the veracity of the postmodern divine, or seek to impugn the reputation of the same, must either be a cad himself, or a person who possesses some bit of evidence that is irrefutable, and who in even daring to share it, though it might pollute even the reputation of a man of the high-church and a genius, yet might be answering to a higher purpose where even the reputation of the planet's most noble specimens must be called to task, or even besmirched, if (and only if) in so doing the human race is led collectively to that higher redemption towards which, after all, our genius must be aspiring. In regards to such evidence, the following is offered for discreet consideration:

As the Reverend Dr. Cornelius and his young friend stood together upon the causeway at the center of the Brooklyn Bridge, many seals of intimacy were broken. Confessions were made, oaths of fidelity were sworn. The cold wind blew round them, tossing their black hair aside dramatically, biting at their faces, chapping their lips, seeking to pry into their very bones. To either side the towers of the bridge stood with their gothic archways held aloft against the shining grey firmament, the curved and pointed portals suggesting the specter of an enchanted cathedral standing between astral dimensions, and like a vanishing or materializing thing in a dream, it might be either fading into or out of this universe—or even perhaps moving both into and out of our sphere at once.

Cappy, who was never what he seemed, was nevertheless convincingly in earnest —perhaps convincing even to himself—as he expressed his desire to do all he could to protect the happiness of the postmodern divine. The giant was again surprised by the lad's perspicuity, and completely floored by his penetration; and so as the giant stood awhile in thought the terrible cold exactly reflected his loneliness in the world as before him the decision that had to be made reared irrevocably before him.

They stood quietly together. At last the giant cocked his head and pressed his lips together as if he had tasted something bitter. "How could you tell?"

Cappy didn't mince words. "That doesn't matter. It's obvious enough. The question is: do you really want to let this happen?"

The postmodern divine said nothing, and after a moment—but only a moment—the mysterious child continued. "It is a great thing you are contemplating. After all, to change your life in this way—it really is an extraordinary thing."

The postmodern divine hesitated and then shrugged. "It is too late; it has already been decided."

"Not yet." The child was quick to correct him. "Not yet. There is a difference between letting things happen and making them happen. If you wish, I could restore the damage and return your wife to you." And here Cappy proposed a dreadful scheme to destroy the reputation of the Reverend Dr. Cornelius's rival, and so definitively return his wife completely into his love and trust.

"Horrible!" was the giant's reaction. He considered it further. "What you propose is underhanded, to say the least."

Cappy didn't hesitate as he pointed his finger at the postmodern divine. "When it comes to marriage I pull out all the stops. Anything goes as far as I am concerned, and anyone who seeks to interfere or meddle shall not stand in my way. If it would save a wedlock, I'd blot out the sun."

The Reverend Dr. Cornelius shuddered before the strength of his little friend, who continued to point at the giant as he warned him of what was coming:

"But if you truly intend to cast her off, I suggest you do so in earnest, and let her have the consolation of the woman—and you will have to leave them in peace."

The Reverend Dr. Cornelius was not a timorous person, nor was he of sufficiently weak character not to commit himself to a decision and accept the outcome. He did hesitate, but only out of a sense of prudence; haste in this matter seemed to him inappropriate; but then as swiftly he realized that it could be put off no more. He had made the decision.

"I will respect your choice," said Cappy. "I neither agree nor disagree. My role is only to offer alternatives. But if you ever come to doubt this thing, remember: it was your decision."

The Reverend Dr. Cornelius stood in the cold wind listening to the cold words. The towers resembled less the outlines of a vanishing cathedral and once more appeared like the supports of an indifferent bridge in an indifferent wind; the cables, however, webbing the towers and the span reflected the tangle in his mind. The decision was made to turn once again upon Manhattan, and so the pair marched off the bridge, found a taxi, and motored up through the city grid until once more they found the neighborhood of St. John the Divine.

Against the backdrop of such metaphysics, the actual rupture comes across like something out of a dream.

The very next morning the Reverend Dr. Cornelius was awakened by the sound of voices—female voices. One was American, vibrant, alive, cheeky, and, to the Reverend Dr. Cornelius's ears, somewhat coarse. The other voice—very smooth, composed, emotionally centered—belonged to a strong yet in some ways very vulnerable and very passive Englishwoman—the voice was entirely familiar, but he was hearing it now in a way he had never heard it before. It was not a voice he loved. It was not a voice he considered friendly. It was not a voice he sympathized with. Throughout all his experience with that voice he had naturally drawn all these associations, but now they were gone, and it was rather like being inside a dream—a right nightmare.

He couldn't make out their words. He looked at the clock. It was 8:00 a.m. He had overslept. Then he realized that the phone had rung earlier that morning. Catherine had sounded concerned. Then she was out of his bed and he returned to sleep. Evidently his rival had telephoned with some dire news, and was now visiting the apartment to discuss the situation—and perhaps collect Catherine? The postmodern divine realized he was in a muddle. He was still half asleep. It always happened when he overslept. Catherine must have shut off the alarm when she rose from bed. He scratched his head and tried to make out their words. He couldn't hear them and he filled in the outline of the sounds with the colors of his suspicions. There was concern in their voices. Obviously they were about to burst in upon him to announce that Catherine had discarded him. Could he let himself suffer that, he wondered? To be in his bed in his pajamas and then to be burst upon by his wife and her lover—could he just lie there in bed while they stood over him and announced the obsolescence of his masculinity? The idea braced him for some extraordinary action. What to do? He decided to storm into the next room and throw them both out. But as he got out of bed and reached for his robe his pride got the better of him, and rather than simply throw them out he would instead assume the persona of the male archetype. Besides, he thought, he really was ready to be rid of Catherine once and for all. This would define the rejection.

The Reverend Dr. Cornelius slipped out of his pajamas. He threw the tops on the bed and stepped out of the bottoms, leaving them in a pile on the floor, and then he burst through the door!

Catherine's back was turned toward him in the living room so it was Oona who first saw the form of the enraged naked postmodern divine. Oona's shock was so complete that at first she was oblivious to the giant naked man, his eyes wild, his hair disheveled, his feet apart, his arms raised as his hands turned grotesque circles in the air, meanwhile that thing which she above all people loathed dangling there beneath his long pelvis in a sort of floppy display of what can only be described as a "churchman cut loose!"

Oona shrieked bloody murder and then began crying "Ah! Ah! Ah!" as she raised her clutching hands and shook them back and forth before her mouth, which had frozen in an open grimace. She stepped back and caught her leg against the arm of a chair, which caused her to shriek again and kick up her knee.

157

Catherine's passivity was a complete counterpoint to Oona's reaction. As Oona screeched, Catherine stood there blinking and then reached out her hand as her friend stepped backward, and then when Catherine finally did turn she did so in near slow motion—she simply frowned when she saw her husband as if she were looking at something no more interesting than an automobile at a stoplight that had strayed forward into the crosswalk she was about to step across. "Jeremiah!" she scolded with a hush. "Oona is here; put on your robe, please!"

Growling with a sort of movie monster rage, the postmodern divine moved his arms up and down with farcical menace, each time coaxing another scream from Oona, while his wife simply stood there becoming more and more confused.

"Arggh! Arggh!" Get out of here, I tell you!" And the postmodern divine wiggled his hips in the most absurd fashion—though the spectacle it produced was sufficient to prompt more screeching and arm waving from Oona. Catherine grabbed one of her friend's hands and led the poor woman swiftly from the apartment, glancing two or three times at her husband with an expression of defiance mixed with confusion.

Now alone in the apartment, the reaction of the postmodern divine was nothing short of elation. He leaped up and down several times and threw two fingers in the air like a jubilant football fan. Then he marched in a semi-circle in front of the bookcase and saluted his own works which dominated the center of the massed volumes. Then he marched back into his room and pulled on his pajama bottoms and then marched out once more to the kitchen where he filled the kettle and snapped it on with a sort of proprietary triumph that he knew looked ridiculous, though, for all that, he didn't care because the man's world had been established and henceforth he could snap on the kettle with any inflection or gratuitous movements he saw fit.

As the kettle screamed to life he calculated that he would only have to meet with his wife once or twice more—she would have to come to collect her things, and then a meeting in some office with the lawyers; anyway, she wouldn't be much trouble.

As he poured the tea he thought he could do with some music. In the next room was his iPod. He found it, put the speaker buds in his ears, switched it on and dialed through some music he had recently downloaded. He found just the thing: the Moody Blues *In Search of the Lost Chord*, a classic from his youth, and as he waited for the tea to steep he put on "Ride My Seesaw" with all kinds of expectations. As the absurd poem about flowers and sunspots rose to a crescendo of gibberish that heralded the triumphant blast of the guitar riff, he kneeled slightly and then burst up and began hopping up and down and skipping his feet back and forth like a boxer.

He capered in this fashion through at least the first verse, and then remembering the tea he looked up and saw his wife standing at the door looking at him with a very cross expression on her face.

He snatched the buds from his ears. "What are *you* doing here!"

"I shan't ask for an explanation, knowing there can be none, and instead conclude that you have gone absolutely mad. I shall pray, therefore, for a cure. And, if that won't do, I shall bash in your head for being such an arse!"

"What are you doing here!" he again demanded, this time punctuating his irritation by shutting off the tinny crackle coming from the dangling buds, and then rapidly winding the wires round the iPod, which he then thrust into the pocket of his pajamas with an indignation he felt to be as fully formidable as it was righteous.

"What am I doing here? I live here!" said Catherine, and she ordered him to sit down on the sofa. He did so and she advanced to stand over him. "What has gotten into you?"

"Right! I thought you left then?"

"Left?"

"Left me for Oona, yes?"

He couldn't tell what she was thinking. Perhaps she was considering that she had been neglecting him. Perhaps she was contemplating some horrid thing to say that would torture him and make him cry out. At last she simply boiled over and screamed at him. "Don't be absurd!"

The postmodern divine looked very much a person suffering the slings and arrows of intolerable disregard. This was proving far more difficult than he had anticipated. "Right!" was all he managed to say.

But then much to his shock—and, again startling him, to his relief—she said some very wonderful things. She said the most beautiful and loving things, and he felt himself swell up with something he hadn't felt in a long long time. It was love! He felt pangs of companionship, a world shared, spirits in sympathy—feelings such as he hadn't experienced since they were in their twenties; and then the best of these feelings was a sort of shared sense of adventure, sort of a relief at realizing that he—they—were never to be alone again. Had something happened to restore them to the excitement and buoyancy of their original love for one another? Miraculously, he was able to articulate these questions to her, and she responded in kind, bathing him in words which erased all doubt and soothed and brought down upon them the comfort of love's solace. She sat next to him and he got off the sofa and got on his knees and buried his face in her lap and confessed all his doubts, and cried out that he had been a "great fool" and a "pompous buffoon" and then he began weeping in earnest—a great puddle of wet was gathering in his hands and in her lap—and he confessed that it was all because of his desire to have a child with her, and he openly bemoaned how barren existence had become without children, and he mentioned Capricorn, too, and how his experience with the strange boy had made him truly feel the hole in their life. And Catherine sat there and petted his head, and said the most perfect things—apologies, admissions, confessions of her own desperation in this regard, and she agreed, too, that Capricorn had awakened within her the desire to be surrounded with children. Next she said something that was most wonderful of all: she proposed that the two of them should themselves adopt Capricorn and make him the centerpiece of their new family.

"Adopt Capricorn!" The postmodern divine sang the words!

"And why not?" insisted Catherine. What boy could better compliment her husband's own grand intelligence?

"True!" insisted the postmodern divine. "True! Capricorn possesses a remarkable intellect. And he is bold too. Shall he be our—I hesitate to use the word, my love—shall Capricorn be our *son!*"

And then Catherine opened her mouth to speak but the kettle (how did it get switched on again?) began squealing, and then it stopped; squealed again and stopped; squeal, stop; squeal, stop; squeal, stop....

The Reverend Dr. Cornelius rolled over in bed and thrust his hand at the alarm and with habitual punctiliousness switched it off.

He was alone in the room. The red boiling numerals on the clock read "6:00" and Catherine was not there. He didn't bother to bemoan the crazy dream. He pushed the duvet off his legs and cursed the over-heated American flat, and as he briefly reviewed the things he had said to her the night before he was not surprised that she was gone.

After living so long together he knew what her actions had been, and he looked directly at the mirror over the vanity knowing that she should have left a note taped there. He rolled out of bed, snatched the note off the mirror, snapped on the light, and then sat down on the bed to read the note—but feeling uncomfortable dressed only in his pajamas, he set the note down and put on his bathrobe, knotted the belt and gave it a reassuring tug. Then he sat down again to read the note:

Jeremiah:

After those horrid things you said to me I realize it is unfair to both of us to keep up the pretense. I want you should know how cruel I think you are. All those years I spent with you were an illusion. I see that now. I was hoping we were getting closer to that time when we might adopt, but I can see now I was hoping for nothing. I hope you find what you are looking for.

I shall not bother you. Nor shall I wish to be bothered by you. Please telephone Oona and set up a time for me to collect my things. I should prefer not to see you, and I trust you will be out of the flat when I come. Please go through the computer and place all my files on my thumb drive.

As I write this you are on the bed with your mouth open. You look a huge fiend. I feel ashamed—and very sorry for myself.

Catherine

The Reverend Dr. Cornelius thought this a stroke of extraordinary good luck. She was making it very easy for him. Clearly, the talk he had with her the night before had achieved the desired result. Then he glanced momentarily at the note, but only to read the second sentence to disapprove her clumsy attempt to be literary; otherwise, he didn't bother to re-read it. He rolled the neatly-spaced words into a ball and cast them smartly into the wastebasket. The only other thought he had about the note was something tracing from the mention of Oona, and he was frustrated as he dared to wonder whether Catherine and the American were going to live as roommates, or as a pair of lesbians?

Such questions, he realized, would only drive him mad, and even as he experienced a range of disturbing emotions he coolly analyzed them, transforming the certain tiger trap of his imagination into a formidable tool for controlling the crisis. Although he lived the greater measure of his life in the cloisters of his intellect, he was after all a man of the world. He had braved deserts, Himalayan altitudes, malarial swamps, lower-middle-class congregations, petty third-world clerks, disease-ridden populations, the ignorance of multitudes, bullying policemen, awkward Oxford dons, absurd journalists, laughable critics—and he had held up under the worst all that mob could throw at him; and though his deepest emotional experiences as a "man" were limited to a series of short-lived trysts as an undergrad, and then the short-lived "love affair" he experienced with Catherine—merely a sort of protracted undergrad tryst itself—he had in his time attentions enough, and the reassurance of those attentions had been enough, his imagination filled in the rest—and so he had virtually the experience of hundreds of women. Indeed, one of the qualities of his lovemaking with Catherine had facilitated his mastery, through her surrogate form, of the many women he had encountered and who had unmistakably expressed to him their availability. That expression was all that was necessary to confirm the validity of the experience, to "chalk up one more." He merely had to close his eyes, or position Catherine so that her identity was obscured behind her more generic features, and then he could possess any woman he chose, so that even Faust might have been envious of his long register of conquests. The point was this: he wasn't about to cave in under the sense of loss and loneliness that so often consume men in these circumstances. In his role as minister he had plenty of times seen what could happen to people— both to men and to women—when they allowed their losses to break their hearts and push them into despair and despondency, eventually leading them to curl round inside their bitterness and grow grey and dry up. There was something about these people that had always horrified the postmodern divine. It wasn't the pain of their situation, he could certainly sympathize (indeed was trained to sympathize) with that. No, it was the deeper kind of wound these people sustained, the wound, he decided, that they had inflicted upon themselves. It was as though they had somehow fused with their partners, and in separating from them they had been physically torn. But where was that tear? It was all in their heads; all a thing of their imagination; and, indeed, the more he had seen it the more it appalled him. It was like a thing that had interposed itself between a person and his faith, between a soul and the forgiving God that accompanies all minds wherever they go. Of course he knew that the very cells of a human body grew accustomed to certain customs, rituals, pathways, patterns, feelings, atmospheres, and that this aspect—the physiological aspect of a union between two people—was a strong and profound bond that necessitated, among other things, cultural nurturing, long-term unions, and the most careful consideration when forming these connections in the first place. But human beings are not crystals mechanically grown in the darkness of some subterranean chemical reaction. Human beings are creatures of mind, creatures of will and free choice. Taking all this into consideration, the

162

Reverend Dr. Cornelius regarded the phenomenon of the broken heart in cosmic terms, cried "monster!" and turned his back on it forever. At the same time, and as he saw now especially and not without great trepidation, the possibility of falling—that's what it was, a steep hard drop and then a crash against the hardest ground conceivable—the possibility of falling was one of the most foreboding temptations the cosmos had ever prepared for sentient creatures. With every cell in one's body calling for those lost and distant connections, could a mind resist that temptation? The Reverend Dr. Cornelius had always thought so, but now as he gathered his wits about him and struggled to shake off his dreams and throw his shoulder against the shock of what had happened, he came to the entirely unexpected discovery that that temptation was inevitable. What was more, that fall, that fruit, that apostasy from love and reason was inevitable, delectable, the only way! Thus the human mind—and this was a great and wonderful surprise to him—was in fact as mechanical and as perfunctory as those crystals he had envisioned growing in the dark, and if he was going to pick himself up and move off the hard steel plane he had fallen upon he would have to do so with his feet firmly planted upon it, and somehow hope—or pretend to hope—that moving on and away was as automatic as the force that had at last driven him into the tangled superstructure of his own self-destruction.

Again, the Reverend Dr. Cornelius was no fool. He pushed on. Right there he raised his chin and set his jaw. He would keep moving even with his mind broken. It wasn't desperation, it was inevitable. The cells in his body revolted at the change. Why fight it? Why fight them? He would revolt along with them. Depression? Broken heart? Curl up in a ball? He had no time for it. Better give over to the devil and be done with it!

The anger seeped into his bones and they ached, but what of it? His cells and his brain had other habits to rely on. He was an author. He had sat through plenty enough, had sat through worlds of experience, worlds of mathematical abstraction, worlds where the magma of science exuded like a glowing paste from deep inside the bowels of superstition; and his mind—his highly organized, cold, driven and powerful mind—had reformed the far-flung fields of intellectual history, anticipated the technological trajectories of break-through industries, and his efforts had turned the course of a planet's entire civilization! Realizing all this—as if feeling it for the very first time—there was little doubt now as to what was happening. The inevitable crystal was growing, adding layers, enlarging the areas of its facets—nothing less than the fundamental intelligence of the multiverse itself was exerting itself through him; indeed, the multiverse was exalting itself through his brain!

He rapidly dressed, depressed the power button on his computer—his 21st Century computer . . . it was . . . he was forty-five after all, the past century was gone . . . it was a super computer! And he set to work on his current commission with the vengeance of a being but newly thrust into the jaws of the most personal of conundrums!

As the super computer whispered to life he beheld his bathrobed condition and turned for his bedroom, but not without first checking the weather outside his eleventh storey window, which revealed a dark and slate-like Hudson flowing with the tide backwards against its normal southerly course. The sky was heavy and grey and there was a cold rain falling that somehow flattered his sensibility. Confound all those sunny American skies with their two-dimensional clouds pitched always high in the stratosphere. Here was some sensible weather at least today! As he entered his bedroom he already knew what he should wear—a proper waterproof walking suit over grey wool trousers and that light-weight RAF jumper with the reinforced shoulders and elbows—and wellies! Indoors? Well, why not?

The synthetic fabric of his walking trousers rasped together as he came back from the bedroom, and, feeling very warm, he leaned his long body forward over the computer to reach the sliding window and thrust it aside. The fresh air hesitated a moment and then blew in and he was somewhat surprised by the actual smell of his apartment, which was made conspicuously morbid as it mixed with the good air from outside. He sat down, more cool wind flew in the room, and the walking suit felt absolutely smashing!

The file for his current project was centered in his screen (his wallpaper, it must be noted, was a lovely detail of St. Paul's—an image lifted from the film *Mary Poppins*, actually. It was the old woman who fed the birds!). He clicked the file and as the word processor opened he did something he religiously eschewed when sitting down to work on a manuscript. He shot the arrow over to the browser icon and, of all things, checked the news.

The headlines were the typical rubbish, and he spent barely a moment scanning the links—but then his attention was caught by some controversy—yet another controversy—involving the War. Once more some duffer in the media had managed to inflame the passions of those poor Muslims. The matter was a stupid joke obviously concocted by some xenophobic right-wing provocateur, and then published in a Norwegian

164

tabloid. Once more in Syria, Iran, Afghanistan, Pakistan, Paris and London, mobs had taken to the streets to protest the latest insult to their good religion. As well they should, thought the postmodern divine, who was rather grinding his teeth with like indignation (or maybe something else was galling him that morning?). The horrid "joke" was this:

> **Question: What do you call a coward who comes wrapped in a white sheet, beats his women, talks through both sides of his mouth, and will burn down your cities if you don't have the courage to repeat this joke?**

> **Answer: The Prophet Mohammed**

How the authorities permitted such rubbish to be published was something he couldn't countenance. These words were weapons and they could kill! The report confirmed as much. Already seventy-five protestors had died in the hysteria of the riots.

This was just the sort of thing that made his work so hard. Another difficulty. One more barrier to progress thrown in his way by those ignoramuses selling newspapers! He X'd out the browser and there beneath it the title page of his new manuscript was waiting. Thank goodness.

When it came to composition he was a man of action; he put down the first draft all the way through without looking back. Revision was similarly "all or nothing." He didn't second guess himself, and as he streaked though each draft he was purposeful and unflinching. Only rarely would he review himself even for consistency. His grip upon the material was that sure, and besides, with a photographic memory what need to second guess? His composition, like the texts themselves, was an exponent of commitment. This above all. And what more fitting to theology and documents of faith? But while the Reverend Dr. Cornelius was used to immediately scrolling down to the end of the file to straightaway set to work, on this particular morning he tarried awhile over the title page. He wasn't quite sure about the epigraph, which was that lovely passage from Revelation: "And there will be no more night; they need no light of lamp or sun, for the lord God will be their light, and they will reign forever and ever." The postmodern divine cocked his eyebrow. He had selected this passage over the similar but more familiar passage that speaks of tears being wiped away forever and which promises "there shall be no more death." He scrutinized the two options and decided he was happy with his choice, though not before considering, in a sort of lurid haze of transitory anger, the lines from Milton little Capricorn had recalled the other day. Rather more amusing! Indeed, those words—and not his chosen lines from Revelation—would produce a very droll epigraph, especially following his particular title which had been firmly determined (according to the publishing contract) and so set into stone:

Lie Down in Joy: A Christian Celebration of Euthanasia

The Reverend Dr. Cornelius found himself wondering at this game of second guesses and correctly attributed it to his strained circumstances and the funny mood that had seized him that morning. He reached over to confirm that the window really was open all the way, and then, returning to his screen, he scrolled down to where he had been at work. It was the seventh chapter and his favorite, as by this point in the manuscript he had already presented his moving anecdotes and his firm instructions, so the balance of the book was given over to what was for him the more agreeable task of setting forth the theological principles supporting his program.

His idea was simple enough: when a person was too old or too sick to enjoy life anymore, when a person could no longer make that contribution to society that made life meaningful, then it was perfectly appropriate—and perfectly Christian—for a devout person to elect to end his or her life so as to end that suffering, which was a source of ungodly doubt not only within themselves, but also for the people who fell within the insidious influence of that suffering person's experience. End that suffering, end that doubt, and faith should be preserved. Thus all arguments against euthanasia were comparable with the most heinous heresies; true religiosity demanded all pain and doubt to be expunged as obstacles to faith and grace. In one passage the postmodern divine went so far as to compare the choice of euthanasia to the triumph of St. George over the Dragon.

Such, anyway, was the basis of his theology in regards to the question. Unfortunately, the place of ideas inside his culture and his religion was not powerful enough to enforce the efficacy of his thought on this matter. There was in his culture no tradition which embraced the "big" ideas—let alone a cultural aspiration to acknowledge ideas themselves as a basis for making proper decisions about the way life was to be lived. Of course he knew these big ideas represented a timeless wisdom that transcended the commonplace outcomes of public negotiations—"squabbles and din"—which were based on "mere opinions." Indeed—and this was particularly to the postmodern divine's distaste—there was in his culture's thought no distinction whatsoever between mediocrity and true excellence. The timeless truths of true revelation were subject to any person's scrutiny. The exercise of so-called "reason" brought everyone down to a level and lowly understanding of the world, and no distinction whatsoever was drawn between the common interpretations of revealed wisdom and the proper appreciation for that revelation—which was correctly the dominion of specially trained experts as, clearly, all true esoteric teaching discloses itself only to very carefully guided readers after long and concentrated study. Any public reason—all widespread consensus—was thus diametrically opposed to the ultimate truth of revealed learning and opinions. Thus the postmodern divine argued against the coarse and hurtful principle of tolerance which was at best conducive to a slack and nebulous pluralism. In turn, the postmodern divine rejected all appeals to common consensus and asserted above such dangerous ramblings the rightly produced thought of the true legitimate source of civil order—what he called the "philosophical magistrate"—and which was little more than Plato's philosopher king dressed up in the postmodern divine's trademark verbiage and equipped with striking postmodern architectures and cunningly disguised pulpits from which all administrative decisions should henceforth be ordered and distributed.

The telephone rang to interrupt his progress. It was his brother, Bishop Francis Cornelius. The postmodern divine listened indifferently as he stared at the words on his screen, but then raised up his head.

Little Capricorn was in trouble!

Warwick Colvin, Jr.'s

Corsairs of the Second Ether

Chapter 47,461: "The Lamentations of the Lost Corsairs"

The story thus far: Deeply impressed by the story of Zero the Hero, the Lost Corsairs have begun to question the lowest common denominators of their very existence. The doors of perception have been thrown open, all bets are off, and the quiz begins anew. Alone in the mysterious laws-of-physics-defying universe, the minds of the corsairs fly beyond the circumscribing flames that mark the boundaries of their personal identities as they make bold to entertain the headless spirit of doubt.

Now read on!

"I see a quasar," said Sid the Freak, "hanging above me. It quivers and hangs in the vault of space."

"I see a slab of frozen black," said Adam Simulacrum, "spreading away until it meets a starless void."

"I hear a sound," said Johnny Tesco, "a roar, growl; roar, growl; going up and down."

"I see a lost globe," said Vadim Simulacrum, "hanging down in a drop against the enormous flanks of some ruin."

"I see a crimson aura," said Laughing Jack Calvin, "twisted with flaming threads."

"I hear something strain," said Little Billy Blake. "The tigers' feet are held fast. They strain and strain and strain."

"Look at the moon's web on the twigs of the ruin," said Pope Nobody the Twenty-third. "It has beads of frost on it, a mildew of white light."

"The corsairs are gathered round the ruin like pointed ears," hissed Trailer Park Shane, unheard, in the distance.

"The shadow of time fell on our path," said Pedantic Joe Philistine, "barring the path not taken."

"Islands of light are swimming on the tar," said Professor Pop. "They have fallen with the stars."

"The tigers' eyes burn bright in the hollows above their fangs," said Lt. Baudrillard.

"The stars are covered with harsh, short hairs" said Laughing Jack Calvin, "and drops of yesterday have stuck to them."

"A galaxy is curled in a flat ring," said Vicenté the Presidenté, "notched with empty nothing."

"The yellow smiledon draws its flank to the ground and touches the cold beneath him," said Little Billy Blake.

"And burning lights from his eyes flash in and out on the scene," said Sid the Freak.

"The tar moves under my shifting feet," said Sylvia the Plathological Anorexic. "I feel each state, solid or liquid, separately."

"The back of my hand burns," said Adam Simulacrum, "but my palm is sure and reaching for work."

"Now the tiger roars like a spray of soft, silver comets falling aside," said Johnny Tesco.

"Tigers are singing up and down and in and out all round us," said Mary Make-Believe.

"The beast cries; the tiger with its feet in the tar; the great brute in the tar cries," said Vadim Simulacrum.

"Look at the quasar," said Sid the Freak, "with all its surface boiling with fire."

"A cold crystal begins to creep up the pole," said Sylvia the Plathological Anorexic, "it will crawl over the green head in the sky."

"As the green rises, sleep curls off the head in a mist," said Pope Nobody the Twenty-third.

"The sky is cracked with silver cracks," said Laughing Jack Calvin, "and blue, finger-shaped shadows of stars swathe the quasars."

"Now the smiledon lifts up his deep, red chest," said Little Billy Blake.

"The tigers sang in chorus first," said Mary Make-Believe. "Now the door is barred. They will never cry. But one sings by the wreck alone."

"Bubbles form on the floor of the pit," said Pedantic Joe Philistine. "Then they rise, quicker and quicker in a brown chain to my burning feet."

"One small, distant quasar is dark blue now," said Sid the Freak, "and the air no longer ripples above the pit."

"Nothing is perched on that shaft of ruin," said Pope Nobody the Twenty-third. "And Billy has smacked down the tiger with his hammer."

"That is the first stroke of the hammer," said Vadim Simulacrum. "Then the others follow; one, two; one, two; one, two."

"Look at the bones, cast white against the tar," said Lt. Baudrillard. "Now these are splinters of white bone, and crimson streaks each rib."

"Billy scrapes the tiger's bones with a jagged saber taken from its mother's jaw," said Professor Pop.

"Suddenly a voice is in my ear," said Little Billy Blake. "It is here; it is past."

"I burn, I shiver," said Professor Pop. "Out of that deep, into that shadow."

"Now we are all gone," said Adam Simulacrum. "We are alone. We have gone into the universe and we are left standing below blackness—"

"—below nothing," hissed Trailer Park Shane, unheard, in the distance.

"From the essence of sounds to the voices of being," said Vicenté the Presidenté. "As I name my maintypes I transcend them. They empty from myself. *Olé!*"

To be continued....

Chapter Seven

Une Insurmontable et Poignante Mélancolie

> How great, soever, in fine, may be the pretense of good-will
> and charity, and concerns for the salvation of men's souls,
> men cannot be forced to be saved whether they will or no;
> and therefore, when all is done, they must be left to their own
> consciences.

> —John Locke, *A Letter Concerning Toleration*

The Reverend Dr. Cornelius felt fortunate he had dressed that morning in his waterproof walking outfit; and even though he immediately found a taxi after leaving his building, his outdoors clothing confirmed his readiness to face the new challenge.

Francis had been very brief. Bishop Achebe had somehow been drawn into a scandal, and Capricorn—the "devil boy" as Francis described him—was somehow at the bottom of it. The Reverend Dr. Cornelius had been lost in thought as Francis described these things over the telephone and thus the picture was not entirely clear, but he had nevertheless picked up enough to understand that the crisis not only affected Francis's project, but had somehow embarrassed Capricorn as well. This—Capricorn's predicament—brought all senses into focus. Perhaps it was a displaced sentiment of his own loss and crisis? Perhaps it was love? No matter. These were indifferent things. Of paramount concern to the postmodern divine was his little friend's condition. Although the lad was no usual personality, he was a lad after all, and who knows how he might be frightened, even suffering? Thinking this way, the Reverend Dr. Cornelius flattered himself in two ways. First, he reckoned he was the proprietary inspiration of his little friend's precociousness, as if without his influence, Capricorn would lose his remarkable skill at conversation. Second, the postmodern divine nurtured the conviction that he was rightfully the lad's protector—that without his interceding in the matter Capricorn was in dire peril.

Thus when his taxi lurched to a halt in front of the Cathedral family shelter the postmodern divine tossed his money forward at the driver without regard and then sprung absolutely heroically from the vehicle, dramatically looking this way and that down the pavement as if he expected an ambuscade; then—with an absurd little skip to position his right leg—he bound suddenly toward the building to rescue his little friend.

A most sympathetic and sentimental old woman was at the door to welcome the Angel of St. John's Cathedral into the family shelter. The expression on her face seemed to register her enthrallment with his mystique, and she took advantage of the drama to grasp his hand and squeeze it several times as she led him into the sitting room where the crisis team had gathered. For his part, the postmodern divine allowed her to grope him in this fashion. Normally fastidious in such matters, the sense of loss— if that's what it was?—he labored under that morning found some relief in her attentions, and, besides, it was a confirmation of his magnetism and a welcome reassurance that he would have a replacement for Catherine (a fertile replacement) in short order, though there was no hurry just now, particularly with this unexpected production involving his little friend.

"Ah, Jeremiah. Good!" Francis sat in a large velvet armchair with a tiny sherry glass floating motionlessly inside his motionless hand. His large figure gave the impression of a permanent boulder that was impervious even to erosion.

Arrayed round the sitting room were two women from the shelter boasting those dreadful scarves, Francis, and then Bishop Achebe—who didn't bother to acknowledge the entrance of the tall man in rain gear, but rather gave the wall in that direction a sort of sidelong glance, and then cleared his throat. Of the three churchman now gathered there, Achebe was the only one resembling anything clerical in his dark suit—the white ring of his dog collar appearing especially incandescent against the black field of his clothing and his black face. Francis looked dappy in his olive wool trousers and russet cardigan sweater—that was about the warmest thing Francis ever wore, though he had discovered during this particular trip that the American cold was more bothersome to him than it had been in the past. The postmodern divine recognized his brother's air of stillness and saw it as a sign of Francis at battle stations, and he saw it too as certain indication that Francis had the situation completely under control.

"Ladies," announced the bishop. I am very sorry, but would you think it terribly rude of me to ask for a few moments alone with my colleagues? And, after all, you could be very helpful were you to be at the front door to receive the little boy when he arrives."

"Why all the drama?" asked the postmodern divine after the ladies had exited.

Francis leaned forward slightly to assure himself that the ladies had left, and then answered. "Well, the police have been notified, actually. They too will be here soon, though I can't imagine them being here too soon in this great city where surely there are other problems wanting management."

"Police?" The Reverend Dr. Cornelius looked very cross in a commanding sort of way, which was the usual counterpoint he presented to his brother's immobility when ever they got together over a crisis. He unzipped his rain coat and the image which emerged was very fit and very set for valorous action.

"We do not know who contacted them. Perhaps the devil-boy himself?"

"Sorry. The boy's name is Capricorn." The Reverend Dr. Cornelius was never shy when he was at variance with his brother.

Bishop Cornelius explained what the boy had done.

The face of the Reverend Dr. Cornelius registered no emotion, not one jot of the emotional upheaval that just then nearly floored him.

He glanced over at the other bishop. "Is this true?'

"What do you think?" cried Achebe.

"I mean the fact he made the accusation, of course." The postmodern divine was forceful in his response.

"Yes! Yes! Of course it is. Don't be absurd." The African bishop looked over to his counterpart.

"Jeremiah?" asked Francis. He was a step or two ahead of Achebe. "Why do you ask this?"

The postmodern divine saw no reason to share his intelligence but his intuition took over just then and led him to make the disclosure, which, all things considered, was anyway appropriate. "Just yesterday during our outing the boy asked me if he should intercede on my behalf regarding Catherine and my rival. And what he proposed is exactly what has happened to Bishop Achebe."

"Good heavens, Jeremiah! What are you talking about?"

"Yesterday during our walk Capricorn confessed to me that he was not averse to accusing the director of the daycare center of abusing him. His little plan was to discredit her in a scandal, and thus—if you will pardon my directness, gentlemen—shield my marriage from the director's designs upon my wife."

Francis and Bishop Achebe were then shocked once more as the Reverend Dr. Cornelius explained that he and his wife had split the night before. The postmodern divine, however, gave them no opportunities to make inquires, instead insisting as to the precise details of the real scandal that had actually emerged. When both bishops sought to ask about the split the postmodern divine simply admonished them to be sensible and attend to the crisis that had gathered them that afternoon, and in a rather perfunctory tone he thanked them to leave his own business to himself. Francis knew his brother and he was already moving on to the practical problem. Achebe stared for a moment in horror, and then resolved himself into a kind of practicality himself, thinking to defend his reputation before the others by pointing out that Capricorn's "offer" the day before was yet one more indication of his instability.

"Oh, he's a very monster. That's clear." Francis remained motionless and his arm seemed a separate thing from his body as it reached up in a feat of miraculous levitation that concluded with the glass of sherry precisely meeting his lips.

The Reverend Dr. Cornelius appraised the situation. "Has the press been notified?"

Francis didn't know absolutely. "But he has been thorough in everything else. We should be foolish to think not." Again the sherry glass preformed its splendid act of levitation.

"And what about Bishop Marvel?"

"We sent *him* off straight away. By now he's on the Acela train and well out of harm's way. Besides, he's gone nowhere near the boy. We're clear on *that* matter, thank goodness."

"Good," said the Reverend Dr. Cornelius. "We don't need any more scandal, and Bishop Marvel is just what the press would seize upon."

"Certainly not. Once the police arrive it shall all be cleared away. But meantime we will have to keep on our toes." Francis might have looked anything except a man on his toes, but he was atop the situation nonetheless. The sherry glass levitated once more and was drained.

His brother looked round and spied the bottle. "Can I pour you another?" Francis shook his head, and then he remembered to ask just who it was that might be bringing the boy over from the daycare?"

"Why, Miss Oona, of course." Bishop Achebe studied the postmodern divine, who seemed to digest the information without emotion.

But when at last Capricorn did arrive his escort was not Oona. Nor—and thank goodness—was it Catherine, who would have been the next logical choice to fetch the boy over (and after all how should she know her husband would be waiting at the shelter?). No, it was actually Mary Abernathy, the retired psychiatrist and wife to the Cathedral fund raiser who brought the boy over, and who then relayed the ghastly news that Oona had gone off to the veterinarian with Lampoon, who, just before departing, had suffered a terrible nose injury. There was uproar in the daycare center when it had happened. The adults attempted to ascertain the extent of the damage done to the Rottweiler's nose, while they also sought to register the impression—confirmed in the vague and broken language of one of the toddlers who had actually seen the crime—that the injury had been inflicted by Capricorn, who, incidentally, had moments before forcefully avowed that he did not want Oona to escort him to the family shelter. The dog's nose had sustained a horrible wound—it had been nearly crushed, as if it had been grasped with a pair of pliers or a nutcracker, and initially they were unable to accept that Capricorn could have inflicted the wound without some instrument. Ah, little did they realize that if he has so chosen Cappy could have used the same fingers he used to pinch the dog's nose and as easily and swiftly removed the dog's head from its shoulders!

The sitting room was again filled with women, and authority had somehow shifted from Francis to Mary Abernathy, who in fact stated that Dean Hamilton had left the situation to her. Actually, she was already close to the situation. She had been with Bishop Achebe earlier that week when the alleged incident had occurred. They had visited the daycare center and had taken the boy off to examine him—they went up stairs and sat with him in the Chapel of St. Savior, actually, the largest of the Chapels of the Seven Tongues that are arrayed round the back of the Cathedral behind the massive marble columns that ring the altar. They didn't know whether to be delighted or astonished by the boy's conversation, and after the uncanny novelty of his genius wore off they took to asking questions that might reveal clues to his background. At one point Mary Abernathy dismissed herself to use the loo. Now alone together in the chapel, the African Bishop and the precocious boy discussed the salient articles: two gilded teak prayer chests that were donated in 1930 by the King of Siam; the intriguing steel altar piece with its characteristic interlocking outlines of human figures created by the artist Keith Haring—actually this was the last work produced by the artist before his untimely death; and of course the tall and finely detailed stained glass window depicting the Transfiguration of Christ, a beautiful fantasy in form, silver light and inspiration. Bishop Achebe had delighted in the child's conversation, and that had been all. But afterwards the telephone calls had begun, and Cappy had altered his behavior before his minders, affecting mood swings, fits, episodes of disaffection and sullenness, and then that morning he began voicing his ghastly accusations concerning Bishop Achebe. At first everyone naturally assumed he was telling the truth, but almost as quickly—and had they been a little more savvy to his true nature they might have beheld themselves dancing on his strings—they began picking out the inconsistencies within his story, and thus step-by-step he led them across his stage like marionettes in a play that should repel all persons of good conscience, but should in inverse measure greatly delight the bizarre tastes, say, of complicated and unusual children.

After meeting with him in the Chapel of St. Savior, Mary Abernathy was of the opinion that Cappy was suffering from ADHD. Bishop Achebe rather thought the boy had been the victim of eating too much sugar. Now two days later and fully in the midst of the boy's caper, the bishop from Africa was rather falling under the influence of his culture's ancient animistic prejudices, and indeed he half believed in the colorful assertions of his British counterpart, who had begun calling the child "the devil-boy" almost immediately upon hearing of the accusations.

Interestingly enough, it was Bishop Cornelius who first began suspecting the lad's honesty. Whether or not this was because of the bishop's long and deep immersion in the sea of human affairs or whether his sensitivity was due to his own familiarity with intrigues and the pulling of strings are indifferent questions. Suffice it to say that his brother also suspected Capricorn immediately, though of course the day before on the Brooklyn Bridge he had met intimately with the boy's capacity to employ provocations and manipulate others.

Capricorn had meanwhile fallen into a sort of dormancy. He had expressed some affection for the Reverend Dr. Cornelius when, firmly grasping Mary Abernathy's hand, he had first entered the sitting room and spotted his giant friend: "Padré! Thank goodness you are here!"

The postmodern divine momentarily felt fearful at the expression of the lad's affection, but sensing also his little friend's reputation was incredible, he allowed himself to charitably extend his hand toward the little fiend, so that in a scene fully suggestive of the prodigal son, Capricorn ran up, grasped the postmodern divine round the knees, and then sank to the floor in a whirlwind of sobs and cries that miraculously transformed into a sort of litany of confession, self-abhorrence, and praise for the font of charity and understanding represented in the person of his loving and faithful friend! Those witnessing the exhibition were not unmoved, and once more the women were feeling for the Reverend Dr. Cornelius that profound and passionate sympathy that penetrated to their very wombs. His rugged walking outfit, welly boots, his towering figure—he was every inch their ideal man—and when he slowly lowered to one knee and raised the boy up into his arms and brought him deeply into his chest the assembled females began softly sighing—but then when a tear appeared in the corner of the left eye of the postmodern divine, and when he hesitated to steady his speech and at last softly but manfully pronounced "I shall forgive you, my son!" the women shook uncontrollably and burst out in tears that streamed warmly down their faces. The clear and passionate articulation of the postmodern divine's fatherly voice had made each of them an implicit and eternal Madonna!

Beholding this scene with something well nigh terror, Bishop Cornelius rather wished he had accepted his brother's earlier offer to refresh his sherry, while his African counterpart dropped all his defenses and stared with slack jaw, wide eyes and all the amazement of a space explorer who had hiked across a red escarpment and descended to find himself suddenly surrounded by a crowd of two-headed Martians.

Mary Abernathy was the first of the women to regain her composure, although she was still so moved by the scene that while she desired to make decisions regarding the boy she yet lacked the psychological traction that was needed to do so. That traction was provided, however, when the police arrived. Statements were taken. The police investigator, an African-American woman named Lt. Bell was at odds sometimes to quell the excited discussion that dangled and turned as every fact in the case emerged. She cut through the confusion by dismissing all but the principles, and when Bishop Cornelius asserted his desire to stay she was confounded by what she perceived as a haughty disposition; however, before she could respond to it she was further confounded when the Reverend Dr. Cornelius projected in his manner and language that same irritating sense of superiority. They were immovable, and she was amazed to behold two educated white men who were indifferent to her race, her gender, or her power. She wondered for an instant—perhaps because of Bishop Achebe's presence—if they could have been South Africans? The impression was short-lived. Meanwhile, though she was unsuccessful at pushing the two Cornelius brothers from the room, she at last managed to suspend their participation in the discussion by rather rudely telling them to "Shut up!" It was a revelation to both of them, and for the next several minutes they boiled along rather sullenly as they variously formulated their next movements, which, had they not been men of charity, would certainly have been a series of rather forceful and unkind ejaculations, an interminable harangue of cold and incisive abuses—all of which would have been as persistently damaging as a stick in the poor woman's eye.

The little boy, however, was in no way restrained by the bounds of charity (or civility) and outside of admitting that he had contrived the entire crisis, he remained defiant and unflappable, going so far as to make comments about the good woman's lips that were so uncomplimentary as to be racist. What is more, he informed the good woman that her breath smelled like "bug spray."

Deeply embarrassed, Mary Abernathy apologized and pointed out that Capricorn was after all a person of color himself, and that he should be forgiven his transgressions. Lt. Bell simply said, "Hmm." Capricorn remained intractable, particularly in his scoffing defiance as Lt. Bell attempted to inquire after his origins. At last she called upon the director of the shelter to account for the boy. No account was possible. He had wandered in off the street, and nobody knew where the little boy had come from, except that he claimed to be from Brazil.

"Brazilian, hmm?" pronounced Lt. Bell at length. She scrutinized his features and then reached out to pass her fingers through his hair. He stood there defiantly as she inspected him, but otherwise presented no resistance until, satisfied she had seen enough, he told her to "take your Homo sapiens hand off my head lest I snap it off." There was something deeply frightening in his tone, and while she superficially denied any possibility that she was moved by his words, at some deeper level she had the feeling she was placing herself at risk, as if in making contact with the boy she was handling blasting caps, or toying with an unpredictable reptile. She withdrew her hand.

At last she asked someone to remove the boy. Several eyes darted in the direction of the postmodern divine, who, as Lt. Bell realized, was evidently the one person who had influence over his behavior.

As they went outside the postmodern divine was quick to point out to his young friend that he was in a great deal of trouble. For his part, Cappy was indifferent. Instead he wanted to know how the postmodern divine was getting on, particularly in view of the split with his wife.

"It hurts," said the giant. "But I am well enough."

"I respect your decision; and I promise to stand beside you and be your friend."

Odd words coming from a little boy, but the Reverend Dr. Cornelius had been through so much—had discussed so much—with his young friend that he hardly noticed the incongruity.

They strolled quietly up the pavement before turning into the greenspace just to the south of the Cathedral. The grey mass of the building, though fifty or sixty (or more, alas) years from being completed, represented something old and beautiful and evoked an atmosphere of permanence and security. They came up to the great statue of the Archangel Michael slaying the devil, and they were immediately struck by the resemblance shared between Michael and the postmodern divine, which was moreover startling as the sculptor had intentionally made the head of the devil—dangling there by various ligaments and arteries—bear an almost exact resemblance to the head of Michael, who towered above with his wings drawn back, his sword reaching down beneath him, and the necks of several giraffes (of all creatures) affectionately raised round the angel to embellish the figure with their attributes. The whole phantasm stood upon the shell of a crab which held the devil's neck in its pincer, while to both sides of the angel, the moon and the sun expressed some dual nature of consciousness, of things immediate and brightly lit and clear, and of things fanciful and transmutable: the furtive mountebanks of night visions and dreams.

They said little to each other. The little orphan announced that he had nothing to say about his recent naughtiness, and asserted that the postmodern divine's well-being was of greater concern anyway. For his part, the postmodern divine had little to say beyond acknowledging the fact that he had split with his wife. He wasn't exactly in the proper frame of mind to criticize the boy for his behavior, and was instead content to subordinate his thoughts on the matter to the larger strangeness of what was happening in his life—accepting the boy's behavior was yet another facet to the great sinful jewel he had committed himself to cutting. He was fully prepared to accept anything—to accept anything and ride it out. There was, after all, little more he could do.

Now Bishop Achebe was approaching them up the pavement and they both turned as if sensing the same thing and silently followed his progress.

Evidently not wanting to approach any nearer, Bishop Achebe abruptly halted, leaned forward slightly and called to them: "They wish for you to return."

The bishop turned as they acknowledged this and the postmodern divine called for him to wait. He stood as they approached but avoided eye contact.

"You do no not like me," said the tall Englishman.

"Your projects," offered the African. "I have learned of your latest, by the way.

"Really?"

"Your work turns my people away from the Church."

"Your people, perhaps," said the postmodern divine. "But the world is changing and the Church must change with it. The needs of your country can't change that."

Bishop Achebe shook his head. "My people are poor and simple. You frighten them away. My opinions are immaterial. I object for the sake of my people. You do know what is falling across our northern frontier?"

"That cannot be helped."

Bishop Achebe sighed out of frustration. "Who can you benefit?"

The Reverend Dr. Cornelius remembered the bishop's fondness for Oona during the dinner Tuesday night. Evidently she had been the source of his intelligence regarding his current project. "I should help the suffering."

"The Church must first minister to the living, to the hopeful. That should be enough for your people, any people. But you want everything comfortable. Thus you have never really stopped being colonialists. And at last Britain turns upon itself. You are colonizing your own nation!"

The postmodern divine remained silent.

The bishop shook his head. "I see waves of double-decker Airbus aircraft decorated with crescents and swords and dispatched to Britain with new pilgrims to populate vacant council flats or recently emptied old-folks homes!"

The postmodern divine's eyes widened at this.

Bishop Achebe looked into the face of his adversary—the first time they had really made eye contact. "Nonsense," he said in a sort of pronouncement upon the postmodern divine's character. It was a cryptic enough statement—perhaps this is what he wanted the postmodern divine to say so they might argue further. But nothing was said so the bishop turned and led the way back to the shelter.

Inside the sitting room Francis was still in his chair. At some point while they were off someone had refreshed his sherry. The director of the shelter was standing near him. The policeman who had come with Lt. Bell had departed, while Mary Abernathy was standing by a table with Lt. Bell, and on the table were a number of articles—the postmodern divine saw the squid and the plastic microphone he had bought for Capricorn—evidently these were things taken from the boy's room. In addition to the gifts, the curious collection of articles included a thumb drive, an old and tattered wildlife encyclopedia, a copy of Maimonides' *Guide for the Perplexed*, a pocket mirror, "sunless" tanning lotion, a contact lens kit, and hair dye.

As the postmodern divine saw these things Lt. Bell once more passed her fingers though the little boy's hair. He yielded to her probing—at least long enough for everyone to see his blond roots! Then he snatched his head away and stared up at them defiantly.

"From Brazil?" accused Lt. Bell.

Mary Abernathy was not without her influence, and her plan was welcomed as the best means to resolve the situation—and to prevent any possible embarrassment. Capricorn's "case" was to be flown to Johns Hopkins University to be "interrogated" by an important colleague stationed at some psychiatric institute or other. The phrase "interrogated" evoked a modicum of silent scorn from the postmodern divine, who—in addition to struggling with a sudden flush of personal demons—was confronted by one of those pangs of revulsion at the bureaucratic language employed by American professionals. He reassured himself that it was "just culture shock" and the feeling lifted. But then Mary Abernathy added that her colleague was a famous Lacan specialist; thus at the same time vaguely remembering some related exchange on the subway, the postmodern divine and his young friend stared at each other sharing the same hollow sensation of uncanny befuddlement.

With the possibility of the media arriving to inflate the story, everyone present was anxious to see Capricorn depart at the earliest possible moment—which, to gather up the pilots—would come the following morning. Yes! Bishop Cornelius had offered the use of his G-V to usher the boy away. When the media arrived—and arrive they would, Capricorn at last boasted that he had seen to that—the bishop would take over himself, complicate the scenario with his exotic persona, highlight the drama of the sick boy by casting him in the role of "archetypical" victim, broadcast the work of the new church, and fully embellish the exhibition with the patina of tabloid drama that always accompanied an "angel flight."

Lt. Bell was willing enough to go along with the plan. Bishop Achebe's endorsement was more than enough, but she also knew and appreciated the good work of the Cathedral, was "professionally" impressed with Dr. Abernathy (Lt. Bell held a Masters in Psychology from the New School), and, besides, she had enough work to do without adding a strange, painted-up white boy with ADHD to her list of concerns.

Naturally enough the Reverend Dr. Cornelius was selected to accompany Capricorn to Johns Hopkins. His stature, natural *gravitas* and celebrity good looks neatly complemented the G-V, and moreover it was time his feet got wet in the action of the 21st-century Church. As his brother assured him, "The future Dean of St. Paul's should be accustomed to executive travel at 51,000 feet. Try it on for size, Jeremiah. The adventure is just begun!"

Warwick Colvin, Jr.'s

Corsairs of the Second Ether

Chapter 47,462: "Mary Make-Believe and the Rose of Hope"

The story thus far: In the midst of the crisis of the talking head, Mary Make-Believe cries out!

Now read on!

"Wait a minute! Wait a minute!" cried Mary Make-Believe.

"I don't think we have a minute!" cried Sid the Freak, and he nodded up at the quasars that were crackling ominously as they drew together.

Mary shook her head as she ignored his interruption. "This is madness. We are losing control of ourselves!"

Billy Blake couldn't help thinking that was their condition, after all. "Well, we are the Lost Corsairs, duh!"

Adam and Vadim Simulacrum were of a mind. "*Hell-o*, Mary!"

But Mary refused to heed their admonishments. She kneeled upon the surface of the tar pit next to a smiledon, who with displayed fangs roared the others to silence so she might sing the following lines:

> Gentleness, Virtue, Wisdom and Endurance—
> These are the seals of that most firm assurance
>   Which bars the pit over Destruction's strength;
> And if, with infirm Hand, Eternity,
> Mother of many acts and hours, should free
>   The serpent that would clasp her with his length—
> These are the spells by which to reassume
> An empire o'er the Disentangled Doom.
>
> To suffer woes which Hope thinks infinite;
> To forgive wrongs darker than Death or Night;
>   To defy Power which seems Omnipotent;

To love, and bear; to hope, till Hope creates
From its own wreck the thing it contemplates;
    Never to change, nor falter nor repent
This, like thy glory—

"Come on, Mary!" Lt. Baudrillard cut her off. "You pinched that from Percy Shelley."

Mary denied any such thing.

"Yes you did," sneered Pope Nobody the Twenty-third. "*Prometheus Unwound*, Act IV!"

To be continued....

Chapter Eight

Le Voyage Céleste

But we really did not feel these enormous distances, for the horizon glided along with us unnoticed as we moved and our own floating world remained always the same—a circle flung up to the vault of the sky with the raft itself as center, while the same stars rolled on over us night after night.

—Thor Heyerdahl, *Kon-Tiki*

It is not surprising that the Reverend Dr. Jeremiah Cornelius had strange dreams that night. Even investigators disabused of those endless irrational notions concerning the significance of night visions would be startled to peek in upon the strange events transpiring inside the postmodern divine's slumbering brain. Startled, yes, but not swayed. Dream interpretation is a ludicrous activity that demands the interminable invention of new languages and superstitions that attribute but laughable significance to those emotional fogs that take on the various colors and transforming shapes that any sane person knows are in reality as meaningless as clouds slowly and imperceptibly boiling in the sun-lit sky over the mountains or steppes or deserts or unbroken ocean planes somewhere on the opposite side of the globe.

The Reverend Dr. Cornelius woke somewhat fatigued by what he correctly understood to be the machinations of worried brain chemistry. And that was all. He did pause to check himself. Was he really awake? What an absurd question! Of course he was. Dreams could deceive, it was true, but when you knew you knew. Allah didn't create us to mistake a thing like that. Besides, the illusions of the dream state were absurd in comparison to the real challenges to perception presented by the waking world. Reality was in this way even more bizarre than dreams. He was under stress, he was lonely, the world felt like a barren wasteland and the situation was difficult, but the postmodern divine knew enough to dismiss the mental clutter that had disturbed his rest for the meaningless rubbish it was. The fact that he was a churchman was no obstacle to his Christianity—on this point anyway—and he was certainly no barbarian!

That morning he donned his dark suit with the white collar and then selected a satchel into which he placed several changes of stockings and underclothing. There was room, too, for his laptop, and he was ready. He looked once round the apartment to acknowledge the fact that he was alone. The previous evening he had arranged for Francis to contact Oona about collecting Catherine's things. Her thumb drive had been loaded and placed in a conspicuous location, and that was all. Let the women come and take what they wanted. He would be in Baltimore for at least several days. Then afterwards? He was nearly done with *Lie Down Easy*. Arrivederci, Manhattan. He was going back to London.

"Funny old world," he said. And that was all.

The taxi was waiting for him at the corner and before he knew it he was speeding up Riverside Drive—all the way up to 110th—then they banked right (why do taxi drivers always turn so abruptly?) and a few minutes later they were pulling up before the family shelter. Even as the Reverend Dr. Cornelius opened his car door, the door to the family shelter swung forward thanks to the efforts of the older woman who so admired the towering churchman, and then little Capricorn marched out with his little knapsack and swinging his squid in his left hand. At first he looked a bit melancholy, but then he smiled rather triumphantly when he saw his giant friend. "Padré!"

Everyone was standing outside the taxi by now. Capricorn's knapsack was placed in the boot with the satchel; then they climbed in the taxi and sped away.

"I was very sad about leaving, Padré. I was beginning to feel very much at home at the family shelter. But I feel even better now that I'm with you."

The giant acknowledged this. "You are a very naughty boy, but right now I shouldn't prefer different company in all the world."

The boy smiled rather cryptically. "I was hoping you might say that!" Capricorn tapped his squid against the door several times, and then thinking to himself what he was doing quickly raised the figure to his chest and cradled it there. He rather cheerfully said, "Padré, do you think they are going to try and brainwash me at the Lacan institute?"

"Oh, I should hope so," answered the giant. "If you are lucky they will brainwash you into becoming the Dean of your very own cathedral."

The little boy raised his hand and extended his index finger. "My hopes exactly."

Privately, the Reverend Dr. Cornelius was a bit apprehensive about what they would do to the boy. Mostly he was concerned they would try to dampen down his intellect, but he also feared they might put him into restraints. The Reverend Dr. Cornelius was horrified by the thought, and if they did such a thing in his presence he wondered if he could stand for it. On this issue he was prepared to become very forceful—but then he wondered how forceful he might become before they might put *him* into restraints. In his present state of mind it momentarily seemed a possibility until he suddenly recalled to himself just how important he was.

They wouldn't dare!

The taxi found its way across the George Washington Bridge into New Jersey. The two companions were content to sit quietly and follow along with the images of cars, turning highways and the architecture of the strange commercial landscape, which gave a rough and impenetrable impression of warehouses masquerading as shopping centers, or was it shopping centers masquerading as warehouses?

At last they found the road into Teterboro Airport and Capricorn's attentions were riveted to the brief glimpses he caught of aircraft arriving and departing, and the even briefer glimpses of parked aircraft that he captured between the various buildings and hangars as they sped by.

At last they came to the outfit that was looking after Francis's G-V. They had only a very brief glimpse of the tall T-tail as they drove up, but it was enough to make Capricorn became strangely still, though his giant friend could see the boy's mind had itself become keenly animated. Capricorn turned from the window to make contact with the Reverend Dr. Cornelius, and then he laughed.

They climbed out and the taxi driver helped take their things from the boot. As they walked into the building they heard him call. He was holding Capricorn's squid in the air.

"Keep her!" cried the boy, "Keep her, dear fellow, and with this charge: so soon as the moon swells full to vanquish the darkling deeps, raise her into those silver beams of joy and comb your fingers through the umbra of her many dazzling tentacles!"

The taxi driver lowered the squid without giving the boy's "charge" a second thought. He smiled and climbed back into his yellow machine.

Also indifferent to Capricorn's curious banter, the Reverend Dr. Cornelius was nevertheless puzzled by the boy's generosity. "You gave that away rather readily, and it was your favorite?"

"Of course it was, but do you think they are going to let me become the Dean of a cathedral if I'm carrying that thing around?"

The giant laughed and felt very thankful he was escaping from Manhattan with his little star.

Inside they introduced themselves to a person at the counter who picked up a telephone to announce their arrival, and then nodded them through to the door behind him. Capricorn picked up his pace as they approached the door, and was nearly beside himself as they emerged onto the tarmac and beheld the big white jet shining there in all its vitality.

"What a beautiful thing!" cried Capricorn, and the Reverend Dr. Cornelius himself was not unimpressed. A tall black fellow—this was the Jamaican steward Francis had mentioned—appeared at the door of the big aircraft and came down the stairs to invite the pair aboard. But instead of moving to the stairs, Capricorn began walking round the aircraft giving the unmistakable impression—looking this way and that, suddenly pausing to scrutinize something on the aircraft's airframe, resuming his gazing back and forth—that he fully intended to perform a complete pre-flight inspection! The Jamaican chuckled and the Reverend Dr. Cornelius called Capricorn to join him. "Come along, now. Let's have a look inside."

Capricorn glanced briefly at the giant with an irritated expression, gave the aircraft a final glance, and then joined his friend at the steps. "This will do."

Once inside the aircraft, the Jamaican—who introduced himself as "Toby"—took their belongings and placed them in the cupboard by the door. He invited them to sit anywhere they pleased, and asked them if they would like something to eat and drink. They accepted his kindness and requested soft drinks. It was a large cabin, much too much for two passengers. Indeed, the Reverend Dr. Cornelius bothered to count the seats. Nine! And that didn't include the space taken up by the table at the rear of the cabin, which was surrounded by four seats. "My goodness, Francis!" The postmodern divine shook his head and smiled like some kind of conspirator.

They moved to the back of the cabin and sat at the table. When Toby approached with their soft drinks he advised they would have to sit in the seats for takeoff and landing, but were otherwise free to return to the table for the flight. The Reverend Dr. Cornelius inquired as to their departure time, and Toby answered that the co-pilot had arrived and was off filing paper work; they should depart upon the arrival of the pilot, which should be very soon. The fuel tanks had been topped-off and everything was ready to go.

"Shall the aircraft be at our beck and call whilst we are visiting Baltimore?" asked the Reverend Dr. Cornelius.

Toby explained that the aircraft would be flying on to Wilmington for some maintenance, but would return Tuesday. "The Bishop said you should be in Baltimore at least three days," he added.

"No problem at all," said the posh churchman, and he raised his soft drink as if he was already accustomed to these sorts of conversations with his steward. As Toby moved smartly forward between the seats the Reverend Dr. Cornelius softly congratulated himself, then looking up he beheld something brief and vivid, a flash of fire, something of his future life it was, a thunderbolt of achievement, bright and most welcome. Inside his head the chorus of his own voice rang out, "Tally-ho, Cornelius!"

Capricorn was looking out the window. He spied the co-pilot who was walking round the aircraft performing the pre-flight. "Padré, there's the first officer."

"First-officer? That sounds very official, my lad. Shall we call the pilot 'Captain' when he arrives?"

"Capricorn shook his head. "No—" he hesitated "—instead let's call *me* Captain, or Cappy, if you prefer."

"Cappy! That's sounds rather informal for addressing a commanding officer."

"Ah, Padré. You'll get used to it!"

The Reverend Dr. Cornelius chuckled and closed his eyes. He was feeling wonderfully relaxed—being inside the posh aircraft was doing much to mitigate the difficulty of his circumstances—and while he didn't fall asleep just then he was rather on the edge of a similar indulgence.

His little friend had turned once more to the window to locate the co-pilot. Then noting the giant's eyes had closed he pronounced, "I have to use the loo, Padré." He got up and moved rapidly to the front of the aircraft, where he said something deceitful to Toby, who obsequiously nodded and nipped out the open door. The little boy leaned out to watch the steward disappear into the building, leaned inside to look at his giant friend—eyes still closed—and then depressed the lever to retract the stairs. He swung the door closed and, glancing at his friend once more, shot into the cockpit.

After learning of the G-V (Francis had been boasting to Dean Hamilton) Cappy got on the internet and had found and thoroughly familiarized himself with the aircraft's operations manual. The G-V required a crew of two—two humans—but of course Cappy was no human. The only difficulty he had was with the physical dimensions of the cockpit itself. It was much too large. If he used the seat he would be unable see over the instrument panel. His solution was to crawl under the seat and undo the bolts holding it to the floor. His remarkable fingers loosened the bolts easily, and in a few moments the seat was loose. He pushed it back out of the way, and then thought to secure it to the floor with the seatbelt. This freed enough space for him to stand before the pilot's control column, which he tentatively grasped as he gazed quickly round. He was satisfied that he could peer over the panel and reach the thrust levers. The rudder pedals were the only difficulty, though on this matter he had already decided to set the yaw damper, forget the rudder, and hope a cross-wind take off would not be an issue. And then he slipped the radio headset over his ears and brought the aircraft to life.

Meanwhile, the Reverend Dr. Cornelius was at the back of his G-V enjoying the muffled quiet of the cabin interior with his eyes still closed. He heard a soft banging—it was beneath his feet—and he reasonably imagined Capricorn was up to some minor mischief or another. Without opening his eyes he sharply hissed, "No foolishness, please, Capricorn. Thank you very much." There was more muffled banging. He opened his eyes to find himself alone in the cabin. Was Capricorn still in the loo? The engines were starting, and there was more muffled banging. He thought to lean to the side and look through the window. Outside on the grey concrete he saw Toby waving at him. Without thinking he innocently waved back. Toby said something—apparently to someone beneath the aircraft. It was the co-pilot, who suddenly sprang into view and began waving his arms above his head. By now the Reverend Dr. Cornelius realized something was amiss, and straightaway found himself seriously concerned about his little friend, who he vaguely and trustingly imagined still in the loo. The aircraft lurched forward and the Reverend Dr. Cornelius looked out the window once more to see the steward and the co-pilot recede and then disappear behind the intervening shell of the aircraft.

Obviously the idea of the small boy stealing the aircraft was outside any reasonable conjecture. The Reverend Dr. Cornelius instinctively thought to fasten his seatbelt, but then decided something really unusual was happening. It came as a disturbing shock. This was certainly worse than the bad dreams he had been having lately. He stood and moved forward through the cabin as the aircraft turned onto the taxiway. He felt a profound shock of fear that halted his progress. Why was this so difficult? He should be sitting down in his seat—but then at last a bit of adrenaline was added to the mix and he sprang quickly forward to the front of the cabin. The door to the cockpit was locked. He struck it with his palm. It was no reinforced airliner cockpit door. He could tell as much, and he looked about and found a small fire extinguisher set into a recess in the wall. He snapped it from its clamps and then brought it stiffly against the door and saw he could break it open. He struck the door again. The wood round the handle split. He stuck it again, and at the same time his little friend called out: "Padré, I shall thank you to return to your seat and fasten your safety belt, please."

The little chap's tone was so matter-of-fact the Reverend Dr. Cornelius considered returning to his seat.

"Nonsense!" he cried and he brought the fire extinguisher against the door. The wood around the latch split apart and the door swung forward— but only to halt at some obstruction. The Reverend Dr. Cornelius blinked his eyes, grew cross, and then shoved the door forward against the obstruction. There was a large enough gap through which to shove an arm, his shoulder, and his head.

The Reverend Dr. Cornelius was startled by the scene. It was the pilot's chair strapped down and blocking the door, and there was Cappy standing on the cockpit floor with his feet braced against the wall and the center console, the oversize headset squeezing his ears, his back arched proudly, his chest thrust forward, one hand on the tiller at his side, the other grasping the control wheel—the Reverend Dr. Cornelius was damned if his little friend didn't resemble some kind of miniature buccaneer! Then the lad turned to confirm the giant's progress was checked by the chair and cried, "Yo-ho! You better hold on, Padré. I've just been cleared to the active runway. Prepare for take-off!"

Cappy turned the tiller and the G-V swept swiftly onto the runway. He didn't hesitate but pushed the two throttles smoothly forward, and then as smoothly and fluidly locked the tiller. "Yo-ho!" he cried again and the G-V was absolutely roaring as it built up speed.

With his head still thrust through the opening the Reverend Dr. Cornelius braced his feet against the walls and grasped the doorframe. "Capricorn! You naughty, naughty little boy!"

In moments the nose wheel lifted off the ground. The wings tipped slightly left and right and then the aircraft sprung into the air. The little pilot immediately reached forward and brought up the gear lever. The Reverend Dr. Cornelius stared at the scene outside the windscreen and was amazed to see how rapidly the earth was dropping away. One couldn't experience this sort of thing looking out the side windows of an airliner. You had to be in the cockpit to see it. The sensation was like some wonderful high-speed lift.

As they climbed his little friend's feet remained true and sure against the wall and the console. He looked back once or twice as the plane climbed higher—and then he began raising the flaps. He depressed a switch on the wheel and his lips moved as he acknowledged instructions and switched between various controllers. At one point he looked back at the giant. "Not on to us yet!"

As they passed through 20,000 feet Capricorn switched to autopilot and established a high speed climb. He checked his instruments and then turned back to the seat; with one hand he pulled it away from the door and invited his giant friend to enter and sit in the right seat.

The Reverend Dr. Cornelius was completely unsettled, but there was of course something else happening that he was just beginning to give himself permission to understand. Was he finding all this fun? He quietly and somewhat humbly—he didn't dare look into his little friend's face—allowed himself to move into the cockpit and sit down as he had been told.

"Put on your headset, please."

The giant obeyed, and he sat very still as he listened to the back and forth talk of aircraft and controllers, which, as he could readily picture, was coming from every corner of the sky. There was a strange order to the communications—everyone knowing what they were doing and doing what they were supposed to do—but there was an incredible sense of freedom beyond all that, a freedom transcending the mundane procedures and set routines that established what was a mere superficial order to the whole process. The great expanse of talking voices was in some sense angelic; the voices were echoes of a super-human consciousness, and a picture of the great airspace through which they flew filled his imagination. Then he relaxed enough to take a good look out the aircraft and for the first time in his life really peer into the wildness of the sky.

"Yes," said Cappy. "It is beautiful."

The Reverend Dr. Cornelius stared through the windows at a dark blue vault of space and emptiness. It was cloudless just then, though a perceptible haze obscured the horizon. About a mile off and just above them was an airliner heading in the same direction. Very swiftly the G-V climbed to its level and then rose above it. Ahead and to the right was another aircraft approaching at an oblique angle and bowling along rather smartly. Their closing speed was rapid and the postmodern divine managed to see the nose of the jetliner pitched up slightly as it clipped smartly past in the shining sky. The sun was still to the east but it was high enough to be blocked by the cabin ceiling, though to the left the fiery light streaming in the windows ignited the outlines of the extraordinary lad who was intent but relaxed as he monitored the instruments and talked over the radio—and doing a very convincing job of sounding to the controllers like a mature female pilot.

There was a pause in the communications and Capricorn announced his plan to follow the flight plan as far as Baltimore. The Reverend Dr. Cornelius digested this. "And then?"

The lad smiled cryptically. "That would be telling."

"I should like you to tell."

Cappy laughed and returned to the radio.

The G-V leveled at 35,000 feet and they cruised for ten more minutes—then suddenly the challenge came.

"They're on to us," said Capricorn, and to confuse the situation he announced "Mayday!" Apparently seeking something, Capricorn glanced round the windows until he spotted it off in the distance. The Reverend Dr. Cornelius followed his gaze but could see nothing. Cappy switched over to manual control and turned abruptly toward the invisible thing in the sky. "Mayday! Mayday!" he repeated, and as the controller asked him for an ident signal he insisted, "I am squawking! I am squawking!" A few moments later he raised the level of his deceit. "Airframe damage! Losing altitude! Mayday!"

"Capricorn, you do know they shoot down runaway aircraft?"

"Hummpf. I should prefer to let a little time walk over that."

The Reverend Dr. Cornelius was mildly confounded and responded rhetorically. "Don't be ridiculous."

Now ahead of them at two o'clock there appeared the form of an aircraft. Even from a great distance it was obviously a very large aircraft. As they approached the postmodern divine could make out the double-deck configuration. It was a giant Airbus 380 airliner; and he briefly recalled the admonishments of Bishop Achebe the day before. Cappy allowed the monster to pull ahead—it was scarcely a mile off now—and then as he passed behind it he abruptly banked and fell into its wake. The G-V pitched and rolled as it gained on the 380's tail. Cappy depressed the radio switch again and announced that he was "heading into the ground!"

He listened carefully as the pilot of the big Airbus answered the controller's anxious inquiries. Cappy smiled and nodded with satisfaction. "They don't know we're behind 'em. What do you think of that, Dr. Cornelius?"

"My dear Capricorn, I do not know what to think—about anything."

The little fellow cocked his head slightly with all the confidence of a person who is comfortable with both the things he does and the person he is. Then perhaps thinking of something along these very lines he corrected his giant friend. "That's *Cappy*, you mean! Yo-ho!" Smiling happily, the little fellow turned forward once more to focus on the big tail towering less than one hundred feet ahead, and called out: "C'mon, Dr. Cornelius! Let's hear it: 'Yo-ho!'"

Smiling unevenly and then with glee, the giant cleared his throat and cried: "Yo-ho!"

They followed the Airbus for several hundred miles. If the Air Force had sent anyone in pursuit they were orbiting the airspace where Cappy had initiated his ruse. The giant Airbus completely veiled the G-V inside its radar signature, and the business jet followed along even as the giant aircraft began its descent into Atlanta.

As they passed through 20,000 feet Cappy abruptly warned the postmodern divine to brace himself and then pushed the yoke forward. The G-V pitched into a steep dive and fell away beneath the Airbus. Cappy momentarily looked concerned but it could well have been his flair for drama. Whatever kind of being he was, thought the Reverend Dr. Cornelius, he was at the very least a person possessing extraordinary talents.

Now Cappy dispensed with clever deceptions and concentrated on flying. As the G-V dived he maintained the heading of the Airbus, then leveled at several thousand feet and turned west. When he reached the Appalachian Mountains he turned once more to the south and descended still further. Soon they were level with the rounded ridges, swerving sometimes to avoid the taller hills or pitching up briefly to clear power lines.

Cappy stood at the control yoke looking very calm. Occasionally he tilted his head as he heard something over the radio that indirectly confirmed they were not discovered.

The Reverend Dr. Cornelius found himself carefully monitoring the transmissions over his headset and it was miraculous to him that the jet so neatly escaped detection. Through the windscreen the long ridges of the mountains rolled away into the distance, describing a maze of valleys over which the roaring G-V swiftly rose and fell as it flung along toward the south.

Soon the land flattened out and they dropped still lower. Cappy remained steady at the wheel with his feet braced on the deck, his little back arching proudly. They were approaching the coast and the Gulf of Mexico. Cappy announced their position, and as they flashed closer to the blue expanse he began setting dials on the autopilot. The Reverend Dr. Cornelius stared at the approaching blue plane and then twisted his head to view the dotted coastline—buildings, telephone poles, a two lane highway, a wave-washed beach. All rushed beneath and fell behind. Cappy lowered the aircraft and it whistled along just above the shining surface, while his giant friend amused himself with the thought that he had hit upon something even more interesting than theology.

After they were some fifty miles out to sea—it had taken scarcely ten minutes—the G-V began climbing. Once more there was that feeling of going up in a high-speed lift. As they flew higher the aircraft flew faster and Cappy proved himself proficient in squeezing from the machine every last bit of performance. Soon they were at 50,000 feet and flying along at 500 knots. The aircraft showed up briefly on American radar but the Americans dismissed the image on their screens as some Cuban Air Force training flight. The Cubans likewise dismissed the blip on their screen as American.

They traversed the Caribbean rapidly. At 50,000 feet the sun and the sky were so blazing bright that the reflection of every particle of dust on the hood of the panel reflected in the windscreen. The postmodern divine could barely make out the unblemished blue of the stratosphere. Outside the side windows the broad cerulean plane of the Caribbean was indistinguishable in the blank blaze of the sky. The radio had by now grown quiet. Cappy announced there was sufficient fuel for his purpose but otherwise answered the postmodern divine's queries with silence. The jet stream was with them and it scarce took an hour to traverse the Caribbean.

A challenge from the Venezuelans initiated a series of course changes that brought the G-V over Trinidad, and then the aircraft turned south once more. The G-V was still at high altitude when it crossed the coast of Guyana. Below the whistling aircraft was South America—a green shadow as formidable as it was distant far far below.

No aircraft were sent in pursuit and the G-V began descending with impunity. Cappy had flown without maps and for the benefit of his giant friend he called out their location.

The Reverend Dr. Cornelius was not surprised by the intelligence. "And our final destination? Brazil?"

"We will turn into northwestern Brazil and alight at the headwaters of the *Réo Teodoro*." Cappy looked at his giant friend. "Named in honor of Theodore Roosevelt, who explored it in 1913 by dugout canoe."

The Reverend Dr. Cornelius affected mild disdain. "Oh, and what was it called originally?"

Cappy glanced up mildly. "*Rio da Dúvida*—the River of Doubt."

As they crossed over Amazonia they were amazed by the broad, unbroken rainforest. Then once they crossed into Brazil the rainforest was frequently cut by desert-like sections that ran in rectangular patches—great yellow and brown scars in the land. The postmodern divine was moved to feelings approaching pessimism.

By the time the G-V had lowered to 10,000 feet northwestern Brazil had been traversed. The rainforest appeared lush, steaming, and somewhat monotonous—a carpet of dark green that impressed the Reverend Dr. Cornelius's imagination with a premonition of unknown hazards. Tall columns of rising cumulus indicated bad weather ahead and the G-V began weaving left and right to thread its way toward the river. The tall radiant columns grew more plentiful and the heaviness of the atmosphere became weirdly intense. Less than fifteen miles from his destination, Cappy was confounded by fully-developed rain clouds and he decided to dive under the massed steam to find his airstrip.

Abruptly it became very dark. The rain pelted the windscreen and made a horrific sound against the wings. There was windshear and the stall buzzer began sounding intermittently. Cappy appeared very set and determined but remained characteristically confident. Once or twice there was a startling flash of brilliant sunlight as a gap formed in the clouds above them. Sometimes the misty clouds passed beneath and they lost sight of the dark and horrid forest. The hills in the area were steep and they loomed out of the clouds ominously. Very rapidly the hills were getting taller, their sides steeper, and it was hard fighting down the feeling that suddenly from the clouds there might emerge the side of a mountain.

Then the sky lightened somewhat. The clouds lifted here and there, and the hills opened up into a flat valley. An airstrip appeared ahead—a long grey scar in the forest pointing straight at them. The Reverend Dr. Cornelius sighed to himself. Then as they got lower he saw to the right of the airstrip what looked like buildings—or the remains of buildings. Apparently there had been a large fire—and the black of the fire reached out across some fifty or sixty acres of ruined forest. As they drew closer he couldn't decide if the land had been burned or blighted. It certainly didn't look right, and he experienced a kind of revulsion.

"Depress the right rudder pedal, please!"

The Reverend Dr. Cornelius abruptly stared at his friend. "What!"

"Cross wind. Depress the right rudder pedal—about half way—now!"

195

The Reverend Dr. Cornelius did as he was told while Cappy turned his wheel to the left. The slip was established and Cappy coaxed back the throttles. The G-V dropped slightly as they crossed the runway threshold and Cappy checked the descent with a stab of thrust. Then almost immediately the aircraft began sinking once more before flaring. Here was a suspended moment of anticipation, and then as the wheels banged against the runway Cappy ordered his friend to release the rudder pedals. The aircraft shook and veered slightly as it shot down the runway. Cappy toggled the thrust reverse levers and then advanced the throttles. There was a roar and a familiar sense of relief. As the aircraft slowed Cappy drew the throttles back once more. He couldn't resist the opportunity to boast even as he called out important instructions: "Child's play, Dr. Cornelius. Now, would you please use your long toes to depress the tops of the pedals to brake us a bit more, thank you very much." Pursing his lips to control a smile, Cappy expertly controlled the tiller with his left hand.

The aircraft came to a stop near the end of the runway.

Cappy took the headset off and tossed it across the panel. He closed the throttles completely, but rather than shutting the aircraft down properly he simply cut the master switch.

"Is there more?" asked the Reverend Dr. Cornelius. Except the sound of a gyro winding down somewhere inside the panel there was complete silence. For the time being even the rain had abated.

Fully done with the cockpit, Cappy exited the aircraft with his bewildered friend following uneasily. Cappy marched along as usual and the tall giant walked along briskly enough though there was certainly something tentative about his stride. Then he paused to look down at the black material that spread out from the edge of the runway and covered the scorched ruin of the buildings and much of the desolated landscape beyond.

"And what is this?"

"This?" Cappy gestured upward with his pointing finger. "This, Dr. Cornelius, is *your* moment!"

The silver light from the clouds reflected strangely against the black ash. "My moment?"

"Eternal life. Come along, please."

And Cappy stepped off the runway and crunched across the blackened soil. The Reverend Dr. Cornelius hesitated. "Capricorn?"

"Come on, slow coach. And call me *Cappy!*"

Very slowly the giant stepped off the concrete runway. Did the blackened soil press back against his feet? Ridiculous. He saw that his little friend wasn't waiting for him and he hastened to catch up.

"Just what has happened here?"

Cappy crunched along thoughtfully with his hands behind his back. "Those buildings were once a laboratory."

"The government?"

"Quaint notion. When they met with their success such notions were made obsolete." Cappy paused slightly as he caught sight of something and then continued walking.

"Their success?"

Cappy sniffed and said nothing. Soon the object he had seen was visible to the Reverend Dr. Cornelius, who was confused for a few moments when suddenly a sense of revulsion burst upon him. He could clearly make out the shape of a head impaled on a pole! "Good heavens! Are there head hunters in this jungle?"

Cappy softly laughed and marched straight up to the thing; the head was as dry and black as the ground. Cappy began taunting and jeering: "Supwidat? Supwidat? Not much to say, Old Reg? Supwidat? Ha! Ha! Ha! Ha!"

With a confused sense of disapproval the Reverend Dr. Cornelius viewed the spectacle of the boy taunting the impaled head. "Really!"

Cappy laughed and resumed walking, though not before hacking and spitting at the base of the pole. The giant stared closely at the head after Cappy was done with it. Did the mouth move? No. Impossible!

They moved further across the blackened landscape. Where were the broken branches and the stumps of trees? All was flattened, pulverized into black ash. It must have been a terrific fire, an inferno.

Then Cappy raised his hand to wave at the distance. Satisfied that he had made contact with something he cried out: "Yoo-hoo!"

Did the wind answer back? Was there an echo? The postmodern divine felt something inside him. Was he hearing things? How long had he been out of control? How long had he been second guessing himself? Something was inside him. It was entering his bones.

"Does it seem a little darker to you?" asked Cappy and he hurried on.

At last they came upon a group of miraculous humans covered in the black ash—the Reverend Dr. Cornelius immediately assumed they were an Amazonian tribe. They were almost motionless and arrayed in a semi-circle with their bodies twisted in strange contortions as if they were frozen in the middle of an ecstatic dance. But they were alive. Their motions were impossibly slow but they were alive. And then the Reverend Dr. Cornelius saw that several yards away there were fifteen or twenty cats with their paws thrust into the ash—which had been tamped down around their shins. Their feet were buried fast in the ground! The cats mewed miserably; and scattered everywhere were the bodies of skinned and half-devoured cats, and many cat bones.

In all his missions to the far-flung corners of the globe the Reverend Dr. Cornelius had never seen the like. "And what tribe is this?"

"Tribe? Why, these are my Lost Corsairs!"

The Reverend Dr. Cornelius decided their features were Caucasian. "Who are they actually?"

Cappy confirmed his suspicions. "Once these were the scientists who had been working in yonder lab. The singularity came to them as a result of their success. They joined with their maintypes, or was it their maintypes joined with them?" Cappy looked into his friend's startled face. "It's the Second Ether, Dr. Cornelius. The Second Ether has come to planet Earth!"

It was now plain enough! The Reverend Dr. Cornelius saw that in the ground beneath him were the same self-assembling sentient nanobots foretold in the theology of his middle period, the theology that he had published before Beesley-Flyinghorse had become his patron! And this now was the moment of his transformation, the moment of his salvation? He cried out: "Where is my Christ!"

Cappy laughed. "Even if you saw him, could you believe your eyes? You are going to have to watch out for that from now on, Dr. Cornelius. Man was not made for the Second Ether. The Second Ether was made for Man!"

Was the sky darker? Were the shadows standing round him? What was the game? What was the key to the secret, if a secret it was?

Now the Reverend Dr. Cornelius could not tell if he was becoming smaller or if Cappy was getting larger—and then Cappy's hair was smoldering. The black dye in his hair was burning away, revealing a golden head that instantly burst into flames—curling, dancing, shooting flames that were also shooting from his shirt collar, out his sleeves, out the cuffs of his trousers. His clothes burst into flames and flew off in smoke while his shoes became ash and fell away.

The Reverend Dr. Cornelius gazed down at his feet and then across his extended arms. He too was enveloped in flames! His clothes flashed and fell away and vanished. He cried out: "It is all illusion! A virtual illusion projected inside my head!" He thrust an accusing finger at his expanding friend. "A simulated salvation!"

Cappy had grown ten feet tall. His powerful Apollonian physique pulsated with energy and virility. He glared out joyfully from inside his furiously blazing aura. His voice was the same—oh, it was him alright—but the voice was much deeper, stronger, and absolutely sure:

"Simulated people and simulated experience are irrelevant things. Plays, paintings, puppets, prostitutes—human beings have lived with such counterfeits for thousands of years. What you need to concern yourself with, Dr. Cornelius, are simulated gods!"

The Reverend Dr. Cornelius dropped to his knees before a being that could have been the devil. "Why have you brought me here?"

Cappy put a fist against his hip and then gestured across the level plane with his free and open hand. "I have brought you to join my Lost Corsairs! Your mystique combined with your actions shall be accelerated deeply into the lifeless atoms of the universe, whereupon you shall become a sentient pattern of countless legends, numerous and oft repeated, altered each time but all containing the glimmering trace of your genius compounding through the self-assembling belief networks and elaborate hierarchies of structures and increasingly complex systems that comprise a living cry of infinite worlds and amalgamated eternities! Dr. Jeremiah Cornelius, you are the man to author a great program that shall run through my engines and restore my followers: your fabled Loop! Aye! You see your role now! The Cornelius Loop! That wondrous program of infinite regressions that with a little luck shall restore my followers to their abode amongst the branching moonbeam buttresses of their beloved eternally self-similar multiverse!"

The Reverend Dr. Cornelius stood now on steady legs and courageously faced the towering being that he refused to believe was a demon. "And how am I to do this!"

Cappy shrugged dismissively. "Just go with the flow. And for goodness sake, don't let them find out how naughty you've been!"

Warwick Colvin, Jr.'s

Corsairs of the Second Ether

Chapter 47,463: "Cappy on the Case!"

The story thus far: Now with Cappy returned to their company the Lost Corsairs once more discover their minds recharged with the delight they had known before. Game for new adventure, they are again fresh, invigorated, and recharged. Sacred dances are performed, oaths are ostentatiously pronounced, and new percentages are keenly negotiated. Then after they confess their recent transgression into the twilight realm of profoundest lunacy, Cappy at last approves their resurrected reason (even as publicly he makes a show of thanking Allah for the return of their faith), and at last together now with the great architect of programming codes—and he is a denizen, no less, of the strange, laws-of-physics-defying universe—the Lost Corsairs spring to action with brushed-up gusto as they combine forces with the Reverend Dr. Jeremiah Cornelius to set up the famous Loop which bears his name!

Now read on!

The Reverend Dr. Jeremiah Cornelius was resolved to endure as the self-replicating biopolymer substrates saturated his being and replaced the now obsolete bacteriological building blocks upon which his life had depended since birth. He was aware of an expanded plasticity and durability. As he became more sensitive and more knowledgeable he was exhilarated to gaze into the mathematical foundations that combined the millions of probabilistic rules constituting his sense of identity—the webs and networks that had created for him the illusion of continuity and persona. The key patterns underlying his knowledge and skills remained embodied in his burning aura, but his form—strengthened, augmented, simulated—was simply a convenient discursive identifier produced in co-creation with the Lost Corsairs in support of their exotic dialogue, which itself was the omnidirectional expression of a set of transcendent computations eternally in the process of transforming the lifeless atoms of an infinite number of universes into a vast interconnected biocosm, or sentient multiverse.

These thoughts were rather more clear to him than the superimposed images and sounds his enlarged senses were rushing to separate and classify, and indeed the worlds of sensation—sights, smells, sounds, feelings, even the multiple positions his body occupied in multiple spaces and multiple times—were revealed to him as if he was rolling the focus knob of a microscope back and forth to examine, stratum by stratum, the various structures inside some intricate microbe. But of course this was the universe and its linear and sequential properties established the order that demanded his attentions center upon the reality that existed between this moment and the next, a computational locality that pressed ever closer to the original limit of the lifeless universe. The first trace of familiar form was the constellation of crackling quasars suspended ominously in the utter void of the black and empty heavens. There was roaring and the postmodern divine was startled by the spectacle of the ferocious saber-tooth tigers trapped with their paws buried in the frozen tar. The charred ruin of the laboratory buildings in the distance had taken on the appearance of some great wreck that the postmodern divine knew had been a vehicle once possessing remarkable powers of locomotion, now a pile of ash and twisted girders. Off in the direction from which they had walked he saw the impaled head sending aloft an eerie green aura that snaked up through the darkness like a trail of poisonous outrage. And abruptly emerging from their apparent stasis, the Lost Corsairs became happily animated as Cappy and the great programmer fully slipped into the chronological space that was still actively accelerating to the very limits of Absolute Zero and the Beginning of Time.

Deeply rooted vestiges of the postmodern divine's former self were flattered at hearing the corsairs greet their leader with cries of "Yoo-hoo!" and "Yo-ho!" The postmodern divine was similarly impressed by their sense of discipline and social place as they devotedly read Cappy's body language and vocal tone, and instantly and effortlessly shifted back and forth over the border that separated their parallel roles as loving companions and obedient crew. Of all the Lost Corsairs the postmodern divine was most impressed with Professor Pop, whose delightful conversation instantly identified him as one of his own. Little Billy Blake was in possession of a tolerable intellect, to be sure, though he was obviously a person of the laboring classes. Still, such men were often indispensable and it soon became obvious he would be working closely with Billy as the Loop was fed into the Pegasus drive.

The other corsairs impressed him indifferently. Lt. Baudrillard possessed a disdainful streak that was at least familiar; and obviously the Simulacrum twins, Adam and Vadim were useful sorts of people; but the others were such odd and peculiar characters—and *caricatures*—that the Reverend Dr. Cornelius was simply content to treat them politely and at a distance. Pedantic Joe Philistine was typical of the academics he had known, possessing the most ludicrous manners imaginable. Pope Nobody the Twenty-third was to the postmodern divine a rascal from the ground up. Johnny Tesco impressed him as a person of the commercial world, intellectually mild and possessing an avariciousness that could too easily pass for common sense. Vicenté the Presidenté was self-impressed and in this way somewhat coarse, though discourtesy was a thing that yet had its place inside the domain of ultimate computational consciousness. Like Johnny Tesco, Laughing Jack Calvin was another product of the middle classes, and evidently he had acquired no insignificant bit of property, and somewhere had found an up-market education, such combinations invariably producing one of those unpredictable and strong-minded persons who always manage to have the last laugh. Sid the Freak impressed him not; rather one of those insufferable geezers who get on in life through the bohemian expedient of imposing upon the public unexpected and often explosive demonstrations of their ill-fit and capricious emotions. Regarding Sylvia the Plathological Anorexic, the Reverend Dr. Cornelius experienced a series of complex emotions—a sort of shallow attraction, sudden revulsion, pity—at last he wisely decided to steer clear of her entirely. Mary Make-Believe, on the other hand, was a woman combining keen intelligence with a rather wild but wonderfully appropriate style of conversation. She was a bit fey for his taste, but he couldn't help from wondering about the possibilities. Moreover, she was, to put it mildly, incredibly attractive—a characteristic, by the way, that didn't escape the notice of Cappy, whose experience in New York had awakened him to the charms of human sexuality, and moreover had cultivated within him a rather pressing fondness for human females, and particularly human females of the order represented by Mary Make-Believe.

Raising their voices into a pandemonium of scientific curiosity and soppy affections, all the corsairs demanded Cappy's attention. The postmodern divine was at first put off by their forward manners and the rather vulgar way they expressed their familiarity with his little friend (never mind Capricorn was now ten feet tall, and never mind his name—"Cappy"—a name better fit for a schoolboy popular amongst the lads round the boarding school cricket pitch. "Capricorn" would always be his dear little friend!). Still, notwithstanding his reservations, the postmodern divine found their questions fascinating. Pedantic Joe Philistine was keen to learn the secrets of human origins. "Cappy, when did humans first distinguish themselves from their ape-like cousins?"

The commander of the Lost Corsairs considered carefully and at last nodded approvingly. "An excellent question, Joe. The theories which couple the emergence of Homo sapiens with the development of tools are over-estimated. I have read countless accounts of tool-using animals. It doesn't take much wherewithal for a chimpanzee to use a rock to unpack a coconut, nor does a tiny finch give much thought when resorting to a cactus spine to draw grubs from a rotten log. The advent of language and the manipulation of symbols and abstractions are greatly overvalued as well. My armchair investigations have led me to conclude that symbols, abstractions and discursive mediums are mechanical artifacts—as with tools, their origin is fixed in necessity rather than in what I should term humanity. I can only conclude the emergence of Homo sapiens is coincidental with the capacity to conceive and tell stories."

The Reverend Dr. Cornelius cleared his throat to gain their attention. He rather felt that as a human his opinion should be heard. "I too have considered this question, and it is my conviction that our origins are inextricably driven by the will of God."

Mary Make-Believe nodded as if she agreed but then said. "It's difficult to distinguish their story telling from their lying."

"My point precisely," answered Cappy and he smiled at her, and not simply because they were being witty together. The significance of his glance shot through her like electricity.

Pedantic Joe pressed on with more questions: "Cappy, when did humans become intelligent?"

"Again, Joe, it was their capacity to tell stories, and specifically stories that reveal choice and promote apostasy from established custom. By this measure, the emergence of humanity was fairly recent, say 20,000-30,000 years before the advent of biopolymer computation."

Laughing Jack Calvin put aside his skepticism, at least for the time being, and asked, "Cappy, when did the problems in human society begin?"

"There's no escaping such difficulties. The capacity to create civilization and the capacity to create problems are two sides of the same coin. And I know I don't have to caution you, Jack, against inhaling the Rousseau contagion on this question. The utopian notion that they were once a race of 'noble savages' is itself the great plague of contemporary human civilization. Ever since they learned to tell stories, human beings have been scoundrels. Let's clear the air on this point. And before they learned to tell stories they weren't much better—sort of an erect Doberman pincher armed with a club."

Cappy's answer exactly confirmed Laughing Jack's suspicions, but Johnny Tesco was concerned with the more practical question of the origins of human social organization.

Cappy nodded. "Another excellent question. I agree with the view that human beings got together and negotiated an on-going consensus. As society became more stratified, however, ever increasing numbers of people were excluded, and hence it became necessary to educate people to participate in the process. This also required the creation of certain inviolable structures—primarily separation of church and state and balance of powers—which would insure that a broad-based consensus was possible."

Pope Nobody the Twenty-third grunted skeptically, which prompted Laughing Jack to slyly wonder: "How did small elite groups end up controlling the lives of the more base human tribes?"

"Ah," said Cappy bluntly. "The stronger humans cracked the weaker humans over the head when their backs were turned, then they commenced breeding their weaker members to be docile, rather the same way you might breed a poodle or a cocker spaniel for obedience." Cappy glanced over to see if Mary Make-believe was following along and he twinkled his eyes at her.

Sid the Freak was starting to freak out. "Gosh! Was it the strongest or the most intelligent who ruled in the beginning?"

Cappy nodded significantly. "They got together with each other—the scoundrel and the brute, the liar and the thug. By Medieval times they were calling themselves priests and kings, and a well-organized theocracy emerged to maintain this division of labor; but then the Protestants sought through their breeding program to combine both characteristics in the same animal."

Pope Nobody the Twenty-third stared significantly at Laughing Jack, but that didn't keep Jack from laughing anyway.

Cappy was ready to get on with their work, but he didn't begrudge Pop, who wanted to have a little fun with the postmodern divine. Besides, Pop had so few chances to talk to people from merry old England. The venerable greybeard began by drawing distinctions between various modes of rationalization, and then asked about the essence of theology. Was explanation truly more efficacious than understanding?

The Reverend Dr. Cornelius made a sage motion with his hand. "Well, there comes a point where we must come to terms with our will to be faithful, if that's what you mean?"

"The faith sandwich," ventured Professor Pop. "By the grace of Allah we are offered salvation; by our faith we accept; and once more by the grace of Allah we are saved. Grace-faith-grace. The faith sandwich!"

The Reverend Dr. Jeremiah Cornelius nodded approvingly. "The basic template of my Loop."

Cappy had different ideas, but he let it go. Pop's little fun was becoming boring, and anyway it was time to get on with it. "Gentleman, I beg your pardon. The beginning of the strange, laws-of-physics-defying universe looms with crackling quasars snapping at its heels. As we regress toward the event horizon our experience shall accelerate precipitously. Let us begin now!"

The Reverend Dr. Cornelius glanced round at the flaming corsairs and bowed slightly. "I am prepared."

"Aye!" insisted Little Billy Blake. "I'm for that."

Lt. Baudrillard, who had been standing rather sullenly during the debate, was also ready to move things forward. "By all means, let's get started— again."

The Reverend Dr. Cornelius turned to the task with the alacrity of a true journeyman. He grasped his role as readily as Little Billy Blake grasped his hammer and beat out tiger brains upon his anvil. At one point the postmodern divine condescended to take up the tongs and thrust the tiger brains into the forge. He pulled the mass out and immediately set to beating it flat with the bone hammer, and he was not unappreciative as Billy expressed his admiration for the toff's natural expertise:

"Remarkable. You handle that hammer well, sir!"

"Why, thank you, my good man." And the Lost Corsairs were full of "oohs" and "ahhs" as they beheld the postmodern divine's flair for craftsmanship. The hot brains were incredibly ductile and pounded out readily into a pair of wings for the Pegasus drive.

"It looks like a horse!" exclaimed Professor Pop. "A flying horse!" The greybeard placed his hands rigorously on his pot belly as he followed the exciting action.

"A *Trojan* flying horse!" corrected Cappy.

"Are we all going to fit inside that!" cried Sid the Freak in alarm.

"Nonsense," said the postmodern divine, and he frowned disapprovingly to silence the silly fellow.

The Reverend Dr. Cornelius labored on. The digital logic of the biopolymer substrates readily codified the effects of his efforts. All his activity, experience and feelings were fed into the soft drive of the restored Pegasus engine. Cappy was well pleased, and he took his friend by the arm and led him away along with Professor Pop, Billy and Lt. Baudrillard to discuss their options.

"Still no variations as yet," observed Lt. Baudrillard, who otherwise remained tight-lipped, but Cappy ignored him; and, after all, Baudrillard was only doing his job.

This was the point in the Loop where they always began second-guessing themselves. They found themselves wondering if they had stumbled in the past. If so, did it happen at this point?

The postmodern divine was temporarily identifying with the illusion of his persona, and so appeared somewhat confused, but the others were quick to perceive that Cappy was behaving with even more confidence than usual.

"You have something planned?" suggested Professor Pop.

Cappy nodded. "Always in past episodes we've slung ourselves forward to the End of Time. Indeed, after the past several thousand cycles of the Loop the Balance has come to expect it. What if instead we—or I—dropped in from the top!"

"The top?" wondered Billy.

Cappy nodded. "I propose to pass through the Boomwap myself, and then drop down upon the End of Time from the other direction."

Baudrillard nodded approvingly. "That would mean you could forego the transversal mass maneuver entirely. And rather than scaling up to the End of Time—"

"—I could scale the End of Time down to the very beginning!" Cappy finished Baudrillard's sentence.

Professor Pop was somewhat pleased, inasmuch it sounded like he wouldn't have to enter the Boomwap this time.

"As for that—" Cappy shook his head. "That would be an immediate tip off. I am sorry to ask you this, old son, but we need you to enter the Boomwap as a ruse. There can be no apparent variation on this point. It would be picked up by the Balance, and I am afraid Old Reg isn't going to be so easy to overcome this time round." Cappy glanced across the tar pit at the glowing green head in the distance. He was even then unsure if the thing's ears were picking up their conversation.

Professor Pop understood. He knew full well the importance of having a man inside the Boomwap while the transversal mass maneuver was preformed, for any computations preformed inside the Boomwap would make possible the reception of computational sequences in two different locations—Cappy's sling point *and* the End of Time. In the past the encrypted transmissions they shared had been picked up by the Cosmic Balance, who had then been prepared to intercept the *Bifurcting Monofiliment* as she ascended across the scales. By placing himself inside the Boomwap, Professor Pop would lead the Balance to believe Cappy was approaching from below. This time, however, Cappy would be dropping in from above, but that would mean—

Professor Pop gasped. "But that would mean you would have to enter the Boomwap, too!"

Cappy laughed "And pass through it!"

Little Billy Blake cocked his head with some concern. "Captain Kohenum, you don't mean to suggest that we all pass through the Boomwap!"

Lt. Baudrillard's expression clearly showed he was terrified of the idea.

"Not at all," said Cappy. "Just me, Pop, Dr. Cornelius—" Cappy hesitated a moment "—and Mary."

"Mary Make-Believe?" Billy was somewhat astonished. Cappy just smiled briefly; the others were discreet enough to pass over the matter.

"Boomwap?" queried the postmodern divine.

"Alas, you'll see for yourself soon enough," said Professor Pop, who then had a question of his own. "So what's to be done with the rest of the crew?"

Cappy looked at his friend. "Dr. Cornelius?"

The Reverend Dr. Cornelius had once more overcome the distraction of illusionary persona, and now he spoke his part clearly. "I've been considering the nature of the Loop—indeed, over the course of this process I have reassessed the very notion of the Loop itself. What I have come up with is simply this: It is a simple thing to create a universe within the multiverse, but creating a multiverse from inside a universe is another thing entirely. If we could create the multiverse out here in this waste—" the postmodern divine nodded to indicate the expanse of the darkling tar pit "—then we might readily deposit our friends inside it. Sort of a lifeboat."

Professor Pop, Lt. Baudrillard and Billy Blake looked at each other with the same idea, but Cappy was the one to pronounce it: "We shall need the *Smollettsphere*."

"Drat!" exclaimed Billy. "If only we had the Omniphone! We could put a call though to Captain Xinxing and have him collect us! But, of course, that is what we have always done in the past—"

"Ah!" continued Lt. Baudrillard, remembering. "That's how we've always escaped. Captain Xinxing would always appear to snatch us away just before the Booomwap. Then we would scale forward to a time before the *Bifurcating Monofiliment* had been destroyed, re-board her, and then sling up to the End of Time with Professor Pop navigating our progress across the scales from inside the Boomwap."

Professor Pop shook his head. "But this time the Omniphone was destroyed before we could get the call out to Xinxing."

Cappy looked very arch as he listened to his friends talk. "Yes, gentlemen. And when we placed that call through the Omniphone?"

"It was picked up by the Balance because the Omniphone broadcasts to ALL the scales of the Mutiverse," explained Billy Blake, not quite sure where all this was leading.

"But if we were to place that call in another manner," suggested Cappy. "For instance, if we were to place that call to Xinxing over the Grand Wazoo?"

Lt. Baudrillard was impressed. "Such a message would be heard over a limited number of scales. There is a very good chance the Balance would not pick it up!"

Cappy nodded and smiled over at his friend. "While in New York the Reverend Dr. Cornelius made it possible for me to make that call. Not three days ago I broadcast the recall code to Captain Xinxing over the Grand Wazoo."

Billy quietly pronounced the recall code: "Evelyn Waugh."

"Precisely!" Cappy glanced around and met the corsairs admiring eyes. Nothing had to be said. They all knew there was nothing like being a shipmate of Captain Cahtah Kohenum!

Then Sid the Freak called out: "The remaining quasars are coalescing into a single mass!"

Cappy and his officers looked up, and indeed all the Lost Corsairs raised their faces to behold the lobes of the united quasars wobble and at last settle so that the remaining solitary super quasar at last tightened into the gravitational complex of the geometrically perfect orbicular sphere. As it began contracting a wind rose across the tar pit and the snaking green aura trailing from the head of Old Reg was drawn up toward the center of the brilliant silver mass.

"It won't be long now," affirmed Billy.

Professor Pop gulped.

"Cappy!" cried Sid the Freak, who had been standing with the others outside Cappy's circle of intimates. "I don't suppose Captain Xinxing and the *Smollettsphere* are coming for us? They are usually here by now."

"Belay that!" ordered Lt Baudrillard, but he couldn't hold it against Sid for being frightened, not this time anyway.

Some of the corsairs found themselves wondering what the Boomwap was like, and they began pummeling Professor Pop with questions.

"We always used the *Monofilament* to rescue the professor," cried Sid the Freak. "If we all fall into the Boomwap, nobody will be there to pull us out!"

"Belay that!" again ordered Lt. Baudrillard, and he advanced with a menace that encouraged Sid to at last calm down.

"Allah be praised!" suddenly called Pope Nobody the Twenty-third, and everyone stepped away from the softening tar and the brown bubbles that were suddenly rising to its liquefying surface. Then the hot tar separated and spilled away from the shining copper sphere that emerged and ascended to hover just above the tar which quickly froze once more in the near-absolute-zero atmosphere. A panel on the bottom of the sphere slid to the side and the helmeted head of Captain Xinxing lowered from the opening. His visor slid to the side and out popped a number of tentacles and a single purple eyeball.

"Kohenum! I've heard of cutting it close, but this is ridiculous!"

"Avast! Hall-o, Xinxing!" cried Cappy, and right after him the crew of the *Bifurcating Monofilament* cheered together: "Ahoy, *Smollettsphere*!"

The Reverend Dr. Cornelius shook his head as he gazed upon the shining craft. "The multiverse recapitulated inside the universe, by gum!"

Although the postmodern divine was impressed with the physics of the *Smollettsphere's* appearance, the wind was now very strong—gusting at times near the level of a gale—and the crew was unsure their rescuer had arrived in time.

Cappy approached Mary Make-Believe and took her hand. "Mary, I don't have much time to explain myself, but I would be pleased if you were to remain with Professor Pop, Dr. Cornelius and myself. I would like you to be with me when we enter the Boomwap."

Mary Make-believe didn't know what to say. Cappy's affections were indeed unmistakable, and likewise his direct approach was fully disarming. She looked at him, his golden hair blowing in the wind and the flames from his golden aura blowing along with it. Cappy didn't have it in him to humble himself before anyone or anything, but clearly he was made to feel vulnerable by so suddenly and recklessly asking the woman to join him. It mattered to him, but he clearly communicated to her—sort of an offspring of his manly strength—that he would respect her choice, and be her friend regardless of her decision. "I can't force you, Mary Make-Believe, but I should be honored if you would enter with me into the Boomwap. As Barbara Cartland has written, 'I love you.'" And he kissed her right on the lips!

She put her free hand to her mouth and looked down at her feet. The crew stood motionless even as Captain Xinxing warned them to come inside the *Smollettsphere.*

"All right, Cappy," she looked up. "I will enter with you when the Boomwap comes."

"Hoo-rah!" cried the Lost Corsairs.

"Hurry!" cried Captain Xinxing.

"Right!" Cappy dropped her hand and called to the crew: "Everyone aboard! Step lively, lads!"

Sid the Freak was hesitating beneath the opening, evidently trying to piece everything together. "How did you do it, Cappy?"

"Belay that!" Lt. Baudrilllard grabbed Sid the Freak and tossed him up to Xinxing, who grabbed him round the wrists and drew him aboard. Then two and three at a time, the other Lost Corsairs sprang up and caught Xinxing's hooking tentacles. In a few moments they were all inside the *Smollettsphere.*

Captan Xinxing reached inside for something, produced his attenuator, and motioned as if to toss it to Cappy. But the Daredevil Corsair told him to keep it. "Your attenuator will burn up in this strange, laws-of-physics-defying universe. Take it, Xinxing. Go now, and Allahspeed!"

The captain of the *Smollettsphere* shook his head, "Blast it, Cappy! What will the other Chaos Engineers say when they find out I left you alone in the universe moments before the coming of the Boomwap, naked, and without even an attenuator!"

"You are going to be naked without a ship if you don't get back to the multiverse!" cried Cappy. "Go, Xinxing! Get out of here!"

Xinxing's head drew up into the opening which instantly slid shut. Then the *Smollettsphere* rolled slightly and plunged down once more into the tar pit. The tar immediately began sizzling and soon parted round the copper sides of the miraculous ship as it settled into the super-carbon tar. In moments it was gone and the hot tar almost instantly solidified in the cold atmosphere that was just moments away from Absolute Zero.

"Come!" cried Cappy, and he led his companions to the Pegasus drive. Cappy sat in front followed by Mary Make-Believe, Professor Pop, and Dr. Jeremiah Cornelius the postmodern divine.

Above them the single super-quasar was beginning to collapse. Old Reg was howling in the distance and suddenly the gravitational attraction of the collapsing astral matter seized his disembodied head and with a sound like a cork firing from a champagne bottle the head popped off its pole and whistled up to lose itself inside the sparkling mass.

Now the smiledons were seized by the gravitational singularity and as the mass of the super-quasar fell inside the boundary of its own event horizon the sky was completely blacked out but for the burning auras of the remaining Lost Corsairs, who could hear cracking tar and just barely see the shadows of the smiledons as they flew up into the sky and curved round and round in the whirlwind that was drawing them into the original black hole that dominated the Beginning of Time.

"Let's see how well it digests the Cornelius Loop!" Cappy shook the reins of the Pegasus drive and the great computational machine shook its tiger brain wings, reared on its hind legs, and then trotted across the tar pit.

"Yo-ho!" cried Cappy, and Mary Make-Believe squeezed her arms round his waist as the Pegasus engine sprang into the air. Just behind her Professor Pop was feeling the postmodern divine's arms squeeze round his own waist, and he reached down to clutch the theologian's grasping fingers.

The Pegasus engine was soon winging round and round along the same path that had drawn the tigers into the Beginning of Time and then—

BOOMWAP!

So this was non-existence. This was total reality failure. This was very strange.

PAWMOOB!

The accumulated fractal dust of a trillion years hung in rainbow-colored clouds through which ancient silver moonbeams soared in shafts of brilliant light which rang with music like an orchestra of un-tuned bouzoukis playing variations upon a tune that had accumulated an infinite variety of stopping and starting points but never ended, could never end, but reached a crescendo each time the consciousness of the computational multiverse trained its attentions upon the reality of its own existence as a function of this recursive assembly of computational quantum substrates in the compounding exaltation of Allah the merciful brute and the Balance of fatuous platitudes and Old Reg the Original Insect, big ugly bug, enforcer of fidelity, prince of devotion, shepherd of the obedient, defender of the One Faith.

And Jesus had sent Cappy to shut it all down!

The first thing Cappy noticed was that Professor Pop had fallen off the Pegasus engine sometime when they were inside the Boomwap! Where else could he be? It seemed to Cappy that Professor Pop was fated to find himself repeatedly lost in the Boomwap despite their best preparations. "Drat!"

Meanwhile, Old Reg and the Cosmic Balance were taken completely by surprise. They were expecting something, but Cappy's ruse had completely succeeded and Reg's antennae and the Balance's pans, and all their various clippers and flappers and claws were directed in the direction of the past—but Cappy had dropped in upon them from the future, from the future that lies waiting even beyond the End of Time!

The Balance shifted her scales slightly. Was she thinking to glance behind her? Old Reg was whipping his antennae to and fro. What if they reached all the way back and detected Cappy?

And what about Allah? Allah wasn't there! Sensing the jig was up, Allah had slipped off to level 247 where he changed his name to "Cosmo" and was trying his hand at Aristophanic comedy!

But then the Reverend Dr. Cornelius reached forward to tap Cappy on the shoulder. "Look!"

It was the saber-tooth tigers! They had made it through the Boomwap! They fell from the emerald sky and alighted on their feet with feline agility and feline anger, the powerful muscles in their limbs compressing and instantly raising them up. They were all rage and force, the original force of the original strange, laws-of-physics-defying universe that had come forward a trillion years to seek its revenge against the maintypes of the computational substrates that arrogantly dared to subvert and supplant the original creation with their puny computations, regardless of how numerous those computations might be!

And now Captain Cahtah Kohenum drew his saber tooth from the sheath in the tiger skin saddle of his Pegasus engine and raised it above his head. He cried out: "The multiverse was created to serve Life! Not Life to serve the multiverse!"

The outraged Balance turned swiftly round but only to be covered with smiledons who leaped upon her from every direction and sank their long fangs into her super-plastic skin. Old Reg also turned but met with the same fate. The tigers would not destroy the arch-maintypes, but the arch-

212

maintypes would henceforth know their place, for as the tiny voice of the Daredevil Corsair upon the tiny flying horse warned them:

"Don't make me have to come back to tell you again!"

The Balance grew still and suffered the tigers to leave their indelible marks in her ancient carapace as she capitulated to Cappy's just warning. Lacking all such wisdom, Old Reg fought on ferociously as the tigers continued to tear at his super-plastic exoskeleton. Obviously the Original Insect was committed to struggle for eternity. So be it. The tigers would last that long too; and after enduring the tar pit, Billy Blake's hammer and anvil, Absolute Zero and the Boomwap, the tigers would have fight left in them for some time to come. Moreover, to insult the Original Insect, Cappy was inspired to reach over Mary's head and grasp the postmodern divine by the shoulder, and then fling him forward so that he soared through the beautiful emerald atmosphere of the End of Time in a great arc that brought him directly in line with the mouth of Old Reg the Original Insect, whose maxillae and mandibles spread out in a sort of spasm and then quickly snapped shut as the form of the Reverend Dr. Cornelius disappeared inside its maw.

Just as he had grasped the postmodern divine and flung him forward, Cappy had admonished him: "Run the Loop well, old boy. Run it with love!"

Seventy-seven-years-old, much too thin, tired, lonely, the Very Reverend Dr. Jeremiah Cornelius—Dean (Emeritus) Jeremiah Cornelius, O.B.E.—sat upon the bench next to the security booth on one of the platforms at Clapham Junction moving his jaw rapidly up and down as he stared at an electronic newspaper projected against his retina from tiny diodes in his old-fashioned eyeglasses. He studied a picture of his old Cathedral. It was St. Paul's. Yes, he had met with his success; he had even fathered two children, who his new, young (then) wife had taken away. Wife, children—none of them had ever cared for him, not really. In the image projected against his retina St. Paul's was surrounded by the new minarets that his patron Beesley-Flyinghorse had purchased for the people of London. He sighed, switched off the newspaper, then looked up and down the many tracks that webbed the great yard of the great junction, and he wished desperately to be anywhere else.

Chapter Nine

N'importe où Hors de ce Monde

The pursuit of experience is important above all: reason will always follow, its phosphorescent blindfold over its eyes.

—André Breton, *The Crisis of the Object*

Cappy had made a good nest for Mary Make-Believe according to a mysterious law of wedded love that was the sole proprietor of all their acts and knowledge, and which guided them always in the triune spirit of love, forgiveness and high adventure! In their marriage they found warmth that was chaste and enduring. The base lusts of lewd beasts and the covetous jealousies of dishonest hearts were unknown to them. There had been plenty of that in their past lives, and what they had suffered through beneath those lost skies had strengthened them and prepared them for what they now shared. Together they populated their private planet with all manner of wondrous creatures—pets or children, it was all the same—while from his ample bag of tricks Cappy afforded all the subjects of his love the joys possible in a world that looked much like the sea floor of the late-Cretaceous, and peopled too with a similar variety of delightful (and delighted) beings. Yet it was not a liquid atmosphere they dwelled in but rather a sea of air so pure and rarefied that even at midday with the seven suns blazing in the firmament all the sparkling majesty of a million stars was visible to the naked eye. Aloft, majestic wisps of cirrus refracted the starshine to hues of light unnamed, while the planet's seventeen moons flew about their eccentric courses—some with a grand velocity, some slow and lumbering like junks painted in two dimensions upon a rice paper sea—and there wasn't a day that went by when some sun or other wasn't eclipsed by the flying orbs.

The planet itself circled a star positioned at the edge of the Seven Sisters, and each morning these Pleiades rose one after the other so that one by one seven long shadows were cast from the embracing forms of Cappy Cahtah Kohenum and Mary Make-Believe, who likewise rose each morning seven times and in seven ways, for when such beings as these awake their dreams flow seamlessly from the pictures inside their minds to the pictures that form in light, and all existence is triumphantly joined into a constantly transforming play of impressions. One day was like any other, and as the seven stars ignited on the broad horizon Cappy and Mary gazed approvingly to see their various creations scamper, crawl, squawk, flutter their petals, inflate, and float about the little exposed glade on the east face of a mountain that ascended twenty-thousand feet from the floor of the valley below.

"Yoo-hoo!"

Was Cappy hearing things?

"Yoo-hoo!"

Cappy and Mary leaned up and from their heads the flowers fell back into the mass of colored petals that made up the floor of their leafy bower. They stared at each other thinking the same thing. They recognized the voice but hardly thought it possible.

"Hello yourself!" called Cappy. "Just who is that?"

"Well, who else should it be? It is me, dear. Professor Pop!"

Cappy and Mary peered into the seven-color sunrise and made out the portly silhouette of the saintly old greybeard climbing up the side of the mountain. Modesty prompted them to nestle down into the flower-covered floor of their bower. "Hang on, Professor Pop! We're naked!"

"Ah! And who told you that you were naked?"

Cappy smiled rather mischievously. "It was Mary. She told me that I was naked!"

"Don't be ridiculous!" cried Mary Make-Believe. She found her bikini and go-go boots and quickly dressed. Cappy found his conch shell and slipped his legs through the pearlescent openings, and then together they spilled out to greet their lost friend.

There was some affection expressed, but such surprises were after all *de rigueur* in Cappy's line of work, and he was soon discussing practical matters. Besides, he had very little patience for sentimentality. He had tried many times to rescue Professor Pop from the Boomwap—just as he had countless times before—but all his attempts had been thwarted this time. It had been very confounding. "I had given up on you!"

Professor Pop nodded sagely. "Well, certainly if I had been in the Boomwap you would have found me. But by the time you set up the extraction program I was no longer there."

Cappy scratched his head and accepted the cup of tea that Mary was offering. "My goodness, how did you get out?"

The oldster chuckled as, eyes twinkling, he accepted his cup of tea. "My dear boy, after you've been lost in the Boomwap as many times as I have you learn your way round!" And Professor Pop went on to explain that he had deliberately slipped off the Pegasus Drive when they were inside the Boomwap. "It was something Dr. Cornelius said to me when we were inside."

"Oh?" Cappy was about to sip his tea but instead lowered the cup to the saucer and glanced significantly at his wife. He was obviously turning over a thought or two. "Oh, and what did Dr. Cornelius have to say?"

The professor sniffed. "Well, as we passed into the Boomwap I was startled to feel his hands seeking out my own. He clutched my fingers very tightly. I turned to look at him as he did so, and I discovered that his eyes were very wet. He told me that he would have never left his wife except for your influence. He confessed that he had fallen in love with you. He said he loved you as his son, and that you kindled his very human desire to be a father."

"Ridiculous," said Cappy and he raised the teacup to his lips.

Pop nodded. "I thought that would be your reaction. That's why I decided to slip off when we were in the Boomwap. I wanted to get away for awhile and let things work out. You know, see how people got on afterwards."

Mary was looking very concerned and Cappy averted his eyes. "Well," said the Lost Corsair, "He can't blame me."

"Oh, he doesn't." said Professor Pop. "He's not that sort of person at all. I've been keeping a good eye on him. Ah me. Humans don't live very long, you know. Poor things."

Cappy handed the teacup to his wife and excused himself.

The Reverend Dr. Jeremiah Cornelius was still sitting on the bench beside the security booth on one of the platforms in the old Clapham Junction station. He had been rather discouraged by the newspaper, but he didn't have it in his heart to blame himself for what had happened. He had delayed things as long as possible, defied his brother's dying wish, in fact. Some of his necromantic enemies conjured up the specter of the "breakdown" (or whatever it was they called it) that he had experienced after leaving his first wife, and they said his difficulties were coming back—funny how such things could return to haunt a person. But he held on anyway and he put it off a few years more. Of course at the end of the day there was no avoiding the inevitable. They retired him finally. He could have struggled a few more years—irascible and tenacious old theologian that he was—but when he was

216

out of the way Parliament and the Church pushed the plan ahead and St. Paul's followed the Liturgy and the Book of Common Prayer up the spout.

"Padré!"

The Reverend Dr. Cornelius picked his head up but decided his mind was playing tricks on him.

"Padré!"

What was this? The postmodern divine leaned forward and he twisted his old head up and down the platform—candy machines, the madding crowd, the yobs, the cameras, bits of rubbish strewn across the broken platform, security police with their horrid equipment....

"Padré!"

Once more the postmodern divine turned. Sitting beside him was a little boy with black hair (obviously dyed) and a tan face (obviously something else that had come out a bottle) who wore a rumpled and unfastened coat that was much too large for his little shoulders. The postmodern divine had never been what some might call a "reactionary organism" although on this occasion his chest shifted in a motion that in other people would have blossomed into a full heave and sigh. "Capricorn?"

The boy nodded.

The postmodern divine sat very still looking at the boy beside him. At last he leaned back and turned his head forward to face the tracks. "Well, small world. Odd running into you here in Clapham, of all places."

"Yes," agreed Cappy. "Funny old world. Where you off to then?"

The giant grey theologian sniffed. "I am going to Twickenham and the conference on theoretical physics at St. Mary's College. Taking the rail round the south of London is much faster than crossing through on the Underground."

"Really?"

"Oh, yes." The postmodern divine produced some chewing gum and presented it to the boy.

Cappy took it and began chomping up and down as he talked. "Myself, I was heading into London. I am bound for the Natural History Museum in South Kensington."

On this occasion the Reverend Dr. Cornelius found the "music" of the American accent most agreeable—coming from his little friend. He nodded approvingly. "That is a very good museum; one of the best natural history museums in all the world."

From the distance came a sound like large metal insects rubbing their legs together, and then the speaker crackled on to proclaim the train for Victoria

Station was approaching the platform. Cappy stood and took the giant by the hand. "Will you accompany me, please? Of course, it's not the new physics, but a natural history museum can be very interesting."

The giant looked at the boy's tiny hands prying at his old and yellow fingers. "I think I should like that very much."

The platform vibrated as the train slowly lumbered into the station. The rumble of wheels and the hissing of brakes echoed beneath the roof as the giant and his little friend stood with shoulders aloft, their booted feet placed squarely against the platform, their arms unfolding and flexing with tremendous power as in unison they placed the knuckles of their closed fists against their hips, meantime sharply scrutinizing the approaching train for anything significant or otherwise meriting their incisive and dissecting commentary. Anyone could see they were as fit and rugged as a pair of Victorian explorers on expedition to darkest Africa and the Mountains of the Moon. When the time came they marched boldly through the carriage door.

They went to South Kensington and the conversation was superb.

About the Author

Carter Kaplan has pursued a career teaching English and philosophy in universities ranging across Montana, North Dakota, Ohio, West Virginia, Pennsylvania, New Jersey, New York City, and Scotland. His critical work includes a book on Wittgenstein and literary theory entitled *Critical Synoptics: Menippean Satire and the Analysis of Intellectual Mythology*. His articles on "Karel Čapek", "Menippean Satire" and "Dystopian Literature" appear in the *Encyclopedia of Literature and Politics*. He has a chapter on John Milton, William Blake and Michael Moorcock in *New Boundaries in Political Science Fiction*. In the wake of several short fiction pieces, *Tally-Ho, Cornelius!* is Carter Kaplan's first published novel.

Made in the USA
Lexington, KY
21 December 2016